THE
CIVILIAN WAR ZONE

Also by Lance Peters:

The Red-Collar Gang
The Dirty Half-Mile

LANCE PETERS
THE
CIVILIAN WAR ZONE

ANGUS & ROBERTSON PUBLISHERS

*Angus & Robertson Publishers'
creative writing programme is
assisted by the Australia Council,
the Federal Government's arts
funding and advisory body.*

All characters in this book are
entirely fictitious, and no reference
is intended to any living person.

ANGUS & ROBERTSON PUBLISHERS

*Unit 4, Eden Park, 31 Waterloo Road,
North Ryde, NSW, Australia 2113;
94 Newton Road, Auckland 1,
New Zealand; and
16 Golden Square, London W1R 4BN,
United Kingdom*

*This book is copyright.
Apart from any fair dealing for the
purposes of private study, research,
criticism or review, as permitted
under the Copyright Act, no part may
be reproduced by any process without
written permission. Inquiries should
be addressed to the publishers.*

*First published in Australia
by Angus & Robertson Publishers in 1988
First published in New Zealand
by Angus & Robertson NZ Ltd in 1988*

Copyright © Lance Peters, 1988

*Lyrics from Hoagy Carmichael "Stardust" reproduced
with the kind permission of the copyright owners
D. Davis and Co. P.O. Box C156 Cremorne Junction Australia 2090*

*Acknowledgement is made to MCA Music Aust Pty Ltd
For permission to reprint the lyric to
"Boogie-Woogie Bugle Boy" — D. Raye/H. Prince*

*Excerpt from "Serenade in Blue" by Mack Gordon and Harry Warren.
Copyright © 1942 Twentieth Century Music Co. assigned by Bregman
Vocco Inc., Con.; reprinted by kind permission of J. Albert and
Sons Pty Ltd, 9 Rangers Road, Neutral Bay, Australia 2089.*

*National Library of Australia
Cataloguing-in-publication data.*
Peters, Lance.
  The civilian war zone.
  ISBN 0 207 16050 3.
  I. Title.
A823'.3

*Typeset in 11pt Times
Printed in* Singapore

For Laura, Lucinda and Luke — the loves of my life

AUTHOR'S NOTE

You can, if you wish, call this fiction, faction. For the setting, the institutions, the military procedure, the uniforms, the political manifestations and some of the incidents, are all authentic, as is the general wartime atmosphere.

Although some of the details in the book might seem rather strange to contemporary readers, they are all the result of exhaustive research and further authentication by the indelible childhood memory of a small boy who hob-nobbed with the "Yanks" on a chewing-gum level during those fateful war years. That small boy, of course, grew up to become the author of *The Civilian War Zone*.

The main characters however, with the exception of Detective Sergeant Joe Church, are fictional and entirely invented, with the customary disclaimers. The character of Joe Church has been modelled on a real police officer, whose astonishing crusade against vice, crime and corruption spanned some thirty-five years in the NSW police department. His background is sketched in much more thoroughly in my novel *The Dirty Half-Mile*, which is set in the 1930s.

I would particularly like to thank the following for their Civilian War Zone research assistance:

(Pfc) Woody Larimore, who was one of the Yanks down under in World War II; my good friend and physician Dr Debbie Saltman for her medical expertise; (Captain) Ray Cooper — Military Historical Society; Alison Hartley Lichtenstein, who knew just where to look in the Public Library when my eyes failed me; and my wife Laura, who was my eyes during that long period of near blindness (now thankfully past) whilst I was writing this novel. Doubtless this affliction added some salt to the wounded in these pages and some vitriol to my writing.

Lance Peters

"A good soldier has his heart and soul in it. When he receives an order he gets a hard-on, and when he drives his lance into the enemy's guts, he comes."
BERTOLT BRECHT *Mother Courage*

"Never shall our enemy set foot upon the soil of this country without having arrayed against it the whole of the manhood of this nation, with such strength and quality that this nation will remain forever the home of sons of Britishers who came here in peace in order to establish in the South Seas an outpost of the British race."

"Without any inhibitions of any kind I make it quite clear that Australia looks to America, free of any pangs as to our traditional links with the United Kingdom. We know the problems that the United Kingdom faces. We know the constant threat of invasion. We know the dangers of dispersal of strength. But we know too that Australia can go and Britain can still hold on. We are therefore determined that Australia shall not go. We shall exert our energies towards the shaping of a plan, with the United States as its keystone, which will give our country some confidence of being able to hold on until the tide of battle swings against the enemy."

JOHN CURTIN
Prime Minister of Australia
December 1941 (after Pearl Harbor)

PROLOGUE
3

BOOK I
MOBILISATION
9

BOOK II
MILITARISATION
87

BOOK III
HOSTILITIES
177

BOOK IV
CASUALTIES
279

EPILOGUE
313

PROLOGUE

The enemy was wearing a tan shirt, olive drab trousers and jump jacket, and an olive drab garrison envelope-type cap fronted by a small eagle within a brass circle and trimmed with Air Corps colours of ultramarine and orange. He had a (US) badge pinned on his right shirt collar and an aeroplane emblem on the left, as well as wings above the fruit salad on his breast pocket. His tie was light tan and his shoes were highly polished dark tan. The two railroad-track silver bars on his shoulder sleeve indicated he was a captain.

Of course the GI didn't know the guy was the enemy. The GI wasn't the type of rebellious enlisted man who considered all officers to be enemies. This enemy was dressed, and spoke, as a compatriot. He also had a comforting smile on his round cherubic face with its almost invisible plucked eyebrows. Furthermore, he seemed to be that rarity — an officer who showed respect and friendship for a lowly private. Almost as if they were equals.

The GI was feeling pretty low, right in the middle of the depression stage of a long drunk. He'd lost his buddies and his footing. He was sitting on the pavement against a boarded-up shop window, watching the blurred passing parade of servicemen and their women, chatting gaily, frivolously, flirtatiously, and he wondered how long it would be before he next threw up or pissed in his pants.

It was raining gently — a damp spring afterthought. No umbrellas. You couldn't buy one today for love or money. Not even on the black market. The people who normally manufactured umbrellas were manufacturing guns. The GI wished it were raining beer, so he could have another drink without having to stand up.

He couldn't remember where he was for a moment. It was a city like most others. It could have been Baltimore or Boston Massatwoshits. He could never pronounce that properly even when he was sober. No, he was down under. In more ways than one. Somewhere called King's Bloody Cross, so some local told him. Two- and three-storey buildings closing in on him, bigger apartment buildings, restaurants with rationed apologies for food, nightclubs that forced you to drink until dawn and then kicked you out when they'd taken all your dough. Wasn't it amazing what life did to you. Only an hour ago he'd been able to stand up of his own free will. Now, he had no free will.

This kindly army air force officer was the first not to ignore him. The first one to stop. He asked him if he needed help, a hand up, a friendly shoulder, anything.

Of course he needed help. Anyone could see that. He was sick, pissed as a fart, having been one full day stinko on a two-day pass. And now he couldn't stand up, not for anything; not for the MPs, not for Rita Hayworth, not even for "The Star-spangled Banner".

The enemy, the benevolent, poolball-faced enemy, helped him up. He even guided him down the street with a supporting arm and a reassuring phrase.

"Take it easy, soldier. We'll look after you. That's our duty."

The enemy certainly looked after him. He took him to "headquarters". Headquarters? That's what he told him it was. But it looked more like an ordinary old house. A suburban bungalow. Not surprising. The US military command had taken over hotels, guesthouses, warehouses, mansions, churches, office buildings, apartments, even a huge underground tunnel built for the never-completed Eastern Suburbs Railway — all for personnel use. So headquarters was a bungalow? Not inconceivable. And inside it was stuffed with all sorts of military bric-a-brac.

The brew-addled GI was not really capable of disputing anything, least of all with such a friendly enemy. After helping the GI remove his uniform in the "officers' quarters" the captain proceeded to ply him with black coffee, sponged his face and neck with a cool flannel and applied iodine and Zambuck to his cuts and scratches.

The GI wondered why he had had his uniform removed, and then put it down to the fact that he was going to be given a nice comfortable bed to sleep in. All part of the R and R. Rest and regurgitation? No. That didn't sound right either. Still, it was no worse than Massatwoshits.

He also wondered why the kindly captain removed one of his dog tags and read it aloud.

"Anthony Costanzi. Type O. Tetanus 5-16-42. Gk. Orth. N.o.K. — Gina Costanzi, Greenboro, N.C."

"Is that your wife?" the captain asked.

"My ma. Hi ma!" Giggles.

"You not married, soldier?"

"Hell no. I'm just a kid."

Costanzi did vaguely wonder why an officer would go to such lengths to help a vomitously shickered enlisted man.

Don't look a gift-horse's ass in the mouth, he thought, and that thought too joined the others in semi-oblivion.

The captain, who was quite a few inches shorter than the GI, and at least fifteen years older, in his late thirties, asked a few more personal questions.

"Do you have a girlfriend, soldier?"

Costanzi held up three fingers. "Two," he said. "Both of 'em North Carolina gals. From North Carolina. An' I'm gonna marry one of 'em one day. But I ain't sure which. Mary with the big boobs or Sarah with the big boobs? Whatta you think. Sir? It's a very confusing shituation. Whatta you think. Sir? I'm only a kid."

Oddly, the captain didn't answer the question. He obviously heard him. He was listening intently, with his round head cocked to one side, but he showed no emotional reaction.

"What do you think of the Aussie girls?" the captain asked, advancing the conversation.

"I think . . ." Costanzi answered, "I think . . . there's lots of 'em. All over the place. That's what I think. Sir. Whatta you think?"

"What's your outfit, soldier?"

Costanzi pondered, waiting for the fog to clear. Then he saluted. "Signal Corps. Thirty-Second Infantry. Sir! Red Arrow. Sir! And I love the army. Sir! Beats the hell out of topping tobacco plants. Sir!" Grinned. "Sir!" Foggy again. So grateful to be made so comfortable. "You're my favourite officer, sir. I'd give you a purple heart, if I had one."

The tall, too trusting, dark-haired young GI was nearly unconscious when the enemy helped him onto a bunk and gently eased him over onto his front. He thought it was just the booze and fatigue. He didn't know there was a gram of chloral hydrate and sixteen fluid drachms of whisky in the black coffee, which constituted a swift Mickey Finn. He had actually liked the black coffee. The best-tasting drink he'd had all night."

Every night and every morn,
Some to misery are born.
Every morn and every night
Some are born to sweet delight,
Some are born to sweet delight,
Some are born to endless night. . .

the enemy gently recited.

The last thing Costanzi ever heard was the enemy starting to breathe heavily. Not from passion, but a kind of asthmatic heavy breathing — the last gasp of a coal miner with silicosis.

In his mental blear and terminal state of unreality, the GI felt sorry for the pulmonary enemy. He wanted to help him. One good turn deserved another.

His last wish was granted.

When the enemy produced an M1 carbine bayonet and plunged it into the base of Costanzi's skull, behind the left ear, it was a great help. The satisfaction involved was cathartic. For the enemy. Only seconds after, as the GI expired from the severing of the auricular branch of his jugular and the ripping of his medulla oblongata, where the spinal cord became the lowest part of his brain, the enemy's breathing returned to normal. Sweet lung reflation. It made him smile again. Proud of his skill. Minimal blood flow. Almost clean as a whistle. Practice made perfect.

Then came the next phase — stuffing the GI's second dog tag in his mouth and stripping his uniform of insignias, valuables and personal effects, including the excessive US army pay. This turned out to be a disappointment. The sly grog merchants must have got their greedy hands on most of it. Didn't matter. It wasn't the money but the glory. His valuable contribution to the war effort. So he thanked his lucky stars and stripes and carved off the GI's pinky for his war souvenir collection. Then he called in his warrant officer and master sergeant to handle the disposal of the remains.

Finally he stood immaculately to attention, saluted and held two minutes silence, for the fallen.

"God save the king," he breathed.

BOOK I
MOBILISATION

"How many patterns of life were based on kindred misconceptions, how many wolves do we feel on our heels, while our real enemies go in sheepskin by?"

MALCOLM LOWRY
Under the Volcano

1

There had been a tree on the street outside the brothel. One tree — a Moreton Bay fig. When it dropped its figs in autumn, the pavement was a squashmire underfoot. There was a certain symbolism in this for the GIs who used the brothel. In the dark, figs underfoot felt like discarded condoms. In truth, there were those too.

Being the only tree in this downtrodden vicinity, it was very popular with stray dogs. It provided them with a respite from the telegraph poles. And it also provided some limited camouflage for the patrons.

The US military command, however, decided that the tree was a hazard. It interfered with the orderly lines of horny troops queueing outside the brothel, and made the search and control duties of the MPs more difficult. So they had it removed, despite protests from the "respectable" civilian residents, who complained to the city council.

But there was a war on, and the city council's influence had been partially usurped by the US military. Not that the US military had official jurisdiction over the area, but they considered it to be their temporary territory. The military bureaucracy had become almost almighty in these parts, since MacArthur landed in March 1942 and became the godlike Supreme Commander of the Allied Forces in the south-west Pacific. Eight thousand miles from home, Uncle Sam, in the person of Douglas MacArthur, messiahed in and changed the landscape.

Not that it was the general who had had the tree removed, although his name was dropped as the authority for removing it. It had been found that dropping MacArthur's name worked miracles, even when MacArthur knew nothing about it.

It's doubtful if the general had intended to become the

leading madam in town and yet he was. For there were quite a number of brothels under his supreme command in East Sydney, to say nothing of Melbourne and Brisbane.

War was the great liberator.

Young men, freed from all domestic constraints and theocratic apron strings, thousands of miles from Mom and Pop (who didn't approve of anything more stimulating than lemonade and necking) and with the spectre of the Angel of Death and Disablement hovering in the wings, demanded, and received, instant succour and spice, most of it at black market prices. Their foster parents — General MacArthur and Uncle Sam — seemed much more enlightened.

Salome and Adam felt like they were married. They slept together, in the same perimetrical tent, ate breakfast together, showered and shaved together, dressed together, drilled together and now, on their first seven-day furlough, touring the treeless back streets, they were contemplating getting laid together.

That was the army for you. These two young men — Pfc Albert Salamandini (Salome to his friends, Salami to his enemies) and Pfc Adam Goldhart — had become engaged, in the comradely sense, in Camp Roberts, a boot camp near San Luis Obispo, California.

In just six months, after being designated replacements to 41st Infantry Division, they felt like they'd been shunted all round the world together. From their homes on the east coast, by train to California for basic training, then to Fort Lewis in Washington state to pick up their gear and multifarious vaccination shots, then, to confuse enemy agents, by train back across to the east coast to New York to board ship for wherever. On board the *Santa Paula* troop transport they bunked together and speculated about their destination together, until they were told it was Guadalcanal. At Bora Bora in the Pacific, after retracing their steps through the Panama Canal, they were told the marines had Guadalcanal under control and their destination was now down under.

Their comradeship stemmed mainly from being originally allocated adjoining bunks at Camp Roberts. They

• MOBILISATION •

had different backgrounds. Salome was Italian working-class from Newark; Adam was Jewish middle-class from upstate New York. Salome was a gangling six three in his socks, Adam a compact five nine in his. Salome had dark, thin, parted hair and sad brown eyes, Adam had fair curls that wouldn't lie down, much to his dismay, and blue eyes that sparkled and questioned. Both had clean-cut, open faces, but Salome's nose was prominent, like a roller coaster he avowed, whereas Adam's stopped short and wouldn't have been noticed in a nose parade. Adam had a sense of curiosity tinged with scepticism that frequently brought him into affable conflict with Salome, who tended to opt for face value and conformity.

Camp Seymour, north of Melbourne, their training camp for three months, was no better and no worse than Camp Roberts — except for the food. Until the US Command set up their Purchasing Commission this was basically Australian which, muttonwise, hard tackwise and meat piewise, deeply offended the Yank stomachs and bowels.

The frequently interrupted train journey — thanks to differing gauges — from Melbourne to Brisbane, seemed to take longer than their journey from New York, and the train carriages were like prison cells on wheels. They had months of amphibious training at Terrible Point, near Brisbane, which all agreed was aptly named, if only for the absence of anything remotely diverting. Then came their first seven-day pass and all the hot-blooded members of A Company, 162 Regiment, 41st Division nicknamed Sunset, of the US 8th Corps (a talent for numeration was helpful in the US army if you were going to remember what outfit you belonged to) entrained uncomfortably, through several gauges, for Sydney — the Paris of the Antipodes.

Before sniffing out the brothel district, Adam and Salome had spent a long, rather tedious day, filling in till night-time, which was purportedly when the ladies came out.

They'd taken a toastrack tram to Bondi Beach, marvelled at the camouflage-painted double-decker buses, chewed over the benefits of DeWitt's Antacid Powder as opposed to Dr Mackenzie's Menthoids and settled for Toohey's Oatmeal

• THE CIVILIAN WAR ZONE •

Stout, all of which beckoned to them from ubiquitous twenty-four sheet posters. Then they hired threadbare costumes and towels, hurdled the barbed wire and tank traps on the sand and floundered around in the Bondi surf, virgin territory for these city-bred east-coasters, who had never attempted a dip in their own Atlantic shores.

Lunch was a compromise. All the restaurants offered five shilling limited meals — austerity snacks. They had asparagus soup which, as Adam put it, "tasted as if it was tasteless", one meat, one veg, one potato, and ice-cream Melba for dessert, consisting of one scoop and one teaspoon of flavouring. Tea and coffee were rationed, so the café offered them a substitute brew made from maidenhair fern and lucerne, the taste of which made them yearn for one of those DeWitt's Antacid Powders or Dr Mackenzie's Menthoids.

"They sure picked the right country to make an army base," Adam commented. "Everywhere you go — army cooking."

"I wonder if they have pasta here?" Salome said longingly. "I would desert for some linguini."

"I doubt it. Not the Italian kind. They don't have too many Italians here. They got lots of Scots and Irish here though. So they might have Scottish pasta."

"What the fuck are you talkin' about? What is Scottish pasta for fuck's sake?"

"Macaroni."

Adam managed to keep a straight face as Salome chewed this over without a mite of mirth. Then:

"Was that a joke?"

"Not any more."

Come dusk Adam, the fairer of the two, felt pretty sore from sunburn. All over. Earlier, in the concrete Bondi men's dressing sheds, they'd watched some flabby, elephantastic middle-aged men sunbaking nude and they followed (birthday) suit.

"I think I even burnt my balls," Adam said. "That place is a frypan."

Salome had done chin-ups on the pavilion wall, trying to see over into the women's section, hoisting his long body

• MOBILISATION •

up with amazing dexterity.

"What do you see?" Adam asked.

"Dames. Lots of 'em."

"Are they . . . are they bare-assed naked in the altogether raw?" Hopefully.

"See for yourself." Salome jumped down. Adam tried to chin-up but was neither tall enough nor strong enough in the shoulders, and couldn't make it. "Give me a leg up, will ya?"

"No way."

"Shit!" Adam fell. "Why should you have all the fun?"

"Like the sarge instructor said — if you can't scale the wall, you're dead!"

Adam ruefully brushed some sand off his burnt legs. "Thanks for nothing, you asshole! Anyway, I don't believe you saw any naked dames in there."

"You'll never know, pal."

It hadn't been the best day of their lives, but they didn't mind too much. They knew in their hearts the night was going to be much better. Around seven o'clock a southerly buster blew up, helping to cool down Adam's scorched skin, and they trammed their way back towards the city and the sordid, well-regimented brothel area.

The dark streets were full of uniformed bodies, some hiding out in doorways, drunk but smart enough to avoid the baleful eyes of the vigilant MPs. Some back alleys and dank doorways were stuffed with couples doing a desperate stand-up version of instant fulfilment or vertical refreshment, with spread legs, overstretched spines and contorted shadowy faces.

Tones were muffled, spiced occasionally by an indistinct shout or an unbridled groan quickly suppressed. The total absence of streetlights and house lights made the area ripe for covert activity, but there was just enough half moon and glowing cigarettes to thwart total anarchy. Like an omnipresent watchful, wrathful God, the white MP brassards seemed to glow in the gloom, promising retribution.

Some of the houses sported long lines of soldiers outside, suggesting that business was booming. The dichotomy of

• THE CIVILIAN WAR ZONE •

wartime: population decrease in battle offset by copulative repopulation behind the lines.

"I don't believe it! Do you see that, buddy? That really stinks! I mean it!" Adam nudged his lofty companion and pointed to a fifty yard line of black GIs outside a two-storey, stucco, semi-detached dwelling made of sandstock brick and pit-sawn cedar adorned with wrought-iron fretwork on the front fence and balcony. It had red lamps glowing insipidly through the upstairs windows, almost, but not quite, defying the brownout.

"The army supports Jim Crow, pal. Didn't you know that?" Salome fluffed it off with a wave of his arm. He had a reach like the Brown Bomber, Joe Louis. "Why do you think there ain't no Negroes in our outfit? Did ya think they forgot to draft 'em?"

"Hey! I know all that! Just that I didn't think it went that far. I would've thought that all Americans could at least dip it in the same hole in wartime. Whatta you say?" Adam pushed back his envelope garrison cap with the light blue infantry corps piping.

"Don't bother me none. But seeing as how you're so riled up, why don't you join 'em? I'll watch."

"Do you think I should? What'll they do to me?" Adam surveyed the calm, patient queue that probably was thinking of anything but segregation at this moment.

"Those MPs'd bust your ass and mail you to the stockade. And that's just for starters. Then they'd put you on a sub and make you sleep inside a torpedo."

"Is that all?"

"Then they'd tie your balls to a depth charge aimed directly at the submarine whose torpedo you're sleeping in."

"You really think so huh?"

"Well, actually I'm just guessing. Why don't you join the line now, while that big nigger MP's got you in his sights?"

"That's the trusty system. It sure stinks. What happened to the Bill of Rights?"

"Suspended for the duration."

"Well, I think I'll pass. My balls and ass are indispensable."

• MOBILISATION •

The streets were an urban wasteland. They smelt of gas and garbage. Some liked it slummy. The brothels were housed in ostensibly residential areas where the rents were low, so the residents could hardly complain about the nefarious goings-on in their midst.

"Basically I'm not impressed," Adam said, as they moved on.

"With what?" Salome lit up a Camel, thumbnailing a match.

"You'll stunt your growth, you giant asshole! With this. It's depressing. Anyway Wishbone told me that the local hookers are cold biscuits, maiden aunts in the looks department."

"Old Willy Wishbone wouldn't know a good piece of ass if he slept with one."

"He has. He showed me his scars. The choice down here, Sal, is between condoms or clap. Take your pick. Sore or sorry." Adam eyed the line of white troops outside another tenement brothel.

Captain Fréjus of the Medical Department Corps had delivered the "clap briefing" to Company A, 162 Regiment, soon after they'd arrived in Sydney from Melbourne, prior to their first familiarisation pass. At first it was received with jocularity, until the specifically nauseating details set in. It wasn't just the blunt, less-than-scholarly medico captain's humourless verbiage, it was the charts, drawings and photographs he projected — many of them stomach-churning reproductions of penile discharges and infected, inflamed urethras.

"Before this war is over, you may get parts of you blown away by the Japanese, and about ten per cent of you, at least, may not live to see the end of it. But before you actually get into combat, there's another enemy you'll probably all have to contend with. And that's the seductive little ladies who, unwittingly or knowingly, are out to infect you with an insidious little germ, which you can't see, called the gonococcus. It's the most common and most infectious of all the sexually transmitted germs, known to one and all as gonorrhoea. The gonococcus principally attacks the linings of the genito-urinary organs. It spreads on and under the surface of the cells forming the linings of these organs, and sets up an inflammation. This leads to the production of pus, which usually gives rise to discharge. The incubation period is usually from two to ten days, so don't count your chickens until they're hatched, so to speak."

This comment got a guffaw or two, despite the fact that Fréjus delivered it with the same expressionless tone and serious face, as the rest.

"What you have to realise is that half the women who have gonorrhoea have no symptoms, so there's no way that you're gonna know if the woman you're lying with has it or not. Most times. She can look as clean as your kid sister, but still be a carrier. Now, when you get infected, you will feel a tingling inside the penis about two to five days after sexual congress. This'll be followed by a thick yellowish-green discharge from the penis. You'll also get a burning feeling when you pass urine. And you'll probably want to pass more than usual. The discharge will continue to increase by amount, the tip of your penis will become very red, and your undershorts will be stained yellow or greenish yellow. If you don't report it at this stage, then the disease will increase and spread up and back to the urethra, and you'll be pissing blood before you know it. From then on you'll have abscesses, warts, inflammation of the prostate gland; you won't be able to piss properly or screw properly — if anyone in their right mind'd let you that is — and you'll have a golf ball-size swelling, which'll hurt like hell every time you want to even think about anything below your waist, and you'll end up sterile and impotent. And about as much use to this man's army as you'll be to any girl or wife you might have. So remember, the enemy is waiting for you out there. The enemy has big tits and a nice smile, and open thighs. And she's mostly wearing camouflage. So don't take chances. Wear a raincoat. The quartermaster has 'em for you. It's your only protection. Don't plunge in with your eyes open. For Uncle Sam's sake, wear a sheath."

"Fuck Uncle Sam! It's my balls I'm worried about,"

• MOBILISATION •

someone said.

"Even if you fuck Uncle Sam, you'd better wear a sheath," someone else responded.

"If you catch it soon enough," Captain Fréjus wound up, "there are some tablets we can give you. Sulphonamide-type drugs. However, the cure rate is going down because the disease is spreading in these here parts. So don't count on getting cured if you do catch it!"

False ending.

"Oh, and also, if you've got it down below, you'll also stand a good chance of infecting your eyes with pus from your fingers. So try and save yourself for the real enemy, if you can. You're here to fight the Japs, not the clap!"

"I'm here to fight the Nips, not the crabs," a smart-ass corporal chipped in, and capped it off with a big laugh.

"Condoms or clap eh?" Salome asked Adam, down where the red lights twinkled salubriously in the dark. "That's like choosing between Hitler or Tojo."

"Right," Adam said. "Let's quit this sewer and go on a virgin hunt."

Salome hesitated, covetously eyeing the line of white soldiers. "You're too finicky. Where I come from, a piece of ass is a piece of ass."

"I know where you come from and it's time you aspired to higher things."

"Like what? What's higher than a piece of ass?" Salome pulled a face and flicked a tenacious mosquito off his face. "Don't answer that."

"I wasn't going to. There's no answer to that. So are you comin' or aren't you?"

Salome was actually moving to take his place on the end of the white line. "Where?"

"Somewhere with lights, where the beer is flowing like booze and the pussies aren't overflowing from the four hundred guys who went in before you."

Adam's suggested odyssey wasn't completely practical. Beer and girls were abundant but the brownout meant few streetlights and windows covered with brown sticky paper.

• THE CIVILIAN WAR ZONE •

It also meant neons doused for the duration and bureaucratic air-raid wardens who blew their whistles and their tops at the sight of a careless candle.

The night-life was there alright, but you had to hunt for it, or peer for it. Shop windows were unlit or boarded over, which meant less competition for the black marketeers, who operated best where it was blackest.

Salome reluctantly followed his buddy away from the Palmer Street floozy dens, stopping briefly at a water bubbler.

Adam flipped. "You crazy? You want your lips to turn green? Drink from that and you'll get clapped lips!"

"What are you talkin' about, Goldhart?" Salome angrily shook Adam's restraining hand off.

"Do you know what they use those things for? Obviously you don't! The gals around here get their guys to hoist them up. They use those bubblers for douches!"

Salome tried to look amazed, but actually looked confused. "What's a douche?"

"Christ! Where've you been? It's like . . . well, it's like . . . an upside down shower."

Salome tried to figure this out. "You mean — they stand on their heads?"

"You're kiddin', I hope. I mean they squirt in between their legs. Up their snatches."

"I know that."

"Sonofabitch! You just said you didn't know what a douche was!"

"I didn't know it was called a douche. My mom and my sister both have those hot-water bottle things. I seen 'em in the bathroom."

"You mean douche bags?"

"Sure." Salome looked longingly at the bubbler. "You sure they use those things?"

"Wishbone told me. He said he was with a dame the other night and she got him to hoist her up while she douched. Still want a drink of water?"

Salome frowned. "Let's go find a beer."

2

They were beautiful, these American gods of war. So clean, so sleek, in their immaculately tailored green uniforms with their wreathed eagle brass badges on their collars, their garrison caps with gold and black piping, their gold and silver bars and the gold (US) cap badges, mirror-polished shoes and razor-sharp creases in their trousers. They all had good teeth, burnished complexions, eyes that caressed you all over and soft smooth voices dripping with honey: "Ma'am" and "Miss", and "Pardon me, do you mind if . . .?" and "Sorry to disturb you, honey, but I'd be much obliged if. . ." They made Cynthia want to lie down in their arms. They made her legs turn to jelly. They made her dreams of handsome princes seem real. They brought fairytales to life and for some — not her — turned yearnings into earnings. So different from the local Aussie boys with their rough skins, neglected teeth, dissonant speech, oafish manners and coarse clothes.

At the Hyde Park Canteen, where the Yanks outnumbered the Aussies three to one, Cynthia competed nightly with the hundreds of other smitten local girls for American attentions and warm American arms, as they chatted and drank and smoked, or else foxtrotted to the Glenn Miller soundalike band that Chattanooga choo chooed them around the temporary wooden dance floor.

It made the daily production-line grind seem worthwhile. It made her spirits soar, it made the enemy seem a million miles north. During the day the oppressive grinding noise of the machinery seemed like a lullaby as she thought about the night before or fantasised about the night to come.

Work? Her mother had pleaded with her not to work. But today, everyone was working. The women were taking over all the men's jobs, except they were being paid a third

THE CIVILIAN WAR ZONE

less. She didn't mind. It was more than made up for by the gifts — the stockings, the orchids, the chocolates, the cigarettes — from her handsome military princes who whirled her around the canteen each night.

She wasn't quite as secure about Colonel Bastien Tunks of the Military Police, despite his gorgeous, all-white, full-dress uniform with two lapel insignias of crossed flintlock pistols, and matching all-white service cap. Some of the other girls thought he looked like a fancy bus driver. She overheard one of the GIs refer to him, behind his back, as "Snowdrop". And another as "Colonel Bastard".

Cynthia's view was more romantic. To her, Bastien Tunks looked like one of those splendid military types from nineteenth century Hungary or wherever in Europe. Yet something wasn't quite right.

To start with, he was almost middle-aged and had long ago lost the fresh naivety that so imbued most of the other, younger officers and enlisted men. No doubt he also had a well-wrinkled, unsuspecting wife tucked away at home.

Certainly, like all the others, he was polite. But there was a quiet ruthlessness about him, underneath it all. He obviously wanted her. She didn't mind that so much. It was the way he kept pursuing her. Almost every time she was dancing with one of the other men, he'd cut in. Without warning. And the enlisted men always released her and faded away, no matter how close they'd been. As if they were scared of him.

Well, why not? He was, after all, an MP. And a colonel. She'd heard that MPs were hated by the rest. She understood that. Her own father was a civilian policeman. A celebrated crusading detective sergeant. A brilliant man. Obviously tough on the job though kind at home. And absolutely incorruptible. But almost everyone seemed to dislike her father.

So she felt some affinity for the unpopular, feared Tunks. Perhaps she didn't even mind his cutting in. Like her father, she had sympathy for the maverick. Except, Tunks wasn't tender like the others. When they danced, she felt his harsh hands digging into her flesh, cruelly. He also didn't smile as

• MOBILISATION •

much as the others. He had a very strong chin and thin lips that curled back somewhat. She wasn't sure if that was the sign of a smile trying to get out, or a sneer. He reminded her a bit of a bulldog, although he wasn't ugly like that. It was perhaps the fleshiness of his wide face and the pinned back ears. She supposed it was overall an aggressive face; despite her interest, he frightened her as much as he did his compatriots.

Oh, she wouldn't have picked him herself. There were all those other, younger, prettier boys. But he had picked her and she didn't feel self-confident enough to reject him. And, of course, a colonel was something of a trophy.

"Say honey, you're not descended from the Mona Lisa, are you?" he asked her, the first time he cut in.

"I very much doubt it." She laughed. It was a corny line, but he said it as if he meant it.

"You got a smile that could destroy the whole US army, honey."

"I think you're exaggerating, colonel, is it?"

"That's right, but I'm off duty right now and you can call me Bastien. My folks lumbered me with Sebastien but I shortened it, and I never exaggerate."

"I bet you say that to all the girls."

"Say what?"

"About the Mona Lisa."

"What other gals? Since I first laid eyes on you, honey, all the other gals just disappeared."

Mmm, she thought. That's better. He wasn't quite as devoid of wit and charm as she first thought.

"Flattery'll get you everywhere."

"I'm just statin' a fact, honey. A fact."

"Shouldn't you be at the officers' club? I don't see any other colonels round here."

"It's dull there, honey. Kind of starchy. Like Buckingham Palace. Besides, you ain't there. So I ain't there."

The colonel had heavy legs. Cynthia felt like she was dancing with a truck. He was ponderously behind the beat all the time.

What Tunks didn't tell her was that all the girls at the

23

officers' club were strictly vetted "nice" girls. Selected according to height and conventionality. They were there strictly to dance and chat. It was the respectable "front", the public relations club, the one that proved that Americans were upright, noble, moral soldiers and that Aussie girls were virgins until wedlock. Besides Tunks preferred to be top-ranking dog. At the officers' club, surrounded by his peers, he felt insecure.

This sticky hot January night, Cynthia noticed that after her sixth compulsory foxtrot with him, dancing as it were, cheek to jowl, his gorgeous uniform was getting a bit stained round the armpits. And there was a strong case for Lifebuoy. It certainly reduced his attraction. Some of these gods were perhaps human after all.

About midnight he asked to take her home.

"I'm not going home yet, colonel." She couldn't bring herself to call him Bastien.

His left hand was exploring her back, just above her strapless cocktail dress, as clumsily as an amputated octopus. Every now and then one of his stubby fingers would slip down and touch the band of her bra. He made out as if he had no idea what his fingers were doing. Maybe they were somebody else's. Definitely not his. He was, after all, a colonel of an elite corps. The one entrusted with authority over all the rest.

"You're not going to stay here all night, are you honey?"

"You can call me Cynthia."

"You're a very pretty gal, honey. And you got real class. And you're tall. I don't like shrimps of any kind, honey."

She wondered about this. Maybe he hadn't heard her.

"Cynthia."

"And I like the way you walk. Tall and straight, with your head up. You're some kind of filly."

Maybe he was so egocentric he always walked through tables. She also didn't relish the equine analogy.

"Cynthia. My name is Cynthia."

"I heard!" he snapped.

"If you heard, why don't you call me by my name?" Colonel Tunks would have to learn that he was dancing with

• MOBILISATION •

the daughter of a tough detective. Perhaps a tougher cop than he was.

"Don't go off the deep end, honey. I didn't mean nothin'. So let me take you home."

She chalked one up to herself.

"Why? Don't you like dancing with me?"

Number two. She felt like taunting him. She felt she had the advantage because he wanted her more than she wanted him.

"There's some things you just can't do on the dance floor, honey."

"Cynthia." She wasn't going to let him win. "Like what?"

"Let me take you home and you'll find out. Do you like nylons?"

"What has that got to do with taking me home?" She was beginning to enjoy this. You couldn't conduct this kind of repartee with an Aussie boy.

"Everything." Tunks' eyes narrowed. He knew he was getting out of his depth.

"You mean — if I let you take me home, you'll give me some nylons?"

This riled him. He always got riled when he felt his catch slipping away.

"Now listen here, honey! I didn't say that! One thing at a time! Whatta you say?"

"I agree. One thing at a time. Where do we start?"

The band stopped for a break and everybody rushed the bar. But Cynthia and her broad-beamed colonel held their ground in the middle of the dance floor, in the huge temporary, prefabricated, hangar-like structure amongst the trees and fountains in the mid-city oasis.

"I got a jeep outside. Let's ride!" He tried to steer her towards the exit. She resisted.

"Hey! Colonel! Just a moment! I didn't say yes!"

He stopped. "Okay. Say yes."

"I don't think I should."

A tic developed over his left eye. She had pressed his inner agitation button. He didn't reply but started to drag her out, his strength making it look more like holding than pulling.

• THE CIVILIAN WAR ZONE •

"I don't think it would be right." With a supreme effort, she tore her arm away and stood her ground.

"What wouldn't be right?"

"I hardly know you."

"Honey!" His blue eyes glinted at her and gave her a prickly feeling. "There's a war on!"

"I know that!"

"We don't have the time, honey. You're a very pretty gal. The prettiest! If Betty Grable could see you, she'd cash in her chips. You deserve a good time. And I want to show you one. What do you need to know about me? I'm from Akron, Ohio. And I hate the dump. Never go back there. I still got four sisters there. I'm the eldest. I been in this man's army for twenty-five years. I fought the Krauts in Europe in 1918. I killed thirteen of 'em, got a silver star and cluster, a hunk of shrapnel in my belly and a whiff of gas up my nostrils. But I'm fitter than any of these hickey-faced ponies today. And I sure like you Aussie gals, honey, but most of all I like you, 'cause you got spirit and brown hair and green eyes and I got this four-wheel drive outside that's jus' achin' to take you home before it's too late, 'cause it's a big day tomorrow, honey. As division Provost Marshal I got to instruct your police force on traffic control, internal security and population control. They got no idea of how to handle a war situation. So let's go, honey. 'Fore I change my mind!"

He gave her the stare — the stare of absolute authority. It was the stare that broke men's hearts before he moved in and broke their bones. And not even the free-spirited Cynthia Church, the tall, svelte, ample-bosomed, lightly tanned, mannequin-featured beauty, could continue to resist.

"On one condition."

"What's that?"

"You stop calling me honey. I like to be called by my real name."

His expression didn't change. She looked for a warm, even humorous glint in his eyes, but there was none. Sure, he called all women honey, irrespective of age, appeal or situation. It was easier that way. If you called them all the same thing, you didn't have to acknowledge their individual identities or take their preferences into account. You didn't have to bow to their wishes, or their needs. They were all honey and he wanted to keep it that way. It served his purpose, protected his invulnerability, asserted his supreme control.

But . . . perhaps, this one was different. She was resisting him. He didn't like that. It could get out of hand. She was a real looker. Way above par. He was bursting to get those pleated, artificial silk clothes off her. In his mind's eye, he could already see the stuff she had on underneath. He'd snap those suspenders, use them like a whip, raise some welts on that buttermilk skin, bring tears to those mocking green eyes. Maybe even rip that silk down the middle, wind it round her throat and pull it tight till she spluttered for air and mercy. Then he'd really lay it on her. He'd ram it into her until she screamed. Sure, she was just a honey like all the rest, but not for now. Just for a fraction of a minute, if it meant getting her compliance, he'd break the habit.

"Okay, Cynthia. Anything you say. Let's get out of here!"

He didn't have to drag her out now. She put her arm through his and walked willingly and gracefully towards the exit.

3

The hunting instinct, having survived tens of thousands of annums, was in full flight again, as Adam and Salome — big dame hunters extraordinary — hailed a taxi in the red-light area. Three stopped, hustling for the reputedly easy bait.

They took the one in the middle and the elderly, over-enlistment age driver, gnarled and knobbly, roared off, making obscene gestures at the disappointed competition.

"Take us somewhere they got lights, buddy," Adam said.

"Right mate. The Cross it is."

"What's the fare, buddy?" Salome asked, when the cabbie disgorged them just a quarter of a mile from where he'd picked them up. It was perhaps the longest quarter-mile in history. Or geography. He had elected to take them the unfamiliar long way to Kings Cross, which meant a minor diversion of about five miles in the wrong direction.

"Just under half a brick, Yank," the cabbie replied. Expectantly. Whenever he wasn't talking his mouth hung open, displaying ill-fitting dentures aching to find solace in a cool glass of water, free of the cabbie's abrasive mouth.

"How much is that?"

"Hard to explain to you Yanks," the cabbie said, scratching his stubbly chin, with a degree of patronising that would've graced a pukka sahib. "It ain't a lot though. We're glad to see youse all here, defendin' us from the Nips, and we want to show our appreciation like. So I'll settle for a quarter of a brick, no matter what the meter says."

"The meter don't say nothing," Adam pointed out.

"Crikey!" the cabbie said. "I must've clean forgot to turn it on! Well, that makes youse extra lucky 'cause now I can charge you even less than I was gonna charge you. Let's call it less than a quarter of a brick."

• MOBILISATION •

"How much is that exactly?" Salome wanted to get it over with. He saw some lights down the street and they seemed to be beckoning.

"Exactly don't matter, mate. Near enough is good enough for me. It's our way of sayin' thanks for comin' Yank. Just give me a look at what you got."

Salome looked sideways at Adam, who looked like a sceptic Yank.

Salome shrugged and showed the cabbie a handful of notes and coins, the value of which he hadn't yet properly fathomed. In camp they'd had everything laid on. This was their first foray into the market place. They'd blithely ignored the army's printed pamphlet on money exchange. Pounds, shillings and pence were as obscure as quetzals and just didn't add up. Two hundred and forty pence to the pound was a hopeless mathematical tangle, as was twenty shillings to the pound and twelve pence to the shilling.

The cabbie carefully extracted a one pound note, a ten shilling note and nine shillings and sixpence in change.

"That should just about cover it, mate. It's actually a bit less than would've been on the meter, but crikey, there's a war on!"

The cabbie slammed the door and roared off, his gas producer producing a puff of polluted insolence to cap off his victory. Salome and Adam stood on the footpath slightly bemused, having made a most generous contribution to the cab drivers' benevolent fund.

"That guy suckered us. I'm sure of it," Adam said.

"Maybe. Cabbies always do. Least he didn't hold out for a tip like the New York hacks do."

"I got an idea we just paid him about a ninety per cent tip. How many bucks are there in one pound?"

"I thought it was the other way around."

"Listen, Sal. From now on, let me handle the dough. Okay?"

"Sure thing." Salome was happy to relinquish the responsibility. "But why didn't you say something before?" Salome screwed up his nose and eyes, an involuntary mannerism denoting embarrassment, as if trying to hide his face.

• THE CIVILIAN WAR ZONE •

They cased the bustling street. It felt good. There was action here. They smelt bear and their young loins were enervated in anticipation. Yet they weren't quite sure of their moves. What came first? Perhaps a little fuel for the long night ahead. They tried a pub, quickly sank two beers and left, disappointed at the marble tiled and glass decor, which had all the ambience of a public toilet, and at the absence of females. Public bars, it seemed, were segregated male domains.

They wanted lights. There were lights. But Darlinghurst Road was taking a risk. It wasn't exactly Times Square, but while the rest of the city was either blacked or browned out, Kings Cross was yellowed out. The authorities tended to take the view that, in the case of an air-raid, Kings Cross was expendable. It had a dubious reputation. Bohemian in the extreme. Not a fit place for nice middle-class people. At least, not with their wives. The Japanese, the air-raid wardens reasoned, bombed Pearl Harbor because of the navy yards, but they didn't bother with Waikiki.

This theory ignored the fact that the docks and submarine bases were less than a quarter-mile from the Cross. Nevertheless, some of the cautious establishments in Darlinghurst Road had sandbags piled up outside their frontages.

Adam and Salome joined the throng, in which American soldiers and sailors predominated. Minority groups included some Dutch sailors and a few Aussie troops, but beside the sleek olive drab Americans their khaki uniforms — the worst in worsted — made them look like poor relations. On the pavement a few shoeshine boys, light tan Aussie kids with pimples, kneepants and grey school shirts, were inexpertly elbow-greasing the already shiny US boots, all in return for a few coins and sticks of Juicy Fruit.

Many of the Americans had local women in tow — girls with frizzy hair and adoring eyes, wearing their best, pre-ration-book cocktail dresses and hats with flowers on them. Morale boosting had become a patriotic duty.

When the air-raid siren sounded the alert, its bent contralto going up and down like an aural roller coaster, it didn't exactly create a panic. Adam and Salome and a few others approached a public air-raid shelter but found it padlocked. Apparently the authorities were concerned that shelters were used by drunks and disreputables for unsocial and unsavoury purposes. Clearly a clean closed shelter was preferable to an open seamy one.

As the siren receded Adam and Salome bought hotdogs — a recent innovation — from a street vendor and felt a little more at home. Then the all clear siren, a prolonged johnny one-note whine, relaxed the tension. No bombs tonight. Except in Darwin, three thousand miles north.

Salome wanted to try the Roosevelt nightclub, just off the main stem, lighting up a dark alley. But Adam vetoed.

"My folks'd blow their stacks if they knew I went in there." As usual, Salome had difficulty telling whether Adam was serious or joking.

"Whatta you mean?"

"They're registered Republicans. GOPs to the core. The name Roosevelt makes them nauseous."

Salome shook his head. He didn't find that particularly funny. He was sick of strolling around. He wanted a base.

"You're kiddin'. Let's go in. And if you're not kiddin', how they gonna find out?"

"My old man knows everything I do. He's like a witch. If I don't write he knows I'm hiding something. If I do write, I have a compulsion to tell him everything. I can't help it. I can't keep secrets from them. We're a very open family."

Salome grabbed Adam by the lapels of his class A uniform jacket and lifted him several inches off the ground. The sturdy cotton chino material held its seams. For such a lean young stick, Salome showed surprising strength, holding Adam's one hundred and sixty pounds as if it were nothing.

"You're bullshitting me again, pal!"

"Put me down! You don't know where I've been!" Adam kept a straight face. Then spiced it with a crooked grin. Salome dropped him. Adam smoothed his uniform and tossed back a bothersome cow's lick.

Salome looked longingly at the Roosevelt's entrance. The paunchy, slightly punchy, retired pugilistic doorman gave them a welcoming sneer."Come on in boys."

Adam turned to Salome, serious now. He shook his head. "This is a clipjoint, buddy. I heard that. Wishbone told me.

They eat wallets for supper."

Salome approached the doorman. "Hey buddy? Is this a clipjoint or what? My friend wants to know."

"A clipjoint?" The slow-off-the-mouth doorman looked confused. "Clipjoint? I'm new on this job, boys. I wouldn't know what a clipjoint is. Is that like a shearing shed?"

"Forget I asked."

The doorman agreeably managed to forget immediately. His problem was retention. He held the padded door open for them, but Adam had steered Salome away, down the street.

"Are your folks really Republicans? I thought all Jews were Democrats."

"All Jews are everything, pal. Just like everyone else."

Salome accepted that piece of wisdom without further comment. He wasn't looking for anything more than something not to write home about. He zoomed ahead of Adam now, and then a sign caught his eye. The Reflections Club.

Salome waited for Adam to catch up. From the outside it didn't look nearly as pretentious as its name. Nor as expensive as the Roosevelt. It had an unlit neon, a glass shopfront window completely pasted over with brown sticky paper for blastproof purposes and there was some white lettering scrawled across the glass on the outside:

"Servicemen admitted free. Others 5/- cover. Dine, drink, dance. Floor show twice nightly."

"I got a hard-on! This is the place! I heard of it! They got everything! Let's go!"

Salome's enthusiasm was so potent that Adam couldn't resist. He followed him in. He had no reason to doubt this place. Not a shadow. He'd never heard of it. The omnipotent Wishbone hadn't been there, or warned him against it. Maybe it was a piece of okay. Maybe it was a haremesque funfest of boozy enjoyment. Maybe it was the Stork Club down under? Maybe.

The night wasn't getting any younger. It was commitment time.

They might've been better off at the Roosevelt. Or better still, they might've been better off going back to their bivouac hotel and playing craps. For they had just ventured behind enemy lines, without knowing it.

4

Colonel Bastien Tunks, Provost Marshal of the Military Police, 41st Division, dismissed his driver, the sad-eyed Corporal Simpson, outside the Hyde Park Canteen. Simpson took the opportunity to go inside and join the jitterbuggers. It was his first break away from his demanding CO for weeks. Tunks also dismissed his adjutant staff officer, Lieutenant Kobovsky, who had been drinking steadily at the bar whilst his colonel besported himself on the dance floor.

Tunks hoisted Cynthia into the passenger seat with a little too much hoist. She toppled sideways and nearly hit her head on the steering wheel. Tunks didn't apologise, possibly because he had mentally shifted the blame from himself to his victim, a reflex MP action. Cynthia fumed inwardly but stilled her tongue.

"I like to drive," Tunks confessed, as he belied his middle-aged paunch and vaulted into the driver's seat like a high jumper. "I got to be where I am by taking the initiative, doing everything myself. Now they want to load me up with slaves to do everything for me, to neuter me. It's not my style."

"I thought you'd be the type of man who likes to have others to push around, colonel," Cynthia said, with overt irony.

Tunks accepted this as a compliment. "Sure I do, honey. That's why I like my job. It's what I get paid to do. Pushing round dogfaces is an honourable and necessary occupation. Most of 'em are street rubbish and have to have law and order knocked into 'em before they learn to act like soldiers. That's what I'm here for. But that don't mean I need servants to wipe my ass . . . 'scuse me, honey. I forgot myself."

Cynthia was almost touched. He had apologised. Not for his actions but for his words. She marvelled at the distorted sense of honour. Here was a violent man wielding great

• THE CIVILIAN WAR ZONE •

authority, who appeared never to apologise for anything except for using cuss words in front of ladies. Her impressions were confirmed as he outlined his credo for her, at a word rate that rivalled his driving speed.

"You know honey, up until Pearl Harbor most Americans didn't want to get involved in any world war. Didn't want to fight the Germans. But I did. I believe in war. The isolationists don't realise that America's always been involved in wars. It started with the British, the Civil War, Mexico, we even sent troops to fight Russia after their sonofabitch revolution. Should've continued that one in my estimation. Now they're on our side. But not for long."

Tunks drove the jeep as if he was in a war zone. He zigzagged along the road, avoiding imaginary mines and enemy ambushes, rehearsing for the day of combat. If it ever came. Oncoming browned-out headlights induced the swerves. Probably he was trying to impress her, which suggested he wasn't as bright as he thought he was. Most of the under thirty-year-old Australian female population was already over-impressed with every male in a US uniform. Tunks was now gilding the lily.

"War's good for democracy you see, honey. Basically, when you got half the men in the country in the armed forces, they're all equal. Except for the officers. But you gotta have officers. You gotta have someone to lead. But the rest, they're all equal. It's communism really. Don't quote me. Now I ain't no commie. Not in civilian life. But when you have all those guys in the forces, it knocks the ambition out of them, keeps them in line, forces them to support their buddies, think about others instead of just theirselves. Sure, some of 'em get killed or wounded, but they get killed or wounded in peacetime too, don't they? But in war, they're equal. That's real communism."

"War teaches men to hate and kill. What's good about that?" Cynthia knew she was supposed to just listen, but that wasn't her style.

"Hate and kill the enemy. Not each other." Tunks glared at her sideways and ran the jeep up over the kerb onto the pavement, then down onto the road again. He seemed to relish the accidental deviation.

• MOBILISATION •

"It rubs off though," Cynthia said.

"If it does, that's where we come in. The MPs. We keep 'em on the straight and narrow. We don't have the constraints on us that civilian police do. We can go in and bust heads whenever we think it's necessary. And it works."

"That's not communism. That's fascism."

"You call it what you want. It works. Most of our guys are happier now than they ever were back home. And when they're on a pass, they can bust out, get drunk, screw, let loose, do all the things they can't do at home."

"When they do, your men bust their heads, as you put it."

"Only if they go too far." Tunks was high on his own polemics. She could argue if she wanted, but he had an answer for everything. He could nail her down without even thinking.

But Cynthia advanced the argument to a new plane. "What do you think war does for women?"

"It keeps 'em in their place. Helping morale, makin' things, working for a change, shows 'em how to stand on their own two feet for a change, while their men are away fighting. It's good for them too."

"You know what I think, colonel?"

"Don't matter what you think, honey. You leave the thinkin' to us."

"Well I think the worst thing about war is that it gives power to men like you."

That shut Tunks up for a moment. He swore softly under his breath. His first instinct was to lash back at her, but he didn't want to sabotage his major objective. Then he lightened up. He had to admire her spunk.

"Tell you what, honey. No enlisted man'd ever say a thing like that to me and get away with it."

"It's lucky I'm not an enlisted man then, isn't it?"

He lost a further advantage when he had to stop the jeep and ask her for directions to her friend's house, where she said she was staying the night. She often stayed there after a late shift at the plant, or after dancing until dawn. The city was almost devoid of signposts, which had been removed to confuse the Japanese invaders. If they ever got there.

Cynthia kept chastising herself for being there with him. It was her biggest mistake ever, she knew that. On the other hand, how could a young, vulnerable, inexperienced girl, captivated as she had been by an entire army, resist such authority as this man possessed? Still, she wasn't entirely defenceless. There was still her tongue allied to her intelligence and, despite lapses, her own built-in sense of reality.

Apparently pleased with his previous unintentional deviation onto the footpath, Tunks swerved again, using a telegraph pole and a tree as a slalom course.

"Aren't you afraid you'll kill someone?" Basically Cynthia was afraid he'd kill them both.

"I'm only afraid of two things, honey. Failure and confined spaces."

"I'll remember that." His frank self-analysis surprised her. "Do you always drive like this?"

"Only when I'm behind the wheel." He laughed uproariously. Another surprise. "These little four-wheel drive babies are built for it. It's a crime to drive 'em any other way."

"Maybe they're built for it, but I'm not. Anyway, you're breaking the law."

Tunks laughed again. But this time it was more malice than mirth. "What law? What do you know about the law, honey?"

"Cynthia. Remember? And I know quite a lot about the law. My father's a policeman."

Tunks was impressed. "That so? Great. I knew we had something in common. That's why you're such a spunky gal. Maybe you'll introduce me to your old man sometime?"

She didn't reply. He didn't mind. He lapsed into silence for a while. Of course he didn't ever want to meet her father. With what he had in mind for her, her father was the last person he'd want to meet.

There was barbed wire along the side of the road now, as they headed south, skirting Botany Bay — another deterrent to potential invaders. Tunks' jeep didn't seem to be out of place here, as it lurched along.

"Your galfriend sure lives a long way out of the city, honey." They'd been travelling a good thirty minutes so far,

• MOBILISATION •

through lower middle-class bungalow territory.

"It's close to where I work. I often stay there. And when are you going to stop calling me honey?"

"We must be nearly there by now." There he went again, walking through tables. She noticed that if he didn't want to answer a question, he just ignored it.

"You didn't answer my question."

"You answer mine first, baby."

Well, maybe that was his idea of compromise. Baby for honey. She wasn't sure which was more annoying.

"Only a few miles further. I didn't ask you to drive me home remember. You offered. In fact, you insisted. I could've caught the train." She had the gloves off now. She felt she had his measure. He had succeeded in disillusioning her — probably a healthy thing. She now realised that all Americans weren't gods. This one was the very antithesis.

"You're sure a sassy little gal, honey. I may have to teach you a lesson."

"What do you mean?" Alarm bells!

He didn't answer. He lapsed back into his own recognisance. Planning his campaign.

"Turn right here." Cynthia pointed to an intersection ahead.

Maybe he heard her, maybe he didn't. He nodded as if he did. But he didn't turn right. He kept on going.

"You missed it!"

"So what?" He had heard her after all. "It's early yet. I thought we might share a little moonlight, you and I." His thin lips pulled back into a significant grin. It seemed clear that their intentions were diametrically opposed.

5

Carl Goyt seemed to be extremely pro-American and on the surface, unlike so many of his fellow Australians, did not appear to harbour any resentment against their presence in his country.

Nor should he have.

Since MacArthur's arrival he had been collecting all things American, particularly of a military nature: uniforms, caps, insignias, weapons, dog tags, pistol belts, magazine clips, mess kits, watches, compasses, sleeping-bags, flashlights, sunglasses, MP peerless handcuffs, pocket-knives, pouch sets, duffle bags, gasmasks, C rations, D rations, K rations, jungle rations and mountain rations — everything pertaining to these noble allies.

Some of them he sold at a nice black market profit; the rest he kept on display at his "headquarters".

The profits from the sales enabled him to give more than adequate service pay to the members of his "volunteer battalion", which in size was not really a battalion at all but more of a special tactical unit. Goyt however had a grandiose vision which anticipated the time when he would command an entire regiment made up of ten companies, led by himself as a full-fledged colonel.

Not bad for a civilian.

This would place him several echelons above his father, who, during his twelve years sojourn in the British army, never rose above sergeant major.

He intended to visit his father one weekend, wearing his best, highest-ranking uniform — that of a major. On the other hand it might be best to wait until he could appear as a colonel. Or even higher. Dare he think it? No. He was a realist. If you aim too high, you might miss your target altogether. Even as a general, he mused, his father would probably confront him, like always, and make him feel lower than a private.

• MOBILISATION •

His father's British imperial authority was the one constant in Carl's life, but one day he hoped to be able to usurp this authority by impressing him with his inventory of military victories which would put Wellington in the shade. To date Carl had been too timid to wear anything but civvies in his father's omnipotent presence, because he knew he might still see right through him. He knew what that would mean. The Punishment of the Picket — in which his hand was fastened to a hook in a post above his head and his suspended body was left to be supported by his bare heel resting on a wooden stump. Or else the cat-o'-nine-tails, his father's most beloved souvenir.

By the same token, his father would not approve of such fear as Carl Goyt felt at the thought of his presence. He always told Carl "a soldier ought to fear nothing but God and dishonour".

He never said anything about fearing one's father.

Carl's headquarters, which also doubled as his home, was an old bungalow in Moore Park, half a mile from the city and Kings Cross. It had huge rooms and high ceilings, dating back to Victorian times. Since he'd taken it over (started renting it), which coincided with the US military taking over so many other buildings in the city, he had transformed it to suit his purposes. Rooms included the Orderly Room (living room), Armoury (toolshed), Mess (dining room), Supply and Maintenance Depot (garage), Officers' Quarters (bedroom), Operations and Logistics Room (sunroom), Reserve Store (pantry), Guardhouse (vestibule) and Communications Centre (attic). Some of the rooms were bedecked with American flags, eagles and insignias. He knew that the Americans liked to dress up their offices with patriotic regalia, just like the Nazis (for whom he had a covert admiration). It was, as he saw it, a post-colonial desire to rival the British, who loaded their headquarters in Chelsea, Victoria and Whitehall with the trappings of imperial splendour. Of course, not having the regal hegemonic background of the British Empire, American military adornments were contrastingly crass and tasteless. In Goyt's eyes.

Nevertheless, for his own esoteric purposes, his head-

• THE CIVILIAN WAR ZONE •

quarters were like a modern American military museum.

Naturally Goyt had tried to join up as soon as Australia followed Britain headlong into the war with Germany. He would have happily gone off to North Africa with the Second AIF, except for his breathing difficulty. They told him it was a health barrier to his induction.

At the recruiting office they even went as far as to call him an *asthmatic*!

That immediately set off one of his most severe and prolonged bouts. He wheezed and whooped and coughed and spluttered and gulped air like an iron lung with metal fatigue, and they couldn't get him out of there quick enough.

Of course he knew he didn't have *asthma* as they'd suggested. He would never admit to *asthma*. He well knew that *asthmatics* are made not born. Parents talk their children into having *asthma* by telling them they have *asthma*, even if they don't. As in his case.

He admitted he had "breathing difficulty". The mere mention of the word *asthma* in his presence was enough to set him off. Which proved his theory.

His mother had always known never to mention that *word* in front of him. But his father had always liked to bait him, liked to see him struggling for air, chest palpitating, lungs like bellows, heart thumping, ribs contracting, semi-asphyxiated. One little word. *Asthma*. Out aloud.

Goyt was spending a long time this night in his Supply Depot, surveying his US military wardrobe. What rank and identity would he bestow upon himself?

He had given himself a one-day pass. He was going to indulge himself, along with all the other American debauchers up at the Cross. It was his rule never to venture out as less than a commissioned officer. It was a matter of being one-up on his father.

Tonight — maybe a captain, or a lieutenant? He liked the way the Americans pronounced lieutenant. Just the way it was spelt. Not *lef-tenant*, like the Aussies and the Brits. How did they get *lef-tenant* out of lieutenant?

Tonight he felt bold. He was going to promote himself. He had a lovely class A major's uniform. Olive drab service

• MOBILISATION •

cap with gold eagle, brown leather peak and chinstrap, a tropical worsted hip-length olive drab jacket with a brown leather belt and bandoleer and contrasting fawn shirt and green tie. The pink/beige trousers had creases you could slit your throat on. This was all set off by his badge of rank — a gold oak leaf.

He thought he'd better pick an authentic-sounding name. He took it from one of the dog tags. It was a private's actually, but the name sounded better with major before it. Major Bradley Theodore. Of the Quartermaster Corps, 41st Division. The Yanks loved to use surnames as Christian names.

He applied a false black moustache, to match his current hair colour. Normally light brown. What there was of it. He was prematurely almost bald. Then he looked longingly at a bayonet in a scabbard and wondered whether he could wear it under his uniform. It was hardly appropriate for debauching occasions. Only the MPs were able to tote weapons openly around town. He could hardly conceal the scabbard under his trouser leg.

He decided on a web pistol belt under his jacket. He could then hook a carbine bayonet, not much bigger than a knife, onto one of the eyelets. It would sit against his thigh, under his trousers. That felt very comforting.

He thought about carrying a .45 pistol in a russet leather holster also attached to an eyelet, but it was too bulky. One night he'd use his MP uniform and then he could stroll around like a human armoury. But impersonating an MP was rather more dangerous than becoming just another officer on leave.

He raided his well-stocked icebox, which was Standing Room Only for food delicacies. He was truly a fortunate fellow. Foods such as these were normally severely rationed or totally unavailable. He doubted if any other Aussie household had cans of American chili con carne, luncheon meat or Vienna sausage. He didn't even own a ration-book, yet he had more cheese, butter, eggs, bacon, rice, flour, pork, beef, biscuits, tea and coffee than he could use. An army marches on its stomach. His father used to say that.

He gnawed on a cold chicken leg and some potato salad. Then he had a little red salmon and a bowl of preserved fruit. Very sweet. The sugar tended to increase his breathing difficulty,

• THE CIVILIAN WAR ZONE •

but it was worth it. Before the night was out, he'd be breathing like Boy Charlton, the famous swimmer. In, out, in, out, he thumped his chest. It felt hard. All muscle.

He wasn't very tall — a lifelong regret. Neither was Napoleon, they told him at school. Or Billy Hughes. Small consolation. He was under five and a half feet. He always felt an urge to cower in the presence of taller men. A kind of twisted vertigo which made him overcompensate and throw his weight around. Well, he had plenty of weight. He was solid. A tree trunk. He also felt ambivalent about his face. In its natural state, it was hardly prepossessing. Almost featureless, bland, unnoticed and unnoticeable. Blank and fleshy. Except for his wide, staring blue eyes. Deep as the sea and hard to fathom. It was the kind of face that was easy to alter. It was fully augmentable. A little make-up, pencil, cottonwool, false eyebrows, moustache, hair, thickening the nostrils, filling out the puffy cheeks, adding prominence, colour to the pale, character to the bland. Only his eyes remained the same.

He felt good, this rather muggy night, as he swaggered down Darlinghurst Road, parrying the come-on looks from the local girls, many of whom delighted in sitting in doorways and on steps with their skirts casually riding high, flashing their receptive thighs, moist with anticipation at the sight of a Yankee uniform, reaching out for a dose of silver-tongued charm and a pair of nylons, offering their souls for a taste of devilry. And he, an American major, resplendent in his hero's garb, hypnotic with his embellished features, attracted them like cockroaches to a garbage can.

Not that he wanted anything to do with them. In fact, he delighted in scorning them. Women weren't his main preference, not even those newly liberated girls in their rush for penetration and even impregnation. He wasn't actually sure of his preference. Sex, no matter who you did it with, meant sharing your body and your fluids. And he didn't really like sharing. Specially not his body, which, because of his affliction, needed nurturing at all times. Sex made you breathe heavily and that was to be avoided at all times. He looked upon sex more as an expression of conflict. You could attack someone

• MOBILISATION •

sexually. Another form of combat. A power play. It was something you did to them, not something of mutual interest.

His mother — that is his ex-mother, she'd passed away many years before — was a very introverted, docile person. He'd once seen his father do it to her. It had been entirely his initiative. She just lay back and put up with it. She always used to let him dominate her, until the one and only time she had asserted herself, by dying. His father had considered that to be a rebuff. He never forgave her for dying on him, it was as if she had no right to do so until he gave the order.

His father used to tell him about the compliant Indian and Burmese women he'd had, when he was in the British army. Serving the Raj. But he couldn't abide the Sydney girls flinging themselves at the Yanks. That was reprehensible in his eyes. Women should be like his mother, and wait to be impinged upon.

The street was dirty. Garbage was only rarely collected these days. Most of the able-bodied garbagemen had been called up, and most of the garbage trucks had been conscripted for military use. The air was full of pungent smells — garbage, beer, urine, cheap perfume, tobacco, sweat. A nice southerly buster would blow it all away.

War was bad for cities, but it was good for Carl Goyt. It made killing respectable, honourable. It made hate and prejudice the norm. People were encouraged to openly hate the enemy, and the enemy could be anyone you hated.

He saw the place he was looking for. A popular nightclub that catered specially for servicemen. It was a bit smoky and that wouldn't please his lungs, but the solution would more than compensate.

He saluted the man at the door and went down into the basement. It was one of those unstarchy, cup-handed American salutes, which were more like a friendly greeting. He liked that. It was so deceptive.

6

For the first time that night, Cynthia felt a gnawing fear in her stomach. Up until now she had felt quite able to cope with this bombastic MP colonel. She had felt secure because she felt she had his measure, as if comprehension was in itself a defence. Sticks and stones could break her bones but words could never. . . But then his words had seemed to dry up and he ignored her directions.

"I need to get home. My shift starts at seven."

"I thought you Aussie girls were romantic."

"I don't think you have romance on your mind, colonel."

He looked sideways at her and there was a different gleam in his eye, a certain fire, not of desire but fury. She wasn't sure what she had done to enrage him.

"What do you know what I got on my mind?" He spat out the words.

Despite the new fear, she wasn't defenceless. "Colonel!" she barked. "Stop the car!"

"Okay." He did. Right on a sandy verge, overlooking the bay, which was navy blue in the half moonlight. The surrounding headland was a dark indiscernable mass without a twinkle of light showing. The air-raid wardens must've been pleased. Tunks kept the jeep's unhooded headlights on, illuminating the slight swell a few yards in front of them.

"I meant — turn the car around!" Cynthia's fear was laced with anger.

By contrast Tunks had assumed a benign front. "You said stop the car, honey. So I did."

"I also said turn right, and you didn't!"

"Well honey, one out of two ain't bad for starters." He slipped his right arm over her shoulders.

"You don't have to do that." She shrugged his arm off.

• MOBILISATION •

"I don't *have* to do anything, honey!" His arm returned.

"Are you going to take me home or not?" Her voice was shrill with emotion.

Again, the walk through tables. "You're shivering a bit there, honey. Gotta keep you warm." His arm gripped her possessively and his large hunk of hand found a squeezing place just above her right breast. He stuck his face against her cheek, which she kept averted.

"You didn't answer my question!"

"Hey? Did you ask a question, honey? What was it?" His lips were carving a trail across her cheek. "Loosen up there, baby."

She turned towards him now, not in a spirit of cooperation but of confrontation. "Look colonel! I don't want to do this! I want to go home! To bed!" She added hurriedly, "To sleep."

His right hand found the exterior swell that denoted her breast, and squeezed hard.

"Don't do that! Please! I mean it!"

Protests, pleas, wriggles, writhing, hard line, soft line: it was all grist to his mill. He wasn't going to be deflected. Total compliance might have been the only resistance.

"You're hurting me!"

He accepted that as confirmation that all was going well, and increased his pressure.

"That's what happens when you struggle, baby. Now, that ain't nice. We're allies, honey. You and me. We're on the same side."

She tried to respond but he put his cruel mouth over hers and kissed her, savagely. She spluttered, tried to turn her head away but he gripped the back of her neck like a vice and almost paralysed her. It was the worst kiss she could remember. Not an indication of love, affection or even desire, but of malignance. In retaliation she bit his lip.

Beads of sweat appeared on his tanned forehead. His almost pleasant facade vanished.

"Well honey, if that's the way you want to play it!" He pulled his face away, but he continued to grip her with both hands, around the breast and the back of the neck. Blood seeped from his lip and Cynthia felt sorry for what she'd done.

She tried to wipe the blood away with her fingers. Her eyes raked his face, pleading with him, hoping he'd understand her impulse. But it was too late. As far as he was concerned, she'd declared war.

"Hell, I thought you were a nice gal, honey. But you've got a mouth like a bitch!" He suddenly realised that his lip was leaking red stuff. He wiped it off with the back of his hand, then looked at it. Saw double red. Boiled over.

He deliberately wiped the back of his hand against her dress. Cynthia gasped. "God! Why did you do that? God! That's awful!"

She tried to clamber out of the jeep, but his grasp was a fixture.

"You asked for it, baby! You sure did!"

She'd played right into his hands. Now he had the excuse he needed. This made it self-defence, he misreasoned.

He ripped the front of her dress open, exposing her slip and bra. Cynthia yelled. He ripped her slip down the front. Cynthia screamed. But her voice was swept up by the night wind and disappeared over the bay.

"Don't, please don't! You can't do this!"

"Do what, honey?" His voice was calm again, with a sinister Peter Lorre undertone.

Cynthia suddenly realised he was taking a sadistic pleasure in her distress. She had enough presence of mind to appreciate that vulnerability was an incitement to him.

She was a policeman's daughter. She would fight back. So she turned on him, tried to scratch his face, but this time didn't draw blood. He grabbed both her wrists in one beefy hand, flesh-and-blood handcuffs. Then he laughed, spraying her with saliva. That and the whisky on his breath made her want to throw up.

"You got two choices, honey. Relax and cooperate and you won't get hurt. Or do it the hard way, and I won't be responsible for what happens to you."

"You'll be arrested for this! I'll see to that!"

"For what, honey? So far I'm the one who's hurt. You talked me into takin' you home and then turned out to be a spitfire. Or a zero. Your cops ain't gonna take the side of

• MOBILISATION •

a cockteaser, honey. 'Cause that's all you are. A cockteaser! I know your kind. You deserve everything you get! Everyone knows you gals are fallin' over each other to make us feel at home."

"Let go of me!" She tried to release herself. "You're breaking my wrists!"

"Aw sorry honey! Sometimes I just don't know my own strength. I realise now you don't want a fight, you want . . . love." He attacked her face with his lips, pecking at her, almost eating her. She couldn't move. His body was like a cement overcoat, weighing her down. His free hand was inside her bra pulling at her breast. Then he snapped the bra off, tugged it down her arms, tossed it out the window. She screamed and cried and tried to pummel him. As he twisted her nipple with one hand he drew the other back for a pacifying punch.

But the jeep was much too cramped for his purposes. He kicked the door open and bundled her out, onto the sandy verge. She was half naked now, with only the bottom part of her torn dress clinging around her hips over her elasticised panty-girdle and stockings. He landed on top of her, pinning her to the ground. Then he tore his white jacket off, oblivious to the fate of his gold buttons, and started trying to unbuckle his white trousers. She didn't know if it was deliberate or not, but his elbow caught her just below the eye with a sickening thump, and she felt a jar in her brain that brought a fresh flood of tears. She nearly blacked out.

"Relax, honey, relax," he kept saying. "Relax, honey, relax," over and over as if he didn't know he was saying it.

He had his trousers and gun holster off, but her panty-girdle was a chastity belt. Thank God, she thought. He was trying to tug them down with one hand and pinched her flesh. She felt his sweat dripping on her. She wriggled her hips trying to reinforce the step-in squeeze and kicked out her legs, damaging his shin. One of his hands was squeezing her left breast and the pain was so intense she felt herself slipping away again. She considered allowing herself to succumb. This seemed a losing battle. But she couldn't. She was a battler, the daughter of a battler. She arched her back, strain against strain, trying to dislodge him, making her body as tight as a board. No surrender. No quarter.

She suddenly found herself with one free hand, and that free hand was gripping one of her high-heeled, ankle-strap shoes that had come loose.

With all her might she swung the shoe up in an arc, towards that thick merciless face.

The heel caught him right on the side of his forehead.

Cynthia shuddered at the unprecedented result. Maybe the heel had contained an exposed nail. The blow hit the unyielding skull bone and split his skin, causing a gush of blood from a pierced extra-dural artery.

Tunks rose up on his knees and howled like a wolfman, cranially contused, concussion to come, haemorrhaging onto his white collar. Her trauma almost matched his. The success of her counter-assault terrified her. Who was the aggressor? Who was the guilty one? She didn't know. Now she wanted to monopolise the suffering. That would be better than the guilt. But she had to get away, not so much for her survival, but to stop herself compounding his injuries. Knowledge that her actions were in self-defence didn't seem to erase her horror.

She wriggled away on her back, wide-eyed, grazing her thigh on a piece of rock, puncturing her hands, caring no longer about her own injuries, obsessed with his.

Tunks put his hand to his wound and then recoiled with blood and trauma. Head thudding, he stood up and stumbled after her, a wounded lion. He was going to get her now. But good.

"You fuckin' little bitch!" he swore, all blood and fury.

He was going to kill her now, she knew that. She didn't have the coordination to stand and run. She couldn't seem to rise up off her haunches. Marooned in the sand. He was only feet away and had his service revolver out of his white holster. She thought it looked like a cowboy gun, a Colt 45. Just the sort of mythical showy obtuse weapon she'd expect him to have.

Her hand grasped the piece of rock that had just lacerated her thigh. She stood up and threw it wildly at his face. Point blank. It hit the side of his head, just above the previous wound, compounding the damage. This time he went down screaming,

• MOBILISATION •

sideways, with his eyes wide open. He didn't blackout immediately. He lay on his side in the sand, just inches away from her, staring at her like a wounded hippo, mouthing silent threats, but unable to move.

The blood rushed out over his eyes until he couldn't see her. She waited, watching him, holding her breath, afraid to move, fully expecting him to reach out and grab her.

Suddenly he did. His hand enclosed her ankle and squeezed until she cried out in pain. All his strength was in his hand but he was unable to pull her towards him. He continued to lie there, with a deathlike grip on her ankle, bleeding away and breathing heavily, conscious but not quite.

She kept one arm over her breasts, trying to keep off the Botany Bay breeze, then she moved her leg. Bent it at the knee. His grip remained but there was no tension in his arm. She was more scared than if he was standing up towering over her. Like this, she didn't know what he was going to do. Like having a wounded snake wound around your ankle. Will it strike? Will it bury its fangs in your flesh? Will it uncoil like a whip and dart for your eyes? The tension was making her head throb and her eyes kept misting over. She wanted to scream but her mouth was dry and her throat had closed up like a choked chimney.

As she stood there shivering like a wraith in the half moonlight, she prayed for his demise or, at least, temporary oblivion.

Suddenly his eyes closed. He seemed to pass out. The power of prayer?

She slid towards him until she was able to reach his manacling hand. She pried his fingers loose from her ankle. She was free. Now she panicked. She couldn't find her bra, scanties or slip. There was flotsam on the sand, lots of it. She didn't have time to dig around. She pulled her ripped dress over her shoulders, started to leave, then hyperactively scraped around next to the jeep for her underclothes. Nothing. But she found her shoes. Not stopping to put them on, she turned and ran into the night. Away. Away from the bay. Away from Colonel Bastard, the MP with the heart of stone. She wondered if he were dead. Whatever the outcome, it was the end of her American period, she thought. No more Hyde Park Canteen. No more bronze soldier gods. No more Glenn Miller foxtrots. No more . . . what? She may have killed a man. An American. An ally. Was it self-defence? She wasn't sure. He'd threatened her body, but not her life. What could she do? Where could she go? Not to her father, the cop. Not home. What if he was still alive? He'd search for her. He'd find out where she lived. He was an MP. He'd comb the city for her, set up roadblocks. If he was still alive. She prayed that he was. And hoped that he wasn't. She knew the type of man he was. His vengeance would be devastating.

If he was dead, she was a murderer. How many people had seen them leave the canteen together? She didn't know. Hundreds perhaps. Maybe none. His driver, his adjutant. Of course.

She just ran, in her stockinged feet, her last pair of nylons, across sand and grass and tar, not knowing where she was going or what she was going to do.

7

Salome and Adam entered the Reflections Club like newborn babes entering the world. Shattering. Loud. Frenetic. Inexplicable. Sobering. It sent them scurrying into their beers and that relaxed them enough to lessen the impact of the overcrowded din den. It was what they were after, but hadn't expected to find.

The key was beer. Reflections floated on it. Yet, thanks to the war, beer was supposed to be like hen's teeth. The Federal government had decreed a strict quota on beer production. Hotels were licensed only until six o'clock and often ran out during licence hours. Unlicensed places like Reflections flouted all the licensing laws, with the okay of the US military. They exploited the black market and even bought wholesale, at black market prices, direct from the breweries, thus further depriving the tied pubs, who were unable to bid above government-controlled prices.

The demand was potent, supplies almost kept pace, but staying liquid was a constant hassle. Of all the wartime shortages, this was the worst. After all, in this part of the world, beer was the stuff of life. Grown men felt they had beer in their veins. Brown, or amber, was the favourite colour. Frothing at the mouth did not denote rabies but that the beer had too much head on it. Sex was alright but beer was better. Work was something you did during the day so that you could pay for your beer after work. And the beer was up to twelve per cent proof, which meant the locals referred to foreign beers, from America or England, as lolly water.

Reflections broke all the rules and instituted one of their own. Sobriety was a sin. Drinking was a wartime imperative. You didn't have to be drunk to enter but you sure as hell couldn't stay unless you were drunk. It wasn't good for the plumbing, or the streets outside, which by midnight somewhat resembled the streets of Venice.

The decor was cheap, disposable and renewable. Fights were as common as worms in a kindergarten. Therefore the tables were bolted down, the cement-rendered walls were painted rather than papered, lighting was set high in the ceiling (adding effectively to the brownout), and the grog store was well out of firing range in a cellar beneath a false floor, out the back. Empties were immediately whisked away before they could be used as weapons. The follow spots for the band and floor show were well out of reach, the microphone and stand were brought on only as required and sandbags were stacked up against one wall, which helped the soundproofing. Artless deco. The new, popular air-raid look. But all was not bleak. There was a large mirror on the ceiling, which reflected the dance floor. Maybe things were looking up. Or people were. Reflections from above. In style it was basic blank, an atmospheric dive with a smoke haze and low lighting. Noisy at night, swimming on high spirits and easy virtue. Tawdry by day, in the cold light of reality.

Salome and Adam reached the compulsory state of insobriety very quickly indeed. Nobody had bothered to warn them about the high alcoholic content of Australian beer. Three beers each and they were anybody's. They regarded each and every visitor to their table with affability, being the kind of people who didn't have vast hidden depths of repressed aggression in their psyches ready to be released with the right amount of lubrication. In their case the alcohol brought out their repressed lovability.

One of their first visitors was a blotto Aussie corporal, a bombed Anzac, who seemed to have the released aggression syndrome. His blue eyes were surrounded on all sides by bloodshot. His speech was slurred and his vowels were as flat as the dance floor. He exuded menace from every pore, although, at first, his tone was affable.

"Killed many Japs yet Yank?" The question seemed to be directed at Salome.

"I didn't know there were any in here." Salome looked quizzically about him.

• MOBILISATION •

A wasted retort.

"Well I killed twenty-five of the buggers so far," the stocky digger slurred. "Twenty-five. Beat that. Eight with me 303, ten with me Thompson and I used me bayonet on the other fifteen. I sliced one Nip's Adam's apple out, picked it up and shoved it in his yeller mouth and made him swallow it before I cut his pecker off and then did the same thing with his nuts. I bet you fairies never done nothink like that!"

"You're right," Adam said. "But don't tempt us."

The digger swung his liquefied gaze onto Adam, who was toying with his beer and trying to will the Aussie out of his sight.

"You Yanks don't know how to fight. I seen youse up there in New Guinea. Youse get wet feet and piss in your pants. A bit of mud makes you puke. Youse may be good at rubbin' up the sheilas and throwin' your money around, but when it comes to fightin', you ain't worth the shit you're standing on. We don't need fuckin' MacArthur to do our fightin' for us, I can tell ya. The Japs are shit-scared of us. They run a mile when they hear us comin'."

"I don't blame 'em," Adam said, but his irony was wasted.

"I seen youse in Buna, didn't I?"

"Sure," Salome said. "We go there all the time."

"Whatta you mean?" The question was staccato, like a rifle shot. The digger's eyes brimmed over with liquid hostility.

"I mean, we'd like to buy you a drink."

The hostility was somewhat diluted as the digger swayed in contemplation of this curve. Then:

"I'll 'ave a beer. But it don't make no difference you shoutin' and throwin' your money around. I still think you couldn't fight your way out of Wirth's Circus!"

"We've enjoyed talking to you," Adam said. "Hope to see you again."

The unshaven digger wasn't going anywhere. "How many Nips did you say you killed?"

"Think of a number," Adam said, humouring the poor sodden bastard, whose memory span was as short as his blurred sight and who seemed to be sinking down towards the cigarette-strewn floor with every gulp of his beer, which he was spilling

• THE CIVILIAN WAR ZONE •

and slurping with alternate jerky movements. The amber fluid seemed to be evincing a new symptom — turning him into Tom Thumb. As he shrank his speech grew bolder.

"What?" A shout.

"Think of a number."

"Why fuckin' should I? I arsked you a simple question. Answer it or I'll bayonet your nuts off before you can say Jack Robinson."

"Who's Jack Robinson?" Salome asked.

The question floated right over the digger's consciousness as he tried to concentrate on the question he had put. "Answer me question!"

"What was the question?" Adam asked, toying with the man.

"Christ! You bastards must be pissed. You Yanks don't know how to hold your beer!"

"We're terrible people," Adam said. "Thirty-six."

"Eh?"

"Thirty-six."

"What the fuck are you talkin' about?" the digger asked, screwing up his face like an old balloon.

"Well, that's the answer to your question. However I'm not gonna tell you what your question was. You gotta try and remember yourself."

"Thirty-seven?"

"I said thirty-six," Adam said.

"I don't know what youse Yanks are talkin' about. Why don'tcha speak the king's English?"

"Which king is that?" Salome asked innocently.

The digger snapped to attention in a slobbish kind of way, and struck a salute. "Don't you dare say nothin' against our king, you Yank bastards!"

"It's been nice talking to you," Adam said again, growing a bit weary of the boozy pest.

"Where's the beer you promised?" the digger said, draining his glass.

"I thought you'd forgotten."

"Forgotten what?"

"About the beer."

• MOBILISATION •

"A man what forgets about beer ain't no man," the digger attested solemnly. "And what's more, we can win this war without your help. And what's more you'd better leave our women alone or we'll show yer what we do to the Nips!"

"You go back to your table and we'll send you two beers over," Adam said.

The Aussie corporal looked slowly around, as if trying to locate his table. Then back to Salome, almost. He actually got an out of focus fix just to the left of Salome. "What'd you say, Stringbean?"

"I didn't say nothin'," Salome said. "It was him."

The corporal swivelled his gaze to Adam's vicinity. "Where's the beer you promised me?" He dropped his empty glass, which bounced harmlessly on the floor. "You Yanks talk big and do nothin'!"

"I said I'd have two beers sent over to your table."

The digger's eyes narrowed as he leaned aggressively towards Adam. "You'd better do that, Yank. If it don't arrive in one minute, I'll be back with me bayonet and I'll have your balls decoratin' me Christmas tree." He staggered off into the crush and Adam and Salome breathed deep sighs of relief.

"Nice guy. I'd like to take him home for dinner. And roast him."

"He's too tough for me. I'd have to spit him out."

"Anything you say, Stringbean."

Salome threatened to pour his beer over Adam's head. "Are we really gonna buy him those drinks?" Salome looked concerned.

"No way. Don't worry. He'll be flat on his back before long."

"Good. Remind me to tread on him on the way out."

Adam stuffed a stick of gum in his mouth. "You know what? This gum tastes like beer." He sucked from his glass, drawing the ale through his teeth. "It must be Beermint."

"It's running down your chin."

"That's 'cause it's in a hurry." Adam wiped his chin.

"You're a slob, Goldhart!"

"Take that back! I resemble that remark. This joint stinks of sweat!" Adam sniffed and cased the joint. Distastefully. GIs

55

• THE CIVILIAN WAR ZONE •

outnumbered everyone else by the tableful. Girls were outnumbered two to one, but sharing seemed to be popular. Some girls had a GI on each arm. Several had a GI on each breast. The few outnumbered Aussie soldiers were womanless. Conversations were shouted in order to be heard over the shouting. The four-piece band, a kind of sub-Benny Goodman combo, provided a rhythmic background that made the sardined bodies swing and sway involuntarily, without denting the shouted inanities that passed for conversation.

"Shhh! The enemy is listening!" Adam said.

"He wouldn't hear a thing in here." Salome looked pleased to have topped his sharper friend. "Don't you like this place?"

"Why?"

"You look as if you don't."

"I think it might just qualify for the Dive of the Year award."

"I don't know what you're complainin' about, buddy," Salome reprimanded.

"Course you don't. You're from Newark."

"Shit! Don't knock it. It beats the hell out of Buffalo."

"Everywhere beats the hell out of Buffalo." The beer was moving Adam from benign to dejected.

"It's okay. Everybody's havin' a good time. Isn't this what you want? Beats the hell out of crap games in the latrine."

"Yeah, well tell me this. How come everybody's got dames and all we got so far is that little Aussie killer?"

"Maybe he's got a sister."

"Shit! I hope not."

Adam was actually ambivalent about Reflections. Back home in Buffalo he never went to nightclubs. He'd once been to a jazz café in New York City. His parents tried to imbue him with moneyed middle-class European notions of good music and culture. Everything south of Mozart was degenerate. Adam had always rebelled. He'd covertly fastened on to bootleg swing, snuck out to saloons with his school buddies, soaked up great gobs of popular American culture whilst paying lip-service at home to Björling, Kreisler, the Philadelphia Orchestra and Dvořák, whom he secretly found more than boring. To his father, Tauber was decadent and a despicable panderer

• MOBILISATION •

to popular taste. So basically Adam loved the din and dissipation of Reflections but his bourgeois background induced him to appear above it.

Salome had no such problems. His family, uncharacteristically, didn't even like opera. They had no pretensions to any culture but that which surrounded them in the working-class streets of New Jersey. His enjoyment was unquestioning.

Salome bought two more beers, for the price of six. Adam had given up on the bartering. Salome seemed hell-bent on spreading money around like a frustrated philanthropist.

"Didn't your folks ever teach you the value of money?" Adam asked.

"How could they? We never had none."

"Figures."

A tall freckled, open-mouthed, pinched-cheeked Aussie private, with his slouch hat strapped to the back of his neck, materialised at their table.

"G'night, Yanks. Me name's Russ, and I just wanted to apologise for me mate Barney."

"Barney?" Adam said.

"The little bloke. The corporal. I overheard some of what he was sayin' to you and I just wanted you to know we don't all think like that." Russ stared down at them, with patriotic eyes — red, white and blue — swivelling about with alcoholic sugared energy, a bit like a punchdrunk fighter, belying the friendly grin on his sunspotted face.

"That's very nice of you, buddy. We appreciate it." Salome stood up and shook his hand. Russ stepped back a bit, not relishing Salome's close appreciation.

"Yeah, well don't go overboard Yank. I mean don't go queening it like a big sis. I mean, Barney ain't that bad a bloke you know. And he's pissed to the gills, so you gotta make allowances." Russ's true face was peeking out.

"That's okay," Adam said, in a peacemaking frame of mind. Didn't work.

"I mean Barney means well you know. But he's had a rough time, thanks to you Yanks." Russ scratched his nose. "His missus ran off with one of you blokes, you know." Russ's grin kept trying to slip off his face.

• THE CIVILIAN WAR ZONE •

"Not me," said Salome. "I never even met her."

"I don't mean you spepifically, Yank. I mean one of youse blokes. A Yankee GI bastard, who don't give a fuck in heaven for a bloke's feelings."

"Sorry to hear that," Adam said, persisting with his olive branch.

Russ snatched it away. "You say that now, but it's too late, see. I mean you waited until Barney was off in the jungles of Kokoda getting his prick shot off, after nearly havin' had it shot off by Rommel in Libya three months earlier. And then you move in on her with your fancy smarty-farty lingo and your fuckin' nylons and your spewy chocolates and poor Barney don't know nothin' about it and then he gets home, fuckin' wounded, hoping his missus'd show up at the Repat and look after him and she's run off with this big Yank bull artist, what's been shoving his mitts up her skirt and ticklin' her fancy. And you call that friendship! Shit!"

"No I don't call it that. No I don't," Salome said, taking it all unnecessarily to heart, sinking slowly into his new beer.

"So I'm warning you, Yank . . ." Russ aimed his index finger at him. "I'm warning you. Don't go takin' it out on Barney just 'cause he's pissed as a snout, or I and me mates'll be down on you like a ton of bricks and youse'll all wish you was in the Solomons bending over for the Japs! So remember that, Yank!" Russ's complexion was a kaleidoscope of red as his pulse rate soared and his index finger rotated like a machine gun. He turned to leave when he saw that neither Adam nor Salome were interested in violent resistance or even rebuttal. Then he stopped. "And it's your shout, mate! You can buy Barney and me a beer see!" He signalled to a waiter. "Two beers! On them!"

Russ returned to his table, where Barney the bedevilled digger was slumped face down on the floor because someone had taken his chair. Not that he seemed to mind.

"Nice to meet you," Salome said, wondering what he'd done to deserve all this attention.

"Nice to be among friends," Adam said, blowing the froth off his fourth beer.

8

Cynthia didn't know where she was running. Her head was in a turmoil, eyes misted over with tears that just wouldn't stop. All she felt was panic.

She was out of breath ages ago. She wanted to collapse and just lie there, panting, drawing in gulps of life-giving air, but her legs kept rotating, despite protests from her stockinged feet, which continued to speed over rocky surfaces, tar, grass, stones, unidentified sharp objects, maybe even glass. She felt that if she stopped, she'd never get up again. The wind penetrated her bare flesh, covered only by a torn dress, her prewar pride and joy, and that blessed panty-girdle.

Now the brownout was a mixed blessing. There was half a moon, no street lamps, just an occasional light leak or faint glow from nearby houses. She heard what she thought was the jeep driving along somewhere behind. The headlights dipped and dazzled then disappeared. Perhaps he couldn't see her in the brownout, but then she couldn't see much either.

If it was his jeep, then she wasn't a murderer. That terrified her perhaps more than the alternative. Should she knock on the door of some nearby house? What house? What houses? She used a piece of her torn dress to wipe the moisture from her eyes and looked sideways, without stopping.

She was running on grass now. Coarse grass. With prickles, bindy-eyes. On her right was the desolate bay, stretching out towards an anonymous headland and the dark blue sea. Not even a twinkle of light on the horizon. The lighthouses were doused for the duration. On her left — nothing. Just land, sand-dunes maybe? Grassy verges. A golf course perhaps? How did she get here? Where were the houses? Where was the road?

She swerved sideways and her feet hit the tar. This was

a road. Now there was a fence alongside, separating her from the . . . golf course? She wanted to stop. But she could hear the jeep revving along somewhere behind her.

Suddenly a headlight picked her up. She swerved again, reaching for the dark. It followed her, picked her out again. She swerved the other way, felt the darkness shrouding her, kept running, praying for continuing dark, willing aside obstacles, thinking smooth, uncluttered, almost flying now. Damn those dastardly headlights. It just wasn't fair. There she was again. Illuminated. A white spectre, fleeing from the enraged enemy, who had four wheels as opposed to her two sore feet. Who did she think she was? Achilles — flying from her heel? Lady Godiva — naked on horseback? Jesse Owens — black as the night? No, just Cynthia, crippled fox, prey to her jeephound.

He had her now. She knew that. The lights had her glued. She was out of swerve. Then she tripped over a small stone wall, just a foot high. She felt herself falling. And falling. She didn't know how far.

It was her head and arms that took the full impact as her body hit the concrete. The explosion in her head and the jarring shock that engulfed her body were short lived, leading to total rest and oblivion, somewhere near Botany Bay.

Here, one hundred and seventy years before, Captain Cook had found a deserted wilderness, except for a few friendly natives. This night there weren't even any friendly natives around.

Bastien Tunks opened his eyes and the first thing he saw was a small robber crab advancing sideways towards his nose. From his prone angle on the sandy grass, it looked enormous and menacing with its nipper claws and four pairs of legs driving its horny shell carapace along — one of God's antediluvian monsters come to compound his suffering.

And what suffering! A throbbing pain in the side of his forehead, and as he raised his head with the intention of moving it out of crab-range, the dark landscape turned over completely and created a whirlpool, mid-cranium. Everything was swimming. Out of water. He managed to roll over onto his

· MOBILISATION ·

back and that put the crab out of eyeshot and therefore out of consideration. But the sky, with its Southern Cross twinkling, kept moving and threatening to spill over into the bay.

Sitting up was a supreme achievement. Like fighting an earthquake. There was a roaring in his head, a kind of cerebral avalanche that only stopped when he attained a semi-upright position. But then it was immediately replaced by a feeling of nausea that started in the pit of his belly and rose up through his gastro-intestinal tract through the twists and bends, up to the oesophagus, moving irresistibly through the entire viscera to his throat. And then he vomited, burying the harmless crab in putrefaction.

Now he felt able to stand. He was about as steady as a paper windmill. The world was still spinning, but he stumbled with it. He recognised the symptoms of oncoming concussion.

Being a veteran of many a brawl as well as a short-lived amateur boxing career, he knew he should lie down, probably for days. It was going to be all dizzy from now on. But he remembered vividly that bitch assailant, who had given him the come-on and then turned to dogshit. She had run off somewhere, he supposed, and he intended to find her, and when he did, he'd probably kill her.

She deserved it. She was an enemy agent. Military justice demanded the death penalty. And he was military justice.

He had blood everywhere, but it was drying, seepage turning to clottage. The throbbing was bearable because it was tempered by the hate in his heart. Soon he'd be used to the pendulum world and be able to swing with it from side to side.

He clambered into the jeep, grazed one leg, felt for the controls because he wasn't able to focus in any one direction in order to see them. He started it up, jammed it into reverse and the wheels kicked up a sandstorm before the tyres gripped enough for traction. Then the brown vehicle shot backwards into a tree. This further shook his brain and spun him out of equilibrium. He kneed the gears into neutral, closed his eyes and waited for the turbulence to subside.

One thought kept crashing through his joggled brain: Get that bitch! Get that bitch!

• THE CIVILIAN WAR ZONE •

She had committed the cardinal sin. She had affronted his manhood and demeaned his professionalism as a military policeman. Perhaps if, in the past, he'd been more successful with women, or even had had a wife who loved him, it wouldn't have mattered so much. But he had needed this one. She was a ravishing beauty, and up to now ravishing beauties had eluded him. Her long tawny hair and warm brown eyes had dazzled his senses. He had had such high hopes. And that body! The fluidity of it when she walked and when she danced, her lissom flesh so pliable but not compliant. And her breasts stood out enough to speak to him. A knockout of a dame. He had horned in on her with a desperation because he was sick of whores, those tired old bats who sucked his cock between their overripe, over-juicy legs, who didn't give a fuck about him and just jerked him off dispassionately. It was no better than taking a piss. There was no conquest there, no triumph, no assertion of his status in the world. But this . . . dame. Bitch! Slut! He toyed with the names. Cunt! That was what she was! A cunt! So promising. So disappointing. A treacherous cunt! The description reinvigorated him. She had to die. It was now the only way he'd get that feeling back, that oh so necessary feeling. The one that said Tunks is king, Tunks is a man, Tunks is a colonel of the military police, a power to be reckoned with, a man to be looked up to and feared. A hero.

He opened his eyes and there was two of everything. Double vision. Swinging double vision. He couldn't clear it. The world in twos. He couldn't tell which was the right one. Which path was the road, which tree the hazard, which eye was true, which was a pothole. But he would cope with it. This little jeep could practically drive itself. He swung it around and roared off, guestimating the position of the road, driving half on the kerb, half on the tar, no man's road in between; not giving a shit, watching his two sets of headlights, side by side, moving back and forth, up and down, picking up twin trees and telegraph poles, and a wall, two walls, scraping one of them, the right one. Crashing through foliage, the landscape was in duplicate, and then a fleeing figure. Or two. Stumbling along, fusing into one, cloning apart, confusing him, almost collapsing but keeping going, blindly. It was her. Two

• MOBILISATION •

hers. Treacherous cunts. Which twin? He had her now. Them. One of her was in his headlights, carved into his brain. She and her shadow. The road was nowhere. Just wide, ever wider track. He couldn't really tell what she was running over or what he was driving over. It was as bumpy as a minefield; the jeep kept shooting up in the air, four wheels off the ground, then landing again with a bump that aggravated his concussion and made him even more determined to catch her. Them.

He'd run her down, if he could get close enough, but she kept disappearing behind proliferating verges and trees and poles.

He soon picked her up again. Now he seemed to be only twenty yards behind. One of them. He would close on her. One of her. Which? A few seconds more.

The anticipation cleared his head a bit, but not his vision. Bed rest. Not now. The concentration on his duplicated vision made him forget the throbs.

Then she suddenly disappeared behind a small wall. He heard her cry, which was louder than his engine and echoed through the night air. He should've stopped the jeep but his hands and feet weren't obeying his brain. He kept going, right in her tracks and he hoped he'd land right on top of her and crush the life out of her. But if he missed, then he'd use his service .45 to blast her away for her treachery.

9

At Reflections, Salome and Adam were playing host to two women on the dark side of thirty, who had approached their table just when the boys were beginning to feel like wallflowers. They were decked out in prewar cocktail dresses with shoulder straps and flared pleats and had wartime frizzy hair (perms and setting lotions were permanently unavailable). It was hard to tell precisely what they looked like because they both wore swamps of make-up. Apparently there was a thriving black market in lipstick, rouge and mascara. They also both had "austerity legs" — brown leg paint — in lieu of stockings, complete with drawn seams.

The platinum-haired one instantly attached herself to Salome, who was wreathed in smiles and exceedingly happy to see her, which meant, in Mae West terms, that wasn't a gun in his pocket. Superficially they were almost a matched set. Her smile matched his, except it seemed to put a strain on her skin, which was stretched and lined almost to parting point. Everything about her was thin, including her bright red lips, eyebrows, nose and neck. She reminded Adam of a walking ration-book. But to Salome, who was after all, something of a stringbean himself, she was female manna from heaven.

The tawny-haired one, with generally much more meat on her bones and a wide but solemn face, wasn't exactly Adam's cup of tea but, in view of his recent female famine, he was prepared to compromise enough to accept her at body value. An early strain was placed on this tenuous relationship, however, when she started combing her abundant locks at the table, with an expression that dared anyone to challenge her right to show such a total lack of decorum.

"What'll you have, ladies?" Salome asked, as friendly as a farmer's daughter.

• MOBILISATION •

"It's alright, we'll order," the tawny one said. "They know us here." She gave a practised signal to the drink waiter, who seemed to know exactly what she wanted. He disappeared through a swing door and then returned in a flash with a bottle of Scotch and two glasses, which he placed in front of the ladies. The price was an economic disaster. Over four pounds.

"Is that a lot?" Salome asked, always the financial pollyanna.

Adam silenced him with a stern look, then turned to the waiter, a husky forty-year-old with a shirt full of muscles. "That's a bit high, isn't it feller?"

"Take it or leave it, Yank," the waiter said, driving a hard bargain.

"We'll leave it," Adam said.

"We'll take it," Salome said simultaneously.

But the ladies had already downed their first nips.

"That's four pounds, two and six," the waiter said. "There's a war on, mate. Scotch is on the black list. You're lucky to get any."

"We didn't order it," Adam said, with a bankrupt expression, whilst Salome handed over four ones and a ten shilling note, as cheerfully as a cheerleader.

"Is that enough?" Salome asked.

The waiter grunted and took the lot. "Just."

"Thanks Yank. You're real generous," the tawny one said. "My name's Doris and this is Dorothy. We could never afford to drink Scotch till you chaps came to town."

"That's nice," said Adam. "Sometimes I'm not sure if we were sent here to fight the Japanese or boost the local economy."

The ladies didn't follow up on this philisophical point. Their concerns were on a more mundane plane.

"What rank are you?" the blonde sylph Dorothy asked.

"Pfc," Adam replied.

"Pfc? What's that stand for?"

"Poor fuckin' civilian," Salome said. Deadpan.

The ladies looked shocked, then Doris started to giggle and Dorothy followed suit.

65

• THE CIVILIAN WAR ZONE •

"Excuse my friend's bad language, ladies, but he don't know any better. He's from Newark," Adam said dryly.

"Aw that's alright," Doris said. "We've heard that word before. Haven't we, Dorothy?"

Dorothy's giggles proliferated uncontrollably until tears poured out of her eyes. Salome topped up her Scotch and offered the glass to her. She took it, gulped a giant sip, sniffed and calmed down. Doris sipped her Scotch and lapsed back into her normal solemnity. The conversation paused for a moment. Adam didn't feel fired up enough to try to keep it going.

"Do you come here often?" Salome offered, as if he'd just invented the cliché.

"Only every night," Doris said. Obviously she did all the talking whilst Dorothy did all the smiling. "We sort of work here. Got any gum?"

"Sure. He's the gum carrier." Salome nudged Adam, who handed them each a packet of Spearmint.

The girls shoved a couple of sticks in their mouths and started chewing like cows. Masticating became their pre-eminent activity, their heavily ringed eyes staring at the never-never land in between the two GIs, making it pretty obvious that there was less rapport at this table than at the Treaty of Versailles. They were only in it for the gum. And the Scotch. Perhaps.

"Did you know," Salome asked Adam, "that this season, DiMaggio made ninety-one hits including fifteen homers, four triples and sixteen doubles? That's an all-time record."

"If he's so good, how come he ain't in the army?" Adam asked.

"I dunno. I guess the Yankees need him more than Uncle Sam does."

"Maybe he's 4F. Maybe he's got flat feet from standing on so many bases."

"Yeah, and maybe he's short-sighted."

"What're you talking about, boys?" Doris asked.

"Baseball," Salome said. "Don't you play that down here?"

"Not that I know of," Doris said. "Is that like rounders?"

"Well, I guess."

• MOBILISATION •

After an interminable pause, Adam picked up the ball. "If you two ladies work here, what does that mean? I mean, what do you do?"

The girls looked at each other and giggled. Doris shifted her wad of gum across her mouth like a typewriter carriage. "We're hostesses."

"What does that mean? What do you hostess?"

"We're hostessing you, aren't we?"

"Well, I guess." Adam grinned, chalking one up to her, but deep down he felt disappointed that the ladies were professionals. It punctured his romantic aspirations.

"How about a dance, sugar?" Salome asked Dorothy. "I bet you can sway like Dottie Lamour."

"Who's Dottie Lamour when she's at home?" Dorothy asked, breaking her silence, resenting any hint of competition.

"A movie star, but no patch on you, baby. Wait till they discover you."

Dorothy giggled again, tickled pink, and practically leapt into Salome's arms.

Adam made no attempt to lure Doris onto the dance floor in the wake of Salome and Dorothy, who had quickly segued into a jitterbugging mould. Dorothy was ideally built for it, being as skinny as a swan's neck and ultra easy to toss about.

"How's about a dance, Yank?" Doris asked, feeling neglected.

"Call me Adam. I'm sorry, I can't dance. It's the shrapnel in my leg see."

"Where'd you get that?" Doris asked, swallowing the line.

"Pearl Harbor."

"What were you doing at Pearl Harbor?"

"Collecting shrapnel."

Doris found nothing to laugh at in this. Adam's dryness confused her.

"Does it hurt?"

"Sometimes, sure."

"Is it hurting now?" Doris's concern seemed genuine. Adam's boyish good looks brought out the mother in her.

"A bit. It needs some pressure. That always eases it."

• THE CIVILIAN WAR ZONE •

"Where is it exactly?"

"Right there." Adam indicated the top of his thigh. "Say, you wouldn't like to put some pressure on it, would you? It'd help a lot."

"I don't mind." Doris reached out to touch his thigh. Adam stopped her.

"No. It really needs a lot of pressure. I think you'd need to sit on it."

"Okay." Doris sat on his lap, put her arms around his neck. "How's that?"

"Well, it takes a while. You can't rush it."

Doris nuzzled his neck. "I think you're having me on. That's what I think."

"Sure. I'm havin' you on my lap."

At Reflections actions spoke the loudest. Most everyone was doing something to someone else. There were American sailors under tables, drunk as admirals, trying to look up their girls' dresses. A burly staff sergeant was lying across his table, dead to the world, with a full beer glass perched on his heaving chest, whilst four GIs were making bets on how long it would be before the glass tipped over. A master sergeant in the Signal Corps was doing handstands on his table, noisily egged on by his companions. Another GI had a girl perched on each knee and was trying to induce them to kiss each other. A dextrous Pfc was juggling three empties in the air with great aplomb until a waiter stepped in, caught them one by one and took them away. Frustrated, the Pfc picked up another bottle from his table and tossed it up. But it was half full and sprayed the crowd. Cries of encore.

Not more than two tables away from Salome and Adam, Major Bradley Theodore sat quietly sipping his beer, old sobersides himself in a sea of inebriates. He was in no great hurry to make his final selection. It really depended on the degree of drunkenness and there was no shortage of candidates. Also, being an aesthete, he tended to opt for the better-looking younger ones. Booze plus naivety was an unbeatable combination. The beauty of Reflections was that all the potential witnesses were in no state to either witness or recall.

• MOBILISATION •

He shrugged off several pick-up girls who were looking for officer material and were not too fussy about looks. After all Goyt was no Romeo in the looks department. But the fairly thick moustache he'd added this night went well enough with his eyebrows which had grown shaggy again after all the plucking. His puffy cheeks were less round than usual, as he'd eschewed padding. The eyes, of course, were the same. Large, mystifying saucers, staring coldly about him, in contrast to the bland, almost benign face.

He shifted in his seat. The bayonet was digging into his hip and it was so hot in this nighthaunt he could feel drips of sweat raining down his thighs. Maybe he wouldn't stay too long. Oppressive. Much more of this and his breathing difficulty would start and then he'd have to leave, or have to do something to relieve it.

"Did you know that my buddy Sal over there is related to Betty Grable?" Adam asked the watery-eyed, comfortably padded Doris, as she snuggled into his lap, applying pressure where it counted most.

For some inexplicable reason, inexplicable to Adam that is, he was finding her more attractive by the moment. It might've been the booze, the dissolute atmosphere, his unwanted celibacy of recent times, or all three, but he decided not to intellectualise about it, but just to roll with the touches.

Doris was quite happy to be gullible. "Is he her brother or what?"

"No, not her brother. Second cousin."

"Is he really?"

"Ask him."

Dorothy and Salome had returned to the table. Dorothy too was now perched on Salome's lap, with her lips exploring his neck, leaving a make-up trail. She looked rather like his puppet with no strings.

Salome sensed a total lack of complication in her, which meant she was willing, and most of all tonight he wanted willing. Dorothy didn't strike him so much as a professional but as a willing amateur. Salome believed what he wanted to believe. He didn't want to flirt, thrust, parry or negotiate. He couldn't recall anybody nuzzling him quite so avidly before, apart from his red setter Capone, who was no doubt still pining for him back in Newark. And she had let her hands fall sensuously on his thigh, only a fraction of an inch away from his little brother, which was his favourite euphemism for his penis. What's more little brother was growing bigger all the time, and any moment now he knew Dorothy's hand would make contact, accidentally on purpose. And who knew what this would lead to. With all this hedonistic matter to dwell upon, he let Adam make the conversation.

"Is Betty Grable really your second cousin?" Doris asked Salome, leaning forward and nearly falling off Adam's lap.

Salome shook his head, not wanting to get involved.

"See. He shook his head," Doris said.

"No no. He nodded," Adam corrected.

"Did you shake your head?" Doris asked Salome.

Salome nodded.

"See! He nodded!" Adam said, triumphantly.

"No, he nodded that he shook his head," Doris argued.

"Look. Are you trying to tell me that my friend here is not related to Betty Grable?"

"Yes."

"Alright, I'll prove it." Adam reached out past Dorothy, who was still obliviously nuzzling, and tore open Salome's uniform blouse. He had a tattoo of a pair of legs on his chest. "Those are his cousin's legs."

"You mean Betty Grable?"

"Ah! See! You made the connection. Now do you believe me?"

"I want to believe you," Doris said, confused. "Say, do you have any nylons?"

"Sorry. I never wear them. They give me a rash," Adam said, straight-faced as usual.

"I mean for me." Doris was quite serious.

"They might bring you out in a rash too."

"Oh, you're a big tease." Doris kissed Adam passionately on the mouth, transferring half her lipstick in the process. "If you want me to be nice to you, it'll cost you lots and lots of nylons."

• MOBILISATION •

"His cousin Betty Grable never wears nylons."
"I bet she does."
"No, she wears mesh."
"Mesh?"
"Yesh."
"Who have you got on your chest?" Doris's hands were at Adam's blouse buttons.
"General MacArthur."
"Let me see." Doris ripped open his shirt and peered at his chest. "I can't see General MacArthur."
"That's 'cause he's hiding under the hair. For security reasons. What have *you* got on your chest?" Adam's hand snaked down the front of her dress, but her bra was an impediment. "I'd like to examine your forward defences."
"It'll cost you a pair of nylons." Doris drove a hard bargain, as she let her hands roam thighwards.
"Careful," Adam warned. "You're getting near to my heavy artillery."
"I hope it doesn't go off," Doris said.
"It all depends on the priming."
Both couples' public gropings were interrupted when there was a smattering of applause and a volley of catcalls as three pseudo Andrews Sisters skipped onto the dance floor in GI jackets and skirts and proceeded to sing "Rum and Coca Cola" in a nicely blended falsetto chorus. At first glance they didn't appear to be overtly talented. At second glance it could be seen that the Andrews Sisters were probably Andrews Brothers, which gave the act a certain flair. Reflections they were.
"Holy cow! What is that?" Salome said, coming up for air from Dorothy's lean, freckled neck.
One of the Andrews Brothers was now touring the tables. She was fooling with the customers, stroking cheeks, stoking fires, lolling on laps, sipping drinks, stealing kisses.
"That's a guy, that's what that is," Adam said. "I think what we're lookin' at is Patti, Laverne and Max."
"Watch out Dorothy baby! You got competition!" Salome said, temperature rising with tempo. He stood up and tipped her off. She looked quite peeved.
Salome stared goggle-eyed at the preposterous imposter,

who was just three laps away from him. He stared at him with drunken intensity and an open-mouthed grin — a mixture of condemnation and awe. He'd never seen a man in drag before.

10

Corporal Bruce Corrigan, a spare, turnip-faced, sardonic young man, and Private Colin Spindle, a stodgy phlegmatic fellow with ginger hair and dull eyes, both gunners of the Australian militia, were bored shitless despite the company of the charismatic American Corporal Sherbrook Wells, Field and Coast Artillery Branch of the 32nd Infantry Division nicknamed Red Arrow. Seven hours in a reinforced cement dugout on the shore of Botany Bay was not exactly the Folies-Bergère.

Wells was supposed to be the expert on the new 105 mm Howitzer artillery piece, which the US army had installed, on a lend-lease basis, for home defence purposes. Corrigan had proved a quick study. Spindle's role was more stand-by muscleman to help them load shells, if and when the time came. This fortification was a good example of allied cooperation and a benefit accruing from the US presence.

The 105 mm Howitzer could fire a thirty-five pound shell 12,205 yards at a rate of six rounds a minute. There were four of them implanted around Botany Bay, protected by ramparts, waiting hopefully for the Japanese fleet to arrive to justify their existence.

So far, since installation, the closest to anything Japanese was the rising sun, which appeared each morning with innocent regularity. The bay, which was basically a small circular harbour with one set of strategically placed heads, was eminently defensible. The men were disappointed that the three Japanese midget submarines, which had recently penetrated Sydney Harbour and unleashed a couple of dud torpedoes before being respectively caught in the boom and depth charged, had not opted for Botany Bay. They needed the target-practice.

The three gunners had smoked themselves vaporous, played poker for loose change, which was all Corrigan and

• THE CIVILIAN WAR ZONE •

Spindle could afford, and compared life in Sydney and Philadelphia respectively, for five nights in a row. Round about midnight, on this particular long muggy night, they'd run out of conversation and ideas. Each was lost in his own reverie, which was mainly to do with the unavailability of the opposite sex, plotting the next damp dream.

Then a minor miracle occurred which banished their boredom and put hope in their chests. It took the form of a beautiful, semi-naked and unconscious girl who suddenly dropped from nowhere — or at least from the parapet onto the rampart, outside their gun turret — like a blessing from heaven.

"Hey!" Corrigan and Wells yelled simultaneously. They scrambled out onto the rampart in the murky night air, picked up the unconscious Cynthia by the legs and shoulders and swung her into the dugout, laying her down on a rug and pillowing her head with Wells' patch-pocket field jacket.

Outside, a jeep hit the parapet and somersaulted onto the concrete rampart, scraped along from the momentum and tipped over onto the sand. The driver did an unintentional swallow dive onto the sand and lay there like a stone, unseen by the guardians of the bay, who were totally preoccupied with their first flying visitor.

Wells uncorked his whisky flask and held it under her nose like smelling salts, whilst Corrigan dabbed her forehead with water.

"She's a terrific-looking sheila," Corrigan said, eyeing her exposed breasts and thighs and almost salivating.

"I don't want to interfere with your education, Corrigan, but we don't want her to catch cold do we?" Wells said, and flung another khaki rug over her body.

Corrigan's disappointment was tinged with embarrassment. "What do you think we should do with her, Brook?" he asked, rubbing her hands between his, feeling it was his consolation prize.

Wells turned her over onto her side, explaining this was correct first-aid procedure for proper breathing and in case the patient should swallow her tongue.

"I guess we should try and return her to her rightful

· MOBILISATION ·

owner," Wells said.

"Oh." Corrigan thought about this. Then: "Isn't it a case of finders keepers?"

"I think maybe you'd better ask the lady first."

Cynthia's smoky eyelashes had started to flutter.

"Oh man," Wells let out a deep breath, "this chick's comin' round."

"She looks pretty beat though," Corrigan said.

The first thing Cynthia saw when she floated back to actuality was this large, shiny, handsome black face, complete with Ipana-white teeth, and sympathetic brown eyes. It was a shock because it was so unexpected, but it was a pleasant shock because that face was wreathed in such a welcoming smile. For several seconds her addled brain sent her garbled messages. The handsome black face was superseded by the enraged white face of Colonel Tunks and this made her scream and shake all over. Then that image puffed away and her tension dissipated. The black Samaritan was there and he was smiling at her, and she warmed to him because his smile made her feel secure and banished the terror.

"You're okay, sweetheart," Wells said. "You're okay. And me and my buddies here want to thank you for dropping in on us like that. It was a beautiful thing. And we thank you."

She didn't quite know what he was talking about.

"Who are you?"

Wells told her and it still didn't mean much. He also told her where she was and then asked her where she came from.

She turned things over in her mind before answering. "Is there blood on me? On my face? It feels wet."

"Not any more, sweetheart, not any more. What's your name?"

"Cynthia."

"Okay Cynthia. Just take it slow. Tell us what happened."

"I feel sick. And sore. And my head . . .?"

"Better buzz for a sick wagon, buddy," Wells said to Spindle. "I think this little lady has a date with a hospital."

Spindle picked up the field telephone.

"There's a . . . there's a . . . one of your MP colonels

in a white uniform . . . in a jeep. . . he's . . . have you seen him?" Cynthia shuddered.

"Hey! Well a jeep, yes. A definite jeep. Better go and sight the jeep, Bruce old buddy." Wells exercised his natural authority, despite his equal rank. His extrovert personality washed all over the two Australian gunners.

"Wait!" Cynthia clutched at Wells' arm. "Don't tell him I'm here! Please!"

"Whoa baby! Just relax! Don't worry. If we find your colonel, we won't tell him nothin'. Colonels are one big no-no in this little echelon of ours. Specially MP colonels. Persona non grata and how!" Then to Corrigan. "Simple syllables, huh Bruce? Non divulgé, okay?"

Bruce Corrigan nodded with a grin. After five long nights he was finally starting to comprehend the American's quaint colloquialisms.

"Now Cynthia, we could all do with a bit of excitement, so you'd better fill us in. I think we got a small serioso incidenté. We been waiting for the Japs to show for weeks and I think they're so fouled up in New Guinea they ain't never gonna get here."

Sherbrook Wells was a dominating character in every way. Big, broad, effusive, theatrical, the life of the army, always drinking in gulps of enjoyment, through good times and bad, dwarfing most other people into insignificance. His mere presence seemed to be acting as a tonic for Cynthia, who began to wonder how she could have met two such contrasting Americans in the same night.

Corrigan came back and told them there was a white ghost of a US officer lying unconscious on the sand, near an upside down jeep. When the US army ambulance came — red cross over camouflage brown — Cynthia refused to go. Instead they just bundled Tunks aboard whilst Cynthia remained in the dugout recounting her version of the night's events.

"Now we got a problem incarnate here, Cynthia," Wells said, by inference amalgamating his group with her. "I don't know how well you know the US army, but the MPs are the law, and a law unto themselves. That Colonel Tunks, he's

· MOBILISATION ·

a mean one. And he's also God. The Provost Marshal in this town. Does what he likes. There's no one to trim his sails 'cept a general who's beat up with booze most of the time or MacArthur himself, and he's full up to here worrying about the Japs. Now, you can make charges against him, but take it from me and I know, because being a poor son of a slave, I am prey to those guys with armbands. Well, they can and do, get away with murder. They hate all enlisted men and look upon civilians as less than dirt. They are the enemy in our midst, baby. Me, I'd rather deal with the Japanese than some of our MP brethren, Cynthia. Let alone the big colonel man. I kinda wish they were on the other side, where they belong. If the Japs ever land here, I figure we should offer them our MPs as hostages. To keep. So you Cynthia, and I can tell you're a nice lady and got fine intelligent eyes, but I guess you weren't to know, but you got yourself mixed up with the number one sonofabitch in this man's army. You might've been better off having a quickstep with Hitler. So, what I'm saying is, Cynthia, and this is my unsolicited empirically justified, not to be treated lightly advice. Best you leave it where it is, try and forget all about it, and make sure you stay one thousand miles away from any MP sonsofbitches from now on."

"But he tried to . . . tried to rape me. He attacked me, tore my clothes." The recollection brought tears, which Wells gently wiped away with his fingers.

"Tell you what, Cynthia. If I ever get the chance, I'll stalk that buzzard some dark night, put sugar in his gas tank and lead in his corpuscles, if that'll make you feel any better. I used to be a golden gloves contender. But I may have to wait till we win the war and I'm about to be demobbed, 'cause I don't want to wait out the duration in the stockade."

Cynthia didn't respond. She knew he was talking sense, but she was confused. She felt her predicament was far from over. Maybe it was just beginning. She wanted to put it behind her, but the beast was still there, in her mind's eye, and she knew she would not erase him easily. She started to shiver now, felt cold all over and her head was swimming. She closed her eyes and a wave of giddiness passed over her.

• THE CIVILIAN WAR ZONE •

"I think you've got some shock waves, young lady." Wells looked to his companions. "I think she's gonna need some treatmenté, you guys. How about we get her to a sawbones someplace? Better than a hospital where they want you to write an essay."

Cynthia started to moan, a kind of dispossessed sound over which she had no control. Wells wrapped her snugly in the rug and picked her up carefully, as if she were a disabled babe. He took her outside to the half track, then drove her to an MD in Brighton Le Sands, who wasn't terribly happy about being woken up in the early hours.

"Just pretend the invasion has started, doc," Wells suggested, and received a curt glance in reply.

Wells stayed with her the whole time, whilst the doctor, a crusty old practitioner, who wore a nightshirt hastily stuffed into his striped suit trousers, gave Cynthia a shot of noradrenaline and examined her all over for external injuries. Despite the large egg on her forehead, bruises, scratches and cut and swollen feet, he seemed satisfied that there was nothing wrong enough with her to justify this early hour's disturbance. He prescribed rest, warmth and comfort and no work or activity for several days.

Wells offered to take her home, but she declined. She didn't want to unnecessarily worry her parents. So he drove her to her girlfriend's house, where Tunks was supposed to have dropped her.

On the way back to the gun emplacement, Brook Wells examined his motives and decided they were a mixture of altruism and Christian charity, with a bit of old-fashioned chivalry for good measure. Sympathy for a lady in distress? Yes, that too. Hours afterwards her face and figure seemed to have been stamped irrevocably on his brain. He couldn't seem to get her out of his mind. He'd have to see her again, that was for sure. Just to prove his objectivity. Maybe when she was up and about, restored to full bloom, she'd be just another gal. Maybe, because he was such a sucker for the underprivileged or hard-done-by, she had appealed to his charitable notions? Maybe hedgehogs made good pillows?

11

Men in drag were as sure-fire to the army mentality as porridge was to the Three Bears. All-male regimentation inevitably produced all-female fantasies. And fantasies produced nightmares. Not that hairy legs in skirts were exactly nightmares — but substitutes, however ambivalent, were always better than nothing.

The touring Andrews Brother was certainly creating a stir, rum and coca-colaing all over Reflections, accompanied by drunken whoops and catcalls punctuating her rhumba rhythms. The whole room joined in the chorus, not quite raising the roof. Male voices dominated, lubricated by beer. The Andrews siblings' appeal was more visual and visceral than vocal, as most of the time they were drowned out by the customers.

The Andrews Brother was now at the table of Salome, Adam and their goodtime girlfriends, having been encouraged by Salome's spectacular height and frame and his incredulous grin, which basically was stoked by naivety but which could have been misconstrued as admiration.

So Max (Andrews) moved in to capitalise on this provocative reaction. Without missing a stomp, beat or lyric, he took a gulp from Salome's beer glass then, perhaps as part payment, bent over and tried to kiss Salome, right on the lips.

Salome's grin turned to grimace, the alcohol in his blood compounding the emotion. He pushed her away. Max pouted. He felt he was a very attractive woman and star to boot. So he tried again.

The scarlet lips actually brushed Salome's cheek and left a lipstick streak, which inflamed Salome as if it were blood.

Salome's fascination stopped short of actual physical

• THE CIVILIAN WAR ZONE •

contact. His interest was definitely academic. He hadn't exhausted the real thing yet. Dorothy, the real thing in question, had stirred his loins before Max wafted in. When she eventually climbed back on his lap, his overriding sexual preference would be plumbed. In the meantime, he had invited, albeit unintentionally, an ambiguous suitor. And Max was a determined young impersonator. He wanted his full GI kiss.

He sank down on Salome's lap, pushing aside Dorothy's reservation. And he spread his less than feminine hands all over Salome's chest, even inside his shirt, fondling his dog tags, fingering the Grable-like legs and the untumescent nipples, still singing so that no one would doubt his professionalism. Then he aimed those scarlet lips once more. This time contact was made. Full rich red juicy contact. The nearby tables cheered. It was truly a sight for bloodshot eyes.

Salome spluttered, turned as red as rhubarb, hated what he thought were the jeers of his peers, started to doubt his own not fully flowered manhood and slammed his fist straight into Max's face.

It was almost an involuntary punch, beyond his control. A clout from his drunken subconscious.

It was a queen hit.

The speed and trajectory of the punch were heightened by the close proximity. The Andrews sibling shot backwards like a rag doll on elastic and cannoned into a nearby table, securely bolted down for extra resistance.

His head hit the wood with a sickening thud, which couldn't be clearly heard over the music, his brunette wig shooting off and landing in the face of a US officer two tables away, who thought it was funny. Max ended up flat on the floor, poleaxed, a stunned soubrette.

It was much more serious than it looked.

The hurried autopsy later would show that the cause of death was twofold: a fractured skull vault with multiple fissures and bone fragments lodged in the brain, caused, it seemed, by collision with the table; and a ring base fracture whereby the velocity of the punch forced the skull to lift away from the spine, thus breaking it away from its strong ring base attachments.

• MOBILISATION •

The femme fatale had become a femme fatal.

Salome's punch opened the bloodgates as now the Andrews Brothers became just two. Their harmonic integration suffered and they rushed towards Salome's table, ending their song in mid-verse. They grabbed some handy bottles for retaliatory purposes. But several Aussie soldiers got in first. They aimed punches which were immediately duplicated. Salome and Adam became targets.

The whole place started to erupt. Fists, bottles, feet and chairs. Women screamed, men yelled and the band played louder, which didn't help.

Before long everybody had forgotten about the fractured Andrews Brother, who continued to lie unattended, the back of his head resting in a pool of blood.

The battlelines were blurred. Not only Aussies versus Yanks but Yanks versus Yanks, army versus navy, officers versus enlisted men and eventually, everybody versus the MPs.

When the latter burst in, gestapo style, with indiscriminate batons, concussion became an instant epidemic. And the brawl was cut off at the pass. The MPs fulfilled their credo of doing unto their own as effectively as if they were doing it unto others.

Salome's face became a punching bag. After his first instinctive punch, he didn't lay another, or even try. He just stood there, hunched over, on the receiving end. His head ached, one eye closed up, his nose bled like a fountain and his lips were split. He was Max Schmelling under the onslaught of twenty Joe Louis's.

A full bottle caught Adam on the side of the head. Stunned, he found himself lying under the table not far away from the slain impersonator, which made him feel sick enough to vomit up a cesspool of bile and excessive ale.

But deliverance was at hand.

Major Bradley Theodore, sober as a statue, came from nowhere and dragged Salome through the mayhem, skilfully evading MPs and other foe, utilising amazing strength and the fact that Salome had had most of his resistance knocked out of him.

The floored Adam recovered enough to see the major

dragging his friend away. Salome looked quite dazed, almost comatose, easy prey for anybody who wanted him. Adam thought it strange. Who was this major? He wasn't an MP. Something sinister was happening. The brawling figures all around him seemed to freeze and fade away, leaving only Salome being helplessly hoisted out the door by some phantom officer with moonscape eyes.

He struggled to his feet, feeling nauseous, stumbled after them, dodging anonymous fists, catching a few, tripping, barking his shins, circumnavigating some club-handed MPs, finally catching up to Salome and his captor at the foot of the stairs, which led up to the street entrance.

"Hey buddy. Where ya goin'? Who is this guy?"

Salome, battered and dazed, became the rope in a tug of war. Adam grabbed his friend's long arm and tugged him out of Goyt's grasp.

Goyt pinioned Adam with his eyes. His bulbous face remained hideously bland, etching itself deep onto Adam's memory. Then he produced a carbine bayonet from under his jacket with magical dexterity and, without a word of warning, slashed at Adam. It was quick as a flash but seemed to be almost slow motion. Adam received an unprecedented fix on a startling pair of eyes, ice-blue, and then he felt a sharp pain in his left shoulder as the bayonet severed all the soft tissue and firm muscle, stopping short of the bone.

The impact spun him around right into the chest of a marauding MP, who retaliated with a well-aimed baton across the back of Adam's neck.

Adam's arms shot up in the air and his mouth opened as a rocket went off in his brain and seemingly out the top of his skull. For a second he froze in mid-dive, then he collapsed face down on the floor for an unexpectedly early night.

Salome's saviour dragged him along the dark laneway with an iron hand on his unresisting wrist. Salome felt sick, his legs kept buckling and he wasn't even sure why they were running. Yes he was. His head was playing tricks. He'd nudged that guy with his fist. Guy? Gal. Whatever. Now he was on the run. No, he was being dragged like a dog on a leash.

• MOBILISATION •

He stopped and the mock major nearly ripped his arm off.

They were in a back lane, deserted except for overflowing garbage cans, dog turds and an old shoe.

"Wait! Wait a moment will you?" Salome's voice bounced off the back walls of a row of tied terraces. Then he doubled up against a fence and threw up, great bellyfuls of overcooked lunch swimming in a sea of rancid lager. Goyt waited, agitatedly, fingering his bayonet, staying just out of range to preserve his shiny boots.

"Hurry up soldier! They're coming after you." The voice was high, a fractured tenor. The accent was nearly Boston with a touch of midwest. Not real. Adopted.

Goyt grabbed his wrist again and led him down one dark lane into another. He seemed to know where he was going and Salome just stumbled blindly along, growing weaker, a fading giant.

"That'll do it. You'll be safe here. For a while." Goyt stopped in a blind alley. No way out but the way in. High walls of stone, the backs of almost yardless terrace houses and shops. Hardly any light. Debris on the ground, empties, garbage, imperfect tar.

Salome sank down onto the tar with his back against a wall, breathing like a hound, his head splitting open from the inside.

Major Bradley Theodore nee Carl Goyt stood a little way away, brandishing his bayonet. Cool and collected by contrast, but with a disturbing wheeze.

"Who are you? Why'd you bring me here?" Salome gasped.

"We're all in this together, soldier. It would've been unpatriotic of me to let the MPs put you away, just because you killed that pathetic civilian."

Salome groaned. "I didn't kill anyone. I just nudged that . . . that guy."

"You nudged him into an early grave I'd say. You pack quite a punch."

"Jesus! You sure?" Salome was distraught. "I never even hit anyone like that before."

"Just as well I'd say. Now, what are we going to do with you I wonder?"

• THE CIVILIAN WAR ZONE •

Goyt's rhetorical question remained in the air. Salome sensed the portentousness but didn't know what to do about it. The odd major with the quartermaster corps buff colour trimming on his service cap seemed to be intent on rescuing him. But why? Officers didn't go around helping enlisted men.

Salome managed to straighten up. He felt a rush of blood from his nose and tried to stem it with his hand.

"Well, thanks ah . . . sir. I'll be on my way now. I'll get back to my hotel. I got a six-day pass to finish. I really appreciate your help, sir." He put one foot forward and hoped the other one would follow.

"I wouldn't leave yet if I was you, soldier." Goyt's eyes flashed like reflective icebergs. They held a message that Salome should have read, but didn't. "They'll be looking for you, soldier. They'll be combing the streets for you. You're wanted for murder, soldier. Killing a civilian. An enemy civilian. But still a civilian."

What did he mean? Salome wasn't prepared to argue with him. He just wanted to go, somewhere, anywhere, away from this odd officer in this blind alley. He felt trapped, helpless, caged. But he couldn't move.

It wasn't just his condition, his weakness, his drunkenness. Eight beers? Or was it twelve? It was the deadly point of the bayonet that the major was sticking into his throat.

Salome didn't dare breathe, or swallow. He had a thousand questions to ask, but didn't. It was all so confusing. He tried to focus on the major, but he became a blur. His head was full of the strains of "Rum and Coca Cola" and the terrible, painted, red-lipped, big-chinned female was kissing him on the mouth, again and again, and it tasted like vomit. He didn't know where he was. He couldn't even see the short sword that was digging into his throat any more. He felt mucus or blood spilling from his mouth because it had to find a way out and still he didn't swallow.

He believed he was about to die and he thought of his mother and his sister and his affectionate slobbering red setter.

"What's your name, soldier? Tell me your name!" Goyt hissed.

Salome couldn't open his mouth.

• MOBILISATION •

Goyt reached out with his free hand and tugged at Salome's dog tags, breaking the chain after it had cut into his neck.

Why did he do that? He wasn't dead. Yet.

He couldn't remember his own name. There was too much else crowding his mind. He wondered where Adam was, and all his buddies. And he hadn't even fought the Japanese yet. How many Japs have you killed? None. Just one Andrews sister. That's all. Would he get a Purple Heart for killing an Andrews sister? A military funeral? Would an officer come to the door of their small brownstone in Newark, the one with all the Italian cooking smells, the perpetual garlic? Or would they just send a telegram, a coldergram, stating he'd been killed in action, a bayonet in the neck, behind enemy lines? God rest his soul.

BOOK II

MILITARISATION

"... and when war was once begun, an utter rejection of all reverence for divine or human law existed, just as if the unrestrained commission of every crime became henceforth legitimate."

RENÉ DESCARTES
(1596-1650)

1

Joe Church looked out the window of his bedroom onto his solitary peach tree and it was either first thing in the morning or last thing in the afternoon. The dying sun suggested the latter.

He stretched and then regretted it. He almost put his back out. How can you feel so tired after a long night's . . . day's sleep? Easy. An abortive, pointless raid last night on a supposedly illegal casino and Winnie had tolerantly let him sleep all day.

"Did you sleep well?" Winnie's knee-jerk greeting. As meaningless as "How are you?"

"Sleep?" He had to answer it anyway. "A passable imitation. I feel like I've been riding a bucking bronco all night. Day." He rubbed his eyes. "Did you notice if there was a horse in the bedroom anywhere?"

Winnie thought for a moment. She had on her apron. As usual. "I heard something that could've been a horse, but I think it was only you snoring."

"That's strange. I didn't hear me snoring."

"That's probably 'cause you were off riding a horse somewhere, instead of sleeping like a civilised human being. What do you want for breakfast? Or should I say dinner? It's five o'clock."

"That early? Why don't you serve me what you've prepared?"

"I intended to."

"I know. Then why ask me?"

"It's a hangover from the old days. Before rationing."

"Rationing? Anyone'd think there was a war on." Joe stood up and removed his pyjama top. "Why is it Win, that ever since Pearl Harbor I haven't been able to sleep properly?"

"Maybe you have a guilty conscience." She stared at his bare chest and marvelled at the still rippling muscles. Certainly there was some paunch and the skin was a bit looser, but her fifty-two-year-old husband still looked good enough to . . . what? Fear? Love? Yes, all that and more.

"That's true. I feel guilty 'cause I'm not in the army."

"At your age?"

"What's wrong with my age? I'm old enough to be a general."

Winnie saluted him. "A general what?"

"I don't know. A general nuisance."

"Just thank your lucky stars you're in an essential service."

"I'm not sure it is essential any more. Now that the city's swarming with MPs and SPs, they hardly seem to need us ordinary cops. Listen, Win. . ." He dropped his pyjama pants and stepped out of them. "Do you think I should have another shot at promotion?"

Winnie drank in the sight of his naked body. He was as magnetising as ever, all six three and two hundred pounds of him. Her lovely big man. Her lovely, famous, tough, complicated big man, who still had doubts about his place in life, who never really achieved what he wanted, despite dedication and determination enough for fourteen men.

"You deliberately failed the last inspector's exam, you know that. Aren't you happy on the prowl any more?"

"Yes and no. I should be earning more. And I think I'm getting too old for the irregular hours."

"You don't look too old." Her eyes were trained on his essential parts.

"What you're looking at is superficial beauty. Behind that facade my legs feel like sponge cake, my back is about to go on me again, and my mouth feels as stale as last week's war news. This famous crusading vice cop is a man of straw."

"You're overtired. You've got no sleep pattern. You're too old to stay out all night. That's your trouble."

Joe admonished her, with a gleam in his eye. "If you think I'm going to argue with that boring piece of sound commonsense, you've got another think coming!" Joe stumbled towards the bathroom.

• MILITARISATION •

"Tell me, are you too old to pick up your pyjamas?"

Joe stopped. "Much." He went into the bathroom, climbed into the old tub and turned on the shower. Icy cold. He shivered and squirmed but relished the stimulation. He hated his daily all-year-round cold showers but stuck to them. A kind of self-discipline. Hot water was a sin. The freeze made his skin tingle. It closed his pores and afterwards, with a brisk rubdown, he felt positively glowing. Except for his back, which had a mind of its own.

"Do you really mean that about promotion?" Winnie stood at the bathroom door. She wanted promotion more than he did. As it was, he had more respect and autonomy than most inspectors or superintendents. He really answered only to the commissioner.

"I might. Well it depends. I've got a meeting tomorrow. I'm not sure what it's about, but I think I may be joining the military."

Winnie was aghast. "You're not serious?"

"I could be. Serious I mean. I actually meant the American military."

He started rubbing soap all over.

"You had me worried for a moment. I really thought you were serious. You'd get a much better lather if you used warm water."

"Warm water's for babies. Anyway most people these days are using cakes of fat."

"See! You always used to taunt me for being a hoarder! Aren't you glad now? We're the only people I know who still have plenty of soap, tea, toothpaste, canned food and pink icing," Winnie said proudly.

Joe was doing his final rinse. "Pink icing? What's that got to do with the price of fish?"

"Didn't you hear? Mr Dedman just banned it." (Dedman was the Federal Minister for War Organisation of Industry and the least popular man in the country.)

"How will that help the war effort?"

"I suppose all those thousands of people and machines involved in manufacturing pink icing for birthday cakes can now be diverted to making bombs."

• THE CIVILIAN WAR ZONE •

"If they pelted the Japanese with pink icing, that could be quite deadly."

"Of course. It would ruin their teeth." That made Joe laugh out loud. He stepped out of the tub and gave Winnie a big hug. She screamed. "You're soaking wet, you monster!"

Later Joe got stuck into the chops and eggs that Winnie had prepared. "That's the last of our meat. No more ration tickets for two weeks. So you'd better enjoy it."

"Don't worry. When I see those American MPs tomorrow they might pass on a few of their excess rations. The US military takes about eighty per cent of all our produce you know. They don't know the meaning of shortages."

"Including pink icing?"

"I'll ask them."

"You *were* serious about the American army? What are you seeing them about?"

"It's hush-hush. The walls have ears."

"So do I. Tell me!"

"I'm not really sure. But I think it's to do with some gang that's preying on American troops. Killing them even." Joe made it sound totally unimportant.

Winnie looked worried. Joe gave her a reassuring smile. He didn't like that worried look of hers. Their relationship had never been better than over the past few years. Most of the past tensions were well and truly buried. In some ways she was like a young girl again, although much greyer, more lines around her mouth and eyes. But she still walked like a ballet dancer and her figure was still slim and firm.

"It's going to be dangerous isn't it?"

"Not as dangerous as joining up. Tell you what though. If they want me to join the US military police, I'll probably say yes." He tried to make light of it, for her sake.

"Does that mean I'll be able to tell my friends I'm going with a Yank? That's a mark of distinction, you know."

"Mmm. Could be fun to be a Yank."

"You were never short of fun, as I recall."

"Don't recall. It makes me nervous."

Winnie suddenly stood up. She started moving dishes around on the table, to no obvious purpose. "This is probably

• MILITARISATION •

nothing, but Cynthia. . ."

"What about her?"

"Well, she's getting more and more like her father. That is, like her father used to be. She just doesn't come home very often at night."

"She's doing shift work at that plant, isn't she?"

"Yes, but I think she's also going out with . . . Americans."

Joe thought about that. He rubbed the front of his neck and felt the extra creases. Shame. One chin was enough for any man.

"Are you saying we should worry about it? You just said it was a mark of distinction. And funnily enough, most of those young men are better behaved than our blokes. I've noticed that. They treat the girls well."

"That's because they want something from them."

"You can't blame them. There's a war on."

Winnie's voice became quite shrill. "Joe! I'm talking about our daughter! Our nineteen-year-old daughter!"

"I know. But she's adult enough and smart enough to stay out of trouble."

Winnie started shaking with anger. "How can you say that? She's not like all those scum you mix with! The Americans turn lots of girls into prostitutes. You should know all about that!"

"Win! Calm down! You've got no reason to say things like that! She's old enough to go out with men. I'm sure she's good as gold."

"You're sure of nothing! You don't care about her! You don't care what happens to her! You don't care what she becomes! In fact maybe one night you can go out and arrest her along with all your other whores! How'd you like *that*?" Winnie flung herself down on a chair and started sobbing.

Joe felt helpless. He hadn't seen her like this for ages. What had got into her? He knew Cynthia as well as she did. She was strong, intelligent, mature. She could handle herself. Americans or no.

"What do you want me to do about her?"

Winnie shook her head, blew her nose, took a deep breath. "Nothing. Absolutely nothing. Like always."

2

Colonel Bastien Tunks lay in a stupor or partial coma for twenty-four hours, after the ambulance brought him in. Then, unpredictably, he surfaced, with almost total recall, the details of which he didn't divulge to anyone. Despite shock and a plurality of injuries to his face and head, he demanded to leave the Royal Prince Alfred Hospital, a large portion of which had been taken over by the US military.

He had twenty-eight stitches in his lacerated brow, a deep puncture wound in his forehead, which throbbed like a compressor and was covered by a light dressing, and other lacerations and contusions, caused by the jeep hitting the parapet and ejecting him. He looked like Primo Carnera after his last fight.

Tunks was incredibly resilient physically. When the MO put back his dislocated shoulder Tunks barely moaned during the manipulation. He demanded a tetanus booster, which the MO told him he'd already had during his period of coma.

"The concussion will take care of itself," Tunks stated. "I've had my brain shook up before. And I'm not staying here in this abattoir! I can take bed rest back at my apartment. I'm no cream puff."

"If you want to run the risk of knocking out some brain cells, then leave," the equally brusque MO captain told him.

"I got more brain cells than I know what to do with," Tunks replied. "And the black eye is a matter of beefsteak. There's no shortage of that in the officers' canteen."

"Lucky you're not a civilian or you'd have to make do with sausages."

Tunks didn't laugh. He was burning up with rage. He blamed the girl for everything. And he vowed to find her and teach her a lesson. More than that. The death penalty. Nothing

• MILITARISATION •

less would assuage his rancour.

He hadn't mentioned her to anyone and no one had mentioned her to him. Apparently she was nowhere about when the ambulance picked him up. The jeep was a write-off. He explained later to the MO and to General Burden, his ultimate superior officer, that the jeep had run out of control after traversing a soft edge on the side of the road and that was that. Such accidents did not warrant a second thought when there was a war to be fought, and Tunks in any case was a law unto himself. He owed explanations to no one, not even General Burden, who tended to be far removed from his duties most of the time, being a practising alcoholic. Albeit a discreet one. It had never been a bar to his promotion. After Pearl Harbor, in the rush for mobilisation, various low-ranking officers in the regular services, such as Tunks and Burden, received overnight escalations of rank. Burden was happy to let his colonel and local Provost Marshal exercise full autonomy over the military police in his area. He would no more take Tunks to task for anything than throw rotten eggs at MacArthur. Furthermore, Tunks was one of the few who knew all about Burden's alcoholic burden, which placed him in a blackmailing position, thus making him inviolable in the chain of command.

Soon after leaving the hospital Tunks was stricken with a degree of retrograde amnesia, so that he couldn't accurately recall the last minute or so before the jeep jumped the wall and hit the parapet. It didn't bother him too much. He could recall all of the preceding events. Nevertheless he heeded the message his concussed brain was sending him.

It was a slow night at Pete's Tavern on West 18th Street, despite the uncertain future for such establishments, with Prohibition just days away. Outside it was raining with tropical intensity, whilst inside Private Tunks was downing fingers of rye as if it were going out of style. Which it was.

The more he drank, the clearer everything became. He pondered his estrangement from Martha, who didn't seem to appreciate his masculine dominance and his decision to remain in the army despite his harrowing experiences in France and

• THE CIVILIAN WAR ZONE •

his two years of agonising recuperation, but more immediately, he pondered the beautiful red-haired colleen who'd just entered the bar. She was with a moustachioed gentleman of considerable girth, who didn't take his homburg hat off, despite his outward appearance as a gentleman of wealth and distinction.

Tunks had changed booths so as to be nearer to the rubicund beauty, who looked to him just like the birthday present he'd been dreaming of. He'd always had a weakness for Irish red hair with its accompanying milky white complexion. And this one had green eyes as well. He remembered those eyes. They were stamped on his brain forever. And the long slim, nicely rounded figure inside the green velvet brocade dress down to her calves. "Happy birthday to me", he had sung. Aloud. Loud enough for her to hear. And her boorish gentleman with the hat on.

A stunning colleen like this would appreciate a well turned out soldier like him, with his leather leggings over breeches and his heavy brown belted topcoat. He pushed his authoritarian campaign hat to the edge of the table, where he hoped she could see it. Despite Wilson, soldiers, doughboys were still an elite. Weren't they? They had ended the war on a glorious note. Victors. It had taken them less than eighteen months to end the war that had been dragging on for so long, with so many casualties. Including him.

He wasn't a casualty now. He had signed on — a thirty-year man. Silver star and all. Scars, inside and out. But a free man, free of his nagging wife, free on his twenty-seventh birthday, free of bossy friends.

He had to meet her. His sixth finger of rye gave him the freedom to meet her. He caught her eye and raised his glass.

"Happy birthday to me," he sang aloud.

She flushed a pretty pink. The doubtful gentleman friend with the hedgerow moustache looked across at him with a sneer. Rude, thought Tunks. Rude. What's a nice girl like you doing with a rude man like that?

"Would you care to join me for my birthday?" he asked. Aloud.

The girl looked behind her, as if he must've been asking

• MILITARISATION •

someone else. But there was no one else.

Tunks picked up his glass and his campaign hat and presented himself before their booth. Courage and fortitude. Take what you can while you can. His impulsive motto, when a private. The mists of time clarified his motives. He was brash then, and brash now. It didn't matter so much now. In those days, few were brash. Except when drunk. He was drunk. She was a picture. He wanted to hang her on his wall. For his birthday.

"Best you go and sit down, sir," the be-hatted gentleman had said, admonishingly.

"I am not a sir, sir. I am a private. But one day soon I'll be a sir, and then you can call me sir. Sir. However, I will accept your invitation anyway."

Tunks slid into the booth and sat down next to the girl, forcing her to slide along, as he responded to the feel of her thigh beneath that green brocade velvet. It was soft. He remembered that. Magic soft. Almost as memorable as her green eyes. She wasn't wearing all that heavy corsetry underneath, that so many women retreated behind.

"I meant for you to sit down where you came from, private!" the gentleman said, with narrowed eyes and furious frown, no doubt insecure because he was almost twice the age of his lustrous companion.

"Now, would you expect a soldier to sit alone on his twenty-seventh birthday?" Tunks asked, with his eyes on the girl and his vitriol on the man. "However, I do want to thank you, sir, for bringing this fine young lady down to the tavern this evening, so that she and I might have the opportunity to become acquainted and to mutually celebrate my twenty-seventh birthday."

Tunks recalled how he had slipped his palm just above the girl's knee, rubbing the velvet ever so slightly, causing a tingling in his wrist and apparently a small fire in her thighs. She had made no attempt to remove his hand. At first. But she remained silent, allowing the two men to make the conversation, perhaps enjoying being the topic, thinking perhaps, may the best man win me.

Tunks knew he was the best man.

• THE CIVILIAN WAR ZONE •

"May I say that I find your intrusion quite offensive and completely inexcusable, private." Tiny red spots appeared all over the gentleman's face, beacons of repressed anger.

"I don't consider it an intrusion, sir," Tunks said. "I read the lady's eyes from across there and they flashed a welcoming light to me that no man could resist. Particularly not on his twenty-seventh birthday. So allow me to buy you all a drink. Bartender! Three more of the same, whatever they are. To Prohibition!" Tunks raised and drained his glass. "May it last no longer than my birthday. And may your green eyes continue flashing me messages, which I'll be forever too weak to resist."

The girl had actually smiled at this, for Tunks was irresistible. A truly dominating male, with pain and suffering behind him, strength within and a future up the military ladder.

"Young lady, allow me to introduce myself," Tunks said, and did. "And I will in turn allow you to introduce yourself; as well as your father."

The gentleman's red beacons flared again.

But the girl still smiled. A rich organic smile. "He's my fiancé, actually. My name is Glenda Gorman. Soon to be Mrs Aubrey Greville."

The gentleman's demeanour mellowed into a glower at the acknowledgement of his correct status. But this induced Tunks to move one up.

"Congratulations. Do I assume then that this is an arranged marriage?"

Apoplexy from the gentleman. Amusement from the lady.

"Not exactly," she said enigmatically.

"Ah!" said Tunks. "Like a good soldier, I sense a damsel in distress. Never fear. I will rescue you. This gentleman, who claims to be your fiancé, has no future, as of now. For I have decided to take you home, free from harm, and free from him."

Tunks recalled standing up and offering the girl his arm, ready to escort her out. And that was precisely when the so-called gentleman, Aubrey Greville, still with his hat on, threw the contents of his glass, which was bourbon with water, in Tunks' face.

Tunks grinned in retaliation, licked away the stinging wet

• MILITARISATION •

and bowed low in acknowledgement, before reaching down, grabbing the gentleman by the vestfront and hitting him in the face.

The punch, which seemed to break a bone in Greville's nose and caused a rush of nasal blood, sent him cannoning back into the booth. Then Tunks grabbed the girl and pulled her bodily across the seat and dragged her kicking and screaming across the floor.

"Where do you think you're taking her?" the cop with the Irish brogue asked Tunks, just inside the swinging doors.

"I'm saving her from that evil sonofabitch gentleman, who's forcing her to marry him!" Tunks said and then hit the cop as he reached out to try and untangle the girl from his grasp.

The cop went down and the girl screamed and scratched at Tunks' face, drawing blood. So he had to hit her too.

He dragged her out onto the street in the drenching rain, before the other cop, so resplendent in his blue uniform, shiny buttons and sou'wester over helmet, clubbed him down and dragged him away in handcuffs, blowing his whistle like an express train.

They charged him with being drunk and disorderly, assault and abduction and then turned him over to the army for discipline. He spent a year in military prison, where he learnt to hate and then admire the system.

He survived on prison hooch and commandeered privileges. He learnt to throw his weight around. He became kingpin to such an extent that, despite being a convicted felon, at times he identified with the warders and the system, and treated his fellow prisoners as if he was the commandant. But he never forgot the tall, shapely redhead with the green eyes, who, in all his subsequent fantasies, became his prisoner, his slave girl, his compliant mistress, his bearer of bodily fulfilment and masculine domination.

And here she was again, only now her hair was darker, her skin less peaches and cream and more light tan and her spirit more wilful. But this time there would be no cops around to thwart his fulfilment. Now, he had the rank and authority to track her down and realise all his dreams.

· THE CIVILIAN WAR ZONE ·

Perhaps.

He gave himself the next two days off and stayed in bed at one of his billets at the Australia Hotel, which in peacetime was a high-priced hostelry of superior reputation but was now housing high-echelon American officers. He had a severe headache, a high temperature and a burning face, and his major stitched wound and deep puncture felt as if they were being soldered by armies of soldier ants with blowlamps.

He darkened the room, put out the "do not disturb" sign and crashed. In between dead sleep he had fitful dreams of chasing naked women with a 75 mm Howitzer which blasted them into little pieces, which in turn coagulated into more women. So each killing was counterproductive. Eventually he was swamped by thousands of little women, some naked, some in cocktail dresses with snakes in their hair, who ate him up. In his wakeful moments he just lay there reliving the treacherous slut's assault on him. Each recollection exaggerated the assault until, in his mind's eye, Cynthia became an amazon, a gargantuan creature with mountainous breasts, four times his size, who slugged him with her fists, feet and high heels, practically gouging his eyes out, making him roar with fury and impotence. Then he tried to run the jeep over her but her mammoth breasts were like concrete blocks.

A new obsession had been born. The colonel Provost Marshal, the ruthless enforcer of military justice, had pinpointed the enemy. She was a jezebel named Cynthia, who was out to destroy an entire regiment with her lethal body. She was going to make eunuchs of them all and it was his duty, as Provost Marshal to stop her. His patriotic duty. And his head hurt worse than ever as his dreams and reveries multiplied and enlarged, and the enemy was no longer the hateful Nipponese but the treacherous Australian cunt, with fire between her legs and a tongue that could cut you to pieces.

A few slugs of rye calmed him down somewhat and seemed to ease his headache. By nightfall he fell into a long sleep that lasted until hunger pangs woke him after midnight. He got up and called his adjutant, Lieutenant Kobovsky, and demanded room service. The sleepy Kobovsky used the

· MILITARISATION ·

colonel's name to organise a hot meal and some more cold steak for his eye.

The remainder of his bed rest went much more smoothly. By lunchtime the next day he felt almost ready for duty, although his wounds were still obvious.

He had a most important assignment. He would deal with the female enemy on his own time. But there was another enemy abroad, amongst the local population. An enemy who was preying on hapless drunk GIs. The high command was getting very concerned. To date six victims had been found. It was creating a wedge between the US and the Australian governments. MacArthur himself had made representations to the Australian Prime Minister, John Curtin. Curtin had spoken to the State Premier, who in turn had spoken to the New South Wales Police Commissioner. MacArthur had insisted it was up to the civil authorities to protect their allied visitors from harm at the hands of ruthless civilians. Assuming they were ruthless civilians. The sparse available evidence made this a debatable point.

In a city with a population of over one million civilians and, in 1943, tens of thousands of visiting American servicemen at any one time, there was a fine line separating the jurisdiction of the local State Police and the Military Police. Especially when you had civilians committing crimes against servicemen and servicemen committing crimes against civilians. However, it wasn't just a question of which police had the jurisdiction, it was also a question of which laws should prevail — civil or military — and for that matter, US military or Australian military. Military law was not constitutionally entrenched. It was really just a series of regulations and codes of behaviour formulated arbitrarily by the respective high commands. Oddly, many of them were more liberal than the local State or Federal laws. Particularly those in relation to prostitution, gambling and the consumption of liquor. The military considered these pursuits a matter of morale, whereas the state's laws were based on morals.

Tunks had had to wrestle with this very grey area ever since he'd landed in Australia and set up the divisional Military Police company in Sydney. He was under strict orders not

• THE CIVILIAN WAR ZONE •

to alienate the civilian population. Secretly he longed to be able to impose some form of martial law. His brief, however, from the Provost Marshal in Washington, per his CO at the US Army Combat Development Command Military Police Agency at Fort Gordon in Georgia, was to coordinate with the host country military and civil police in internal defence operations.

Personally he didn't give a tinker's cuss about civilians or their delicate feelings. They would have to accept there was a war on and the military, and that meant the Military Police, held sway, even in a land that wasn't exactly theirs. But he was professional enough to know he couldn't let his own, well-blooded instincts ride roughshod over all the political manifestations involved, and whilst he'd ordered his men to be on the lookout for those maggoty gangs who were preying on US troops, he knew he'd have to defer to MacArthur's decree that it was basically a problem for the State Police. It was a bitter pill.

The next night, Tunks, with his black eye at the deflated parachute stage and his worst lacerations and puncture hidden by plaster, returned to the Hyde Park Canteen.

Not that he expected to find Cynthia there. But he was about to launch his own investigation. He hadn't noticed previously if she had mixed with any other girls in particular, so he danced with a bevy of them and casually enquired if they knew this swell doll called Cynthia, about five six tall, willowy, 110 pounds, great figure, long legs, walks like one of those fashion models or beach gals, dark wavy hair, prominent cheekbones, large green eyes, sort of Joan Crawford shoulders, only much better looking. Then he appealed to their romantic souls. He confessed he had fallen madly in love with this goddess, but like Cinderella she had disappeared at midnight, without telling him her second name or where she lived.

The first eight girls didn't seem to know who he was describing. But the ninth — bingo!

"Oh yes. That sounds like one of the girls I work with. At the plant. In fact she's been absent from work for the past

• MILITARISATION •

few days. And I haven't seen her here either. She must be taking a sickie. Although it's not allowed, unless you're really ill."

"Great! I don't mean that she's sick. I mean that you know her. What's her second name, honey?" Tunks took out his notebook.

"Is that your little black book? My, I think you must be a bit of an old roué, colonel?"

Tunks swallowed his anger. "Wrong honey! I have to write things down 'cause I have a bad memory."

"To tell you the truth, I don't know her second name. We just call each other by Christian names. Or nicknames. We all call her Sin. For short. I think she must like to sin too."

"What's your name, honey? I might write yours down too, for one of the other guys I know, who likes real cuddly little dames like you."

She giggled. "My name's Jane. Jane Hervey. Not Harvey. Hervey."

Jane wasn't exactly plain but she was plump all over, with very red cheeks, almost a permanent blush, and short hennaed hair. And she didn't really like this bashed-up all-white officer. He was holding her too tight and pinching her back. She didn't know Cynthia very well. Cynthia was prettier and more popular than she and didn't bother much with Jane. She was surprised that Cynthia had become involved with this heavy abrasive man. She was sure Cynthia could get any American she wanted. Surely she didn't want this over-the-hill creature?

"What's this plant you work at, honey?"

She wished he'd let her go and sit down. She wasn't enjoying dancing with him at all, even though he was the first one to ask her all night.

"It's a . . . well, we make, you know, war things."

"War things?" Tunks' lip curled in scorn. "War things? You mean things that go boom boom?"

Jane's bottom lip quivered. She didn't like people scoffing at her. "We're not supposed to tell anybody where we work. It's top secret. You never know when the enemy's listening.

That's what they tell us all the time."

Tunks patted her gently but significantly on her very pink cheek. "Hey honey? Do I look like the enemy to you? We're allies, honey. Allies. I work for General MacArthur. He's the big boss man down here. He commands all the troops, Aussies and American. And I'm a colonel, honey. We're all in this goddamn war together!"

Jane was near tears now. This bear of a man was impinging on her worse than her own father ever did. She wasn't used to this amount of open communication with a man. Everyone else she knew talked at arm's length, and in polite, oblique or evasive tones.

"So don't hold out on me, honey! Where do you work? What's the name of this plant? You know what they say? All's fair in love and war! Well this is both, honey! So don't hold out!"

"SKG Bearings and Casings at Tempe." Jane bit her lip. She had to tell him. He was so overbearing.

"What do you and Cynthia do there, honey? Sweep up the factory floor?" Tunks laughed sadistically.

Jane pouted. "I work on the production line and she works in the accounts office. We do exactly what the men used to do," she said proudly. "If it wasn't for us, you soldiers would have nothing to fight with. So there!"

"That's great, honey. Really great! I like the idea of women working their butts off for a change. Before the war, you all had it too easy!"

Jane wanted to tick him off, but he really scared her too much and his hands were digging into her back and making her flesh creep. She hoped she hadn't got Cynthia into trouble and yet secretly, she didn't mind. She'd always thought Cynthia was a bit haughty and too pretty for words. It wasn't jealousy, but some people needed to be taken down a peg. Now all she wanted was to get away from this scary warlord, who smelt of whisky, aftershave and disinfectant — a most unpleasant concoction.

"Since you've been so helpful to me, honey — and for all I know you might be responsible for bringing on those wedding bells eventually — well I'll let you have just one more dance before I go."

Jane's heart sank, but she was quite incapable of bowing out.

The band struck up "Tuxedo Junction" and Tunks whirled her round in an inexpert, unbluesy, double-time quickstep that scattered the other deliberate beat dancers.

"Does that hurt?" she tentatively enquired about his facial injuries.

"Not any more," he replied gruffly. "I got that jitterbugging the other night. Threw this little gal right over my shoulder, but she missed and caught me right there with her high heels. Say, do you jitterbug?"

Jane shook her head, vehemently. "Oh no! I wouldn't dare! Was that with . . . Cynthia?"

"Oh no. She's too fine a piece of goods to hurl around like that. It was with some other gal. Don't know her name. That's why I didn't go and visit her in hospital."

Jane's eyes widened at this piece of information and she prayed she'd make it safely through to the end of "Tuxedo Junction".

Tunks was tickled pink to see the terrified expression on her face. That's the way he liked it.

3

Carl Goyt was pleased with his latest enemy find. So tall, lanky, smooth, good-looking, credulous, drunk and vulnerable. He could have killed him there and then in that disgusting blind alley, but the physical imperative of his breathing difficulty had, surprisingly, not evinced itself. Therefore he was able to take a cool, rational, tactical view of the situation. Utilising foresight as well.

Sometimes it was preferable to take prisoners, to build up a stock of readily accessible victims for when the physical imperative was immediate. This lanky one would make an ideal prisoner of war. Already he looked undernourished. No all-American hero this one.

Salome, for his part, couldn't understand the reprieve. He couldn't understand his captor either. The whole thing was like a bad dream. The mad major was a man of fickle moods. After sticking that bayonet in his throat and causing him to bleed, he had suddenly started talking softly to him and leading him through more back streets in the brownout. Salome just tagged along, in a complete daze, with his head somewhere over the rainbow, drunk and punch-drunk, walking on clouds, smelling the garbage and thinking it was angel's perfume.

Maybe he *was* dead. Was this God or St Peter, this major with the soft voice and the ice-blue eyes? It must be God, alternately harsh and vengeful, kind and gentle. Advising him he mustn't go back or they'd shoot him in front of a firing squad, or hang him, because he killed that painted warrior.

"Where are you taking me, sir?" he asked once, in a fit of logical thought. The sir didn't sit right though.

"To a temporary safe haven, where they'll never find you."

Salome could hear the lap of harbour waters now and gently tooting foghorns. The major was leading him down some never-ending stone steps and he kept slipping on the moss, overbalancing.

"We're nearly there." The major seemed to know the steps and scampered down them, sure-footedly.

Now they were in a park, on the water's edge. There were rough wet mounds of grass, then rocks, balance-sabotaging rocks. Goyt kept a firm grip on Salome's elbow, coaxing him from slippery surface to surface. "Nearly there."

Salome hoped so. He was completely fagged out.

Then a cave. A cave? A cold, damp, forbidding cave. "You'll be safe here for the night. Until we can get you to the proper detainee point."

"Detainee point?" Salome's head was full of questions but he felt so incoherent he couldn't get them out.

The major lit a kerosene lamp so there was light enough to see a mattress, a chair and a bottle of drinking water. There were small pools of salt water, sand and shells in crevices and slimy smooth slippery rock, which suggested the cave spent some of its time under water.

"What is this place?"

"Why, can't you see? It's a cave. My own little hideaway. I've sheltered many a deserter here in recent times. I discovered it when I was just a small lad and needed to escape."

"From what?"

"From life, you might say."

"I can't stay here."

"I'm afraid you have no choice. For your own safety, I must ensure that you're secure." Goyt chuckled at his consonance. Then he abruptly handcuffed Salome through a steel clip secured to a snubbing post, ostensibly for tying up boats.

"Why'd you do that?"

"For your own protection, of course. We can't have you running off somewhere and getting caught by the MPs, can we?"

Salome's head thudded. One of us is mad, he thought.

Goyt quickly frisked him and relieved him of his wallet, watch, stainless steel four-bladed pocket-knife (army issue), two packs of Camels, gold lighter, chocolate bar, loose change and a condom, which Goyt held up distastefully.

"You won't be needing that, down here." He stuffed all of Salome's things in his own pockets.

"Why'd you take my stuff?"

"For safekeeping, of course. Now, I trust you have no more inane questions to ask me."

Before Salome could respond, either inanely or profanely, Goyt slipped out of the cave. Salome sank down upon the mattress, which was wet through. His handcuffs restricted him to a crouching position. He shivered as the harbour breeze swept in through the entrance. The alcohol was wearing off, increasing the pain in his jaw, nose and mouth. He cursed himself for not resisting this mad major, and yet, most of the time, he had acted like a saviour, not a captor.

After a while he began to suffer from cold tremors and cramps. His calf and thigh muscles seized up. He bent his feet back and that helped a bit.

"What am I doing here?" he asked himself, over and over.

Nothing made sense. A ribbon of doubts. The war didn't make sense. It had been so clear at home. Here he was, some sort of prisoner, captured by one of his own side. All because of that dolled up fruit. It had just been a puny poke. Was that all it took to change your life? A split second. Before that he'd been as high as a kite. Feeling up that warm, skinny Dorothy, liquefied with the ice-cold brown. Sniffing pussy. About to make that goddamn war seem worthwhile. He had joined the march for manhood at last. After all those years of incestuous fumbling and false promises. Then — a faggot's sloppy kiss, an involuntary jab, and . . . and . . . this! The Count of Monte Cristo. Twenty years in a cave. Starved. Busting for a piss. Why wait? At least his piss was warm. He let it flow and it eased the cramps.

Then he suddenly had company. Two seagulls, pure white against the black night, fluttered into the cave with a series of fishing bay squawks, which chilled him with their proximity, more than anything had previously. They flew around his head, sizing him up for bait. He shut his eyes before they could peck them out. They didn't try. If only his hands were free, he could throttle them and eat them. Raw. Like in that movie

• MILITARISATION •

he had seen in Camp Seymour. Those survivors in a lifeboat.

What the hell! He wasn't even hungry. Yet. They didn't attack him. Non-vultures. This was their hotel. The Hotel Seagull. Accommodation by the sea. They squatted down and cawed themselves into an apparent sleep.

Salome tried to follow suit. No way. He stayed awake until dawn. Shivering, throbbing, aching, barely moving for the cramps in his legs which seemed permanent. Every movement made them ache more.

Maybe he was a POW? Prisoner of What?

Salome's best friend, Adam Goldhart, had less doubts about his status. And about his injuries. He was comfortably bedded down in the US military hospital at Herne Bay about fifteen miles south-east of the city. Unlike his friend, he was not reluctantly incarcerated. He had nothing much to get up for except more amphibious training and probable embarkation to the war zone.

He had sustained considerable shock as a result of the stab wound in his shoulder and the blow to the back of his neck. The morphine they had given him to relieve the pain had relaxed him considerably and made him view the previous night's altercations rather too benevolently. To accelerate the healing process and to combat clostridial infection, they applied sulphanilamide locally and sulphathiazole orally: new drug therapy that worked wonders.

He'd heard about guys who deliberately shot themselves in the foot to avoid war service. He'd never do that. Apart from high school football bumps and bruises he'd never been injured before. Maybe it was better than crawling through mud, swimming with eighty pounds of equipment on your back, studying the characteristics of jungle trees and foliage, doing advanced map reading, making long oppressive marches, hand-to-hand combat, terrain clearing and scaling trees. Tarzan he was not. Tarzan was better off. He only had to wear a loincloth and he had Jane for company.

Sure he hated the Japanese almost as much as he hated the Germans. Pearl Harbor and Hitler's ascension both disgusted him, made him want to join up, made him want to fight for freedom. But it wasn't really his style.

When you joined up you lost everything: your hairstyle, underclothes, clothes, medical and dental secrets, all ambitions outside of promotional ones and, most of all, your privacy. The army wasn't his idea of making a living. He had planned on going to college and majoring in labor relations as well as the history of American labor. Perhaps it was a reaction to his father's inherent industrial conservatism or the guilt he felt from being cushioned against the Depression. This rebelliousness carried over into the army. The army was a totally undemocratic entity. It thrived on exploitation of the underprivileged enlisted man, decreed and enforced totally arbitrary rules and regulations, used a highly repressive police force to preserve its totalitarian structure and allowed no consultation in regard to its structure or decisions. Of course, like most totalitarian regimes, it provided certain benefits to its masses to keep morale up and make the regimentation less a cause for revolution. But basically Adam resented it and, given the opportunity, was prepared to do something about it. Except that the imperative of the war made this impossible.

Armies, he realised, had never been democratic. Not national armies. Although some guerilla forces had and their effectiveness as fighters was often second to none. Surely, he reasoned to himself, if the cause was worth fighting for, discipline and regimentation were unnecessary. Of course, his was a singular view and he had yet to find even one ally.

Maybe he just didn't like the idea of being battle fodder. He realised he should have volunteered for one of the non-combatant corps — the Finance Corps, the Judge Advocate's, or the Quartermaster's. But having no special economic, legal or clerical expertise, he wouldn't have been accepted. As it was he was just a dog soldier, and all his middle-class radical instincts rejected his situation.

Making the most of his convalescence, he read all the recent issues of *Stars and Stripes* and brought himself up to date on the home news, in particular the baseball. Not for himself so much as Salome, who was a ball nut and worshipped the Yankees more than the flag. When he found Salome he'd be able to bring him up to date. He would be tickled to learn

• MILITARISATION •

that Ted Williams of the Red Sox and Stan Musial of the Cardinals, both big hitters he could do without, had been drafted. On the other hand he couldn't find any mention that DiMaggio had been drafted, which would be good for the Yankees.

His recuperation wasn't all peaches though. He was jerked back to reality by two bedside visitors, both of them MPs, a sergeant first class and a corporal, who had no sympathy for his wounds or regard for his feelings.

"You can consider yourself under arrest, soldier!" the barrel-chested, piggy-eyed Sergeant Struther said, in his Oklahoman dustbowl accent. "You'll be facing charges next week at a summary court martial, along with twenty-five other soldiers arrested at the Reflections Club, which has now been designated temporarily off limits."

"I didn't do anything, sergeant!" Adam protested. "I was an innocent victim. I didn't even throw a punch!"

"That's what they all say."

They shoved a photograph of Pfc Albert Salamandini under his nose. In it, Salome, photographed way back at Camp Roberts in California, right after his first crew cut — acne-faced, adolescent sick, a sun-denied over-urbanised civilian drifter — looked much worse than he did now. At least army life with regular chow, exercise and sleep had toned him up, improved his health and appearance.

"Do you know the whereabouts of this soldier? Same company as you."

"I wish I did. He's my buddy. I don't know where the hell he is."

"When did you last see him?"

"At Reflections. After the . . . brawl. He was being dragged out by some . . . major. The same officer who stabbed me with the bayonet."

Both MPs turned their eyes on him with scepticism.

"How much had you drunk that night?" Struther asked.

Adam hesitated. "Oh, I don't remember. Six or seven beers maybe. But I knew what was going on."

"Sure you did. Maybe it was ten beers, not six? Maybe fourteen?"

• THE CIVILIAN WAR ZONE •

"No, not that many! Christ! It was only beer!"

Adam's shoulder started to throb now. These monkeys were tensing him all up.

"Well soldier, in case you been jerkin' off, the beer here is almost as strong as bootleg hooch! So I'd say your story was ten-tenths bullshit!" Sergeant Struther stuck his cleft chin forward defiantly, abusively.

Adam sat forward, rigid as a rulebook, his face reddening, trying to ignore the sharp pain in his shoulder. Old Master Morphine had taken a powder.

"Well, who the hell do you think stabbed me? The Lone Ranger?"

"We don't know who stabbed you, soldier," Struther spoke in a controlled tone, utilising great restraint, mindful of the other soldier patients in the ward. "And what's more, we don't care."

"You got off lightly," Corporal Beeston chipped in, "compared with some of the other injuries."

"If you can't stand the heat, stay out of the bathroom!" Struther said.

"That's kitchen, sergeant," Adam corrected.

Struther gave him a withering look, but didn't make the correction.

"I guess you know something about the killing of that female impersonator? You must've seen it happen."

Adam fell silent for a moment. He licked his dry lips. "I didn't have anything to do with that."

"But you saw it?"

"I didn't see anything. I was under the table."

"Maybe you saw this guy, your buddy, kill that dude?" The sergeant thrust the photo under Adam's chin again. Adam was not about to hand his buddy in for murder. He bit his tongue.

"Well, did you see him kill that dude or not?" Struther's greyish face was only inches away. Adam could've bitten him on the nose. The guy's breath stank of weed and large intestinal malfunction.

"My buddy wouldn't harm a flea. He's not that kind of guy. A big softie. Why would he kill some cotton candy creep?"

• MILITARISATION •

"We got five witnesses who saw him knock that queer off his feet. A fatal punch. How come you didn't see it?"

"I don't have to say anything without a lawyer." Adam clammed up.

"You'll be assigned a legal officer from the Judge Advocate General's Department before the summary court martial. In the meantime I'd remind you you're just a dog soldier and you got no rights. None at all!"

"I'm innocent until proven guilty. That applies to soldiers same as civilians."

"Who told you that horseshit, soldier? You're subject to army laws and army discipline, and you take orders. And your buddy is wanted for murder and going AWOL. And unless you want to be charged as an accessory, you'd better tell us what you know and what you saw."

Adam softened his tone. He wanted them to note the change in his demeanour, which, through its new shade, might convince them he was suddenly telling the truth.

"To tell you the truth, sergeant, I'd had twelve beers and I really couldn't see anything properly. I was seeing things, in twos and threes, you know. I couldn't swear to anything. It wouldn't be right. I was drunk as a skunk. I don't even know who stabbed me. I don't know anything. Wish I could help, but I can't. In all honesty. Sorry."

They stared at him with more, not less scepticism. The MP white-on-blue brassards seemed to wink at Adam. He held his slight smile of simple sincerity until he thought his face was going to break. The sergeant stroked the long white nightstick that was hanging from the eyelet in his webbed belt. No doubt he was fantasising caving Adam's head in.

Not now.

Adam felt he had a slight advantage. They could hardly interrogate him physically in a hospital ward. He also guessed that their investigative prowess was limited to brute force. They weren't exactly psychology majors. So, for the moment, they were relatively impotent. Not that it changed anything, but he would have to stick to this story in the court martial.

But Adam hadn't counted on one psychological rabbit in the hat, which they now produced. The old prejudice ploy.

• THE CIVILIAN WAR ZONE •

"Goldhart? What is that?" Struther asked, with narrowed bitter eyes.

"It's a name. What do you think?"

"That makes you a Jew then?"

It wasn't so much what he said but the way he said it. Adam's stomach turned over. He immediately recognised the anti-Semitic symptoms. To thugs like Struther, the word Jew was an insult. One the victim couldn't refute. Sure I'm a Jew. Why deny it? But if you are one, the implication is that you're inferior or undesirable. Subhuman. But what can you do?

When he was younger the temptation was always to opt for the easy way out. Pretend you're a gentile. Why suffer? Why stick your neck out for an identity you were only half-hearted about anyway? At school he'd heard some of the kids try and deny it and then they hated themselves for so doing. But now, particularly since the events in Germany, to deny was as despicable as the prejudice itself.

"It doesn't *make* me a Jew, sergeant. I am one."

"I thought so," Corporal Beeston said, shaking his muffin, near-shaved head disgustedly.

"What does that mean?" Adam countered defiantly.

"What does what mean?" Struther said.

"Forget it!" Adam said. Why fight these bastards? Let them stew in their own ignorance. He averted his face from them, picked up a *Stars and Stripes* and started reading it, dismissing them mentally and thus gaining some slight advantage. You didn't beat these types with words, Adam reasoned, only with force (which was out of the question) or attitude.

Sergeant Struther demonstrated his sudden psychological disadvantage by thwacking the end of Adam's bed with his club, before exiting. For a moment Adam thought the bed would collapse, but it was iron. An inch further north and it would've fractured his foot. Better bed than head, Adam thought, as he slanted one eye to watch them strut out of the ward like Nazis, and he wondered for a moment who was on whose side.

After they'd gone, Adam lay back with a sigh of relief, then trepidation. He realised a sojourn in the stockade was

· MILITARISATION ·

likely, where, from what he'd heard, the inmates and the guards vied with one another for the Distinguished Brutality Award. Then he wondered where Salome was and who, in the name of Adolf, was that moon-faced sonofabitch commissioned asshole who had stabbed him.

4

Salome, the captive in the cave, remained confused. He did not understand why his saviour had become his captor. Maybe he wasn't a US major after all. Maybe he was a deserter. But he hadn't heard of any officers becoming deserters before. Enlisted men became deserters. He was totally unaware that now such a major could actually be an enlisted, civilian part of the great American war machine.

After the establishment of the American Purchasing Commission in February 1942 "to provide coordination and to control procurement of supplies, equipment and material for American forces in Australia", it was found that this daunting supply facility could not be fully staffed by US military personnel. So the Quartermaster Corps decided to employ many local civilians and keep to a minimum the number of service troops to be brought to Australia.

In all they employed 365 civilians as clerks, stenographers, warehousemen, storekeepers, tent repairmen, shoe repairmen, purchasing experts, statisticians, tailors, motor mechanics, telephonists, carpenters, bookkeepers, janitors, messengers, seamstresses and typewriter repairmen. They even employed an attorney who was an expert on Australian contract law.

One of these civilians was Carl Goyt, rejected by the AIF for reasons of asthma and, in turn, recommended to the US QM as a useful employee. He was a stock record clerk — one of five in Reserve Store 18, QM Supply Depot at Base Section 5. His work consisted of non-stop inventory of subsistence, clothing and general supplies in the reserve store. His salary was not to American standards but was the same as that paid by Australian government departments. However, with something like eighty per cent of all food and consumer items produced in the country going to the US military, for

• MILITARISATION •

a time Goyt's work in the reserve store made him feel like Aladdin in his cave.

The reserve depot was for storing supplies not required for immediate issue. Stocks were not to be withdrawn from reserve depots, such as Goyt's, without approval of Headquarters USAFIA (US Armed Forces in Australia). However Goyt was able to pilfer stocks from his reserve store and cover it up in two ways. One: by understating slightly some quantities on his weekly inventory. Two: by forging requisitions, signed by the Chief Quartermaster himself, Brigadier General Wilson, for the removal of all types of supplies (within reason, so as not to create suspicion) from the General Supply Depot at Base Section 5, which he used to replace all the items he had pilfered from the reserve store, thus keeping his inventory accurate. By alternating the two methods, he felt there was less chance of being caught out.

As the Chief Quartermaster was also responsible for the procurement and distribution of motor vehicles, Goyt was able to borrow a Dodge Pick-Up and an eight ton QM truck at various times, under forged requisitions, for the transportation of his pilfered and replacement supplies and for armaments he had secured from the Chief Ordinance Officer via a Quartermaster requisition. He was aided and abetted in all this by the element of extravagance which was such a feature of all US military procurement and distribution. Abundance meant excessive use, excessive replacement, excessive reserve stocks and excessive paperwork, which so daunted many of the commissioned and non-commissioned officers in charge, including Major Courtney Silverwater, who was Assistant Supply Officer directly responsible for Goyt's section, and his base commander, Colonel Willis Wallis. Thus inconsistencies in procurement, supply and inventory usually went unnoticed.

Goyt loved his work. Totalling abundance was total heaven. Assessing his own needs, and arranging to fill them, at no cost, made him feel godlike. The only thing that could drag him away from his beloved reserve storehouse was his penchant for active service — a service which, of course, was fed from his paid occupation.

He now saw himself in three separate but linked capacities:

• THE CIVILIAN WAR ZONE •

Quartermaster; Commanding Officer of his "undercover battalion"; and Commandant of his POW facility or detainee point. He was a one man military force — supply, combat, punishment — all rolled up in one fleshy barrel of obsession.

"History will record me as the man who saved the British Empire, Carl the Great, Usurper of the Infiltrators, Destroyer of the Yankee Invader!"

He was already writing his memoirs in his head and planning the inevitable invasion that would knock the usurpers out of the war, or at least, out of Australia. His imagination was way ahead of his activity and sometimes he was quite unsure of where reality lay. His Aladdin's cave was reality, his prisoners were reality, his victims were reality, his father was reality, his ambitions were reality, his aspirations were reality. Reality was everything he wanted it to be. Reality was life and death. Reality was war. He loved reality.

5

Salome would not have made a good troglodyte. By the time the sun had risen on the second day of his cave incarceration, he was stricken with pleurisy and well on the way to pneumonia. He was soaking wet. The water at one stage had risen to waist level and he had to stand painfully for six hours until it subsided, with his hands still cuffed to the snubbing post. The wind didn't help either, as it gusted into the cave.

His symptoms dominated his consciousness. Aching joints, aching bones, headache, frequent stabbing chest pains, a persistent cough that just wouldn't dislodge the mucus, restricted breathing, increasing depression.

The fever eventually banished his depression and substituted hallucination. A merciful relief. His head floated from present agony to past frustration, during which the joint aches and all the other nagging symptoms played second fiddle.

His sister Andrea was lying on the floor, in her childish, three little piggies cotton pyjamas and he was sitting on her stomach, which was soft and pliable beneath his buttocks like a cushion of creamy pasta. He was riding. She was his cock horse.

"Get off Albert!" she screamed. "Get off! Get off me, you big centipede!"

Being a boy of long body and many segments, although lacking most of a centipede's appendages, it was a fair analogy; one he didn't attempt to dispute. Nor did he dislodge himself at her command. Nor did she want him to. But it was a natural request to make, because the bodily contact, for all its overt innocence, was slightly disturbing. His hand accidentally came in contact with her satiny smooth adductive breast. This contact, although far less intimate than the one below which was covertly pre-coital, nevertheless caused a charge, almost a spasm in

• THE CIVILIAN WAR ZONE •

the boy centipede. It enveloped in a flash all of his segments and appendages, including the pivotal penile one which was attempting to gnaw a hole in the pubic side of the three little piggies pyjamas. This charge called for some extra fondling, under cover of more innocent playful giggling.

Andrea squealed like thirteen-year-olds do when hurt or stimulated, and writhed, both with and against the pressure. But his pubescent hand had infiltrated her cottons, caressing, squeezing, untrammelled and uninhibited, fired by unfamiliar lust.

"Get off! Get off me, you big centipede!" she continued to scream, without actually knowing if she wanted him to get off or not. He certainly wasn't hurting her and being a long, skinny lad, he wasn't unduly crushing her.

Anyway he stayed until he felt the floodgates; wet ecstasy, uncontrollable, particularly wet; more wet than ecstatic; for the ecstasy was fleeting whilst the wet seemed permanent.

His pyjamas wet, sticking to her, sticking to him, so wet. Afraid to move. Might go away if you don't move? Shame. Like peeing in your pants. What will she think? What will Mother think? Anybody? So wet. Nothing more down there but wet. Limp and wet. The cave was flooding.

Submerged from the waist down. Had to get up now. Doesn't matter what they think, what she thinks. He couldn't move. The wet lapped his chest, spreading ever up. His chest on fire. Why wouldn't the wet put the flames out? Time to get up. He pulled his whole wet aching body up until the cuffs cut into his wrists.

What did his mom say? "Feed a cold and starve a fever." Right. He was doing that. Starving his fever. It hadn't eaten for two days. Or was it three? Where were those seagulls?

Was this the Japanese water torture? His punishment for defiling his sister? For wetting her? Salome. Salami. Dance for me Salome. Salome you big lug, you're going to war! Going to be a hero! Who said that?

Cousin Terry. He was 4F. One leg shorter than the other, flat feet and an unusual spinal defect. Untreatable. What did they call it? Syringomyella. Something like water on the spine. Only worse. Everybody had something, except for him. Now

• MILITARISATION •

he had everything. The big wet.

"Salome, you big lug! You're going to war! Stars and stripes forever. Wish I was going!" Regretful. "Where they sendin' you?"

"Don't know. Top secret. The enemy has ears."

"Sure! And a nose and a asshole! Kill a few fuckin' Japs for me, willya?"

"Sure. How many?"

"Many as you can. Sky's the limit!"

"We'll be thinking of you, dear. Take care of yourself. Where are they sending you?"

"Don't know, Mom. Somewhere in the Pacific. That's all we been told. I'll write to you."

"Write to me too, you big centipede!"

"Sure sis. I'll write you a novel. Providing you write to me first."

"Where'll I write?"

"I dunno. Just send it to me, c/o The Army, Fort Devens, Massachusetts. They'll find me. Somewhere in the Pacific. Swimming around. Wet."

"Kill a few Nips for me, willya son?"

"Sure Pop. I'm dying. I killed a guy. And now I'm dying."

My legs are numb. Wet. What's that sonofabitch playing at? Why am I here? Did he know my sister? How do I pump this water out? No hands. My sister's douche bag. Where the hell is it? In the fuckin' bathroom! What good is that? This ain't no bathroom. It's too wet.

At school they called me Salome. Salome the sissie. Salome the six foot sissie. Why a sissie? A centipede can't be a sissie. I'm dying. Drowning. What's pneumonia feel like? Something to do with the lungs. I can't feel my lungs. I can't even feel my sister.

"Something's eating my balls! Oh Christ! Jesus! Mary! Stop it! Someone!"

A shark? A seagull? I got no balls! I'm dying! Drowning!

"See private, see! You're in the paper!" Whose voice is that?

The commandant. The major.

"Get me outa here, willya? I'm drowning! Seagulls are

• THE CIVILIAN WAR ZONE •

eating my balls!"

"You're in the paper, see! What'd I tell you? Wanted for murder!"

The major had returned. At last. His feet were wet and his beige trouser pinks were soaked to the knee. He read from the paper, breathlessly excited, whilst Salome, half submerged in harbour brine, hyperpyretic, couldn't even hear.

> *The Truth* Sunday 21 February 1943.
> NIGHTCLUB KISS BRINGS DEATH
> TO FEMALE IMPERSONATOR.
>
> Harry Sidney Foy, one of the best known nightclub entertainers in Australia, met his death when he tried to kiss an American soldier during his act at the Reflections Club last Thursday night. Foy danced over to the soldier, later identified as Pfc Albert Salamandini, and made several attempts to kiss him, during the floor show, but the GI pushed him away. On the third attempt, Salamandini punched him in the face and Foy fell backwards and never regained consciousness. The American disappeared and has not been seen since. MPs and local police are searching for him and it is believed he has gone AWOL. Private Salamandini is described as very tall. . .

Goyt looked triumphant.

"Did you hear that, soldier? They're all searching for you. But they can't find you! 'Cause I found you! Didn't I? And it's my duty now to take you into custody!"

Goyt unlocked the handcuffs and Salome sank down in a stupor, almost totally submerged in the rock pool, with his head underwater, spluttering for air.

Goyt summoned his aide, Private "Crowbar" MacPherson, AIF deserter, a swarthy brute of ape-like appearance and retarded personality, who picked Salome up over his shoulder like a giant sausage and transported him out of the cave, across the rocks, through the waterside park, to their camouflaged Willys eight ton QM truck.

· MILITARISATION ·

Salome was now out of the wet, and on the way to an even more horrific incarceration.

6

The US Military Police company, including the provost marshal section, the company headquarters and security, communications zone (COMMZ) and investigation platoons, were all housed in an Edwardian sandstone building, a monument of colonial masonry. Its rectangular dentils under moulded cornices and casement windows gave no clue to the militaristic law-and-order energy inside. Yet the colonial nature of the building was not entirely out of place. The occupants, after all, belonged to a foreign power.

Situationwise it was almost mid-city, just a baton charge away from the New South Wales police headquarters, which was four city blocks east, and next door but one to the art deco marble facade Grace Building, which housed the US military divisional headquarters in Sydney.

Joe Church, wearing his civvies — a three-piece grey suit, a tie and a felt hat — mounted the steps leading to the portico, contemplated the stairwell and opted for the birdcage lift. He was fit, but old enough to be realistic.

A Pfc, wearing the white-on-blue MP brassard on his sleeve and a shiny steel helmet with the white MP emblazoned on it, operated the elevator with dedicated military precision and no sign of the boredom that such a job usually produces. Joe told him the sixth floor and he swung the airfoil control lever with inappropriate satisfaction, as if he was driving the Bluebird.

The lift rose with shaky reluctance, protesting past each floor, then ground to a defective halt several inches too high on the sixth, despite the private's precision on the rudder.

"Mind the step," said the private.

"Would you like to try that again?" Joe responded.

"Why not?" said the private, reaching out to slide the

• MILITARISATION •

doors closed.

"Don't bother," Joe said, stepping out. "I think I can make it. Next time I'll bring my parachute."

"Why don't you just flap your wings, birdbrain?" the private said and slammed the doors shut behind Joe as defiant punctuation, leaving Joe retortless.

Joe shrugged it off and fronted up to another MP-stamped private, who was making like a sentry outside the colonel's office. He was standing at relaxed attention with his M1 rifle resting sights-up on his right shoulder, US style, which to Joe, more used to the British/Australian slope arms mode with the rifle flat against the left shoulder, looked most awkward.

The private saluted and went through the drill to an at-ease position. Joe didn't return the salute. He was still smarting from the flip liftdriver.

"Detective Sergeant Church to see Colonel Tunks," Joe said. Then barked: "Attenshun!"

The MP sentry private instantly snapped to attention, then double-taked at Joe and looked sheepish. Joe felt better now as the private rapped on the office door without turning around, facing Joe but not meeting his eyes. The door opened.

Lieutenant Kobovsky, in an olive drab class A uniform consisting of an open-collar tunic, shoulder straps, trouser stripes, buff dress belt and the statutory MP brassard, saluted Joe and ushered him inside. Again Joe didn't salute back and enjoyed not doing so. The lieutenant was Tunks' administrative assistant and deferred to the colonel, who was standing behind his desk next to a small stars and stripes on a flagpole, staring out the window. He didn't turn round when Joe entered.

"Detective Sergeant Church, sir," the adjutant announced.

Tunks didn't stir. The lieutenant motioned to Joe to wait, apparently until the colonel deigned to turn around. Joe cleared his throat. Nothing. Joe looked at the lieutenant, who had taken up a position just inside the door, standing stiffly at attention.

"Nice day," Joe said. The lieutenant didn't stir.

"Good morning Colonel Tunks," Joe said.

Tunks turned slowly around. His face was fixed in granite. A genuine antarctic welcome.

• THE CIVILIAN WAR ZONE •

"I thought they'd send me someone higher up than a detective sergeant," Tunks said curtly.

He was wearing his dress blues, with commissioned rank cuff stripes, a multiplicity of rank and corps insignia, the crossed pistols in lieu of the MP brassard and the Silver Star medal — a kind of rough rhapsody in blue. His service cap, also blue, with a gold eagle, was sitting on his desk.

"You'd better take that up with my commissioner, colonel. I just go where I'm sent." Joe waited for Tunks to invite him to sit.

Tunks didn't, although he sat down himself. On his spring leather swivel chair. He put his shiny black boots on the desk with all the arrogance of a two-bit businessman asserting his primacy in his own domain.

"Why didn't he at least send me a captain or something?" Tunks complained. He took a Lucky Strike from a carved wooden cigarette box and wet the tip, but didn't bother to offer Joe one.

"We don't have captains in our force. The nearest equivalent would be a chief inspector or a superintendent."

The desk was like the deck of an aircraft carrier — a long sweep of highly polished rosewood, with all the paraphernalia neatly and strategically stacked along the edges. The entire office looked new, or at least completely redecorated. The carpet was high pile, burnished red, the furniture all luxury masculine leather.

"I don't give a horse's ass what your ranks are! But I know what a detective sergeant is and what we've got here is an important investigation, authorised by General MacArthur himself, and your commissioner . . . what's his name?"

"Murray."

"Sure. Well he sends me a detective sergeant."

"That's sergeant first class, colonel."

Joe had the feeling that Tunks' attack was more a means of feeling him out than insulting him.

"What the hell! Would you send a division into battle under the command of a sergeant, sergeant? No offence."

"I don't offend easily, sir," Joe said, with a slight grin.

• MILITARISATION •

The desk paraphernalia was well integrated with the occupant — a magazine clip of thirty rounds, no doubt for the M1911A1 semi-automatic .45 pistol that Tunks was sporting in a light leather holster, a knobbed wood truncheon, a gasmask, a tear gas canister, a patterned Damascus folding knife in German silver with hand-carved bolsters and a pair of inkwells shaped like mines.

"How come you're only a detective sergeant anyway?" Tunks nagged.

"It's my choice. I have all the authority I want." Joe hoped his new-found sensitivity on the promotion matter didn't show.

He decided he wouldn't wait to be asked to sit down. He selected an Eames chair — upholstered, contoured and swivelled; an exclusive American chair, no doubt shipped out specially for the colonel's use.

Tunks picked up a piece of paper and flourished it. "It says here, you got an undercover squad. How good are they?"

Above a wall rack of M1 carbines, M2 submachine guns and M1 rifles, was a gigantic American eagle emblem. Next to this was a framed photograph of General MacArthur. Joe felt it all gave the office a certain fascist flavour, which didn't endear this ally to him.

"As good as any other squad." Joe was pleased to note that whilst Tunks was probably younger than he, he was greyer and with less hair, which he'd taken to combing forward to cover a cranial drought area.

"How good is that?" Tunks was aggravated by Joe's evasiveness.

"Good enough."

Tunks turned red with impatience. He swung his feet onto the floor and picked up the magazine clip, using it like worry beads.

"Good enough for what?" he snapped.

"Good enough to do the job." Joe refused to be intimidated.

Tunks' eyes glittered. He felt this brawny, good-looking Aussie cop with the square-cut face was getting the better of him. So he changed tack.

"You in charge of this undercover squad then?" He tried

to pin Joe down with a relentless gaze.

"Virtually." Joe leant back in his ultra comfortable imported chair. He was enjoying getting under the boorish colonel's guard in such an oblique way.

"What the hell does that mean?"

"It means I share the authority with Inspector Roberts, who does the desk work, while I'm out in the field."

"Ah! Then you aren't in charge of the squad!"

"Yes I am."

"But you got this inspector over you?"

"If it comes to a conflict, he does things my way."

"Now wait a minute! You're a detective sergeant and he's an inspector. What have we got here, some topsy-turvy Walt Disney police force? Or do you have the goods on this inspector? What'd he do, rape his sister? Explain."

"As I understand it, colonel, my commissioner gave you a complete run down on me and my squad. Isn't that good enough for you?" He started swivelling in his chair, feeling quite perky.

Tunks ducked the challenge. "Listen, detective sergeant, basically I'm just a cop like you. And I like to double-check everything, including the folks I gotta work with. Now it says here, you busted more vice dens, prostitutes, SP bookies, sly grog . . . what is that?"

"What you call bootleg."

"Sure. And drug runners . . . you busted more of them than any other Aussie cop. Should I be impressed?" Tunks tossed the paper on the floor dismissively. Then he stood up and started pacing, slightly favouring his left leg. His walk was wary, rising up on his toes, distrustful. Ready for anything. "But it doesn't say nothin' about real criminals — thieves, thugs, killers! What sort of a namby-pamby cop are you?"

Joe flushed. He picked up the folding knife from the desk, flicked it open and with an imperceptible aim, threw it across the office. It lodged in General MacArthur's photo, right between the eyes, splintering the glass.

"Hey! That's army property, feller!" Tunks was ambivalently angry.

"Sorry. My hand slipped."

• MILITARISATION •

"Well, you've made your point. So, how are you in a brawl?"

"Quick."

"Hmm. At your age you gotta be."

"Despite your little boy blue suit, colonel, you're not exactly Bobby Breen yourself."

"Now I know why you're still a detective sergeant. You got no respect for rank." Tunks scowled, removed the knife from the photo. Then he sat down again, folded it, snapped it open, fondled it, tested the blade, looked slyly across at Joe. "You ever killed a man, sergeant?"

"Why do you want to know?"

"Most people, including you no doubt, think that the war is going on up there in the Pacific, New Guinea, Tulagi, Guadalcanal. Bullshit! It's going on here, Church! Right here! And you've been nominated to help me fight that war! And if we're gonna win this fuckin' war, we gotta be killers!" He took his pistol out and symbolically laid it on the desk. "Killers! Don't believe the bullshit the government hands down. There ain't no glory in war. No heroics! It's killing. Nothing wrong with that. Killing is only pre-empting the inevitable. Our job is to get in first. And that's not happening right now. So answer my question, Church! You ever killed a man?"

Joe nodded. He was sweating a bit now. He didn't like the turn of the conversation. "It was self-defence. In the line of duty. But I didn't enjoy it."

"Don't matter. Some do, some don't."

"Does that mean you do, colonel?"

"Depends who it is."

"If you don't mind my asking, sir. What happened to your face?"

Tunks looked as if he did mind. He put one hand up to his black eye. "One of your guys ran into my jeep."

"One of my guys?"

"A civilian!" Contempt.

"What'd you do to him in return?" Mocking.

"Her. Nothing. Yet." Ominous.

Joe didn't pursue this. But he could see that Tunks was a bitter man and, no doubt, a mean enemy.

Something moved behind Joe. He looked over his shoulder. He had forgotten about the lieutenant, who was still there, obediently at attention. Joe felt like offering him a chair and wondered if Tunks kept him standing there all day.

"Okay." It looked like Tunks was going to get down to business at last. "You've been briefed about the killings?"

Joe nodded.

"Here are all the autopsy reports. Our own army pathologists did them." He handed a sheaf of reports to Joe. "And here's all the evidence reports, weapons analysis, witness descriptions — which don't amount to a can of beans — collected by my investigative platoon. Take it home and study it." Another sheaf of reports.

Joe tucked them all under his arm. "At this stage, have you any consensus on the perpetrators?"

"Sure. Some of your guys dressed up in our uniforms."

"Our guys?" Again.

"Civilians. It's gotta be. There's no way in the world that any GI is gonna go round methodically murdering in cold blood a whole stack of his own men."

"What about deserters? I hear you've had a regimentful take off."

"I can't buy that. There's no motive."

"Maybe, like you said before, they just enjoy killing?"

"Doesn't stand up. Why would they desert? If they enjoyed killing they wouldn't desert, would they? No, deserters are yellerbellies. They don't want to kill or be killed."

"So, if they turn out to be civilians, then we arrest and prosecute. But what if I find the perpetrators are your personnel?"

"Then you hand 'em right on back to us and we'll court martial and shoot 'em!"

Joe rubbed his nose. "You sure? After all, if they've been committing crimes on our territory, then we should have the right to try them."

"Let me tell you something, Church. If it was up to me, I wouldn't have you involved at all. I'd handle it all myself. I don't give a fuck in hell about slamming civilians. Nothing would give me more pleasure. Ever since our guys started

• MILITARISATION •

coming here to this limey outpost, your guys have been complaining, robbing us blind, cheating us, stabbing us in the back, giving us the clap and now murdering us! That's the thanks we get for comin' to save you from the Japs. Personally I think we should've gone no further south than Hawaii. Who gives a shit about the rest of the South Pacific? Let the Japs have it! You might learn how to cook some good food for a start. But then I ain't Franklin Roosevelt or Douglas MacArthur. I'm just a thirty-year man, and I gotta obey orders. And those orders say I gotta enforce civil and military laws, orders and regulations in conjunction with programs pursuant to agreement with the host country and that includes advising and assisting host country civil and military police. I don't like it but I have to swallow it."

Joe grinned, mainly to cover up the fact he was contemplating overturning the wretched colonel's desk prior to setting fire to his office immediately after assassinating him with one of those tempting M1s from his wall armoury. As he wasn't in the habit of acting out his fantasies, he utilised his wit instead.

"Now that you've so eloquently outlined your credo, colonel, let me tell you mine. I'll be happy to work with you on this investigation and I look forward to apprehending the vicious killers who have been slaughtering some of our young allies, because my commissioner has requested me to. However, personally I don't think I could warm to you if we were cremated together."

Tunks' annoyance turned to laughter. Not exactly hearty, more scathing like a kookaburra.

"Well that suits me fine, Church. At least we know where we stand. We each hate each other's guts. Nothing wrong with that. We should be a good team. You stab my back and I'll stab yours. Now piss off and read up on all that stuff and then let me have your recommendations for action."

Tunks stood up and turned his back on Joe, making bookends with his flagpole, retreating into non-specific contemplation.

Joe stood up, walked to the door, nodded at the tense lieutenant, then turned back.

• THE CIVILIAN WAR ZONE •

"It's been nice talking to you, colonel. I look forward to our next meeting with a great deal of reluctance."

The lieutenant suppressed a smile.

Tunks didn't stir.

On the way out, Joe took the stairs.

7

Cynthia's head was ringing when she left the plant. They had told her she'd get used to the cacophony after a while and wouldn't even hear it. Like hitting your head against a brick wall — it only hurts when you stop.

After three months, she still heard it. Her office, in invoicing, was only a partition away from the production line and only intense concentration made it possible for her to work. Sometimes the intense concentration made her head ache.

In these dark days, they said, everyone had to make sacrifices for the war effort. She just hoped the war wouldn't last long enough to send her deaf.

Maybe it wasn't the plant setting her on edge. Maybe it was the other night. She always thought of it as "the other night". It would always be "the other night". Her injuries had affected her head and her nerves. She was still shaky. The egg on her forehead had subsided into a tender smudge, which she covered with face powder. But "the other night" was now. It kept recurring. His snarling sweaty face with blood pouring from his lip; wiping his blood on her dress; tearing the fabric; backhanding her; excruciating pain when he squeezed her nipples; her high heel splitting his face; blood, more blood, hate, tears. A recurring nightmare and daymare. And she knew it wasn't over. She expected him to turn up in his jeep anytime, anywhere.

It was eight o'clock. She saw him watching her, twenty yards away down the train platform.

But it wasn't him.

There was nobody on the platform, except some other women from the plant, mostly with their heads in scarves and their faces drawn with fatigue and probably, like her, with their heads ringing. It was her nerves. She kept seeing him,

• THE CIVILIAN WAR ZONE •

but he wasn't there.

In reality, he *was* there. Keeping out of sight. Wearing fawn fatigues and a loose windbreaker field jacket, garrison cap and MP armband. His colonel's silver eagle rank badge was on the shoulder sleeve of his jacket. He'd watched her leave the plant, sitting in his staff car — a brown Dodge sedan without a gas producer. He'd driven slowly along as she walked to the station, then parked his car. He couldn't scoop her up because there were too many other factory workers around.

He'd followed her down the narrow road, past rows of gardenless semi-detached workers' houses, identical company-built industrial dwellings, drone housing with soot-producing chimneys firing back at the factory stacks nearby that polluted day and night to keep up war production schedules. The war casualties in this environment included many dead trees and shrubs. The shell casings and gun bearings took an early toll.

Cynthia's physical ailments were nothing compared with her disillusionment. A week ago she had been carefree, romantic, stars and heroes in her eyes, jitterbugging, gliding, rubbing shoulders and hips with the handsome, well-groomed allies. But now it was ashes. There was nothing to look forward to at night. The music had stopped. She was at war. And scared.

He lined her up on the platform, peering round the corner of the station house waiting rooms, which contained the only light — forty moth-dimmed watts. There were three other women standing near her, waiting for the train. A quiet night. A couple of searchlights fingered the dark sky looking for non-existent enemy planes over the nearby city. The elderly railway ticket seller in his caged box was a witness to nothing. Withdrawn, smoking, half asleep.

Tunks figured his .45 could knock the side of her pretty head off and he'd be gone before those other women had stopped screaming. But he wasn't that sort of killer. That was pointless. He wanted to confront her again, see her squirm, see her cry, see her go down on her knees and beg for mercy, see her offer herself to him in exchange for her life. He was a cop. A military cop. The best. He needed and expected respect, and fear. It was his sustenance. He liked it when they showed

• MILITARISATION •

fear. It acknowledged his authority, his status.

Then the electric train came in rallentando. Tunks boarded three carriages behind Cynthia. Then off again, piu allegro, clattering through the night, picking up shift workers and soldiers, ululating through the urban industrial scape.

Cynthia got off at Central Station, where the city began. It was nearly nine o'clock and the platforms were alive mainly with soldiers, returning to camps in Granville, Ingleburn and Dundas on the city outskirts, or starting their furloughs. The latter boisterous, heading for fun and booze, the former full of it, but downcast. Back to Mama Army, thinking about shipping out to the war zone, heads full of past pleasures, wondering if there'd be any more.

Cynthia attracted whistles and wolf calls from every second uniform, the ones heading for leave inviting her company, the others wondering if she was worth going AWOL for. And fifty yards behind, the stolid solid MP colonel, looking deliberately less immaculate than usual, following her every movement, his face still plastered, his eyes fixed on her bottom and long legs that travelled so gracefully.

She descended a flight of stone steps to a long pedestrian tunnel linking the east and west ends of the station. Her heels clicked and reverberated. There were only a few other pedestrians, well spaced. Tunks stayed well back, in case she turned, ambling along with his head down, almost drunk.

She stopped and turned once, apparently nervous, but didn't pick him out. The tunnel lighting was dim, barely enough to read the inept political graffiti on the walls inciting strike action, abusing former Prime Minister Menzies for selling pig-iron to Japan prewar or suggesting that the now broken treaty between Russia and Germany should keep Australia out of the war.

Cynthia increased her speed. She sensed she was being followed, but when she turned around all she could see were about half-a-dozen nondescript nobodies stretched out down the half-mile long tunnel behind her.

Tonight she was going home for the first time since "the other night". She wasn't going to tell her parents about it. It would only worry them and humiliate her. She was at the stage of her life where she needed success, not failure. "The other night" was a failure. Hers as much as his. She didn't want anyone to know about it. She would pass off her bruises as a work accident. Her father probably wouldn't be there anyway. He still worked many nights. Her father the non-stop cop. A lovely man but, like so many police officers, seldom there when you needed him.

Then she thought about that other lovely man, the black one with the fancy name that sounded like a place in England — Sherbrook Wells. He was one of the few who knew what had happened "the other night". She wouldn't mind seeing him again. He had salvaged some of her illusions about the Americans.

At the end of the tunnel, some relief. Emerging up the steps into the bustle of Broadway and Railway Square, she took a deep breath of the not-so-clean night air. Still, the fumes from gas producers were one polluted step up from carbon and oxide waste. She walked further, ignoring more wolf whistles from stray soldiers, and cursed the war which turned men into skirt scavengers by cutting them off from their families. Since "the other night" she had turned sour on the war and everything connected with it.

Next lap was a toastrack tram ride to Bondi, where her parents now lived. Tunks boarded four compartments behind hers, but couldn't see her. The high seat backs were in the way. The conductor, swaying precariously from the long running board, didn't bother to collect Tunks' fare.

He saw her alight at Campbell Parade, which ran along the park at the beachfront. The sound of the surf thundering in dominated the night air. He waited until the tram picked up speed again and then jumped off, nearly losing his footing in front of an oncoming car.

He watched her cross the road in the pale moonlight. She headed back towards the beach cafés and fish and chip shops on the other side. He sprinted to catch up to her before she got lost in the brownout, and saw her turn down a side street and into a bungalow just a seagull's splatter away from the beach.

• MILITARISATION •

"Nice of you to come home." Winnie actually hated herself for saying things like that to her daughter, but couldn't help herself.

"Thank you Mother, for the warm greeting." Cynthia flung her raincoat, handbag and overnight bag on the settee.

"I'm sorry, but if you treat your home like a hotel, then . . .?"

"Mother! I'm tired! I've been working all day." She sank down upon the settee and put her feet up, after kicking off her shoes. "Is there anything to eat? I'm famished."

"Of course there is. You know where to find it." Winnie hesitated. She just stood there, staring at her daughter, bursting with information but not quite sure how to come out with it.

With a supreme effort Cynthia stood up and padded off to the kitchen in her stockinged feet.

"I'm surprised you're not out dancing again tonight, with your . . . your Americans." Winnie had followed her into the kitchen.

"They're not *my* Americans, Mother! Far from it." Cynthia busied herself making a sandwich, with cold chicken and salad from the ice chest.

"That's not the impression I have."

Cynthia could tell her mother was on the warpath about something. It was the way she was standing there, all five foot nothing of her, with her arms folded as if keeping herself in check. Transparent parent. Normally she was plunged busily into household duties. Now something was needling her and it took all her attention and effort just to keep it in.

"I don't know what you're talking about. Have we got any tea left?"

"Of course! We haven't run out of it yet! Nor should we. I'm talking about some of those Americans you've been mixing with."

Cynthia looked around at her sharply. Did she know something? "Is beetroot rationed?"

"Of course! Everything is. But I have a tin put away."

"Which Americans? Mother, what are you talking about?"

"Not what. Who." Winnie bit her lip, brushed her

• THE CIVILIAN WAR ZONE •

forehead. It was very hard to confront her daughter with these disturbing things.

"Well then, who?" Cynthia's voice almost rose to a screech. Everything was getting to her, including her mother. "Are you going to get me the beetroot or not?"

Winnie didn't move, couldn't move, mentally dispensing with the beetroot. "The one who came round to see you today."

Cynthia transferred her beetrootless sandwich to the kitchen table and sank down on a chair. She needed time to think. Suddenly she was scared again. Dead scared. Too scared even to bite into the sandwich, despite her hunger.

"What'd he want?" Practically a whisper.

"He wanted you of course."

"Oh God! What'd you tell him?"

"I told him you weren't here."

Exasperated. "Mother! What else? What else did you tell him? About me?"

"I said you were probably at work."

"Did you tell him where I worked?"

"Oh no! Do you think I'm stupid? How could you get mixed up with . . . with someone . . . like that?"

"I wish I knew. What else did you tell him? Tell me! It's very important!" She picked up her teacup and realised her hands were shaking.

"I didn't tell him much at all. He did most of the talking. I must say he's quite a talker. I'm just glad your father wasn't here at the time."

"What did he talk about? What did he say?" Cynthia felt her heart pounding and she wanted to scream. She could feel herself getting hysterical. A kind of eruption was building up inside her. That brute! Fancy coming to her home like that! To her mother! God!

"He said he was very sorry to have met you under those circumstances. I didn't dare ask him what circumstances he was talking about. You can imagine how I felt — my daughter leading this sort of life! Oh I suppose it's that damn war! That damn war! It turns all our lives upside down!" Now Winnie sank down upon a chair, looking nearly as distressed as Cynthia.

"Mother, stop feeling sorry for yourself! Just tell me what he said!"

Winnie wiped away a covert tear. "He said . . . he said he wanted to see you again. He said you'd only met once before, but he was quite taken with you. And . . . and . . . he wanted to stay until you came home, but I said he couldn't. I mean, I couldn't have a man like that staying around. I told him I hadn't seen you for days. That you sometimes stayed with a friend. And he said he knew that. But you weren't there now. That he'd tried to find you there and they, I suppose it was Bonnie, had told him to come here. And I said I didn't know when or if you'd come home. And that was that."

"That's all?"

"Well, almost all. He said he'd call back first thing in the morning, if that was alright. He was very polite some of the time, but I could see right through him."

"And what did you say?"

"Well, I didn't know what to say. As you can imagine. I said it would probably be better if he didn't just drop in. Then he said he'd ring up first. But I told him we didn't have a phone."

"Oh mother!" Slight relief.

"But he kept insisting he'd call back. And I couldn't talk him out of it. He was so insistent. I kept trying to put him off. But I'm not sure if I did or not. I said you were very busy with your war work. And that my husband didn't encourage men to call here. It just wasn't done. I tried to put him off. He really scared me, to tell you the truth. He was so large. So frightening to look at. But I have a feeling he'll come back anyway. Oh Cynthia! How could you get mixed up with such a person? How could you?" Winnie's tears came back — a real flow.

Cynthia sat there, tight-lipped, drumming her fingers on the table, ignoring her sandwich. Deep in dread.

"What happened, Cynthia? Tell me, how did you meet him?"

"It doesn't matter. What's done is done. My main concern now is how to avoid him."

"I'll tell Joe. When he comes home. He should know

what to do. He loves you so. He won't let anyone bother you. I'll tell him. He can do something."

"No!" Cynthia snapped. "No! I don't want you to tell him anything! He mustn't know!"

"But he has a right to know!"

Cynthia stood up. She had beaten this brute off once, hadn't she? She scolded herself for feeling like this. She'd been so depressed for the past few days, and so scared. Why should she? Why should she let this man intimidate her like this? She wouldn't put up with it! She would meet him again, head on if she had to. And she wouldn't need her father to help her. This was a private matter, which she'd got herself into. It was no one's fault but her own. If necessary she would arm herself. A gun. Her father had one stashed away in the house.

"Mother! Listen to me! I want you to keep this entirely to yourself! Do you hear? Don't tell Dad! Don't tell anyone! It's my affair and I can handle it. I'm not a child. I work for a living. And I've been around. If this man comes here again, when I'm not here, don't tell him anything! Just get rid of him! And if he comes when I'm here, well just leave us alone. I'll know how to handle him. But I don't want any interference. And I mean that!"

Winnie looked at her tearfully, wiped her eyes with her apron, shook her head. "Sometimes you're so like your father. Maybe you should join the police force too. But I don't think you realise what you're saying. I really don't. I think you've got yourself into something you can't handle, something that will bring disgrace on us all. And I still think your father should know about it. Otherwise I fear for all of us. And that's my final word!"

Cynthia moved towards her mother, her eyes blazing, her voice soaring. "Well it's not mine! I told you I don't want you interfering in this! It's my affair entirely! And that's that!" She thumped the table. "There's more important things to worry about today than some American I accidentally got involved with!"

"Accidentally?" Now Winnie stood up. Her daughter's impingement causing an identical reaction. "Accidentally?" she

• MILITARISATION •

screamed. "How could you accidentally get involved with a . . . with a . . . a Negro? A black man? How could you?"

Cynthia couldn't believe her ears. What was she talking about? A black man? She stared at her mother, the colour draining from her face, then returning in a flush of relief. Then she convulsed with laughter. Hysteria. Beating the table, spilling her tea, tears rolling down her face — a face wreathed in smiles. Laughter. Choking laughter.

Winnie stared at her, perplexed, fearing disaster, quite convinced her daughter was having a nervous breakdown. And all because of the war.

Tunks watched the house for about an hour, burning up, despite the night wind blowing in from the ocean.

There was a pale light glow through the papered-over windows. Once he heard raised female voices seeping through. A family argument? Didn't she tell him her father was a cop? Maybe he was at home too. He wasn't going to do anything so obviously unlawful as break and enter. Nor was he prepared to conduct an all-night surveillance outside. He couldn't spirit her away anyway. He had no vehicle. The important thing was that now he knew where she worked, where she lived and how she travelled in between. He also had an idea of the shifts. So he could plan exactly when and where to grab her. With absolute impunity.

A slight delay wouldn't hurt. He was starting to enjoy the contemplation of what he would do to her when the time came.

8

When Salome surfaced he was still a prisoner. But this time in a dry place — some sort of pen, chained to a railing, lying on smelly straw infected with animal excreta. And he wasn't alone.

Through the gloom he could faintly see a couple of other sick-looking prisoners, mostly in just regulation trousers and T-singlets. Also chained.

Salome felt as weak as a whisper. Even struggling to a sitting position seemed beyond his capabilities. The fever had passed, which wasn't necessarily a blessing. Cold unclouded reality was more painful. No dreams now. Just recollections.

He too was wearing just trousers and T-singlet. Everything else was gone, including boots and socks. It seemed to be night. A few kerosene lamps were flickering, scattered around, threatening the dry straw on which they were perched.

He was still trying to fathom his whereabouts when the ape-like deserter Private "Crowbar" MacPherson brought him his first meal in three days and nights. It was a kind of beef gruel with crusts of bread floating, or sinking, in it. He wolfed it down and asked for more. In vain. It helped. It was a substitute fuel, but fuel nevertheless. It stopped his shivers and the stomach cramps and removed some of the extreme coldness from his limbs. But it didn't help his lungs or the pain in his chest from the upper respiratory infection.

"Where in hell am I?" he asked MacPherson.

Crowbar responded with a monosyllabic grunt. He had an M1 carbine on a shoulder strap and a .45 pistol, a carbine bayonet and an army knife on his webbing belt. He was wearing khaki fatigues. Salome wasn't sure if he was mute or retarded. He took the empty pan away and disappeared into the gloom at the end of the shed, bouncing along ape-like in the straw.

• MILITARISATION •

"Where the hell am I?" Salome screamed out in the direction of his silent fellow prisoners.

"PW camp, pal," one of them called hoarsely. An American voice. "Relax. You're gonna die."

In fact, Salome was in the Sydney Showground, a virtual walled city of 71½ acres of brick, steel and glass pavilions; halls, pig pens; stables; cow sheds; display stands; kiosks; cafés; bars; sideshows; bakeries; kitchens; cattle rings; saddling paddocks; a main arena seating 45,000; thirty miles of sealed roads; banks; gardens; parks; shelters, and offices. Last year it had been taken over by the Australian military for the duration, as a camp, training ground and munitions store. Aussie troops were billeted and slept on straw palliasses in poultry pens and cow sheds. Enough munitions were stored in some of the horse pavilions, the Manufacturers Hall and the Hordern Pavilion, to blow the whole city sky high.

The entire showground was encircled by a prison-like brick wall topped by barbed wire, stretching for about three miles. The four imposing entrance gates and ticket entrances were controlled by armed sentries, who wrote down the number of every vehicle entering and leaving.

Carl Goyt knew the showground like the back of his hand. He had worked there as a gardener for five years. Until the army moved in. He had lived in a garden hut all his own, except for his kelpie dog that is. They had loved each other. Except during the annual ten days of the Royal Easter Show and the occasional other agricultural, horticultural and industrial exhibitions, it was as if the entire place was at his disposal. He had the run of all the public toilets, kitchens, buildings, grounds, nooks and crannies. He was one of the few permanent staffers. The others came and went: casually employed office workers, carpenters, breeders, stable hands, maintenance men and plumbers. It was his showground, his city.

When the army took over, they didn't need any civilian gardeners, or any civilian anythings. They kicked him out and, on the day they arrived, a gun-happy private shot Goyt's dog with his bolt-operated 303.

It was war.

• THE CIVILIAN WAR ZONE •

It was war — and like so many others, for whom peace was a pause, Goyt flowered. Spurred on by hate, twisted opportunism and psychopathic illogic, he came into his own. He also discovered the treatment for the breathing difficulty that had plagued him since boyhood. Not drugs, inhalers or therapy. But acts of violence, preferably fatal ones. You could even say that the war itself unlocked his treatment.

Goyt also retained his affinity with the showground. He wasn't going to let the Australian army dominate his previous domain. He soon discovered that several pig pavilions had been allocated to the American military for billeting Negro troops, thus segregating them from the white Americans, who were billeted, more comfortably, in various camps, hotels and other buildings all over eastern Australia. It didn't seem to bother either army that the black Americans were not exactly segregated from white Australian troops.

This unpublicised US billeting enabled Goyt to gain access to the showground at will. He was able to drive one of the QM trucks loaded with supplies for the black Americans several days a week. No questions asked. All paperwork exemplary. He then later discovered that several goat pavilions remained unused. They had a series of goat pens, railings for tethering, straw galore and total privacy.

Goyt felt, under the circumstances, he had as much right as the Australian or US army to utilise these goat pavilions for his own military purposes.

Carl Goyt marched into Animal Pavilion D flanked by Crowbar MacPherson and two other aides — one a delicate-looking young corporal deserter from the US army named Miles Seldom, tall and thin with pasty skin and reddish hair, and the other a mean-looking slinky fellow with narrow sly eyes and thinning black hair, who was another deserter from the AIF. His name it seemed was Private Blunt. They each carried M1 Garand rifles, knives and grenades. Seldom kept looking adoringly at Goyt, whilst the other two looked at the prisoners in vampirical fashion.

Goyt was now dressed for combat: field jacket with an artillery red silk scarf, olive drab trousers, cut-down boots and the issue fibreglass steel pot helmet, with a colonel's metal

• MILITARISATION •

ranking fixed to the front. He had promoted himself again. For a while he paraded down the centre aisle of the pavilion, sullenly surveying the prisoners in the pens and tapping his knee restlessly with a captured Japanese sword.

Then the delicate Corporal Seldom introduced him to the fragile nest of tortured prisoners:

"Attenshun! For Lieutenant Colonel Forsyth of the 333rd Field Artillery attached to the 32nd Infantry Division, Pacific Theatre, presently commandant of this camp known as Custer's Blood!"

Nobody sprang to attention. A few rattled their chains, another few sat up, Salome barely moved. This man was as ubiquitously demented as Adolf Hitler. Or maybe he was still delirious.

"Attention for the Lieutenant Colonel's inspection!" barked the corporal, in a strident asexual command, with all the authority of a mermaid.

Goyt stopped at the first stall. The prisoner, bleary-eyed, unshaven, dark-haired, semi-conscious, was lying pathetically on his bed of straw like a sick foal.

"Name, rank and serial number, soldier!" Goyt barked in a high-pitched voice with the cut of a chainsaw. His round face seemed almost benign until you saw the liquid eyes which conveyed an impenetrable coldness.

The soldier mumbled something inaudible. His eyes swivelled upwards and they had enough awareness to show fear.

Goyt's breathing was quite irregular and full of puff. He kicked the soldier in the shins with the toe of his steel-tipped, cut-down heavy boot. The soldier clutched his leg in agony. It was already bloody from a previous wound.

"What kind of a fighting man are you? You're not worth pissing on!"

"Oh yes he is!" interjected Seldom, before receiving a withering look from his commanding officer.

Another kick in the other shin. "Straighten up! This is the army, soldier! Not a kindergarten! Let's have some discipline here! When did you last comb your hair?"

Upon a nod from Goyt, Crowbar punched the soldier

• THE CIVILIAN WAR ZONE •

in the side of the head with a sickening crunch. The soldier turned glassy-eyed and blood poured out of his nose.

"That's not good enough for this man's army, soldier! You're a goddamn two-bit Bowery bum! Not fit to wear your uniform!" Goyt put the boot in again. This time it wasn't a kick as such. He just casually stepped on the man's bare foot as he moved to the next stall. He seemed to grind down hard for as many seconds as was feasible. The soldier passed out with the pressure and lay there, like a breathing corpse, with mucus dribbling from his mouth.

"Another thirty days!" Goyt said to Corporal Seldom, who wrote this down with affirmative satisfaction. Seldom seemed to be the 2IC, whilst MacPherson and Blunt were the muscle.

At the next stall the prisoner was more defiant. He was older, thirtyish, more solid, crew-cut light hair, big mouth, prominent teeth, some of them black from decay, and a scarred face that suggested either a veteran brawler or an accident-prone drunk. Some of the abrasions were fresh and his hip was blown out from an untreated infected bullet wound.

"Name, rank and serial number, soldier!" Goyt barked again.

"Go fuck a daisy!" the soldier mumbled in a hoarse weak voice through clenched lips foretelling imminent tetanus.

"What'd you say, soldier?" Goyt's voice came down an octave. He was deeply offended.

The soldier didn't repeat his suggestion. The effort would've been too much for him. He just growled like a sick dog.

"That's not how you address an officer, soldier!" Goyt adopted a dignified authoritarian pose. "Your mouth will be your executioner." Goyt looked significantly at Crowbar MacPherson. "Tomorrow at dawn!" he said. MacPherson grinned in anticipation and stroked his M1.

Goyt was in his element, responding to the times, the prevailing norm, splendid in his madness. Killing, torture, looting, bombing, rape, maiming, mutilating, disfiguring, destroying, executing — words of war. Action, reaction. Defend, attack, assault, the fatherland, motherland, call to

• MILITARISATION •

arms, glory, banzai, love of country, the king, the emperor, the fuhrer, God. A myriad of justifications, rationalisations, motivations. Pages of history extolling victories, defeats, disasters, repression, freedom, bondage. Always with the same result — tears, pain, disillusion, ashes.

At the next pen, Goyt looked contemptuously down at the wreck of a man who had an open weeping wound in his shoulder, the result of a four-inch deep gash that had become chronically infected. The soldier was obviously feverish. His face was covered in beads of sweat, his teeth were chattering and he was mumbling incoherently, communicating with non beings.

"This place is a pigsty, soldier!" Goyt spat out, which was only one animal away from the truth.

Goyt kicked a pile of filthy straw, laced with excreta, in the soldier's face. The soldier remained deliriously oblivious.

"Do you like to live in a pigsty, is that it?" Goyt asked rhetorically. "Was your mother a sow? And your father a boar? Is that it, soldier?" The soldier's eyes were upwards. Unseeing. "Clean this mess up, soldier! Now!" The soldier just lay there and twitched, a quivering heap.

Goyt grabbed one of the soldier's limp hands. "Look at your fingernails! Are you a dirt farmer? Digging for worms? Or are you an insect? A creeping, crawling, malodorous scabby insect?" Goyt crouched down now, putting his face near the soldier's dribbling countenance. And he spoke in his soft, soothing voice. "Would you like to die for your country, soldier? Would you?"

MacPherson, Seldom and Blunt stood behind Goyt, watching, with satisfied smirks. They knew what was coming next and they were looking forward to it. Vicarious indulgence.

Goyt started breathing heavily now and turning red in the face. His chest was constricted and sputum appeared on his lips. His lungs screamed out for air, but there wasn't enough available. He was on the last lap of a marathon, stomach heaving, eyes watering, gasping, wheezing, body stiffening.

"Say your prayers now, soldier. You're going to die a hero. The word is out. You'll be mentioned in dispatches. The insect who died for his country!"

• THE CIVILIAN WAR ZONE •

As Goyt plunged his Japanese sword twice through the feverish soldier's heart, his lungs miraculously cleared and his breathing returned to normal.

"Get rid of him!"

MacPherson and Blunt jumped in, picked the soldier up by shoulders and feet and carted him away, the limbs twitching for some seconds in a cadaveric spasm, and blood dripping from the cruciate entry wound onto the ground.

Goyt wiped his sword on the straw bed that had been the last resting place for his victim and then returned it to the scabbard, which was attached to an eyelet on his belt and tied around his thigh with a thin cord. He took a deep unimpeded breath.

Then he moved on to Salome's pen.

9

Adam Goldhart was luckier than most. He came out of the summary court martial without a blemish. There had been no witnesses to state that he was actually involved in the fracas. His presence in the club, which was not off limits, was not in itself a misdemeanour.

Several other GIs testified to seeing Pfc Salamandini punch the civilian entertainer, the punch which resulted in his death, but Adam stuck to his story that he was too drunk to see anything or remember anything. His advocate argued that for a soldier to be drunk was neither a misdemeanour nor a breach of army regulations. If it was, almost the entire US army would be convicted. One would have to be proven drunk *and* disorderly, which Adam was not.

Adam's shoulder was not yet healed. The MO stated that he could not remove the stitches and that infection was still a risk for at least another seven days. So Adam was billeted at the Granville Showground, along with several thousand other US soldiers from various corps not yet required for active service. Most of the rest of 41st Division were trained to Rockhampton in north Queensland prior to embarkation to the war zone, probably Port Moresby, although that was still a rumour.

Adam was given light fatigue duty in the laundry at the camp, which made his wound weep. He asked to be transferred to lighter duties, possibly with the Judge Advocate General's Corps. He was told to apply for an official transfer which he did; but it would take time.

Salome had disappeared off the face of the earth, despite being wanted by both the Military Police and the State Police for the same offence. If he was caught, it was unclear as to who would have jurisdiction over him.

• THE CIVILIAN WAR ZONE •

Given time to think, Adam's strong sense of justice asserted itself. Maybe he shouldn't have cared that the army seemed to be controlled by knaves, staffed by incompetents and disciplined by thugs. But he did.

Maybe he should have been like most of the other enlisted men, who were happy to be clothed, fed and paid to serve without question. Long as they could play craps in the latrines, get drunk on a three-day pass, fuck a few willing, uncomplicated dames and hope like hell that when they were finally beached in the Pacific, the navy guns would soften up the Nips for them before they got their balls shot off. They didn't give a shit about how the army was run, or who ran it, or whether the MPs or the courts martial were just and fair. MPs were like cops anywhere — to hate and avoid. You didn't expect cops to be just and fair, or to be agreeable. A cop was a cop. An MP was a cop.

But Adam couldn't help himself. It kept nagging at him. Injustice. He really hadn't been that drunk at the Reflections Club. He saw and heard what was going on. He saw what the MPs did to innocent drunk soldiers. They didn't single out the brawling aggressive ones. They just used the brawl to exercise their own penchant for violence and authority. They cracked heads. All heads. Without fear or favour. Then they arrested everyone in sight. And they loved it. Some of those assholes were drooling as they split heads and pistol-whipped the drunkest.

These were their own countrymen, their own colleagues. And they treated them like the enemy. Worse. The enemy would be ready for them, and could fight back.

He wished he could forget it all and go play craps in the latrine. But he couldn't. It nagged at him. It was wrong. It wasn't what the United States was supposed to be about. What about the Bill of Rights? And Gettysburg? And the founding fathers? What about the four freedoms? What were they at war for? What about equality in the eyes of the law? And what about the segregation of black American soldiers from white American soldiers?

This all came to mind once again on his weekend pass, when he found himself down in the tenemented sleaze section

• MILITARISATION •

of East Sydney, outside the segregated brothels. That was an insult to the constitution. Jim Crow at government level. Private Jim Crow he could understand. There were bigots everywhere. But Uncle Sam was a bigot too. General MacArthur was a bigot. It was alright to die together, but not to live together.

He wanted to do something about it. It was eating him up. He wanted to get back at those boy bigots at elementary school, who used to beat him up mercilessly because he was a Jew. And when Germany started rounding up their Jews, the boy bigots at high school sometimes taunted him with chants of "Hitler is right! Hitler is right!" and the graffiti: "How odd of God to choose the Jews." And he was too weak to fight back. The bigots were bigger, stronger, more numerous. In Buffalo at least.

What was the war for? Not words. Not opinions. Deeds. He had to *do* something about it. He didn't want the army, his army, to be like those boy bigots. In boot camp, some of the Southerners were overt anti-Semites. Adam's oft-repeated rejoinders that they were in the wrong army and should join the Axis didn't dent their narrow-minded proclivities. Before they shipped him off to Port Moresby, the Solomons or Guadalcanal, he felt he had to strike a blow for justice. He wanted to fight the Japanese, but he wanted to believe that his side had the edge in virtue. Not words. Deeds.

In Liverpool Street everything was dull grey. A greyout. The houses, roads, telegraph poles, stray dogs, red roofs, filtered moonlight, variegated curtains, white faces, black faces, the green and khaki uniforms, the weather, a dull grey night, converting everything to monochrome. The war made everything grey. Bright was dangerous. The leading colour was camouflage. A cigarette glow was instantly cupped behind a grey fist. Liverpool Street was a grey area indeed.

Adam casually walked up and stood behind the last man on the line. At first, nobody seemed to notice. There were twelve men ahead of him. All black GIs.

"This the end of the line?" he asked the small smiling Pfc with scarlet and white Engineer Corps colours, in front of him.

• THE CIVILIAN WAR ZONE •

"You said it, pal. The end of the line."

"Thanks." Adam stuck a stick of gum in his mouth and waited silently, staring across the grey street at the loitering servicemen trying to make up their minds whether to go for it, or go somewhere else.

A strong breeze was whipping up dust, leaves and wrappers, tempering the hot night with warm westerly inland air that added as much to the comfort of the visitors as roller skates in a minefield. Adam turned the lapels of his olive drab field jacket up to cover his neck against the gusts of biting dust.

"Man, you're in the wrong line!" A tall sergeant, with a Harlem accent, tacked on behind Adam.

"Why?" Adam turned and gave him an innocent stare.

"Why what?"

"Why am I in the wrong line?"

"I don't know why you're in the wrong line, white boy! Maybe you got a tumour in your brainbox? How would I know?"

"No, I mean — why is it the wrong line?"

"You colour-blind? What is it with you?"

"Sure. You could say I was colour-blind." Adam lapsed into silence.

The small cheerful engineer in front of him gave him a quizzical look. "You for real, Joe? Or are you just doin' this for a bet?"

"Doing what?" Adam was starting to enjoy his Andy Hardy role.

"Standin' where you don't belong."

"I hear the gals inside are hot tamales, Joe," Adam said, digressing to the essentials.

"You are askin' to get your ass whipped by the gestapo, Joe."

"I'm not askin' for anything. I'm here to pay."

"What funny farm you from, Joe?"

"41st Division, Company A."

"That's not what I meant, paleface."

"I know what you meant. That's all I know." Adam figured obscurity was the best defence.

• MILITARISATION •

"Don't expect no sympathy," the one behind said. "Rules are rules, even if they ain't writ down."

"What rules? I don't know what you're talkin' about," Adam said. "I'm in the mood for some slash tonight, that's all. I don't care where I get it or who I'm gettin' it with. Slash is slash."

The tall sergeant lifted Adam off the ground by the front of his jacket and breathed a nicotine storm right in his face.

"Don't play games, buddyboy! All you're gonna get tonight is a hot squat, if you don't move on. They won't blame you, they'll blame us! They always do! They'll say we forced you to stand here and then bust all our upper stories, while you go free."

"No they won't. I'll tell 'em I'm here of my own free will."

"Free will? What's that baby? How come you got a free will? This ain't free will territory here. You does what you is told and that's it. So why don't you slam off, back to your own kind?" The words were threatening but the tall, spread-nosed sergeant made no overt physical threat.

"You're an American aren't you?"

"Whatta you think?"

"Well, I'm an American too. So we're the same kind." Adam gave a quick smile and lapsed back into the waiting routine, cracking his gum, contemplating the windswept night.

"Please yourself, Jacko. It's your ass."

A couple of hefty MPs twirling batons (steer clear leaders) approached the line. Perversely both MPs were black.

"Here come the trash!" someone said.

"You better hide your dial, Sunshine, or you might be eatin' through a tube tomorrow."

"I'm okay. I'm not doing anything wrong," Adam held his ground.

"You buckin' for suicide, Joe? Just turn your head!"

Four of the black GIs closed in around Adam, shielding him from the view of the alert, man-crunching MPs, who looked longingly at the black soldiers, praying for an excuse to let loose. Adam turned slightly so that his back was towards them.

The MPs strode by, more intent on finding a black

offender than on discovering the previously unheard of phenomenon of white encroachment on a segregated reserve.

"Thanks guys," Adam said, when the MPs were out of eyeshot. "I owe you one."

"You owe us nothin', Joe. We was protecting ourselves. We would have turned you in, 'cept they'd probably blame us for not turnin' you in sooner."

"Thanks anyway. But I wouldn't have minded if they'd seen me. I don't think they could've done much about it."

"Where you been livin' man? In the Mickey Mouse house?"

After fifteen minutes, Adam was one off the front porch. Then the heavy green door swung open and the small smiling Pfc engineer was swept inside by a heavyset, middle-aged harpie in a kind of floral housecoat, which bulged with excessive mammary fat. And Adam was next.

In the dim light, the durable doxie couldn't really tell that Adam was white and, as such interlopers were virtually unprecedented, it took a while to register. He was inside and mingling with the all-black customers and all-white chippies in the waiting room before someone in authority noticed him.

"Hey soldier? What you doin' in here?" a well-rounded whore wanted to know.

"I guess I'm lookin' to get laid like everyone else, honey," Adam said and patted her predominant bottom, which was enshrined in what seemed to be the statutory housegown uniform of floral cotton.

Miss Rotunda turned and screeched at a peroxided woman in her forties (that included age, hips, waist and chest) who was dressed in a kind of sub-Cinderella prewar ballgown and who seemed to be top bitch of the enterprise. "Matilda!"

Matilda came waltzing through the suburban-style room towards the summons, making a path straight through the communing couples, who parted like the Red Sea.

She plonked herself right between Adam and her informant. "What're you doin' in here, Yank?" Matilda's voice was deep, almost masculine, a result of hormone imbalance, too many cigarettes and a penchant for shouting down all opposition. Her puffy eyes tried to burn a hole in Adam's forehead and her foul breath presaged chemical warfare.

• MILITARISATION •

"Same as everybody else," Adam said benignly. "Did I do something wrong?"

"This place here is for Negroes only, soldierboy!"

"Why?"

Adam's question almost confounded her.

"'Cause I said so!" Not much conviction. "And so did your army!" More weight there.

"Well, I know what my army is, but I don't know who you are." Adam struck a challenging pose.

"I'm Matilda Honey and I own this place. So on your way hotstuff or I'll get your wallopers to take you away!"

"Not until I get laid!" Adam was resolute.

Matilda almost burst into flames. "You'll get laid, sonnyboy! You'll get laid out on a slab! Now scram!" Matilda started to shove Adam through the crowd with her ham-like fists. She was as strong as she looked and would've made an ideal labour camp commandant, Adam thought. But Adam dodged out of her grip and joined a group of three black GIs and three girls of varying superstructures, nursing drinks and softening up for the main bout. One of the GIs was the sergeant from Harlem.

"Here comes the flake!" the sergeant said. "What'samatter boy? You lookin' for your loony vest?"

"Hold him! Hold that white soldier!" Matilda yelled. Then she instructed one of her girls to summon the MPs and shuffled across to Adam with a blackjack in her hand, produced from under her gown.

"Looks like Matilda's gonna crack you open, soldier. Why don't you go home like a good boy?"

"I got my rights," Adam said.

"You lost your marbles!" the sergeant said.

Matilda would've cracked Adam's head except that two MPs burst in, delighted to be of service, guns and white sticks out, sniffing for black bear. They looked positively disappointed when they were led to Adam. They seemed to feel it would be a poor substitute to crack a white head when there were so many black ones about.

"What're you doin' here, soldier?" the lean Texan MP corporal asked, mentally attuning to the fact that this was

• THE CIVILIAN WAR ZONE •

probably a nigger-lover and therefore blacker than black.

"Why does everybody keep asking me what I'm doing here? I like it here. I'm doing the same as everybody else!" Indignation.

"You'd better come with us." The corporal gripped Adam firmly by the arm. Adam shook it off. Angrily.

"I don't wanta come with you! I wanta come with her!" Adam put his arm around the slimmest of the three girls, who looked blonde and vacant.

"Do what you're told, soldier! While you're still conscious!" The MP had his club raised in tune with his voice and temper. "This house is for nigras only!"

"Where does it say that? I don't see no sign! I like it here!" Adam gripped the girl more firmly.

The two MPs grabbed Adam by each arm, tore him away from the girl and handcuffed him. Adam felt a white-hot searing pain in his still healing shoulder.

"Go easy! That shoulder's wounded!" He shouldn't have told them. It became the focal point, like a boxer's bleeding eyebrow.

They frogmarched him across the room, the Texan's hand biting into his weeping shoulder wound. Adam howled, which gave the impression to the assemblage that he was truly off his hinges. "Sheeit! I think you just opened it up!"

"You're under arrest, private!" the corporal said.

Passive resistance. Adam then deliberately went limp and they had to drag him out.

"I haven't committed an offence!" he howled. "You can't arrest me for nothing!"

"We can arrest you for shittin' in your pants, if we want to soldier!"

"I never shit in my pants!"

"You will when we've finished with you!"

They transported Adam to headquarters in a jeep with a big white "MP" daubed on it. He was forced to sit in the back between two heavily armed MPs, who kept jabbing him in the guts with their pistols every time the jeep lurched.

He didn't resist during the journey. There was little point in arguing with these slaves. He felt maybe he was really

• MILITARISATION •

meshuggah for taking this so far. A GI Don Quixote. But it was too late to back out. He had to see it through and try to make his point.

"Where are you taking me?"

"Headquarters first. Then a nice little cell at a detainee point. And then, with a bit of luck, you'll get a nice long vacation in the stockade. They just love nigger-lovers there!"

"I demand to see your commanding officer!"

"You got a better chance of seeing Deanna Durbin."

"What're you going to charge me with?"

"Breaking military regulations and being off limits."

"That joint wasn't off limits!"

"It's off limits to you, soldier."

"Who says?"

"General MacArthur."

"We'll see about that." Quietly determined.

"Who're you kiddin'? You're just a dogface! You got no rights! You were off limits! Mixin' with niggers! Sheeit! You're gonna be in the shitpen! And serve you right! You're worse than a faggot!"

"Thanks. Who's your CO? Adolf Hitler?"

"Watch your mouth!"

The first floor of MP Company Headquarters was a beehive. Drunken soldiers, bleeding soldiers, depressed deserters, resentful black marketeers, sad sack soldiers, MPs gestapoing about everywhere, raised voices, besotted voices, parade ground arrogance, disillusion, military mayhem. The two captors shoved Adam up to an MP master sergeant behind a counter, who took down the reported details and gave Adam a curious stare, the kind reserved for utter contemptibles.

"Maybe you better see an MO shrink? Or a chaplain?" the sergeant suggested.

"I'm a well-adjusted non-religious Jew."

"I don't care if you're a armadillo! Anybody who wants to mix with niggers in a cathouse has gotta be off his trolley!"

"I want to see your commanding officer! The Provost Marshal!"

"Do ya now? Whatta you wanna do, kiss his keester?"

Just then, Sergeant Struther of the piggy eyes and barrel

• THE CIVILIAN WAR ZONE •

chest, who had interrogated Adam in hospital, walked by, recognised Adam and stopped.

"What's with him?" he asked the Desk Sergeant.

The sergeant placed the report in front of Struther, who quickly read it, then joined the list of Adam's contempt-filled critics. "I'll take him!" He led Adam into his office and sat him down, then perched on the edge of the desk and stared down at him, like a lion savouring his next Christian.

"Can I have the cuffs off?" Adam asked.

Struther ignored the request. "I know your type, Goldhart! What are you looking for, a dishonourable discharge? Is that it? Shit scared to fight the Japs are you? Well, you won't get it. I'll see to that!"

"All I did, sergeant, was mix with some of my fellow men at a friendly cathouse. What's wrong with that?"

"That place was off limits to white soldiers, including Jews. And you know it! What's your game?"

"I'm against segregation."

Struther's piggy eyes flashed and his jaw set in a firm line. "I don't give a fart what you're for or against, soldier! Neither does the army! Your job is to obey orders and do your duty. There's a war on or hadn't you heard? If there's something you don't like about the army, that's too bad! You can write your congressman if you want, but we'll still bust your ass if you step out of line! Now, we're gonna let you cool down in a cell overnight and I'll have a word to your company commander and just don't step out of line again. Just 'cause you wriggled out of that summary court martial last time don't mean you got a charmed life. We'll be watching out for you from now on! That means you got no more'n an inch to step out of line and you're gone! And when I say gone, that means you'll be back in that hospital again before we take you to the stockade and then you'll be back in the front line, in the first wave of the next assault, machine-gun fodder, with twenty Jap bullets through your guts!"

Adam was pleasantly surprised. Beneath the threats and bluster, he was getting off with just one night in the cells. Not what he expected at all. Why?

It meant, he realised, they were actually too scared to

· MILITARISATION ·

come down on him hard. The US army segregation of its black soldiers, at all levels, was rarely discussed. It was a fact of army life but not a fact they wished to broadcast. If they threw the book at Adam that could lead to a broadcast. Embarrassment all round. So, let him down lightly. Don't make a federal case out of it. Brothels for blacks and brothels for whites? Never heard of it. Military secret.

He wasn't sure whether to laugh or cheer. Sure, his transgression was only going to be lightly punished. The coward in him cheered. But he hadn't really made his point. He'd stuck his neck out and had his chin dusted. Hardly the sort of impact he had in mind. He'd won but he'd lost.

He decided to accept it philosophically. It was a start. Nothing else. But there was another matter burning him up.

"What about my buddy, Private Salamandini?"

"What about him?" Struther moved away from the desk.

"Have you found him?"

"It's not your concern. He's wanted for murder and he's AWOL. Unless you want to get involved as an accessory, I suggest you forget all about him." Struther shoved an inhaler up his nose and sniffed, suppressing the pleasure.

"Who's in charge of . . . finding him?"

"Are you deaf, Private Goldhart? I just told you to forget all about him."

Adam felt a sense of inviolability. He knew their pressure point. He had penetrated their Achilles heel. He would use it now.

Adam took a deep breath. "Look, sergeant." He stood up, using his body for emphasis because his articulate hands were still cuffed behind his back. "Do you know what they taught us in boot camp? If one of your buddies is in trouble, it's your duty to help him out. That's the American way isn't it? Well, the last time I saw him, he was being dragged away against his will. I tried to help him and got stabbed. I'm still trying to help him."

Struther frowned, pushed Adam in the chest sending him back into his chair. "He's a fugitive! If you help him, you're as guilty as he is!"

Adam stood up again, fighting mad. "Hell sergeant! I'm

sick to the guts of being shat upon by every NCO and officer in this man's army! I thought we were all in this war together! All I'm asking for is some information on my buddy! Who's every bit as good a soldier as anyone else and who has nothing proved against him yet!"

Adam realised he'd reached his limit now. He couldn't push much further or their reaction might overrun their calculated restraint.

Struther's hand was on his club. No doubt he was fantasising caving Adam's skull in, but the wider issue kept him in check. Still. "He's AWOL. How many times have I gotta tell you? That means he ain't your buddy no more! Now get out of here 'fore I throw you in the cooler for insubordination! Corporal!" Struther thundered for the corporal who was waiting outside the office to escort Adam to the cells.

The corporal entered, expectantly.

Adam was a rock. "But what if I can bring him in? What about that, sergeant? I'd be doin' you and the army a favour! 'Cause obviously you ain't found him yet!"

"Shit!" Sergeant Struther slammed his fist down on the desk. "Get him out of my sight! Put him away for the night! And if he gives you any trouble, put him away for the next night as well!" Struther turned away, biting his lip, purple in the face.

The corporal grabbed Adam by the 'cuffs and tugged him out. Adam went quietly. He realised he'd wasted a perfectly good weekend pass, but at least he knew that Salome was still out there somewhere. His war, like the big war, had a long way to go yet.

10

Carl Goyt stood silently staring down at the sprawling six and a half feet of sick and fading lean meat that was Salome with an expression of abject triumph on his round fleshy face. Salome was conscious but weak, unable to sit up without support, flesh crawling with thrips and stinkbugs from the dirty stall, four days' growth and hair like a short fright wig, lice and fleas on his scalp, hygiene just history, dysentery a threat.

"Why are you doing this?" he agonised. After all, the most helpless victim of all is the victim who doesn't know why he's a victim.

"Lord Macaulay said, 'Soldiers must, for the sake of public freedom, in the midst of public freedom, be placed under a despotic rule.' You should actually thank me, soldier. For the more miseries you suffer now, the less terror you will feel when you face death upon the battlefield."

"You're a fruitcake," Salome mumbled. He didn't have the strength to declaim it the way that Goyt was espousing Macaulay's message.

"I'm not what I seem, private." Goyt's accent was suddenly no longer American but a kind of clipped Oxbridge English, which further emphasised the cold and merciless tenor timbre. "When you invade a foreign country, as you Americans have done, you've got to expect resistance. I am a member of that resistance. Leader of an underground army. I uphold the Empire and all that it stands for. The finest traditions of Anglo-Saxon dominance. I represent King George the Sixth, a descendant of that other George, whom your forefathers so misguidedly rebelled against, condemning your America forever to be a land without a soul, bereft of the true and honourable values of the British monarchy that has shaped and inspired all important corners of the globe ever since. Including this

• THE CIVILIAN WAR ZONE •

fair land of Australia — this white European outpost in an alien, barbarian hemisphere. That is why you, and the other half-caste foreign wretches, are my prisoners. For you are attempting to usurp all of the solidly white British traditions that have made this colony what it is today. And like all foreign invaders, you will be repelled, just as Hannibal wiped out the great Roman army and the Caledonians resisted the Roman invaders for fifty years."

Beads of moisture gathered on Goyt's forehead as he lectured, and his words were punctuated by frequent short sharp breaths.

"This country, which was discovered by that estimable Yorkshireman Captain Cook, settled by his English brethren, governed by such as Bligh and Macquarie, maintained by British law and institutions, peopled with mostly pure Anglo-Saxon and Celtic stock, rejecting all other barbarous influences from the yellow hordes of Asia and the inferior melting pots of your bastard nation; this . . . country will retain its rightful place alongside Britain, fighting its wars against the Hun, the Turk, the red and yellow hordes, just as it did in the Crimea, the Transvaal and Orange Free State, at Gallipoli and in North Africa two years ago until certain traitorous politicians with the connivance of your mongrel Roosevelt, withdrew them from their rightful place as expeditionary forces under the direct control of the British army."

Goyt's face was growing red in the dim kerosene lights and his voice was rising in pitch and intensity, reverberating around the putrid goat pen, preaching to the inexorably helpless. Salome was not taking in the words, only the attitudes. He wanted to kick the sonofabitch's face in, but he didn't have the strength. Anyway the three aides — Seldom, Blunt and MacPherson, from precious to thuggish — had their rifles pointed at him and were wearing pleasurable expressions of sadistic anticipation. Salome was a truly captive audience.

"We don't need our Anglo stock diluted, we don't need you traitors to the Empire telling us what to do and who to fight. We are here to preserve king and country and to break the unholy alliance that is sapping our national fibre, turning our women into prostitutes, our currency into confetti

· MILITARISATION ·

and our glorious institutions into contempt!" Goyt snapped his heels and turned, stiff as a ramrod, his face set like cement.

"Execute the Yankee foreigner at dawn!"

"Aye aye, sir!" MacPherson said, snapping to attention, confusing his service jargon.

"Wait!" Salome called hoarsely. Goyt refocused on him. "They're lookin' for me, you told me that! I'm wanted for murder. Why not hand me over to the MPs. Then you won't have to worry about executing me yourself."

"Alright, private. I understand. You don't want to wait to die. You want to die now. Quite right. And so you shall." Goyt drew his Japanese sword. His chest was palpitating, he seemed to be out of breath.

Salome's stomach did a cartwheel. He didn't know if it was fear or dysentery, but he abruptly soiled himself and all his limbs started shaking. He wanted to scream and shout and cry, a mass of shit and sweat, blood pressure skyrocketing, pulses racing, heart thumping, but his voice seemed disembodied and ineffectual.

"I don't want to die. Jesus Mary I don't want to die! You're twisting everything! You're . . . I don't want to die! Let me go!"

Desperation was a fuel. Salome thrashed around on the straw, the chains biting into his wrists, trying to make himself a difficult target. But Goyt's aim was always precise and his target was long and large, despite the frenetic convulsions . . .

Sergeant Major Charles Goyt used to come home from the army at irregular intervals and give his wife Clara and his son a hard time.

"It's only right," he always told Clara in his diluted Lancs industrial accent, "that you give me your full attention when I'm home, because for so much of the time, in the service of His Majesty, I must leave you to your own devices."

He always insisted that the boy take second place. He demanded that Clara should bend to his will, tend to him constantly, obey him at all times, feed him, bath him, fuck him, whip him with birches, massage his feet, rise at five and complete the household chores of cleaning and scrubbing before

• THE CIVILIAN WAR ZONE •

he rose at eight, read to him, polish his weapons and battle souvenirs until they shone and sparkled and then clean and polish them again. And then he would inspect her work — the bedspreads, the curtains, under the rugs, the silverware, the furniture, the bathtub, the toilet, the pelmets, the pots and pans, the linen and all of the ornaments — and if any should show dust, grime, dullness, flaws or follicle mites, mildew or microcosms of foreign matter, he would rant and rave and sometimes beat her about the face and head with his antique quarterstaff, occasioning her injuries which never seemed to heal.

Yet Clara was a benign woman, servile to her husband, caring but undemonstrative with her son, as if she always feared that Charles was watching her, even when he wasn't there. And when Charles was home on leave or, as happened after the Somme, on recuperative leave following his shell shock, Carl would have to be neglected.

When his father was home, he dared not speak at the table. The utterance of one junior syllable would bring a bowl of porridge down on his head, or a saucepan of hot stew in his face.

"Children should be seen but not heard. The traditions of obedience and discipline, so essential to army life, are never out of place in the home," Charles emphasised. His son was his regiment, his wife was his batman. Orders must always be obeyed, on pain of punishment.

Once, when Charles entered his son's bedroom and found a half-eaten sandwich on the floor, under the bed, he berated the boy in a non-stop flow of invective for thirty minutes, in a voice as penetrating as the north wind. Then he tied him to his bed with a rope and kept him imprisoned there for eight hours, further berating him, after release, for wetting the bed.

"Did you know that a Norse soldier who fled, or lost his shield, or received a wound in any part save the front of his body, was by law forever afterwards prevented from appearing in public?"

When Charles was away, Clara insisted that Carl should worship his father, because he was a hero, a British army

• MILITARISATION •

sergeant, thrice decorated for valour, a man of great respect and distinction, whose methods might be harsh, but whose intentions were of the highest order. A man who, but for class distinction, would now be a high-ranking officer. (Sandhurst was not for sons of impoverished Wigan mill workers.)

Nevertheless, although he was away for most of every year, it was impossible to continue the perfection, the neatness and the tidiness he demanded. Clara never knew exactly when he would come strutting home again, barking his orders, demanding her constant attention and complete servility. So she had to be ready, for if the curtain of cleanliness slipped, the pain and the torment would begin.

Yet she endured, because he was all she had and all she was ever likely to have. And Carl looked up to his father because secretly he despised his mother for being so servile and so forgiving.

When, after the armistice, Charles was dishonourably discharged from the army, for what, he never said within his son's earshot, he announced they were leaving Britain, a country racked by class division, strikes, unemployment and, apparently, disgrace for the dedicated sergeant major. They were going to the colonies to start a new life, like so many Britishers before them. It was both their right and their duty as the original civilisers of these formerly pagan countries.

The long ship journey out was a torment as great as any at home. Carl was confined to his cabin for most of the journey, racked with dysentery and fever, hearing voices, mostly his father's, berating him for being slothful, unkempt, dissolute, living on gruel and dried bread, surviving the antipyretic elixirs and purgatives supplied by the ship's doctor. He reached puberty and Australia simultaneously and appreciated neither, at least until his father developed a metastatic tumour that seemed to envelop all his vital organs in less than a year and gave him endless pain and heightened psychosis. Life in their small suburban cottage was hell until he died, and totally mundane afterwards.

But Carl was making up for all that now, conducting an inspired campaign against the enemy, achieving vengeance and satisfaction at every turn, inflicting the worst upon all those who deserved it. In his eyes.

Somewhere, in the darkest recesses of his mind, Salome cursed his friend Adam for not letting them go to the Roosevelt Club. Perhaps then, his life would not now be ending in such ignominious circumstances.

"God save the King!" Goyt intoned, between bouts of breathlessness, as he struck another fatal blow for the preservation of traditional imperial ties.

11

Sherbrook Wells, looking as sharp as Robert Taylor in *Bataan* in his forest-green shirt, trousers and field jacket, his black tie, his field and coast artillery branch scarlet silk scarf, his imperious service cap and all the usual insignia, badges, chevrons, piping and crests, descended on the Church house at eight o'clock, flashing his smile and warming up the fresh morning air.

Joe answered the door and was rather taken aback to find this carved, handsome mahogany face bursting with goodwill at his front door.

"Good morning, sir," Wells beamed. "I came to see Cynthia. Hope I didn't interrupt your breakfast."

"No, no. I'm just off to Bondi baths for my morning dip. I never swim on a full stomach."

Wells felt like commenting that Joe's stomach did look rather full anyway, in his khaki shorts and short-sleeved shirt, but thought better of it. "You must be her daddy. I can see the resemblance. I like a good-looking family. Believe it or not, I have one myself."

"Oh yes." Wells' early morning charm was a bit hard to take. "Ah, can I tell her who's calling?"

"I'd be delighted if you would, sir. My name is Sherbrook Wells, and I'm happy to meet you, Mr ah . . .?"

Joe took his outstretched hand. "Detective Sergeant Church."

Now it was Wells' turn to be taken aback. Where he came from, cops were top of the least-wanted list. But he was perceptive enough to recognise the man behind the badge. "Now you've just knocked the wind out of my topsheet, sir. They say you can never find a policeman when you need one. Well, I just found one. Right out of the blue."

• THE CIVILIAN WAR ZONE •

"I never wear blue," Joe said, dry as a cracker.

Wells' face exploded with mirth. "Say, that's really something. A bolt from the blue. A cop with a sense of humour." Then he frowned. "'Scuse me. I don't mean to be rude. That was very impudent of me."

"Don't worry. I know what you mean." Joe warmed to him now, because of the flash of honesty. "I never met one either. Why don't you wait inside? I'll get Cynthia."

Brook removed his service cap and stepped inside. The bungalow had a long hallway, with all the rooms leading off. There were china objets d'art and framed prints of Australian scenes on the walls. And a grandfather clock keeping watch, halfway down. The wallpaper was a pale tangerine and ivory, grain of rice pattern, of oriental antiquity. It was basically a simple uncluttered house for people who didn't have the time or inclination for lavish living. And definitely not the money. Wells decided, on the available evidence, Joe wasn't a corrupt cop.

Winnie appeared down the hallway, wearing an apron over her housecoat, and saw Wells standing patiently inspecting the grandfather clock. At first she was going to duck back out of sight, but Wells saw her and flashed a grin that careered down the corridor and hit her incontrovertibly between the eyes. So she walked daintily and tentatively down to meet him, with a shy smile.

"Hullo again, ma'am." Brook's voice bounced off the wall with a rich penetrating baritone.

"Hullo there . . . ah . . ." Winnie was not sure how to address him.

He made it easy for her. "My name's Sherbrook Wells, ma'am. I don't think I told you that when we met last night." In fact he had, but she'd forgotten. "Corporal Wells," he smiled. "But as this is a civilian household, albeit a custodial one, I'd be delighted if you'd call me Brook. All my friends do."

Winnie tried to stop melting. But the man had more charm than a roomful of royals. She wanted to say so much to him. She wanted to express the fear she felt at his presence. The embarrassment she felt about her daughter "associating" with him. She didn't think she was a bigot. It was just that she

• MILITARISATION •

had never actually met a black person before. In fact, she'd never met an American before. Certainly Australia had its Aborigines, but she'd never met one. They mostly lived in the outback or on the city fringes.

Of course she was projecting. Cynthia had partially explained to her that Wells was just an acquaintance who had helped her out of a difficult scrape. But Winnie, in her blinkered way, could not fathom a young man with a young woman in a detached way. To Winnie, all liaisons led to the altar. Particularly when, as now, the young man was carrying a corsage of purple and blue orchids. Yet she didn't have the courage to speak her mind. She was quite disarmed by the man.

"I told my daughter you'd called last evening."

"That's very kind of you ma'am. Very kind indeed." Brook's brown eyes sparkled and Winnie melted further. She gleaned a slight understanding of how Cynthia might feel towards this man.

"Would you like a cup of tea, Mr ah Corporal Wells?"

"I sure appreciate the hospitality of your offer, ma'am, but I had an early breakfast not long ago."

"Well perhaps you'd like to sit down in the living room?"

"Sure. Why not?"

Winnie turned, glad to have an excuse to avoid eye-to-eye confrontation. She led him down to the living room, but they were cut off at the pass by Cynthia, materialising out of the kitchen in a pale-blue negligee over her nightgown, a slightly flawed natural beauty, svelte figure, no make-up covering the discolouration of the deflated lump on her forehead.

Winnie couldn't hide her disturbance at Cynthia's domestic bedroom appearance. "Oh Cynthia, that's no way to greet a guest!"

"Don't worry, Mother. Why don't you make us a cup of tea?" Cynthia's request was really a command sugared by a sweet smile.

Winnie flushed slightly and went to the kitchen, thinking disturbed bourgeois thoughts.

Cynthia led Brook into the living room, where a console

• THE CIVILIAN WAR ZONE •

wireless set was playing:

"Men love to be near the girl who's sweet. Lux toilet soap makes you sure of daintiness. This is Barbara Stanwyck saying: nine out of ten Hollywood stars use Lux. I love my daily Lux toilet soap beauty bath."

Cynthia switched it off and turned towards her visitor. Wells enveloped her in a smile of such intense admiration that she almost swooned at his feet before she found the necessary degree of composure.

"Sit down, corporal. I'm so glad you called. I've been wanting to thank you."

Wells handed her the orchids. "I'm sorry. They don't quite match your beauty, but then, what does?" He had a way of making platitudes sound inspired.

"Thank you, but I should be doing something for you." She sank down on a pile of crocheted camouflage nets.

"You have. You smiled at me. No man could wish for more." He tempered this with a self-deprecating smile.

"You're very gallant, Corporal Wells."

"Call me Brook or I'll leave the country."

"Brook." She said it gently, tenderly. Testing it, liking it.

For a moment they just sat there, staring at each other, unblinkingly, drinking in each other's presence, silently cementing rapport. Then Cynthia looked away.

"How are the contusions? Obviously you've got no after effects."

"Thanks to you."

Brook spread his hands. "I did nothing. Say, I don't suppose you've heard any more from that sonofabitch MP? 'Scuse my language."

"Not a peep. Perhaps he's still licking his wounds." Cynthia felt secure in Brook's presence. With him around her nightmares seemed ridiculous.

"I didn't know your old man was a detective. Could he maybe do something?"

"Oh no. I haven't told him. It's not a good idea. Anyway I don't think he could do anything against one of your policemen. Even if he wanted to."

"Okay. Just a thought. Say, what are you doing today?

• MILITARISATION •

I got a two-day pass. How about we go out somewhere? A ferry ride, something like that? Your harbour's just the greatest in the world. I don't think there's any more Jap midget subs about."

"My shift starts in a few hours, then I'm a slave for the next eight straight. Sorry."

"Hey, slave I know. But what time do they set you free?"

"Eight o'clock."

"Great! Why don't I pick you up at your workplace and we'll go have dinner? Don't say no or I might cut my throat."

Cynthia laughed. She could no more say no to this man than cauterise the sun.

Wells was waiting for her outside the factory gates in a borrowed jeep. He jumped out to help her in. She had on a beige dress with a narrow waist and a large white butterfly collar. Barely knee length, the skirt rode up thigh high when she climbed aboard. She had on leg paint, having laddered her last pair of stockings, and Brook had a delightful thigheyeful, which made him feel warm inside.

"Last time I rode in one of these, I regretted it," she said, without rancour.

"I promise you, Cynthia, you won't regret it this time." He patted her shoulder before gunning the motor and manoeuvring the four-wheel drive off the grassy verge onto the road.

"I believe you." She laughed, feeling good, marvelling at her swift comeback from despair to cheerful expectation.

They took the Princes Highway into the city, which, despite its grandiose name, was a mostly grimy dual carriageway, skirting through industrial suburbs and English provincial type shopping areas of ill-matching bungalows. There were enough other cars on the road for them not to notice the khaki Dodge sedan following them.

Tunks clenched the wheel of the Dodge as if he were trying to throttle it. The sight of that tall graceful cunt with the black sonofabitch nearly choked him. This was the greatest humiliation he had ever suffered. In his book of obscenities,

• THE CIVILIAN WAR ZONE •

to be thrown over for a jungle bunny like that was tantamount to treason.

He now had two targets for extinction. It made his head thud and his mouth dry. He could feel his stomach churning like a cement-mixer. He felt like gunning them down from his car as he sped by, like a Chicago mobster. He had an M3 sub-machine gun on the back seat. He could pump twenty rounds in ten seconds into their car and who the hell'd know or care.

No way. Perish the thought. He could do it better than that.

He tailed them all the way to Martin Place, mid-city. Watched them sitting awhile in the jeep, chatting intimately. Watched the nigger's arm snake round her shoulders, just as his had done, only this time, she didn't shake it off, but seemed to welcome it and even leant nearer to him, responding with lover's accord. If he kisses her, he thought, I'll blow their heads off.

He watched as the corporal helped her out of the jeep, hugged her affectionately as she landed and then, arm in arm, guided her into one of the city's few still-open plush eateries. Romano's. An un-austerity menu at un-austerity prices. Maybe, Tunks surmised, they wouldn't let a nigger into such a plush place. He'd eaten there himself, several times. They laid it on for US servicemen, mostly officers rather than enlisted men. Steaks, oysters, lobster, sole, king prawns (the local version of jumbo shrimps) supplied, he suspected, by US military caterers. But Wells and Cynthia were ushered in by the resplendently clad doorman like long lost cousins. Tunks vowed never to eat at Romano's again.

He left them there and drove three blocks away to his headquarters. He was ready to make this official business now. They had inadvertently made it easy for him. He could now utilise his authority and status to bring that bitch and her black consort to a sticky end. And there'd be no questions asked.

Tunks sequestered the services of two NCO MPs, McFarlane and Brackett, who were overwhelmed to be called to duty by so high-ranking an officer.

• MILITARISATION •

Tunks sat in his office and checked his latest reports. Two more GI bodies had been discovered. Seemed like the same elusive killers. But no further clues. He made himself a note to check with that abrasive Church cop. There was real pressure wafting down from divisional headquarters now. They had to break this open but quick. But not as quick as he was going to break his own enemies open.

He drove back to Romano's, sat in his car and waited, just around the corner in Castlereagh Street, where he had a snoop's eye view of the canopied entrance and padded front door.

Four cigarettes later, Brook and Cynthia emerged, arms around each other, flushed and laughing, full of good cheer and perhaps a little drunk. Tunks' night-time fatigue vanished and he sat up expectantly. The couple stopped on the pavement, halfway to their parked jeep, and kissed, long and tenderly and hard, Gable and Lombard, but with the extra non-Hayes office element of locked tongues. It went on and on, passionately, marathonly and to Tunks, sickeningly. Her hands were round the back of his neck, rubbing, groping his ears, pulling him tightly, their bodies pressed together like peak-hour commuters.

They might have continued the kiss long past midnight if the two MPs, McFarlane and Brackett, hadn't materialised from nowhere and interrupted them. One of them, McFarlane, bull-necked and beefy with drooped eyelids, almost prised them apart and stepped between them, isolating Cynthia from her escort.

Tunks heard abusive words spilling out of Wells, which played right into the MPs' hands. Resisting arrest became an extra attraction. Cynthia looked understandably distressed and started shaking all over. Brackett unholstered his .45 and pointed it at Wells, who blanched with fear and anger. Then Brackett, a stocky, cheerful farmboy, relishing his authority, snapped the 'cuffs on him. Cynthia protested vehemently, desperately, verging on panic. But in vain. The MPs ignored her and guided Wells firmly away, at gun and clubpoint, down the street, in the shadows of the grey monolithic city buildings, breaking into a trot, almost dragging him as he tried to resist.

• THE CIVILIAN WAR ZONE •

Martin Place was a tomb at this time of night, with the brownout discouraging street activity.

Cynthia started to follow, until McFarlane turned and shouted at her to go home. It was none of her business! He even briefly pointed his gun at her. She stopped, bit her lip, watched them hoist Wells into a jeep as he looked appealingly back at her. He shouted something, but she couldn't quite hear. It sounded liked "Set-up!" Whatever that meant. And "Get out . . .!" He was obviously trying to warn her. McFarlane sat beside Wells on the back seat, with his gun levelled, whilst Brackett drove. Wells kept shouting back at the fast-disappearing Cynthia until McFarlane ordered him to shut up with his steel persuader.

Cynthia was alone, on the pavement, dwarfed by the office blocks and circumstances. She felt fearful, angry, confused. Reality was staring her in the face again, but she didn't want to accept it. She felt dreadful about her new friend. Friend? Almost her lover. It had seemed inevitable. In the last few hours they had become so close, blocking out the rest of the world.

Ashes again. Dreams into nightmares. Romance into reality. Reality was the war. She felt like screaming. She really didn't know what to do, where to go, who to turn to. Her father perhaps?

It was unbelievable! Her luck. Or lack of it. No luck. Lackluck. What was happening here? They'd eaten so well, best food she'd ever had. No rationing here. Lobster mornay, lashings of potatoes with it, the cheese sauce a delight. Fresh vegetables, greens, cauliflower, some salad. Peach Melba to follow. Champagne. Black market no doubt. More orchids from the management. After-dinner mints, real American coffee, so Brook had told her. Even a photograph for her album. A three-piece band that sounded a bit like Benny Goodman. Dancing. Cheek to cheek. His tangy aftershave was still in her nostrils. Soft lighting. A delight. What she'd dreamed about. And this oh so handsome, charming, cultured, masculine, sweet-smelling, sweet-talking black man. Her very own Othello, without the jealousy, always tending to her needs, asking her permission, assessing her feelings, touching her

• MILITARISATION •

gently, gliding over the polished floor like Fred Astaire to her Ginger Rogers. No pressure. Lots of reassurance. Nice plans. Something for the future. If the war didn't intervene.

Her mother was right. They were destined for a relationship. He was growing on her by leaps and bounds, impinging on her senses and on her heart. Her knight in shining skin. Her prince. Her American lover. To be. She knew it wouldn't be long. They wanted each other and there was absolutely no justification in the whole wide world for her to resist. It was her destiny. At last.

Then — nothing. Her man whisked away, at gunpoint. It had only just begun.

She sensed . . . what? Something there. Something in the shadows of the papered-over streetlights. Someone standing behind her. Dreaming? Not a soul about.

Calm. If she spun around, who knows what would happen? Calm. Turn slowly. Act natural. Smile. Calm. But there were tears in her eyes, compounded emotion. The someone was a blur. Someone solid, she rubbed her eyes; someone wearing army fatigues. Clearer now. Don't sob. Don't speak. Rub your eyes, it'll go away. But no. Army fatigues, greeny brown, a garrison cap, jaunty, with a white-on-blue MP brassard, and .45 pistol in his belt. MP? Dreaded letters. Like the Nazi swastika. Terror. Swallow it. Don't show it. Scream maybe. Someone would come. But all choked up. Screaming took energy. She had none.

She smelt his foul smoky breath, sensed the pent up aggression, hatred, sweat. Clearer now. Veins bulging in the sticky wet forehead. Thin lips. Curled. Truculent chin, bulldog ears, jowls, hooded eyes, red, levelled. At her.

As he reached out for her silently she felt the lovely dinner turn to stone in her stomach. And her head swam. Waves of giddiness enveloped her. One coarse hand clamped over her mouth and stifled her screams whilst the other squeezed the breath out of her.

BOOK III

HOSTILITIES

"When the military man approaches, the world locks up its spoons and packs off its womankind."

GEORGE BERNARD SHAW
Man and Superman

1

Joe Church spent hours poring over the Military Police reports on the GI killings, trying to piece together a common thread.

The modus operandi of the killers (all indications were for plurality) seemed to fall into three categories. Three had been stabbed, two shot with pistols, three with rifles. All the bodies had apparently been transported from the killing scene and dumped outside various US military installations, including Divisional Headquarters, camps at Granville, Dundas and Ingleburn, Herne Bay Hospital, Operational Headquarters (which was situated in a tunnel beneath the Domain) the Stage Door Canteen and the US Officers' Club. The killers had made sure not to use the same dumping ground twice.

All of the victims had one of their two dog tags stuffed in their mouths (normal battleground procedure) and were clad only in their undershorts. Autopsies had been performed and all apparent bloodstains found on the bodies and the undershorts had been analysed meticulously by US army medical examiners.

Apart from establishing through serology that the bloodstains matched the blood types of each particular body, they had tested all the bloodstains by extracting minute samples from the stained undershorts and the bodies, putting them in saline solution, then mixing them with a solution containing phenolphthalein and potassium hydroxide, powdered zinc and hydrogen peroxide. In two cases this test was negative, showed no change, which meant that the apparent brown bloodstains were not human blood at all. Further serological tests had been carried out and these stains were deduced to be animal blood and animal faeces.

The pathologists didn't have the time or the facilities to narrow down the types of animals but they listed a number

• THE CIVILIAN WAR ZONE •

of possibilities including pigs, monkeys, sheep and goats.

According to telltale marks on their wrists, three of the victims, including the two with the animal bloodstains, had been chained. They had also been malnourished and, prior to death, had suffered from exposure, pneumonia and dehydration. The autopsies found skin changes, reduced metabolism and a degree of capillary vascular stasis, all of which indicated they had been kept prisoner in severe cold and damp.

One of the stabbed victims had been killed with a US M1 carbine bayonet. The other two, who had also been kept prisoner under deteriorating circumstances, appear to have been killed with some kind of sword. Probably a Japanese military samurai sword, being the only swords currently in use. The stab wounds — one in the back of the neck, two through the heart — were relatively neat and precise, which showed an absence of passion and either a lack of awareness on the part of the victims or total helplessness.

The rifle victims had been shot in the heart and the brain from a range of approximately fifty feet. This suggested some sort of firing squad. Each of these bodies had received no less than six bullets emanating from three different M1 rifles, issued by the US army. The M1s were .30 calibre, semi-automatic, gas operated, with an effective range of over 500 yards and capable of firing twenty rounds a minute. Being shot at a range of about fifty feet had produced a bone shattering effect. The entry wounds were soiled and split by the tailway of the bullets and were in the fronts of the bodies.

The two pistol victims had been shot at very close range, in the head, with all the tattooing from powder markings and split entry holes. Arm-length shooting was indicated. Again, in each case, the victim was probably tied down or in a prone position prior to the shooting.

Ballistics tests on those bullets still lodged in the corpses, mainly in the heads, thanks to the thick buttresses and bones of the floor of the skull which inhibited exit, were all standard US army issue for the types of weapons used.

The two pistol victims had been shot with the same M1911A1 semi-automatic .45 calibre revolver of the type issued

• HOSTILITIES •

to US army officers. Such weapons were capable of firing thirty rounds a minute and had little accuracy, so the victims had several large entry wounds, not quite side by side, despite the close range.

A further note from the MPs suggested that the use of US military weapons did not indicate they had been used by US personnel. They pointed out that thousands of weapons had been brought into the country, and had been handed out lavishly to their forces during training and before embarkation. A typical armoured battalion of 751 men would have at their base 449 sub-machine guns and 285 machine-guns, whilst all infantrymen were assigned one M1 rifle or carbine, each with enough spares to double that supply. Furthermore many arms had been stolen or mislaid. Replacements were plentiful. Few of the "missing" weapons were ever found. And not a great deal of effort, apparently, went into finding them. In the US army, ordinance appeared to be unlimited.

The report went on to state that there was a lack of proper manifestos with shipments from the States and many crates were not properly marked. This was a direct criticism of Ordinance and the Quartermaster Corps. Also someone had either stolen or mislaid some of the ammunition stock inventories from the Reserve Depot. This was under investigation by the MPs.

The report reiterated Tunks' comments; it seemed that the Military Police could not accept that the killers were US personnel. They could not conceive that any GI could kill his own colleagues in cold blood and get away with it. True, there was one known mass murderer amongst US personnel. That was Private Leonski, who had murdered three women in Melbourne recently before being apprehended. But that was quite different, they claimed, to killing US soldiers. It had to be, for motivational reasons the report went on, some sort of maniac with a grudge against the army, Japanese or German enemy agents, or an insane civilian, probably a foreign national. Furthermore, the Military Police had done a profile on all known US deserters and none had shown any propensity for violence or had any recorded convictions for same. The general motivation for desertion seemed to be to avoid violence rather

• THE CIVILIAN WAR ZONE •

than indulge in it.

Joe found their conclusions highly circumstantial and biased and basically unrelated to the scientific evidence. It seemed to him more a matter of wishful thinking than detection.

It seemed conceivable that the killings were mostly unrelated, in view of the different weapons used. However, the final state of the bodies seemed to cast doubt on this. There were several constant factors. All of the victims had the little finger of the left hand missing. (The pinky as the Americans called it.) It had been severed with a sharp instrument. Obviously something ritualistic. Also each of the victims had been on a leave pass when last seen by witnesses, who were all companions or colleagues of the deceased. Each victim had last been seen drinking at a nightspot of the kind largely frequented by American servicemen. However none of the witnesses recounted seeing the victims with any suspicious persons at the particular nightspots, except for one. A certain Pfc Goldhart had reported seeing his friend, one of the latest victims — Pfc Salamandini — being dragged from the Reflections Club by an unidentified US major. However later, at a summary court martial, Pfc Goldhart had retracted this story, and the retraction had been accepted as fact.

Joe decided this was worth a follow-up. In the meantime he pondered over pigs, monkeys, sheep or goats. The zoo? Unlikely. The zoo had no sheep or pigs. What was it? If the stains were from sheep, pigs or goats, then a farm was indicated. If monkeys, it would have to be either a zoo or a medical research unit. If it were a farm, where would he start to look? There were hundreds of farms in the near countryside. But only one zoo, plus a couple of smaller animal parks.

He decided to eliminate monkeys for the moment. Sheep, pigs or goats? Farm animals. Impossible. No doubt many semi-rural households tether sheep, pigs and goats too. This was a dead-end. They didn't have the manpower. Suffice to say the prisoners had been kept in some sort of farmyard, sheep, pig or goat pen. Not much help.

No, he decided, the best place to start was where the victims had started. Obviously there would be more killings, more victims selected. Pfc Goldhart? He had to speak to him.

• HOSTILITIES •

Why did he change his story?

Joe phoned Tunks. He wasn't there. They weren't saying where he was or when he'd be back. Joe left a message but Tunks didn't call back.

Joe decided to go to MP Headquarters. Tunks wasn't there. He was referred to Captain Duggendale of the divisional Military Police Investigation Platoon, whose name was on the report. Captain Duggendale referred Joe to Sergeant Struther, who had been in charge of interrogating the witnesses.

Joe explained who he was, dropped Colonel Tunks' name and asked the rather churlish Struther about Pfc Goldhart.

"Goldhart? It so happens that that sonofabitch will probably be let out any moment. He's been in the temporary confinement facility since last night."

"Temporary confinement facility? You mean the cells."

"You call it what you want!" Struther bristled.

"What'd he do?"

"Insubordination. Being off limits. The guy's a nutter. I think he may be a commie and he's definitely a nigger-lover."

Joe decided that Struther was cut in the Tunks' mould and was competing with him for Undesirable American of the Year. "What does that mean — a nigger-lover?"

"Sure, I forgot. You don't have no niggers here, do ya sergeant? Well, ain't you the lucky ones? Take it from me, they ain't worth the trouble they cause."

Joe remained contained. "That a fact? Well, we do have our Aborigines here. Don't know how it is with you, but I find it's the whites who seem to make the trouble. They can't seem to look beneath the skin."

"Sheeit! You look wherever you want, buddy! Just you come over to where I come from and try and live with 'em. Now whatta you want with this Goldhart creep?"

Joe realised he wasn't going to win any arguments on racial tolerance. So he just told Struther why he wanted to talk to Pfc Goldhart and wondered when he was going to meet an MP he liked.

"They tell me you're a nigger-lover," Joe said to Adam, as they sat down at the Hasty Tasty up at the Cross.

THE CIVILIAN WAR ZONE

Adam caught the twinkle. "Sure. And I'm colour-blind too."

They ordered tea and coffee respectively and the GI staple diet: two hot dogs.

"So'm I, I think," Joe said. "Or, at least, in view of certain developments, I'm going to have to be."

He told Adam about his daughter's latest attachment and then got down to business.

"Why did you change your story?"

"Well I guess it was because the MPs didn't want to know about the truth. They didn't believe the truth. Are you an honest cop?"

"Well, it depends? What day is it?"

"The day before tomorrow."

"Why do you want to know?"

"Well, you're working with the MPs, and I was wondering whether I can tell the truth about them to you without getting my ass busted."

"Well, I'll put it this way. I'll pay for the hot dogs. Will that do?"

"You've convinced me."

Joe was quite impressed with Adam's whimsical sincerity.

"So give it to me straight and I promise I won't let anyone bust your arse. See. You blokes have only been here one year and already you've changed the language."

"You're a fast learner."

"The American way of speech is insidious." Joe bit into his hot dog. "And so's your food."

"Fair dinkum, you're right, cobber. But she'll be apples." Adam retained his straight face.

Joe grinned. "You were going to spill the baked beans about your beloved MPs. I take it you don't like them much?"

"Put it this way. If I saw an MP drowning, I'd throw him a lead lifebelt."

"Well nobody here likes our police force much either. I personally have found that my standing with the general public is something akin to General MacArthur's in Tokyo. But then I think that has something to do with our convict stock."

• HOSTILITIES •

Adam lowered his voice when a pair of MPs occupied the next booth. "Listen. Our guys treat all GIs like convicts. So there's no point in telling them anything. They're not good cops. They just want to smash heads. They're not investigators. You know what I mean? They're into discipline. Nothing else. I think maybe it's 'cause they feel inferior to normal soldiers, 'cause they're not actually going to get to fight the real enemy in the war. So they compensate. By pushing us around, beating us up, trying to prove that GIs are inferior. It makes them feel more important. You know what I mean? Compensation for not being real soldiers."

"You're a pretty smart young feller for a private."

"I haven't always been a private you know. Before joining the army, I used to be a human being."

"I'm glad to hear it. Now what about this major you saw dragging your friend out?"

"Let me tell you. That guy's face is engraved on my brain. He had the oddest eyes. Like blue moons. Listen. Will you help me find my buddy?"

Joe was stunned. "Don't you know? They found him."

Adam stared at Joe, in mid-mouthful. The colour drained from his face. "When? Where?"

Joe was silent for a moment. Both men seemed suddenly isolated midst the bustle of the soldier-infested café, which was turning over coffee, doughnuts and hot dogs like hot cakes.

"They didn't tell you he was . . . dead?"

Adam shook his head. Tears sprang to his eyes. He tried to stop them, bit his lip and drew blood, put his hand over his face, then looked away, too choked to speak.

"Do you want to hear about it?"

He shook his head, then changed his mind and nodded.

Joe handed him a clean handkerchief. "Your lip's bleeding."

"I'm sorry. I shouldn't . . . I can't help it, you know. He was a . . . well, a great guy. My best friend. Shit! Those sonsofbitches shoulda told me! Shit! I'm sorry . . . I don't know what to say. Why didn't they tell me?"

"I'm sorry you had to hear it from me, like this."

"He's got a big family, you know. Back in New Jersey.

• THE CIVILIAN WAR ZONE •

I never met them. Oh shit! Why did that have to happen? How did he die?"

Joe told him all he knew. Adam listened solemnly. Suddenly he knew he was at war. He'd just lost his first buddy. Probably there'd be plenty more. The first was the worst. He wiped his face. "They tortured him? Why? Who did it?"

"That's what I'm trying to find out. Maybe you can help me. This major interests me. Nobody else mentioned anything about him."

"I want to help! Shit! I've got to. I owe it to him. The military police aren't going to do anything. For all I know, they had something to do with it."

"I wouldn't go jumping to those conclusions. You sure you want to help? Can you get some time off?"

"If I can't, I'll go AWOL."

"I didn't hear you say that. Anyway I think I can pull a few strings. I'll talk to my commissioner. And keep your voice down. Your two friends with the armbands in the next booth might have sharp ears."

"Sure. To match their pointed heads. To tell you the truth, they don't scare me any more. Nothing does. Eventually I'm gonna get killed anyway. That's what this war is all about."

2

Sherbrook Wells, born Germantown, Philadelphia, June 1918. Mother — domestic servant at the Greenfield mansion, home of the wealthy textile-manufacturing family. Father — frequently unemployed compositor. Normal middle-class aspirations — security, home, professional achievement. Wanted to be a journalist. Had enrolled at college when war intervened. Loves people, depressed when isolated, likes to impress, verbal fencer, spent much of his youth at a Quaker school and encountered little discrimination until joining army. Always thinks of himself as extrovert, ambitious and articulate.

When called a nigger, a coon, one of Tarzan's apes or some other such demeaning racial slur, Brook Wells has to think twice as to whom the person is referring. A white man doesn't constantly think of himself as a white man or as belonging to any particular grouping, but always according to his own identity. Same with Brook. Same with everybody.

I am Brook first, a man second, an American third, son of my mother and my father, brother of Daphne and Tiffany. I love sports, boxed three years until winning Golden Gloves light/heavy trophy, refused all professional offers because of pride in clear thinking.

I am Brook. I am a man. That's who I am. Treat me accordingly. Am I a nigger? No. I am a man. What price pigmentation? Call me Brook. I am an individual. Like me or hate me. Don't categorise me.

Why was that MP sonofabitch spitting at him like that, calling him a nigger corporal, referring to watermelon, blackberries, raping white women, black black marketeers. Why? He was none of those things. He was Brook. A man. Now a soldier. Anxious to fight the enemy to preserve freedom. Anxious to protect the American constitution, which had protected him. Or had it? He thought it had. The white Quakers had. He had suffered no prejudice in Philadelphia, although his mother, to make a living, had had to serve those rich white industrialists, who had more money than all the blacks collectively in the city of brotherly love. But she had never complained, she had never envied them.

Now these army cops were treating him like a sub-human. They weren't relating to Brook Wells, a man, but to some stereotype with which he had no affinity at all, except for the colour of his skin.

"Who are you?" he asked the MP platoon leader, who was interrogating him.

"Sergeant Struther, boy!"

"Well I am Corporal Sherbrook Wells of the Field and Coast Artillery branch of the Sightseeing Sixth. That's who I am! And that's who I think I am. You can call me other names, place me in a group, pinpoint my appearance, my supposed race, but that don't mean nothing! It's not accurate! It's not me! It's not fair! And why the hell am I under arrest?"

Struther didn't really know what Wells was talking about. He didn't see Brook Wells in front of him, he saw a nigger, a black man like every other black man.

There was no rapport, only blindness. And Brook didn't know how to fight it, because these people had the authority, the brassard that gave them the right to push him around, demean him, categorise him, dehumanise him. Just like the enemy.

Then his mind lurched. What about Cynthia? What would she be thinking? They had hit if off so well. She was so warm, so beautiful, so trusting. She had never once looked at him the way these MPs did. She looked at him the way he looked at himself. Brook. He saw it in her eyes. She sparkled when he sparkled, laughed when he laughed, touched him when he touched her, stared deep into his eyes.

Then, suddenly they had pounced, arrested him, charged him with fictitious deeds on the black market, whisked him away from her, leaving her standing on a deserted dark street, without explanation. What would she be thinking of him?

Then it all came clear.

• HOSTILITIES •

"Why did you arrest me? Where's the evidence against me? What are the specific charges? Who ordered my arrest?" He jabbed at them with all these questions and more.

They parried, they insulted him, digressed on to race and pigmentation. He asked for a drink of water. Struther started to hand it to him then, accidentally, spilt it all over him. Laughs. He remained calm. He stood up. They shoved him roughly back in his chair.

"Get that goddamn light out of my eyes!"

No response.

"Who ordered my arrest?"

Hesitation. Then: "You're due for the big fall, boy! The colonel has the goods on you! You might even swing." Hopefully.

"The colonel? Which colonel?"

"There's only one, boy! Tunks. The big man! He's got the goods on you! You're on the way out. For good! Now, where do you store the stuff? Tell us and we might let you sleep for the night."

Tunks?

Of course! What a set-up!

"You can't charge me with anything! You have no evidence!"

"We can hold you till the colonel gets back. And that's what we're gonna do! And there's a little matter of resisting arrest too! That's gonna get you a week or two in the stockade."

"I want to talk to my CO Major Lucius Gantry, Field and Coast Artillery Corps, 6th Division."

"The colonel will talk to him. I'm sure they'll get on well together. I'm sure they both love niggers!"

Wells turned livid. His pulses pounded. His wrists strained at the 'cuffs. He stood up again and advanced on Struther, eyes blazing.

"Talk to me like that again sergeant and I'll have your stripes! I'm a corporal in the US army and you'd better learn to respect that!" Brook's voice was low and cutting. His eyes bored a hole in Struther's. He wasn't going to lose control with this thug, but he wasn't going to bow down to him either.

Struther prickled. He slammed Wells in the chest with

189

• THE CIVILIAN WAR ZONE •

his club, jarring his ribs, making him gasp with pain, knocking him off balance, back into his wooden chair. "Don't lower your voice at me, black boy! Or I'll hang your balls on my Christmas tree! You're in enough trouble already! You just might find yourself shipped out in chains next!"

"You got no right to keep me here! You know that!"

Struther grinned — a fat facial concoction half insolent, half cruel. "You know boy; you're right! I got no right to keep you here. You're holding up the orderly flow of police administration. Havin' you on these premises will bring this place into disrepute. Brackett!" Corporal Brackett, the open-mouthed young farmboy enforcer, snapped to attention, his hand clasping his white nightstick to his thigh. "Lock him in the cells for the night! I don't want to look at his ugly black face no more!"

Brook's anger soared. The man still wasn't seeing him as he really was. Ugly? That was one thing he'd never been. Strange that. The big sadistic MP sergeant was basically too scared to see the man in front of him so, in his twisted mind's eye, he converted him into something he wanted him to be. One he was able to push around, without feeling guilty. It made Brook feel strangely superior. He never looked at people like that.

Tunks knew how to kill someone, anyone, with his bare hands. The right amount of pressure on the carotid baroreceptor on either side of the neck, and it was like turning off all the lights with one switch. But he didn't want to do that to Cynthia as yet. Two minutes of pressure would suffice. That should black her out. His timing had to be precise. Much longer than two minutes and she'd never wake up.

The pavement was deserted. The stone, marble and brick office and bank buildings shrouded the road and kept out the moonlight. Subdued headlights on the occasional car didn't reflect peripherally. Down the street the entrance to the Australia Hotel was the only busy spot and could be heard but not seen. So he applied that pressure, with thumb and forefinger of one ophidian hand, whilst the other stifled her screams and clamped her chest.

• HOSTILITIES •

She struggled at first but he was a bear to her squirrel. As his pressure continued, she felt a sense of terror. She was dying. He was killing her. There was nothing she could do. He was snuffing out her life. All she could do was whimper, a strangled whimper. A flood of regrets. Her heartbeat was slowing, pulse retracting, blood pressure dropping. Oh dear life, don't leave me! Her eyes swivelled, looking for a way out. Looking for a light. Blackness. Nothing. Oh dear life. The worst feeling of all. Powerlessness. Oh God, sweet God! I've done nothing. My life is nothing. I've been nowhere, felt so little. Not now. Oh dear life, don't leave me!

Gradually, in a welter of non-specific pain, total helplessness, a sense of utter doom, the curtains descended and she was oblivious.

Tunks took a deep breath as she slumped in his arms, and released the pressure. He hoped he'd timed it right. He didn't want her dead, yet. He figured she had about five minutes of oblivion, that is, unless he had miscalculated, or unless she had a heart condition, or untapped encephalitis. That'd be too bad. But it would be her fault, not his. He'd soon know. If she didn't come to in about five minutes, she'd never come to.

He lumbered her into his staff car, with as much care as for a sack of potatoes. Her body nearly slipped off the smooth leather seat. So he flipped her over against the back.

As he gunned the car, he coolly assessed the situation. He had two choices. Keep her a permanent prisoner or kill her. He couldn't just have his way with her, knock her about and then send her back. Specially not with her father a cop. She wasn't worth his career. A court martial. No way. He liked the idea of having her his permanent prisoner, at least until the war ended. But there was always the chance of her escape.

He could lock her up, feed her, screw her when he felt like it, humiliate her, subject her. Risky. He couldn't trust anyone enough to assist him.

It would have to be death. It didn't matter. She would be just another war casualty. He liked that. The beneficial thing about war was that life became so cheap. Every day the

• THE CIVILIAN WAR ZONE •

newspapers ran the latest war casualty list, compulsive reading for the masses. Here in the hundreds, in the States in the thousands. Worldwide, by the hundreds of thousands. Not all soldiers either. Plenty of civilians involved. He'd heard somewhere that the Germans had death camps for Jews and other undesirables. And Allied bombing was demolishing whole cities full of civilians. It was a good time for the ruthless. You could get rid of your enemies with no questions asked.

He tossed up where to take her. He had, during his duties, mapped the whole metropolitan area. Sydney was a great city for covert activities. It was full of parks, green belts, glades, harbourside bushland, vacant allotments, any number of places where a man could be alone with a woman, safe and sound.

He opted for a bushland park in the inner, affluent eastern suburbs, only three miles from the city centre, yet deserted, overgrown, rocky, hilly and fully protected. He knew it was a favourite spot for GIs on the whorepath or with pederastic tendencies. Those who went there, at night, respected the privacy of others. (Greta Garbo would love it.) No interference during interference. Later he could dispose of her body in Double Bay, only a few hundred yards away. There were rowboats handy. It was an estuary of the harbour, full of submarine cables, shipping obstructions, buoys and even in certain designated areas, mines, he'd heard. Most of the harbour beaches were meshed and full of tank traps and barbed wire, so if her body was washed up, it wouldn't easily be noticed, or, by that time, identifiable.

He liked to plan ahead. Logistics were his cup of tea. That made him both a good military man and a good cop. He'd leave nothing to chance. Before, he had acted impulsively. He'd allowed himself to be carried away by the girl's allure. The result — almost disaster. He was ashamed of himself for that. It was a sign of weakness and that was another black mark against her. She knew he was vulnerable. She mustn't tell. He needed to protect his authority at all costs. If word got out, his entire MP realm would suffer. Discipline would disappear, insubordination would rule and the MPs' place as the army watchdogs in this foreign colonial land would be lost. The Aussies would see not an impeccable fighting force

• HOSTILITIES •

but a dangerous rabble. Undesirable allies. No better than the enemy.

So it wasn't just revenge, he told himself, redeploying his forces for a counterattack, it was also a matter of self-preservation and the maintenance of law, order and the allied war effort.

He knew she'd talk, if she hadn't already. He could hear the voices: "The colonel's a weakling. The great Tunks is a loser. Colonel Tunks got beaten up by a shapely Aussie tart, armed only with a high heel." Great! They could lose the war like this.

"Alright bitch! Dream your prayers! You've got nowhere to go but down." He turned his head and looked at her, as he drove along Park Street, past Hyde Park, sandbagged shopfronts, stray servicemen, aimless civilians, commercial becoming residential, ruminating on the gloomy night, joylessly anticipating the culmination of his plans.

On the back seat, she was stirring. Moaning. A trickle of vomit on her chin. He'd really shaken up her system. But she was breathing heavily. Shit! He would make a great anaesthetist, using only his bare hands. No more risk than a dose of ether.

He'd have to stop soon. Before she fully surfaced. Fortunately he'd had the foresight to handcuff and gag her.

The moon had found a cloud. Not a good night for outdoors. A certain amount of wind. Grey clouds further dampened down the night sky. Maybe there was some rain on the way.

Down the steep hill from Edgecliff, plenty of other cars on the main road, then he turned right at Double Bay and he was alone again. A flat narrow road with nice bungalows on either side spiced with a few two-storeys. A moneyed street. Trees, front gardens. Then, on the left, the foot of the park. Up a steep hill, winding, fenced-in park on left, more and better houses on right. Bellevue Hill. Steep. Not just houses, some mansions. He found the spot he was looking for.

He parked in a cul-de-sac leading onto the park. Just a few winking lights escaping from the houses. The entrance to the park was marked by dark bushes and trees. The wind was stronger now, howling a bit as it blew up from the harbour onto the high ground. A sombre park, befitting the night.

He climbed over onto the back seat and started massaging her hands, bringing her to, ripening her up for the feast. Some feast.

He decided it would be good policy to let her suffer in isolation for a while. And for his own protection, he had to put in an appearance at headquarters. Here, in the concealing foliage of this suburban parkland, no one would find her. Except perhaps the odd bush animal or spider. So he shackled Cynthia to a tree, still gagged.

3

"What are you going to do about it?" Winnie could be quite a tyrant, Joe thought, as she challenged him from the bedroom, earlier that day.

"What do you think I should do?" A little sophistry.

"That's obvious."

Winnie was relentless. Joe was readying up for the big push into assassin territory. He really wanted to avoid all her entreaties regarding action on the Cynthia front. He didn't want to interfere in his daughter's life. He considered her mature enough to make her own decisions. Besides, from his own experience he knew that interference in matters of the heart with wilful people like his daughter, who was tarred with his own contrary brush, was counterproductive. Winnie, however, was becoming obsessed.

She cornered him when he was shaving, showering, dressing, breakfasting, exercising, gardening, brushing his teeth (like now), or trying to read the paper.

"You don't care if she throws away her life on this . . . this Negro?"

"He seems nice enough." That was the wrong thing to say. Winnie choked on this.

"Oh, they're charming alright!" The voice of disdain. "They're charming! All smiles and pretty words. Like salad dressing. But that doesn't alter the fact of who he is, and what he's doing to our daughter!" Winnie used the word "daughter" like a club. It was an octave higher than her other words.

Joe stalled. He really didn't share Winnie's concern. It didn't even strike him as a full-fledged courtship. She was going out with the man. Most local girls seemed to be going out with Americans. Early loss of virginity and innocence was no doubt de rigueur. Blame the war. Did it really matter? Unwanted

• THE CIVILIAN WAR ZONE •

pregnancy seemed to be the greatest trap. Cynthia was bright enough to be careful. He hoped. She was his daughter. He had seen so much, felt so much, perhaps become desensitised, that he had endowed his daughter with these same reactions. Winnie should know better. She had spent some years working with his vice squad as a police agent. And she knew all about his rocky past. So, why was she now acting like such a . . . such a . . . Racial prejudice he supposed. He didn't know she was a "racialist". After twenty-five years of marriage, such latent bigotry.

"Tell me, Win? What exactly is it you think he's doing to our daughter?" A little vinegar. He didn't like scenes. But he wasn't prepared to let her blindness influence him.

"You know what I'm talking about! You know! And I sometimes wonder what sort of a father you really are! No doubt your years working with the scum of the earth has made you forget what common decency is!" A frontal assault. She was scared. Scared of what? Scared of her daughter associating with a black man. Scared of what the neighbours would say. Scared.

"You're probably right, Win. I've seen the dregs, rubbed shoulders with the scum, as you put it. Whores, pimps, razor slashers, drug runners, touts, killers, crooked coppers, women who'd take your pants off with one hand and stab you in the back with the other. I've seen it all. And you know what I've gone through. The broken bones, the blood, the disease, the corruption!" Joe took a deep breath. He could feel his temples pounding, his stomach contracting. She had got to him now. He no longer felt so dispassionate. It was all welling up inside him. "And maybe, just maybe, after I've seen all that, maybe . . . maybe that's why I don't think it's the end of the world when my lovely, grown-up, highly intelligent daughter goes out on a date with a coloured American soldier who is, after all, fighting on the same side as the rest of us!" He stopped, swallowed gulps of air, waited for his heart to stop pounding. Prayed that he'd got through, stilled her fear.

"Is that the sort of son-in-law you want then? A Negro? Is that what you want? How will you feel, walking down Campbell Parade, strolling along the beach, with your black-

• HOSTILITIES •

skinned son-in-law and your black-skinned grandchild? Is that what you want? Are you just going to smile and ignore all the looks, all the hate, all the embarrassment? Do you think people will still look up to you? Respect you? Do you think that?"

Winnie's face was contorted now. Her pupils were tiny black dots, her cheeks red as sunset. Joe had never seen her like this before. Not during the worst days of their marriage. Not even during the syphilitic days, the days of suspension, humiliation, the days when he was the most hated and feared cop in town. Then she had courage, understanding, tolerance.

"Win. I never knew. I never knew." He looked at her with sympathy and sadness. "Win. I hope someday you'll realise just how wrong you are. And I hope you'll learn to love your daughter again. The way you used to."

He turned and left her abruptly, walking out of the house to his car, not wanting to be in her presence again for a long time.

Winnie rushed after him, shedding tears of fury, yelling after him.

"Do you know where she is now? Do you? Don't talk to me about love! Do you care where she is? What she's doing? Do you care that she hardly ever comes home? Do you ever stop to think about her?"

Of course he cared. Her voice kept ringing in his ears as he drove down Campbell Parade, past the concrete beach park wall. He heard the surf pounding in, but the roar wasn't half as penetrating as Winnie's voice. He didn't notice the sun dancing on the breakers, not even as he followed the rising curve of the road directly into the low lying dying dazzle. Of course he cared. But he wasn't really concerned. Would he care if she married this man? Such mixed marriages were rare in this part of the world. He didn't care about the notoriety. He was used to that. The fact was that he didn't really care. If Cynthia wanted the man, if he was good to her, and loved her, why not? To hell with convention! What did he care about convention? He'd always been a lone wolf.

For a moment he wondered where she was, whether she was having a good time. Why not? She deserved a good time.

• THE CIVILIAN WAR ZONE •

Jitterbugging no doubt. Dancing cheek-to-cheek with her black American. He wasn't worried. Maybe, just a little concerned. Then he pushed her from his mind. He was about to embark on the most important case in his long career. Mass murder was more important than his daughter's latest dalliance.

4

Cynthia surfaced feeling nauseous, sore and breathless. She also felt strangely relieved. For a few seconds she had to think hard why. Then she recalled the colonel squeezing her neck and the black cloud of death descending on her and she began to cry. Great sobs of terror and relief. She couldn't recall ever crying like this before. A veritable flood of tears and mucus. It blinded and choked her and she couldn't stop it until it ran its course.

Eventually she was able to take stock of her situation and her relief at being alive was quickly drained. He had her handcuffed round the trunk of a tall tree, putting her in the position of a forcible embrace of the trunk, with her legs spread, her skirt up around her bare thighs, her posterior on a hard rocky surface and most of the strain of her unnatural posture on her spine. Looking up, she could barely see the night sky and the twinkle of a lonely star through the waving branches and leaves of the trees. On each side there was dense foliage almost touching her.

She remained like that for ages, the pain in her back and shoulders increasing by the minute, and the chill night air cramping her bare limbs. Her cotton dress did little to keep the cold out, and leg paint wasn't exactly protection against the elements. Thank God she'd worn her blessed panty-girdle, for that provided a little warmth. Since "the other night" she'd looked upon her girdle as indispensable, although in the past she'd seen it as some kind of fashion tyranny.

What to do? She thought about sleep, but her cramped position and vulnerability kept her mind and nerves on edge. She did manage to unwind her legs from her squatting positon around the tree trunk, but the alternative was resting on her knees on the rough rocky surface, which was also very painful.

• THE CIVILIAN WAR ZONE •

It forced her head to rest against the trunk, which seemed to be a workshop for ants, but it did ease the strain on her spine.

Then she managed to sit on her buttocks again, with both legs to one side of the trunk, but that still strained her shoulders and back and forced her face against the trunk. Standing up was not entirely impossible, except that there was a thick branch jutting out just three feet up the trunk, which meant she could only stand partially bent forward, which was fine for about thirty seconds. Hobson's choice. Cramp or constriction. Pain or agony. She decided to vary the three possible positions constantly. About one minute each. Movement was better than atrophy.

Then there were the ants and other nondescript bugs that kept crawling up her legs and arms and which she couldn't brush off. Didn't insects sleep at night? These ones seemed to be nocturnal or else very light sleepers.

She tried to dislodge the gag, which was an army issue green scarf, by rubbing her mouth against the tree trunk. But Tunks had clamped it firmly into her mouth and there was no dislodging it without scraping skin off her face.

At least I'm alive, she thought. For not so long ago, she had felt death descending. And then another thought struck her. He would be back. Perhaps soon. He wouldn't have imprisoned her here permanently, as she would certainly be found when daylight came. So he would be back. And then what? The possibilities were too horrific to contemplate.

Carl Goyt, wearing the mess dress uniform of a US colonel, his highest rank to date, visited his father. Ostensibly to impress. But his father's diatribe thundered through his brain and he began to regret coming. But he stood there amongst the overgrown grass and weeds, staring down at the tombstone in Rookwood Cemetery.

The tombstone read: "Charles Trevor Goyt — 1879 to 1936. Loving father of Carl. 'A soldier who feared nothing but God and dishonour.' Rest in peace". Carl had omitted any mention of his mother. She had unasserted herself right out of his reckoning.

• HOSTILITIES •

He apologised to his father for not having visited him for over a month. "Like a good soldier, I put the battle before personal considerations," he told the overrun grave. "You should be proud of me now. Your only son a colonel. I am winning the war. The enemy are dying. The Empire will be preserved."

His father's voice echoed through the desolate cemetery, bouncing off stone, penetrating the green, one of a chorus of ghosts, heard only by Carl. Words emblazoned on his consciousness, penetrating words confirming an unshakeable spirit of turpitude.

"The trouble today is that politics is in the hands of politicians." The Goyt credo. "Down through history, the most successful political leaders were always military men. Napoleon, Alexander the Great, the Caesars, Gordon, Kitchener, Smuts. To name a few. What've we got? Lloyd George. A bloody civilian! Weak. Hopeless. We would've won in 1916 if we'd had a military man as Prime Minister. And in this country, the civilians defeated conscription. Now, nothing but defeats. Gallipoli. Ugh!" A spit. Always a spit.

"When we defeated the Turks at Gaza, we were ordered to cut off the little fingers of all the dead Turks, as proof of our victory and our superior casualty rate. If you mislaid your rifle you were shot! War isn't for pansies! War is the great unifier! It makes men out of boys and empires out of countries. War purifies corruption. The history of progress is the history of warfare. Without conflict there is no progress. The British are not only the greatest fighters, they are the greatest inspirers. The British army used and trained Indians, South Africans, Canadians, Gurkhas, Malays, Australasians, West Indians, Africans, the fruits of empire. In the British army these vassals turned into heroes, only because of the flag they were fighting under and the king they were fighting for." Now a hand over the heart. Piously. Then the clenched fist again.

"Put generals into parliament I say, and our nation will win all its battles. Civilian politicians are whoremongers! They pollute parliaments with their effete brayings, their socialistic solutions which solve nothing, their suffragette manifestations

• THE CIVILIAN WAR ZONE •

which demean all our masculine military accomplishments. The Burmese girls are the most beautiful in the world. Do anything you want. . ." Always the digression. ". . . if you were a British soldier. Just leave your rifle on the bedside and you couldn't keep their legs together. Not that you wanted to." The Burmese girls were quickly relegated to their rightful place. "We didn't take prisoners at Salonika. No point. There were too many of them. We shot all the wounded in the heads as they lay there, saved the country a fortune, gave the enemy a message to pass on. Gas? I never smelt gas. You couldn't smell the mustard for the gun powder and the cordite. I was sorry when it was all over." The hand on the heart again.

"Armistice? We could have had unconditional surrender! The civilians sold us down the river! That Yankee pinkslip Wilson. Scared of his mother's milk. Turned victory into betrayal. It would've been better if those doughboys had never entered the war in the first place. With allies like that. . .?" An obscene gesture here.

"At Hamel, north of the Somme, the British Empire forces, Australians mainly, and a company from the 132nd US Regiment, fought and beat the Huns. But who did all the fighting and dying? Not the Americans. They had only 134 casualties. The Australians had 775. Fighting for Britain. That's the kind of sacrifice we need." A salute. Stiff as a ramrod. "Remember this! You don't need the Americans! Ever! We have our Empire. You can control your colonials, mould them, inspire them, turn rabble into warriors. But you can't turn traitors into allies. You're better off without them. Stick with the people you know and can trust. The traditional friend is the only true friend. Men without imperial titles are not men at all. You can't govern a country without royalty! You can't have civilians at the helm and expect to gain respect. You can't subjugate the inferior races without men of royal blood and military bearing to do it for you. Democracy is a veneer as thin as ice. Presidents are for banana republics. Monarchy and manhood go together. Remember that! You can't have democracy without monarchy."

Carl Goyt remembered his father's words vividly. Which was surprising. For his father's words were manifold ravings that poured out in torrents of verbiage that filled the ether with confusion and prejudice. He knew his mother never listened and never understood, but reacted with nods of agreement and a blank expression, curbing whatever propensity she had for conversation of any kind. But at times, to Carl, when he was old enough to comprehend words of more than one syllable, much of it stuck. Bits and pieces of imperial rhetoric and bloodthirsty grandiloquence. It was much more satisfying than the bits and pieces of logical thought he heard occasionally at school. It soothed him, even inspired him, without exactly knowing why. It was like the preachings of an evangelist. Instead of loaded words like Jesus, love, sin, he that believeth in me have everlasting life, faith, temptation, life after death, come forth and be saved, his father's rhetoric was hard-edged, disturbing, undermining in its confusion, inspiring in its inconsistency.

Yet Carl hated him, but not as much as he hated his mother for bowing to him, for going back on all her kindness to Carl when her husband came home, for neglecting her son when he was around. Now it was all clear in his mind. The war had clarified everything, turned his father's frustrated rhetoric into a creed for action, giving purpose to his life. Now he knew who the real enemies were and how to deal with them. And how to win the war. The war of his life.

Above all Goyt remembered the words of his father: "We never took prisoners at Salonika." So, later that night, together with his three trusty colonial vassals, he waited until small arms training was in progress in a nearby converted cowshed at the showground, and then put a bullet in the head of each of the remaining chained prisoners.

They bundled the bodies into a commandeered army laundry truck and drove out, past the unsuspecting sentries at the main gates. In the very early hours they deposited the bodies on the doorstep of US Divisional Headquarters at the Grace Building in King Street.

Then Goyt rang the newspapers, and using his Oxbridge English voice, told them that five traitorous American soldiers had been executed by loyal members of the British Empire

• THE CIVILIAN WAR ZONE •

Territorial Army.

To date he was most annoyed that army and government censors had kept all news of his victories out of the papers. This time he felt the news was too hot to suppress. He would really have liked a permanent war correspondent attached to his army, but he realised that this was, as yet, too much to ask for. First his cause must come out in the open, so that the population at large could learn the truth about the nature of the real enemy in their midst and stop being taken in by the glamour of the American traitors.

As long as he was able to pursue his ideas, his father would never die.

5

Cynthia heard a car grind to a halt somewhere beyond her bushy prison, and froze. She was back in her original position with both arms and legs embracing the tree trunk. Her teeth were chattering, her skin was bluish, everything was aching and now the sound of the car made her heart pound so much she felt it might burst. Was it friend or foe?

She knew the answer before she framed the question.

The sound of boots tramping over the dirt and stones and the snapping and parting of the branches was almost Frankensteinian in portent. She couldn't see anything, for the sounds were coming from directly behind, and that made it worse. She felt herself whimpering and her imagination summoned up visions of a knife thudding between her shoulder-blades and piercing her heart and lungs or a bullet blowing the back of her skull off. She imagined pieces of herself spraying out over the foliage.

Then he was there beside her, squatting down, a cruel hunk shrouding his viciousness behind a thin-lipped grin, spicing it by playing with his .45 revolver, absently pushing the safety catch on and off, deliberately holding it up near her nose, making sure she saw it, relishing her fear. Then his voice, almost jovial:

"Bet you thought you'd never see me again, *honey*?"

Cynthia moved her head from side to side, willing him to remove the gag.

He did. She parted her lips, licked them, took a deep breath and couldn't stop the tears that coursed down her cheeks again. At first she couldn't find her voice. When she did it was hoarse and her throat hurt when the words came out.

"You're a sadistic pig!" she croaked.

"Flattery'll get you somewhere, honey." He grinned. Her

• THE CIVILIAN WAR ZONE •

distress and discomfort seemed to amuse him. "I bet you're tickled to see me, right?"

She spat at him. And missed. Then she tried not to groan, and failed.

"Hey! I thought you were a lady!" Mocking.

She was far too scared, pained and angry to play his games. "This is killing my back!" she gasped, and hated herself for complaining.

"Oh sure honey. I can see that. But don't worry. Soon you won't feel a thing."

Playing for sympathy with Tunks was like trying to kiss a giraffe.

"Please! Take these handcuffs off! Please!" She hated having to plead with him but she couldn't help herself.

"Well now, I'd really like to honey, but I'm kinda scared of what you'll do to me. I mean, you jus' might scratch my eyes out now."

"I would if I could!"

He stood up, struck a scolding pose. "Now, is that any way to talk to a friend who just came to give you a picnic in the park?"

He put his gun back in his holster and pulled a packet out of one of the deep top pockets on his field jacket, then unwrapped it. "Roast beef on rye or red salmon, honey?" He proferred the sandwiches to her.

She almost choked, shook her head vigorously.

"Oh I guess you ain't hungry then. Well, I'm not surprised. I guess you ate up a storm at that Romano's with that nigger friend of yours? Well, you won't mind if I just have a munch here. I ain't had the good fortune to have a slap-up dinner tonight. It's been mighty busy out there keepin' law and order."

He sat down on a rock and started eating, chewing like an ape with his hooded eyes fixed on her like searchlights.

"You can't keep me here like this. There might be a war on but there's still laws you know."

"Oh I know that, honey. I'm a law man remember." Speaking in between chomps. "I'm a colonel of the law. Military law. You're under martial law now honey, whether you like it or not. How about a little fruit cake?" He unwrapped several

• HOSTILITIES •

slices of fruit cake. "Just like my mammy used to bake." He thrust it at her mouth.

She angrily shook her head and kept her lips tightly clamped.

"Oh sure, I keep forgettin'. You're all full up with lobster, oysters, cheese sauce, peach Melba. Now what would you want with little ol' fruit cake? You're a lucky gal you are, honey. I bet all your friends would like to know what you had for dinner tonight. And who you had it with? How many ration tickets did it cost you, honey?" Laughs. Jowls shaking. Eyes merciless.

He stuffed a large slice of cake in his mouth, brushed crumbs off his jacket and his hands, then stood up, still chomping, staring down at her. "I think this calls for a little celebration, don't you honey?"

He produced a flask from his jacket, unscrewed the top, squatted, thrust it at her.

"Just open those luscious lips of yours honey, and tip your pretty head back. This is genuine corn-fed real American bourbon. Help you get rid of those shivers and shakes. Sure it ain't champagne, but then beggars can't be choosers, can they? *Honey?*"

He shoved the flask between her lips and tipped it up whilst holding her chin with his other hand. The strong liquid burnt her throat and nearly choked her. Some of it spilled down her chin. She hated the taste, not ever having had spirits before, yet the burning inside, all the way down wasn't unwelcome. It halted her tremors and brought sweat to her brow.

He took the flask away. "Don't overdo it, honey. We don't want you drunk now, do we?" He wiped her chin with his hand, an addendum to his derisive game. "We want you to be fully aware of all the good things that are going to happen to you. *Honey!*"

"How long are you going to keep me here like this?" She couldn't help the bubble in her voice, caused by the spirits.

"Long as it takes, honey. Long as it takes. Now just excuse me for a moment. Have to see a man about a dog."

He turned away from her, moved several yards towards

a clump of bushes, unbuttoned his fly and pissed, aiming the long stream into the darkness, then turning his head to look at her.

"Just keep your eyes to yourself, honey. This is man's business." He chuckled and sprayed half a gallon or so. Then he shook his penis and put it away, turning back towards her with a familiar grin.

The bourbon had helped restore some of Cynthia's resolve. She realised that no amount of pleading would work. In fact he seemed to like her helplessness. Perhaps the only thing he understood was strength.

"Whatever you're planning won't work!" The catch in her voice was regretful but she couldn't help it. She hoped the resolve in her heart was enough. "I told my father about you! So no matter what you do to me, he'll know it was you!"

Tunks' jaw hardened a bit and he just stood there, looking down at her, fingering the handle of the Mark II combat knife which was sheathed on his belt.

"Well, I said I'd like to meet your old man sometime, honey. I'm sure we got a lot in common. Trouble is you never did tell me his name."

Without hesitation Cynthia spat out her father's name, hoping it would stop him short, make him think twice.

It did.

"Church? Detective Sergeant Church?" Tunks mouthed the name with disbelief. His mind picked out scattered thoughts and converted them into one. There was almost dead silence for a moment, punctuated only by some distant hoots from ships in the harbour and the shrill staccato of an isolated cricket signalling to his choristers.

"You're lying!" he snapped.

"I don't know what you mean. He knows all about you!"

"Church? Your father? You're a lying little dozo! He works for me!"

"Works for you?" Cynthia looked confused. That didn't make sense, but she held further comment.

Tunks' mind was working overtime now. This was a whole new ballgame. She wouldn't make this up. How could she? Father and daughter? Figures. Both of them too smart for

· HOSTILITIES ·

their own good. Both of 'em sharp-tongued. Abrasive. Both of 'em. Both of 'em!

Was it a coincidence? Sheeit! Was it a coincidence? Was there a connection? His paranoia was overwhelming. Conspiracy. There was something going on he hadn't even suspected. It was not just a personal vendetta now. Not just wounded pride. It was some sort of espionage. A frontal assault on his position and his esteem. Something so unnerving he was bound to take action. Now. He unsheathed his seven inch knife and squatted down at her side.

6

Major Gil Mitchell towered over his adjutant, Lieutenant Adam Goldhart, temporarily promoted for purposes of this particular operation. Mitchell was an immaculately uniformed mountain in his class A forest-green belted and bandoleered tunic jacket over beige pink trousers. His service cap was olive drab with brown leather peak and strap. His gold oak leaf rank insignia was on the shoulder of his tunic, his US cyphers were on his upper lapels and below these were his crossed Rifles Corps badge. The shoulder patch on his left arm was a red arrow pointing upwards, crossed by a short red horizontal line indicating the 32nd Infantry Division.

Joe was pleased to be back in uniform again. He felt good. Americans, he noticed, seemed to love wearing uniforms whereas Australians looked upon them as an occupational nuisance. Joe was an exception. Uniforms were one of his favourite disguises. Just donning this one had transformed him into a major character. It gave him bearing, authority, military precision. Nevertheless he'd added a small moustache as a further embellishment.

Major and adjutant emerged from their staff car, which was lacquered brown and had no gas producer, much to the envy of passing civilian motorists.

The major even towered over the club-happy MP blocking their way outside the Reflections Club. It wasn't just size, it was Joe's aura of authority which placed him head and shoulders above everybody else, even those matching six-plus footers.

The MP spoke with a mixture of respect, for the gold oak leaf badge, and brutishness befitting his status as an enforcer.

"This place is off limits, major!"

• HOSTILITIES •

"Since when?" Joe's accent was a dry-mouthed Texan drawl, which he'd copied from a recent Randolph Scott movie.

"The order came down from General Staff Corps, major."

"That's mighty good to hear, soldier. Now would you mind steppin' aside?"

The MP turned red in the face. "But you're not supposed to go in there, major. With respect, sir."

"It's off limits to enlisted men, right?" Joe challenged, thinking how enjoyable rank could be. Maybe he'd go for that promotion after all.

"That's right, major."

"Well, do I look like an enlisted man to you?"

The MP started to buckle. And he needed a shave.

"Sorry, major. I guess it's okay if you go in."

"Wal, that's fine soldier. And it's okay with me if he goes in too." Joe saluted. He shepherded Adam past the MP, who looked ambivalent. "It might be an idea if you had a shave, soldier."

Three other US officers, a warrant officer and a naval lieutenant, who'd been dallying outside, took Joe's cue and stormed in past the beleaguered MP. Adam felt good. Joe pulling rank was music to his ears.

Inside, Reflections was just a pale reflection of itself. Drinking soberly were a smattering of Aussie servicemen, a couple of Dutch sailors, some ageing civilians. Women were as scarce as deodorant in Tibet.

"I wouldn't have thought our man would come here now that it's off limits to GIs," Adam said.

"Neither would I." Joe had a cursory glance around the room.

"Then why did we come here?"

Joe grinned. "To tell you the truth, I just enjoy baiting your MPs. You could say I did it for you."

"I'll drink to that." And he did.

"How many's that?" Joe asked.

"A birdie. One under par."

"What's par?"

"About eight beers."

They only stayed five minutes. On the way out Joe

· THE CIVILIAN WAR ZONE ·

confronted the same MP.

"What's your name, soldier?"

The MP looked most unhappy. "Felton, sir."

"Well, Private Felton, I'm afraid I'm going to have to report you to the Provost Marshal, Colonel Tunks. Dereliction of duty. There's three officers, a warrant officer and a naval lieutenant in there, and this place is supposed to be off limits!" Felton gaped at Joe, reddening with confusion. "And get a shave!"

It had been a hectic couple of nights. They'd appeared, seemingly drunk, at practically every watering hole in town that catered to Americans, including the Trocadero Dance Palais, where they'd enjoyed dancing with several willing girls to the music of Artie Shaw and his band, on tour for the USO. But there'd been more than a thousand other servicemen there and the chances of picking out their target had been negligible.

Then came Ziggy's Underworld Nightclub in King Street, awash with whores, pimps and crooked coots battening off the few foolish GIs who ventured in unknowingly. But no sign of Adam's vicious US major or anyone resembling him.

The Stage Door Canteen had been too respectable — chaperoned ladies and servicemen behaving themselves with an eye more to public relations than fun.

The Empire Club in George street was ill-named, being neither imperial, British nor traditional. It was a lowish dive overflowing with sly grog, gambling, unrestrained carousal, girls of easy virtue or none at all but, for a change, the Aussies outnumbered the Yanks, which meant it didn't fit the pattern. Everywhere they went US MPs were checking every soldier's leave pass and papers, a new security measure, but Joe was sure their quarry would have valid documentation.

The York Hotel was a popular pub with GIs, so they stayed there through three rounds, which Joe surreptitiously spilt whilst Adam consumed, despite Joe's warning about the need for sobriety. But Adam, though acting as Joe's deputy, was still a soldier on leave, in his head, and such discipline was beyond him.

"I think that's a bogey."

• HOSTILITIES •

"No sir. I'm still putting along."

Joe was rather tickled that everywhere they went, attractive young women practically threw themselves at them. Adam had to be contained a number of times. Unlike Joe, who had spent so much of his life in the after-hours, seedy, twilight gloom of feckless indulgence and disparate disillusion and who was now able to seemingly indulge and stay coolly removed at the same time, Adam was more and more swept up in the flow of bacchanalian fever, searching faces for their quarry but really only seeing the faces that attracted him.

The Roosevelt, through Adam's eyes, seemed almost haremesque, with available women outnumbering GIs almost two to one. Joe had to remind Adam what they were there for.

"How long do you think this is gonna take?" Adam asked.

"Had enough already?"

"No siree. This is the best pass I've had. I was just hoping it wouldn't stop."

Joe smiled grimly. "When it does, you'll probably be face-to-face with a man who wants to kill you."

"May it never stop." Adam raised his glass.

The Roosevelt was a plush nightclub decorwise, with waiters, polished dance floor, padded seats, tablecloths, mirrors, discreet lighting and an ornamental bandstand, but the conduct of the patrons was no better than at any of the dives. Grog was king, sex was queen, escape was the royal decree.

"The secret of success is to be a drunk on the outside and a priest on the inside," Joe said, intercepting Adam's hungry survey of the distaff patrons.

"With me it always seems to be the other way around."

"Maybe you try too hard."

"You could be right. You know, you're not a bad guy for an Aussie."

"I'm not sure that's a compliment."

"Sure, I guess that's kinda narrow-minded. But well, most Aussies I met so far seem to resent us being here. So you can't help stickin' it to someone who sticks it to you. Know what I mean?"

"Well, we've never had such an influx before. Up to now

• THE CIVILIAN WAR ZONE •

we've been an isolated island. A homogeneous people. Now, think about it, suddenly there's half a million of you people passing through. You get twice the pay, wear smarter uniforms, you always seem to be on leave, living it up, all the women are falling for you. . ."

"Not me."

"You're not looking in their eyes."

"Right. I hadn't ever got up that far."

"Then, a lot of the Aussie soldiers have just come back after fighting the Germans and Italians in North Africa; the Australian army puts them in pig pens, moves them from city to city in uncomfortable trains in the middle of the night with just a cup of tea and army biscuits to keep them going, and they look at you blokes and little green devils light up in their eyes."

"I don't blame 'em I guess."

"It's like Rockefeller suddenly walking into a poorhouse. All the inmates are (a) going to want some of his money and (b) hate him 'cause he's got more than they have."

Adam raised a supplicatory hand. "I guess I'd probably feel the same. Just that most of our guys mean well, you know."

Joe toyed with his beer. "That makes it worse. Aussies tend to distrust the well-meaning. You'll get on better if you insult them. Openly. Then they'll think you're just like one of them."

"I'll try and remember that."

"Fartface."

"Fartface."

"That's better. You'll get on. Listen! I hate to break this up, but I'm sure we'll do better if we split up. Separate tables. Outside we walk apart. Our man is probably looking for solitary bait. More likely to be you than me. A full-blown major of my age and size will scare him off. So I'm going to leave you to it. Get as drunk as you like, lay around, indulge yourself. On the outside. But keep a cool head. I'll be in range the whole time. If you recognise your man, stuff some chewing gum in your mouth."

"How long should we stay here?"

"I'll let you know. It's all a gamble really. The odds are

• HOSTILITIES •

good. It's crowded. Three of the other victims were last seen here."

"Return to the scene of the crime, eh?" Adam's speech was slightly slurred.

"Just remember what I said. Drunk outside, priest inside. I think you'd better just sip from now on."

"Yes sir! Whatever you say, sir! I'll be as sober as a grudge, sir!" Adam saluted.

"That's judge, son."

"Grudge sounds better."

Joe left, found another table, from which he could still see Adam. He immediately fluffed a rather attractive blonde girl off, as she started to sit down. Then changed his mind. Good cover. Long as she didn't get too many ideas. But something was preying on his subconscious. Something he'd said before. Accidentally. What was it? He bought the girl a drink, smiled at her, but kept going over words in his mind. Re-ran his conversation with Adam.

"Hallelujah!" he yelled.

"I beg your pardon?" the girl said.

"It's alright. I just remembered something."

The girl looked away. She knew this handsome mature hunk of US major had more than her on his mind and she began to look around for greener prey. But for Joe, it all started to fall into place. What he'd said before was: "The Australian army puts them in pig pens." "Pig pens?" What did that forensic report say about those bodies? Blood and faeces from animals; either pigs, monkeys, sheep or goats. Pig pens? He knew that the Australian army was billeting soldiers in various animal pavilions at the showground. But what did that mean? Were the killers members of the AIF? Hallelujah! The showground! Scene of the crime! Probably. Well, they'd have to finish off this scene tonight, but tomorrow — the showground! Of course! It was so obvious. Had been staring him in the face. Not a farm, or a zoo. He felt good now. So good, he celebrated with a large sip of the beer he'd been nursing.

Adam had to keep reminding himself he was on duty. He

• THE CIVILIAN WAR ZONE •

thought of Salome, the fun they'd almost had. Half of him wanted to continue that fun whilst the other half wanted retribution. Trouble was, at the moment, the fun side was predominant. The atmosphere, the beer, the crowd and, in particular, the brunette who suddenly plonked herself down at his table, kept subverting his main purpose.

It was like magic. A moment ago she'd been sitting at a nearby table with a heavy, mean-looking Aussie soldier; now she was his. He took Joe's advice, looked in her eyes, which were clear green, and they were semaphoring the ultimate. But, unlike his previous compromise candidate, this one was a real looker. Non-frizzy hair neatly bundled in a roll to the neck, good figure, just the right height for him, good complexion with not too much make-up, nice smile, full lips, slightly parted. "What cloud did you drop from, angel?"

Adam, as an amateur investigator, knew he was looking for a certain male face. He was not remotely prepared to be suspicious of any female in the vicinity, let alone one as appealing as this one. Joe, on the other hand, watching from afar, wondered why this girl had decided to leave the Aussie soldier for the Yank, without any obvious complaint from the Aussie.

"Hello, Yank, where you from?" the girl asked, quite unable to match Adam's creative greeting.

"I'm from Mars and I've been looking for someone like you all over the universe."

She held out a soft, delicate, unlived-in hand, which he shook ever so gently.

"My name's Adam, and if you tell me yours is Eve I won't believe you."

"My name's Virginia and I'm pleased to meet you. I hope you don't mind me sitting here?"

"That chair was nothing until you came and sat on it. Can I buy you a drink?" As soon as he'd asked, Adam recalled the previous inflated transaction at Reflections. This time he resolved to make the selection himself. He needn't have bothered.

"Something soft," she said, in a plaintive voice.

Adam liked that. "Very appropriate."

• HOSTILITIES •

He bought her a Coke, reserved specially, the waiter said, for their American friends, seeing as how it was unavailable to civilians.

Adam couldn't comprehend such a shortage. To him a civilian without Coke was like a dog without fleas.

It didn't take long before the soft and pliable Virginia was sitting very close to him, caressing his hands, finger-straying over his thigh under the table, making small sighing noises and making his eyes water with her strong perfume, which Adam suspected must have aphrodisiac qualities because he was getting his first hard-on in weeks. She seemed to sense this because those delicate hands kept gently traversing his thigh and stopping just a tantalising hair's-breadth away from his involuntary throbjob. Such sweet potential removed all thoughts of Salome, Joe and the dreaded major from his mind. His entire intellectual capacity was temporarily overwhelmed by the blunt end of his unreasoning pudenda.

"Did you know they had bedrooms upstairs, Adam?"

Adam almost melted. "Who wants to sleep?" he covered up.

"Silly. Who said anything about sleep?" Her eyes were all dewy.

"But you hardly know me. How do you know I'm not a ravening beast who likes to eat young brunettes?"

"I'll take my chances." Virginia's hands were playing a tingling tattoo on his upper leg. He dragged his attention away from her for a moment — a supreme effort of willpower — and looked across at Joe, who seemed not to be watching him, but was. He knew he shouldn't leave his post, but Joe had said indulge yourself. Maybe it was all good cover. Priest on the inside. His hard-on was on the outside. Act natural.

He sank his eighth beer, or was it his tenth, and felt light-headed. Virginia was looking at him, hypnotically. The music from the bandstand was "Poor Butterfly" played by a sub-Goodman clarinet, but it added to his mood. The thought of turning down such an invitation seemed positively treasonous. His body and psyche were crying out for sexual succour. Opportunity knocks. Open the door.

Joe could follow them, if he liked. Long as he stayed

• THE CIVILIAN WAR ZONE •

outside the bedroom. Bedroom? What a lovely word. He hadn't been in a bedroom since leaving home. Bivouacs, dormitories, tents, with a hundred sneezing, farting, snoring, smoking soldiers in them, side by side. Bedroom?

"Did you say bedroom?"

She nodded, with a sweet smile and gripped his hand under the table.

"Is that a room with a bed in it or a bed with lots of room in it?"

"Would you like to find out?"

He nodded, unable to speak any more because of the thickness in his throat.

As they threaded their way across the club through the labyrinth of tables and partying patrons, he didn't notice her surreptitious signal to the heavy Aussie digger at her previous table. The digger, Crowbar MacPherson, licked his scaly lips in anticipation as he watched them pass by without raising his head.

7

Cynthia's father had never hit her, not in all her born days. Smacking was anathema to him. He was never less than tender with her.

Strange for a tough vice cop. He'd hit other women, she knew that. He'd never hit her mother though. When he was home, he was a gentle giant. Always. Sometimes otherwise engaged. But a man of love. Secretly, she admitted, she had always cherished the hope of finding a man just like her father. A not unreasonable object. But perhaps there weren't any others like him. There were policemen and policemen.

The other one in her life was a different drummer. He was hard, cynical, self-involved or perhaps the word was obsessed and he was releasing her handcuffs.

Her mind swam now. He was breathing hard, had lapsed into silence and his combat knife was at her throat. But she wasn't convinced he was going to use it. She sensed his inner confusion, his mixed motives.

He put the handle of the knife between his teeth and flipped her over onto her back. The back of her head hit the hard rock and she saw fireworks, tears filled her eyes again and her brain, that miraculous jelly, seemed to slide around, causing her head to throb like a jungle drum.

Now he was recuffing her wrists round the tree trunk, so that her arms were imprisoned behind her head and she was stretched out, ready to do backstroke.

"How's that? Comfortable?" he asked.

He didn't really expect an answer.

"Bear in mind," he lectured solemnly, "that this is entirely your own doing."

"No! Not here!" she screamed. And her voice was lost in the trees and the night wind and the flowing waters of a

• THE CIVILIAN WAR ZONE •

nearby stream.

Then he deftly tied the gag around her mouth again and ended direct communication. She made strangling noises in her throat and her saliva saturated the scarf and tightened it, making it bite into the corners of her mouth.

"Ah ha ha, hee hee hee, little brown jug don't I love thee?" She was back in the Hyde Park Canteen and the Glenn Miller soundalike band was swinging in dreamtime and the impeccably uniformed fresh-faced young men were whirling her around. And he was removing his jungle fatigues. The man had boxer shorts on, with a trapdoor. Her eyes were on the trapdoor. The cricket chorus started up, in answer to the chorusmaster's call. Don't they ever sleep?

"No! Not here!" she screamed again, inside her head. The rock bit into her back and buttocks, the disturbed ants crawled up her bare legs and stung, and explored. She pulled herself back, using the cuffs round the trunk as a pulley and slammed the top of her head into the trunk. Everything was spinning. Life was a merry-go-round. "Ha ha ha, you and me, little brown. . ." He was prising her legs apart. She held them rigid, her muscles aching, pulling against his iron grip.

The gong sounded, the people yelled, half for her, half for him, a tug of legs. And arms. She wasn't going to give in. She looked up, away from his tense, vitriolic face. There were lights in the sky. Searchlights. Looking for who? She wasn't up there.

"I'm down here!" she called, inside her head.

The lights swung around, criss-crossing, single, searching, but up in the sky. She was on the ground. On a rock, chained to a thousand-year-old gum tree with peeling bark, riddled with worms and tree lice. And in her hair too. Looking for wood. She had plenty or she wouldn't be here. She couldn't tell the good guys from the bad guys. They all wore uniforms. They all had smooth tongues. They all danced to Glenn Miller and Artie Shaw. They all stood to attention for their flag.

Did they all rape when they couldn't get what they wanted?

"Ha ha ha, you and me, little brown jug don't I love thee. . ." Love? Where was love? A casualty of war. She was a casualty of war. Her legs were apart. He had won, with

• HOSTILITIES •

his brute strength and his law-enforcing determination. Her calves had cramped. Agony. She ached to bend her legs. He had them tied now, with just enough give to suit his foul purpose. One to each bush. More ants. Violating her. Bull ants. Bull cop!

A voice: "You were drafted, baby. Military service. That means you service the military. Or else you're a deserter!"

"I am a conscientious objector. I think you're on the wrong side." Inside her head. "When I hear that serenade in blue. . ." Conquering armies always raped. The fortunes of war. The unfortunates of war. Her undies were shredded. But he wasn't that strong. He couldn't remove her panty-girdle.

He was slashing it away with his knife. Blood on her belly and in her pubic hair. She was only partly a virgin. Can you be a part virgin? This boy, the terrible Timothy, had partly penetrated her once. Before they were interrupted. In the toolshed. How appropriate, she had thought at the time. He'd cut her with his knife. Careless. "Sometimes I wonder why I spend the lonely night. . ." Where was the music coming from? Why was he punching her face? Each punch landed with a sickening crunch that disturbed her reverie, made her teeth ache and slammed the back of her head against the tree. She was slipping away again, but she didn't want to. She wanted to stay awake. She wanted to stay awake in case he killed her. Oh God! He would kill her if she blacked out, wouldn't he? Either way. What did it matter? It was the helplessness she hated most. That bastard! That cowardly bastard! He had her pinned down so she couldn't fight back. The bastard! She was slipping away. The music was growing softer. He was prodding her. Down there. Wounding her with his baton. His MP club. Hard and long, like wood. Made for cracking heads and cracking vulvas.

She couldn't see the lights now. His head was in the way. The mean lips, he needed a shave, the hateful eyes, the grey crew cut, as sharp as wire, the lined forehead, the bulldog ears, the strong ugly aggressive chin.

His face was creased with effort, strain, pushing, prodding, jerking in and out, trying so hard, hating her, fighting her with every pore of his body, tearing her in two, trying even

• THE CIVILIAN WAR ZONE •

harder, for what? For revenge? Hell hath no fury like an MP scorned! The military defied. Action — reaction. Attack — counterattack. He was chafing her, tearing her, sweating all over her, the only fluids were his, apart from her blood. She hoped she was bleeding all over him and that he'd never be able to rub it off, that he would carry her bloodmark till the day he died. Let it be soon.

He was pumping away, like the Atchison Topeka and the Santa Fe. Steam escaping. And blood. Hands squeezing her breasts, the pain competing with the rest. All parts aching now. All muscles straining. All limbs cramped. "Oh God! When is it going to end?" Her face bleeding, her belly bleeding, her vagina torn, legs bitten, nipples crunched. "I'm the boogie woogie bugle boy from Company B". She'd had enough! She raised her head and crashed it down on the tree roots, praying for oblivion. They jarred her brain, didn't split her skull. Maybe she hadn't tried hard enough. Maybe she wasn't suicidal yet. She just wanted to black out. But she could still hear the music, feel the pain, taste the disgust, see his spiteful eyes, feel his foul smoky breath, taste his cruelty. And it seemed to go on for ever. Then it started to rain.

It was the only ejaculation that was going to occur. This beast couldn't come. He could only try, and try, and hurt, and torture. Thank God for the rain!

8

All was not as it should be with the British Empire Territorial Army, Goyt thought. It was really a matter of recognition. They had none. One line had appeared in the newspapers to the effect that US military police were investigating unsubstantiated reports that a number of missing GIs had been found dead in the city. Nothing else. Almost a complete blanket. Censorship. Yet, the papers were full of stories of what the Aussies and the Yanks were doing to the Japanese enemy in the Pacific. Nothing about what his army was doing to the American enemy in occupied Australia.

The public had a right to know; a need to know. Goyt knew all about censorship. Public morale. Well, this news would be good for public morale.

He rang the news editor of the *Daily Telegraph* and asked him why there had been nothing printed about the work of the British Empire Territorial Army's defeat of thirteen American soldiers, all members of the US occupying force.

"Who is this?" the news editor asked, signalling his assistant for assistance.

"It doesn't matter. I am the commanding officer. You'll learn my name in due course."

"What's the secret? We know the names of all the American and Australian commanding officers. Surely you want yours printed as well?"

Cunning. "You can't trap me like that, sir. I want to know why you didn't print that story. It's important news."

"Well, listen here . . . what's your rank anyway? General is it?"

Pause. "That's right."

"Well general, there's a war on. You should know that. We're not allowed to print everything."

Goyt seethed. The wretched man was humouring him. "Who censored you?"

"I can't tell you that."

"Was it the Americans?"

"We only get censored by the State government. Sometimes the Americans put some pressure on, I suppose."

"You suppose? Don't you care? What sort of a person are you? Don't you have any national pride?"

Pause. "I'm going to hang up now. We're not interested in crank calls."

"Wait!" Goyt yelled. "I haven't finished."

"Make it quick. I've got a paper to get out."

Goyt wanted to put that wretched editor in his place, but first he had to clarify the essentials. "Which Americans?"

"Listen, mate. I haven't got time to waste."

Goyt changed tack. "Well, you'd better hang up then. I'm sure the relatives of those dead Americans would like to know how important you think their sons were. Particularly the Salamandinis, the Cathcarts, the Murphys, the Nelsons . . . shall I go on? I have all their dog tags here."

The editor started signalling frantically now. He wanted the police in on this. "Alright. I heard you. Now what exactly are you after?"

"I don't want these great and significant military victories ignored."

"We know about them."

"Good. Now who censored you?"

"Why don't you ask the US Military Police? I'm sure they can help you."

"Perhaps I will."

"Look, general. You want some news printed? Tell you what. We'll do a story on you and your army. But we gotta get together somewhere. What do you say? We can't just take things down on the phone. We need verification. We need to meet you, and the others, get all the facts. Do you understand me?"

Pause. "We demand a war correspondent. Permanently attached."

The editor grabbed at this. He now had a reporter listening

• HOSTILITIES •

in on the other phone, scribbling furiously, and another trying to raise the police and the MPs.

"A war correspondent? Alright. That's a good idea. I'll assign one immediately. Where'll I send him?"

Long pause. More cunning. "Tell him to wait there. I'll send someone for him." Goyt hung up. He had to think about this. He didn't trust them. There were so many traitors about today. Who could you trust? Definitely not the newspapers. They were propaganda arms of the government, allowing themselves to be censored, printing army handouts verbatim. You couldn't trust anybody. Why were people so confused when choosing sides?

The Military Police? Why the Military Police? He hadn't thought about them much before. "The Military Police were investigating unsubstantiated reports. . ." That's what it said. What about the State Police? What were they investigating? Furthermore the editor had said: "Why don't you ask the US Military Police?" Why didn't he? Ask them what? Ask them why they are censoring the war news? Ask them if they know who their enemies are? Ask them why they are trying to keep news of their defeats a secret from the public? Well, that's not unusual. No army liked having their defeats trumpeted. Although, look how they trumpeted Gallipoli.

Goyt felt confused. He also felt some breathing difficulty coming on. Confusion always did that. He needed clarity. Soldiers always needed clarity. Confusion was for politicians.

It was time for another assault on the enemy. Which enemy? That was the confusion. The Military Police. They were the enemy. They were investigating him. Everybody hated the US Military Police. He knew that. He had heard it from Aussies, from some of his American POWs, from deserters, from civilians, even from some of the US Quartermaster Corps personnel. It slowly dawned on him that if he launched an attack and defeated the US Military Police, then the papers would print the story and everybody would be on his side. Of course. One of the weaknesses of his war so far, he admitted to himself, was that his victims were young, good-looking boys, favourites of those brainless Australian sluts, lauded by the treasonous press, fawned on by the government and authorities.

• THE CIVILIAN WAR ZONE •

They were winning the propaganda war, even if he was winning the real war and inflicting severe casualties.

But the MPs were as hated as the Japanese. They were the true invaders and occupiers, the gestapo. If he was able to defeat some MPs, everyone would cheer. Thousands would cheer. The press would trumpet. The British Empire Territorial Army would become heroes.

At headquarters, Goyt summoned his regiment, which was not yet a battalion, nor even a company and, for that matter, barely a platoon. They now numbered five. He had recently conscripted two more deserters, an Aussie and a Yank. He didn't mind utilising an enemy deserter. He probably hated the Americans more than anybody.

Corporal Seldom, his loyal acolyte, had brought them along. Goyt suspected they were both deviates and had met at one of those pubs that Seldom frequented. That didn't bother him. His father, in one of his unguarded moments, had told him how members of his regiment, in Egypt and India, had importuned Arab and Indian boys for sodomistic purposes at various times, using, as always, such devices not for physical pleasure as such, but to assist in the subjugation of the civilian population. Rape and sodomy were legitimate military tactics for occupying forces. The Americans knew this as well as anybody. He had seen some luring pre-pubescent schoolboys into a newsreel theatre with promises of chewing gum and candy. The delicately vicious Corporal Seldom was no doubt a prolific sodomiser of vulnerable civilians and deserters. Goyt could use a few more like him.

He could hear his father's voice shouting and singing in the bathroom: "One two three four, Kimalio Kimalio *war*! Hold him down . . . the Swazi warrior, hold him down . . . the Swazi king. Hold him down . . . the Swazi warrior . . ."

One problem. Crowbar MacPherson, his normally trusty lieutenant, was nowhere to be found. Perhaps he'd gone AWOL. That was treasonable. He had his orders. He had to be on hand every evening at the beck and call of the regiment commander. Still, knowing MacPherson's underworld background, Goyt wasn't altogether surprised. The man was

· HOSTILITIES ·

a bit demented and endemically forgetful, but a strong fighter and an amazing marksman. Nevertheless, discipline must be maintained. When he turned up, it would have to be the cat-o'-nine-tails, he told Seldom, who seemed delighted at the prospect.

Utilising the underground stratagem that he felt should eventually win him a decoration, Goyt dressed his men in US noncom uniforms with MP brassards on their arms and steel half-pot helmets, and the MP Corps insignia of crossed flintlock pistols.

Goyt felt a surge of power and authority as they strapped on their .45 pistols in russet leather holsters together with their twin clip pouches, their MP peerless handcuffs, white batons, flashlights, combat knives in leather sheaths — all attached to the eyelets on their webbing belts. Goyt, as MP captain, added some dark glasses and a 30 round mag clip for his M1 carbine, which he intended to carry. Being able to openly tote an arsenal around the city combat zone was what he'd always dreamed of. Tonight, they were inviolable conquering heroes. Previously he'd thought such a ploy was too dangerous. The sort of exposure that could lead to their downfall. But now, after all those successful secret missions, it was time to stand up and be noticed.

"Attenshun!" he barked, with quivering jowls and owlish eyes, and his sub-platoon snapped to almost attention. "Inspection!" They remained frozen as he peered at their uniforms and their weapons. Then he trod on a pair of their unshined boots with instructions to polish them until they bled. Because of a sudden tightness in his lungs, he had no option but to smite the new American deserter recruit across the cheek with his baton, which temporarily stunned the man and brought forth a bounteous swelling which would make his head and face ache for days.

Goyt pointed out that an untied bootlace was ample justification for such a punishment and he must quickly learn that his new military mentor was a man of high standards — which were reflected in his success on the battlefield.

As MPs they could openly sport any weapons. He had two M1 carbines in his armoury and a Browning automatic

THE CIVILIAN WAR ZONE

rifle or BAR, which were only issued very sparingly. This was a devastating piece of hand-held artillery that could demolish a building. He wondered if they dare carry it. It might be too obvious. He would think about it. They had practised with them at his secret training camp at Windsor, thirty miles from the city. He issued a riot shotgun to Seldom, took one of the carbines himself and, as a sop to his injury, issued the other to the US deserter, a disreputable overweight wretch called Kroeger.

His father's voice: "War isn't for pansies!" Now his: "Remember, our object, as always, is to confuse the enemy first, before destroying him. Your main targets will be other MPs. Unsuspecting MPs. But on no account are you to take action, except when I command. Discretion is as important as valour, if we are to continue and eventually conquer. We are too few to be wasteful with our own lives. Anyone who disobeys, will be shot."

His words didn't seem to faze them. They looked at him expectantly. It wasn't really an ideal situation. Unlike the British army and its deployment of colonial conscripts, he had not been able to really inspire his men with a sense of empire, king and country. When he lectured them on these matters, as he so frequently did, they reminded him of his own pathetic mother not taking in anything his father said to her, despite its prickly potency. They weren't really interested in imperial glory or patriotism, only brutality and money.

"There'll be a bonus and back pay for you. Fifty pounds for each MP you conquer, plus all the rations you can eat. And drink. And I'll let you keep your weapons this time. Something no other army does for its soldiers."

Their faces lit up. He wished that Kroeger had shaved though. Now he wouldn't be able to because of his swollen face. He felt like taking a cutthroat razor to him, but sometimes discipline had to take second place to combat expediency. Later, when he had more men at his disposal, he would brook no sloppiness. He would institute some of those admirably severe disciplinary measures his father treasured. His eyes burned into Kroeger's unshaven face, but the man didn't seem to notice. He was communing with hidden beings inside his bloated head,

· HOSTILITIES ·

which accounted for the constant slight movement of his lips and the involuntary humming noises he made all the time. But at least the man took orders without question, and took punishment without obvious resentment. He was like a robot. The make-up of a perfect soldier. Perhaps, if Crowbar MacPherson didn't shape up, he would make Kroeger his lieutenant. No doubt, in time, he would unquestioningly die for his CO. Goyt preferred soldiers who were prepared to die. That was what soldiers were for.

His father's voice: "One two three four! Kamalio, Kamalio *war*!" They all joined in, as they paraded: "Hold him down . . . the Swazi warrior, hold him down . . . the Swazi king. Hold him down . . . the Swazi warrior, hold him down . . . the Swazi king!"

As they hit the warpath, Goyt's confusion passed. Everything was crystal clear. Kill the enemy!

9

Joe watched Adam and the girl called Virginia leave their table, cross the main room out through the doors and up the deep pile burgundy carpeted stairs, past the paunchy middle-aged chucker-out. He knew where they were going. He knew this place well, having raided it several times for selling liquor without a licence and using the premises for purposes of prostitution. None of it seemed illegal any more. Or even immoral. What was immoral today was the war and all the killing. It put sex and sly grog in the shade. The laws hadn't changed, but the times had. He wasn't a vice cop now, he was on a homicide mission. More than that. A combat mission.

He was annoyed with Adam for deviating from his duty and danielling into the lion's den, for he had noticed the covert communication between the girl and the heavyset Aussie soldier on the way out. If he'd been on a vice mission then Adam would have unwittingly set himself up as a bunny prior to a raid, which would've suited Joe's methods admirably. But that's not what they were here for.

Nevertheless, Joe realised he had to protect his new partner and the busting of what purported to be a gingering racket was a useful spin-off.

He didn't follow them upstairs. He waited at his table, keeping his eyes on the Aussie soldier, without obviously neglecting his blonde companion. She was trying to come on with him. She was nearly as young as Cynthia but, although her face was fresh and unlined, it was also empty. His daughter's was alive, intelligent, searching, perceptive. He was proud of her. He wouldn't have been as proud if this girl had been his daughter. He knew she had soiled credentials, as did most of the women at this club. She could work her little arse off, but she wouldn't get him upstairs.

• HOSTILITIES •

Virginia led Adam into a nicely appointed bedroom and closed the door, without locking it. She removed the chenille bedspread and sat down. Adam couldn't keep his distance. He tried to kiss her, but she placed her hand over her lips.

"Business first, dear. Sorry but you understand."

Adam was stunned. An innocent in army issue clothing. Maybe the beer had lubricated his romantic illusions. But she looked so clean, regular featured, so pert, friendly, Anglo-Saxon. He had rashly assumed it was the normal attraction of the glamorous Yank for the trophy-hunting local girl. He was prepared to offer nylons, gum, gifts, anything, as a sign of goodwill or an exchange of favours. But cold hard cash . . .?

"I didn't know." Embarrassed. His anticipatory tumescence turned flaccid.

"Didn't know what, Adam?"

"That you were a . . . you know."

"Oh my! I thought you Yanks knew everything. Fancy that."

"Just that you look so different from the others."

"I am different. I didn't do this before the war. You might say it's my contribution to the war effort. On a fully professional basis. Now it costs five pounds for me and five pounds for the room. And another two if you want me to take everything off. The room money goes to the little man who owns this club. I have no say in that."

A true professional keeps her finger on the pulses and impulses of her client. Virginia worked hard to rearouse Adam's flagged interest. Business had temporarily taken the pleasure out of his business. She kept smiling sweetly, her ruby lips slightly parted and her tongue just showing, as her hands played a sensuous tattoo on his uniformed thigh, letting her pinky lightly brush against the bulbous phoenix, whose period of sulk had been extremely short-lived. Then she let her eyes tilt down from his chunky, slightly bronzed face with the slightly spread nose and full lips and slightly lost intelligent blue eyes, down to the slightly raised portion of trouser where her hand was resting.

• THE CIVILIAN WAR ZONE •

Adam, after months of storage, fruitless anticipation, endless exaggerated anecdotage from his compatriots and the biological imperatives of his age group, forgot about his mission, about Joe downstairs, about his dead friend Salome and his still sore shoulder wound, and succumbed to the oldest procession, along the sexual route. Twelve pounds worth.

She removed her dress, which left her with just bra, half-slip, lace panties and the usual austerity leg paint.

"How do you get that off? Turps?"

"Hot water."

Adam marvelled at the simple act of a woman reaching behind her back with one hand and unhooking her bra. It seemed to him to be the epitome of sensual expectation. A graceful and supple act of allegorical divestment. And when she turned to him, bra-less, with bullseye breasts joyously uplifted, seemingly winking at him, the cost and consequences became irrelevant.

Dragging his magnetised gaze downwards, Adam found she was wearing a suspender belt under her panties, which in view of the unavailability of nylons, seemed somewhat of an indulgence. Albeit a delicious one, as it promulgated the lingerie mystique that, to the inexperienced Adam, was almost as alluring as the female body itself.

Before removing her underwear, she tenderly eased Adam out of his uniform, folded it neatly and placed it on a chair by the door. That left only his cotton T-shirt, shorts and dog tags.

"Shall we synchronise our underwear?" Adam suggested, with a dry smile that hid his tentativeness.

"Yes darling," the unshopsoiled Virginia said, her lean brown legs creating a lovely vista of smooth flesh leading up to a dark undergrowth that camouflaged her deep ravine, where so many soldiers had recently fallen.

Her hands massaged his staff with tactical dexterity and encirclement, bringing him almost to the front line, then retreating, for it was just a diversionary tactic. He tried to explore her slit trench, but she cut him off at the pass, admonishingly.

"I'm ready for you darling, so no need to touch. I have

a little something for you to wear, dear."

Camouflage. No naked assault. Keep the weapon inside the scabbard.

She slipped on a sheath, despite his reluctance. A muzzle on his musket. Her bargaining power outstripped his. Then she guided him inside for the first wave frontal assault.

It was a roomy trench, big enough for a platoon, he felt. He was a mite disappointed at the lack of expected friction, at first. He had anticipated a tighter fit from such a slim, neat young ally.

"Welcome to headquarters, dear," she whispered as she primed his piece. Then she clamped her legs tightly around him and pitched back and forth, clutch and thrust, bringing him up to the firing position sooner than expected. It was a prolonged burst of rapid fire, a fusillade of shots, which brought him waves of pleasure all down his spine and into his flanks.

He didn't complain, although he had intended to hold his fire longer. But then he had seen the whites of her eyes.

Virginia had also misfired. She had also intended he hold his fire longer, for the benefit of the versatile pimp, part-time soldier, deserter and executioner Crowbar MacPherson, who had not quite finished rifling Adam's trousers on the chair by the door by the time he had shot his bolt. And when Adam, alerted to the presence of the swarthy ape-like soldier figure in the Aussie army fatigues and brown slouch hat, struggled out of Virginia's rather desperate clutches and turned his head, it was almost as big a surprise as Pearl Harbor.

It was the fastest unbuckling in the west, as Adam leapt off, all damp shiny flesh and spent energy, and flung himself at the crouched soldier. But he wasn't quick enough. MacPherson straightened up and slammed him on the chin with a haymaker, dropped and retrieved Adam's wallet and shot through the door before Adam stopped seeing stars and an exploding moon, flat on his naked back.

Virginia sat bolt upright in bed, her breasts bobbing with emotion and bit her lip, explanations at the ready.

Tunks returned to his office and stared blankly at the various

• THE CIVILIAN WAR ZONE •

reports on his desk. Words, words, words. He couldn't read them. His mind was in combat. Even the document on the Psychological Operations Program for Internal Defence, prepared by the cold and brilliant Captain Floyd P. Guyle of the Perimeter Security Platoon for the main command post in the Sydney area, was pushed to one side. This concerned Tunks' pet project — the establishment of a limited (in the first place), covert form of martial law. Oh, he definitely wanted to get to it. It was about plans for the distribution of leaflets and posters, plus loudspeaker addresses and radio broadcasts, to inform the civilian population of the rules and regulations pertaining to curfews, blackouts, travel restrictions and identification documents. All that was needed was an extension of the current crop of murders and unrest simmering between the US and Australian forces and resentful civilians. And then, when he did institute his martial law, the civil authorities would probably be grateful. But not yet. Such formulation of plans and paperwork was beyond his capabilities tonight. He wasn't aware that the unrest he'd been anticipating, and secretly hoping for, was on the brink of realisation.

Duty last. What a night! He'd finally shown that bitch who was in charge. If only his mother was still alive. There was the number one bitch! She'd died nagging him, putting him down, fondling his four sisters, favouring them, ignoring his younger brother, abusing *him*.

What a night! He had to find that bitch's father now. That uppity cop! He felt sure there was a conspiracy. Whilst he was giving it to her, he kept thinking it was all a set-up. He knew that cop didn't like him. Envy. A fuckin' detective sergeant! He was probably trying to use his bitch daughter to bring him down.

Well, he wouldn't succeed. That's why he hadn't chilled her yet. He wanted the old man to see what he'd done to his bitch daughter. He constructed an inflamed scenario in his head. The cop had really got to him. He hated insubordination. Most of all. He had spent half a lifetime gaining his rank — ignoring that he'd jumped four places after Pearl Harbor — and he deserved respect. The whole system was based on respect for authority. And he was authority.

• HOSTILITIES •

Anyone who didn't show it was a fuckin' commie. Like that crummy cop, fifty years old and still a sergeant. Yet he acted like a fuckin' major. It was getting to a crisis stage now. His life. Maybe it was the war. The pressure. Controlling thousands of snotty nosed draftees, in uniforms they had no respect for. He felt he was under attack the whole time.

Maybe he should forget everything, grab a bottle of rye and get drunk, all on his ownsome. It usually worked. He realised he wasn't in a fit state to do his job properly. It was after midnight anyway, but in this furlough city, that's when most of the action started. Sometimes the topsy-turvy hours got to him.

Shit! What was he going to do with that bitch? He'd left her there, cuffed to a tree in the rain, looking like she was catatonic. The truth was, when it came right down to it, he couldn't kill her. Didn't have the guts. He'd held the pistol at her head, squeezed the trigger, but kept the safety on. She'd gone into shock. He thought he'd leave her there to cool off. Give himself time to think. He wasn't a cold-blooded killer. Not like those fuckin' fiends who were rubbing out GIs. Certainly he had killed people, but in the line of duty. Or self-defence. He could kill her in self-defence. Give her a knife and let her come at him. Squeeze her carotid baroreceptors again. She was probably going to die anyway. She had to die. She would accuse him. It may not stick. But . . .? His paranoia, ebbing and flowing, rose again. Of course she'd have to die, after that cop had taken in his handywork. Accidental death. He'd have to think it through properly first.

A new report hit his eye. The British Empire Territorial Army. What sort of a nuthouse group was that? They'd rung the *Daily Telegraph* claiming responsibility for the GI killings. Christ! The editor wanted to print the story. Tunks made a note to contact the New South Wales government censor who, under the National Security Act, could censor anything likely to affect public morale or relations between the allied forces. Perhaps he would get a D Notice issued.

Maybe he could use his juice to get the post office to put a trace on the newspaper's line in case they called again. The British Empire Territorial Army? Who the hell was fighting who?

235

• THE CIVILIAN WAR ZONE •

He buzzed for Struther.

"See if you can find that Detective Sergeant Church! Get him over here! Or find out where he is. I have to see him. Tonight! Call his commissioner if necessary. Make it quick!"

Struther mumbled a response.

He'd have to get back there soon, to that hillside park, when he'd formulated his plan. The back of his neck was aching now. Tension perhaps. His life was full of tension. Always. Never any release. Not even tonight. He'd had to keep pumping it into her. Relentlessly. Feeling no real pleasure. No satisfaction. If it hadn't been for the rain, he'd still be there, driving at her, pumping her into the ground. The only release he could find was in dreams.

He buzzed Struther again.

"Did you find him yet?" Pause. "Well, where the hell is he?" Pause. "Well keep trying!" Flicked off the intercom. Shit! He wasn't going to be able to move his head in a minute. He buzzed Struther again. "Find out anything you can about the British Empire Territorial Army. If there is such a thing!" Off.

It was self-defence now. He'd have to silence her. Maybe he already had? He had pushed her into shock. He knew all about shock. She was in the second stage, when he'd left her. She had lost the ability to respond to stimulation. Her pulse was weak, her skin clammy, her pupils enlarged. Next stage unconsciousness. Unless she was treated, she may not come out of it. He'd wait another half-hour or so and then return to her. If she was well and truly in coma, he'd take her to a hospital, stating that, in the line of duty, he'd found her in a back street in the rain and that he was conducting the investigation into her . . . well, death. Because by that time they wouldn't be able to revive her.

What about her old man? Just how good a cop was he? Not in his class that was for sure. No doubt if he did get close to those killers, he'd become their next victim. He knew Church's MO. He was going to disguise himself as a US officer. That was his specialty. Disguise. A fuckin' actor! What sort of a cop was that? When they found his body it'd be just like the other poor dogfaces.

Right. He'd worked it out now. Shit! What a war he was having. The front line was here. He buzzed Struther again.

"What's takin' so long? Where the fuck is he?" Pause. "Well find him! They gave you a description of what he's wearing, didn't they? Find him! Send every available man and find him! Bring him in here! I don't care how they do it! Arrest him if necessary! I want him in here within the hour! There's only about ten joints he's likely to be at!" Off.

Fuck! The guy was posing as a major. Intercom again:

"Listen! Tell 'em to book him for impersonating an army officer! Yeah, I know he's on duty! But that doesn't have my approval! It's a felony!" Off.

What a night! His neck! He could barely turn his head. Struther buzzed:

"What do we do about that nigger, sir?"

"What nigger?"

"That corporal you had brought in. Black marketeering. Name of . . . Wells. "

"Oh sure. I'd forgotten about him. Ah . . ." Tunks considered the possibilities. He wanted to punish that black bastard for stepping out of line, but it didn't matter now. He wouldn't see that bitch again. And he didn't want this incidental aspect blown up. "Release him. Tell him it was mistaken identity. All those coons look alike anyhow. Get rid of him."

"You sure, sir?"

"Sure I'm sure! " Tunks snapped. "Are you questioning me, Struther?"

"No sir."

"Just do what I say. And if you haven't located that Church in half an hour, you'll be on fatigue duty yourself! For insubordination."

"Yes sir."

10

Brook was surprised when they released him from the temporary confinement facility in the rear of the headquarters building. It had all been a mistake, Struther reassured him, in a manner that suggested if he'd had his way, such a mistake would be perpetuated.

They obviously didn't expect him to take any official action about his detention, because he was a Negro, and Negroes did what they were told and knew that occasional injustice was all part of their burden.

At first all Brook could think about was being free. He didn't dare enquire about Cynthia. MP Headquarters was a nest of vipers. He casually asked where the colonel was and Struther's reaction indicated he didn't know. He wondered if the man had done anything to Cynthia. He demanded to see the colonel. Struther told him the colonel was very busy in his office and would see no one, least of all him, who had no right of access to such as the Provost Marshal.

Well, at least Brook knew that the colonel was there. And he wasn't going to take this lying down, like some Uncle Tom nigra. There was no point in appealing to his own CO, whose southern deprecation of his worth was an insurmountable barrier. But he could go to the Judge Advocate General's Department and swear out a complaint against Tunks and the MPs. And if not them, he would go to the Adjutant General's Department. But first he had to see if he could find Cynthia.

He took a taxi to Bondi, overtipped the grateful driver and knocked on the Church's door.

Winnie, with a wrap over her nightie, rubbed the sleep out of her eyes and answered the door. When she saw who it was she nearly collapsed.

• HOSTILITIES •

"Mrs Church, I'm sorry to bother you at this late hour. Is your husband in?"

"My husband?" Why did he want her husband? "No. He's out. On an assignment. Police officers work strange hours you know." She didn't really need to explain this. "Is something wrong?"

Something was wrong all right. She didn't want this man to keep intruding into their lives. Why doesn't he go away? Her mind screamed. But outwardly she retained a civilised facade.

"Well, I'm not sure, Mrs Church. May I come inside?" He looked around, as if afraid of eavesdropping neighbours.

Winnie was torn in two. She hated the idea of him coming inside again, and yet it was better that he wasn't seen on her doorstep. So she let him in.

"I suppose you know the time, young man?"

"Yes I do, ma'am, and I'm truly sorry. But well, I don't suppose Cynthia's at home?" Hopefully.

Winnie stopped in the hallway. She had been going to lead him into the living room. Well that was it! The same old thing. He was here lusting after her lovely daughter. She wished Joe were home.

"Why do you want to know?" It was a stupid question, but she really didn't want to tell him anything. She didn't want him to know she was home at this hour, entirely on her own. She also feared for her daughter. She assumed that Cynthia had escaped from his clutches and he was now pursuing her. Perhaps even terrorising her.

She hated the war. If it weren't for the war, none of this nightmare would be happening. Cynthia would probably be married to some nice local boy, setting up a home, having a child. She'd always prayed Cynthia wouldn't marry a policeman. But now, this dark-skinned American seemed a much worse fate. But what could she do?

"I'm sure she doesn't want to see you now." Surely this would make him go away.

It didn't.

"Then she is here! Thank God!" Wells practically beamed.

Winnie couldn't understand this at all. What did he mean?

Thank God? What was he going to do now? Push her aside and rush for Cynthia's bedroom? And what would he do when he found she wasn't there at all? Better play it all the way.

"She's asleep."

"Oh." Disappointed. Obviously he did want to see her. "Maybe I'll just wait around here till she wakes up. If that's alright with you." He smiled at Winnie, trying to melt her down. He sensed her fear.

"No, I don't really think that's a good idea. I mean, it's very late. She probably won't wake up till morning."

Wells looked worried now. He rubbed his shiny forehead, indecisively. "Well, look. Could I just speak to her for a moment? If that's alright."

Winnie totally distrusted his politeness. He wasn't supposed to be so well mannered. She knew it was a trick to disarm her, so he could get into Cynthia's bedroom. She remained firm.

"I'm sorry Mr er . . . corporal."

"Call me Brook, ma'am. Please."

She had no intention of calling him Brook. So she called him nothing. "Really I don't think it's a good thing to wake her up. In fact I don't think it's a good idea for you to come here at all. I'm sorry to say this, but we do have certain conventions in this country that may seem strange to you. I think you'd best go now. I'll tell her you called in the morning, when she wakes up." Winnie circled warily around him, heading for the front door, hoping he'd follow. When he didn't, she felt she'd made a fatal mistake. No doubt he'd take this opportunity to dash down the hall into Cynthia's room. But he just stood there. Unsure of himself. And her.

"You really don't understand, ma'am. I thought she was in trouble. I just came here to find out if, first of all, she was home and if she was okay. She is okay, isn't she?"

Winnie frowned. "Okay? What do you mean?"

"Well, I mean . . . she's not hurt?" Brook really wasn't sure how much he should tell this woman, who struck him as a little odd and very nervy.

"I don't understand. Has she been in some kind of trouble?"

• HOSTILITIES •

"Well, that's what I want to ask her, ma'am."

"Why do you want to ask her that? You are thoroughly confusing me, ah corporal."

"She didn't say anything to you when she came home?"

"No." What was he talking about? Now Winnie's fears were heightened. "I haven't spoken to her." Winnie's first truthful statement.

Wells wasn't sure why they were both getting so upset. "Well, I guess if she's home asleep, there's nothing to worry about. Everything must be okay. I'm sorry to get you out of bed at this hour." He moved to the front door.

Winnie just stood there, watching him. Ambivalently. "Maybe you'll tell her I called, when she wakes up? Say that I'll see her again soon. And I apologise for leaving her so abruptly last night. But it wasn't my fault. Can you tell her that please?"

Brook opened the door, pulled his jacket up against the rain and trotted up the path to the front gate.

He was on the pavement and starting to head towards Campbell Parade when he heard her voice calling to him.

"Corporal Wells!" He stopped. It was the first time she'd called him that without a degree of hesitation. It wasn't quite Brook, but it was an improvement. He turned back and the rain drenched his face, fanned by a wind from the south-west.

Winnie was standing at the open front door, almost wringing her hands in distress.

"I'm sorry. Really I am. I think maybe . . . well, is she in trouble? Tell me!" Her voice was shrill. All her imaginary concerns were now being replaced by genuine ones.

Wells stopped at the front gate. "Why don't you ask her?"

Winnie's voice broke. "Please." She beckoned to him. He strode up to the front door. The only sounds were the rain beating down and the distant roar of the surf. "I can't. I'm sorry. She's not home. I haven't seen her since yesterday morning. I'm sorry. I thought . . . ?" She was near tears now.

Brook shook his head and swore under his breath. He stared at Winnie with disbelief, his heart pounding and the skin on the back of his neck crawling.

• THE CIVILIAN WAR ZONE •

Cynthia, saturated with rain, disgust and pain, drifting between insensibility, violent shivering, hallucination and plain terror, lay on her back in Cooper Park, shackled to the tree trunk with not even a marsupial for company. During her increasingly rare lucid moments, she wondered when the dreaded beast was going to return and stick a knife in her. Her own mind told her he couldn't afford to leave her alive. When he had held the pistol to her head and pulled the trigger, just after he withdrew his other fruitless weapon, leaving an agonising burning sensation behind, she thought her number was up. In terms of shock and terror, it almost was. Perhaps if she'd been older and in poorer health, she would have had a fatal cardiovascular reaction, but much to her surprise, when the gun didn't go off, despite a staccato heartbeat and sprinting pulse rate and, no doubt, elevated blood pressure, she survived.

Because she had closed her eyes when she felt the gun at her temple, she didn't know he had gone until she dared open them again, several minutes later. She hadn't heard his departing footsteps. There was only the rain now, which washed away her tears and some of the blood from her face.

No part of her body was unaffected. She felt that if she ever went free, she would be crippled, unable to bend, sit up, walk, dance. Her shoulders ached from the unnatural posture forced upon her by the cuffs which kept her wrists embracing the tree trunk, behind her head. But despite everything, her head kept thudding thoughts of escape and salvation. But how?

In fact it was the desire to somehow get free, before he returned, which kept the hallucinations and coma at bay. She felt that if she let herself drift into a coma she would never wake up. Life was dependent on consciousness. She utilised the pain to keep her awake. She began to count the throbs and waves of agony, totalling them up in her mind, almost marvelling at the fact that in between every agonised beat there was a fraction of a second of sublimity. There was no such thing as constant pain. Just perpetually intermittent pain, which she could live with. For a while.

11

Tunks was ready to explode. Joe Church was proving elusive. He'd been seen, as Major Mitchell, by several MPs, but none had yet approached him. Tunks was now torn between pursuing him himself or returning to his helpless harrier in the park. Then there were also the nagging official duties pressing in on him. But his inability to choose what to do kept him boilingly ineffectual.

Struther buzzed. "What is it?"

"Lieutenant Ralph wants to see you, sir." Struther's voice was guarded but his sub-text was spilling over. Ralph was the officer in charge of the Negro Military Police platoon. Tunks wanted nothing to do with him.

"Tell him I'm tied up. You handle it."

"He's very insistent, sir. He has Corporal Wells with him."

"Who the hell's Corporal Wells?" Tunks screamed into the intercom.

"He's the corporal you told us to arrest for black marketeering. You know the one. Sir."

"Sonofabitch! What do they want?"

"They want to see you, colonel! I think the lieutenant wants to lodge a formal complaint."

Tunks was about to continue to fob them off, but didn't. He needed a fight right now. A conflict with a couple of uppity niggers was just what he needed. Balm to his tortured soul. "Send 'em in!" He'd court martial both of them. "And come in here with 'em!"

Struther hesitated. "I'm still chasing up that Church for you, colonel."

"Put someone else on it and get in here!" Tunks sat down on his swivel chair, placed his pistol on the desk, then his feet next to it. His balls ached. Like always. That slut! Why couldn't he come? He had to see about that one day. Some sex psychologist. Some civilian shrink. He didn't know if it was psychological or physical. Maybe that bitch would be dead by now, with a bit of luck. He should get back there soon.

Sherbrook Wells and Lieutenant Ralph, who was a slim six footer with a superior attitude that tended to inflame his white colleagues, entered and stood to attention in front of the colonel's desk. Struther followed them in and parked himself near the door, in an observer capacity. Tunks remained seated, with his feet on the desk, refusing to show any respect for his coloured visitors.

"I'll give you two minutes, lieutenant. That's all. It's late as hell and a busy night."

Lieutenant Ralph prickled. His nostrils flared, but he maintained the required respectful attitude towards a superior officer.

"I'd like to know why you issued an order to arrest and detain Corporal Wells, colonel."

Tunks looked up at him with a sneer. "Would you now? And what gives you the right or the rank to come in here and question the actions of your commanding officer? Got a little mutiny on your mind, have you lieutenant?"

Ralph ignored that last jibe. "First of all, colonel, as I'm sure you're aware, it has been decreed that my platoon has the responsibility for disciplining coloured soldiers. Part of the segregation regulations. Furthermore, I think that in the case of Corporal Wells here an injustice has been done."

Tunks smiled. Like an iceberg with teeth. "That's quite an assessment of the organisation and functions of this here Provost Marshal section of this divisional Military Police company, lieutenant. Very impressive. Maybe you ought to be reassigned to the Combat Developments Command of the Military Police Agency back in the States. Or maybe we can arrange to have you reassigned to the stockade, for a year or two. Whatta you say? Lieutenant?"

Ralph kept his mouth shut, but sweat broke out on his forehead and he felt his pulses ticking like a time bomb. But he knew that Tunks was trying to undermine him so he continued to exercise self-control.

· HOSTILITIES ·

"What you choose to ignore, lieutenant, is that the Provost Marshal has control over all platoons, no matter what the individual functions of those platoons are. Next time you peruse the regulations, don't be so selective. Or maybe it's just your inferior southern education that gives you such a one-eyed view. Tell me, where'd you get your commission, lieutenant? Down on a watermelon farm?"

Inside, Ralph's ire subsided. The colonel was just like all the other bigots. No point in increasing the antipathy that was already there. He knew it was impossible to win on this man's level. Better to stick to the real issue.

"It's the evident injustice perpetrated upon Corporal Wells that mainly concerns me, colonel."

Tunks swung his legs down and stood up, timing his movement for ultimate dramatic advantage. "Injustice? Is that your baby? Injustice?" He put his hands on the desk and leant forward. "Let me tell you about injustice, lieutenant. The Japs are unjust! Did you know that? The war is unjust! My grandmother was unjust! Hitler's unjust! The whole fuckin' world is unjust, lieutenant!" Tunks crowned his speech by slamming his fist on the desktop. "God is unjust! Don't come in here and talk to me about injustice, lieutenant! You're supposed to be a Military Policeman not a fuckin' jury! Law and order, discipline and military regulations! That's your concern! Not injustice!" Tunks sat down, put his feet back on the desk and looked at the flag, away from his visitors. Pause for refreshment before round two.

Lieutenant Ralph kept his counsel and his dignity. "Why was he arrested, sir?"

Sergeant Struther piped up from the rear. "I told the lieutenant it was a case of mistaken identity, sir."

Tunks took a cigarette from the box on his desk and lit it. He didn't offer one to the others. He deliberately held a loaded silence during the tobacco ritual. He could have capitalised on Struther's lead and probably assuaged Ralph and Wells, but he really didn't feel like it. He didn't believe in apologies, excuses, compromise, consensus or democracy. He believed in the correct exercise of authority and preferred pulling rank to admitting error.

• THE CIVILIAN WAR ZONE •

"He's free now, isn't he? So what are you crying for? Do you think a few hours in the cooler is hardship? This is the army, lieutenant! Our function is to kill and be killed. It's none of your concern why he was arrested. If he don't like being free, I'll arrest him again! And your two minutes is up."

Tunks swivelled around in his chair until his back was towards them, which was an incontrovertible sign of dismissal. Ralph held his ground and Wells felt proud of his lieutenant. This was a man worth serving. "That's not all, colonel. Corporal Wells wants to know what you did with the lady he was in company with, when you had him arrested."

Tunks swivelled slowly round again, like an artillery piece taking aim. His eyes were red-rimmed and the colour had drained from his face, making his daylong whiskers stand out. And there was an ominous twitching near his eyes that forewarned a manquake. His hand automatically grasped the pistol on his desk and fingered the safety catch. His previous insidious air of sarcasm had been replaced by unrepressed anger.

"Get out of here, lieutenant! Now! All of you! Or your commission'll be withdrawn forthwith! At a court martial!"

Still Ralph and Wells didn't budge, although Struther half turned towards the door. Ralph reasoned that the last thing Tunks would want would be a court martial which might uncover his alleged involvement with this girl. Provided, of course, that Wells' allegations had some substance.

"Is that all you have to say on this matter, colonel?"

Tunks stood up, visibly shaking with anger. "Damn right that's all I have to say! And that's all you have to say too! Now, get out of this office or I'll have your black asses in the stockade so quick you won't have time to think shit! Now get outa here!"

The beauty of military hierarchy was that rank meant autocracy. The chain of command was inviolable. Explanations to subordinates were not required. Discipline, correction, punishment was always from above. No rank was answerable to a lesser rank. There were no checks and balances within the military machine. Lieutenant Ralph and Corporal Wells had made a cardinal error. If they had wanted something done

HOSTILITIES

about Tunks, they should have gone to a general in the Adjutant General's Department or perhaps to MacArthur himself or his Chief of Staff. Tunks was the military government and you can't oppose a military government, except by appealing to God. On the other hand, they had caused Tunks to lose his cool and this somewhat diminished his authority. But it was a tiny victory and not the one they sought. Furthermore they had now revealed their hand and Tunks could move to cover his tracks, if he felt in any way threatened.

Struther whisked them out of the colonel's lair, for their own protection, and his. Ralph knew when he was licked. He apologised to Wells but said he could do no more. Unless Wells came up with some unassailable evidence, which could be placed before the highest command through the Judge Advocate General, he'd do better to forget all about this colonel and the civilian girl.

Brook decided that, as usual, his own resources were the only ones he could rely on. He vowed to hover around, shadow the colonel night and day, wait for him to slip up, perhaps even lead him back to Cynthia, for he was now sure in his own mind that Tunks had somehow spirited her away, or, God forbid, even killed her. Yet, at this stage, it was all based on suspicion. Perhaps, when he eventually located her father he would have a useful ally. But for the moment he too seemed to be incommunicado. Police headquarters only stated that Detective Sergeant Church was out on a case and no information was available as to his whereabouts. How could he lick Goliath without even a slingshot?

Tunks now had his priorities worked out. Those insubordinate blacks had done it for him. He stormed out of his office. He was going back to Cynthia, to finish the job. He left orders that when Church fronted, he should remain there until he returned. "Tell him I said his assignment has been changed. We have a positive lead on the case. And that he's to do nothing until I return and rebrief him," he told Struther.

Tunks had just reached his staff car when Struther and two privates caught up with him.

"Trouble up at Kings Cross, sir! I thought you ought

• THE CIVILIAN WAR ZONE •

to know. It sounds like a riot!"

Tunks kicked the wheel of his car and dented his boot. Nothing was working out right.

12

When Crowbar MacPherson dropped Adam and stole his wallet, it set off a chain of events beyond all reckoning.

Joe had been alerted when he saw the big Aussie digger leave the table he had formerly occupied with the new girl in Adam's life. Now he was at the foot of the Roosevelt stairs, just as Crowbar came hurtling down as if he'd just been goosed by a red-hot poker.

He tried to bar the big ape's way, suspecting that this was a felonious flight. Crowbar shouldered Joe aside with all the strength and finesse of a Panzerkampfwagen tank. Joe spun around before crashing into the wall. Then, after a moment in which to assure himself that all his bones were intact and to extend sympathy to his doubtful back, he set off after Crowbar, who had taken the main exit into the street.

Not far behind, taking the stairs three at a time, was Adam, who had managed to put on his shorts and beige pink trousers and, for decorous purposes, his garrison cap. Nothing else, not even shoes. He was not going to take this lying down, even though he had been.

Once Crowbar MacPherson had turned the corner from Orwell Street into Macleay Street, the main traffic artery with a pavement teaming with servicemen and their women, as well as with women who wanted to be with servicemen but weren't, he stopped to inspect the contents of Adam's wallet, letting greed get the better of survival.

Joe saw him first, and behind him he heard Adam yelling: "Stop that guy! That big ape stole my wallet!"

When Joe reached Crowbar, who was standing in the gloom of a sandbagged shop doorway, he snatched the wallet out of his hand and Adam's money fluttered to the pavement. Crowbar, enraged, came at Joe with a marine combat knife

THE CIVILIAN WAR ZONE

held out in front, jabready. Joe backed away, then circled, reluctant to draw his .38 automatic from his holster which was hidden by his officer's jacket. He figured that a drawn gun would panic the passers-by.

Nearby, a group of three Aussie soldiers watched the confrontation between the Aussie with the knife and the supposed Yank with the fists. They didn't intervene, as the odds seemed to be with the Aussie. But Joe's weight and age were no handicap. He feinted with his left and kicked out like a brumby, catching Crowbar on the ulnar nerve at the elbow, sometimes called the funny bone. Crowbar's knife shot up in the air, descending blade down and lodging in his musclebound shoulder.

Crowbar howled like a wounded digger, which he was, and his blood spurted out like a geyser. The Aussie spectators, already smarting from an earlier rejection in the street by three Aussie girls with Yankee stars in their eyes, howled in nationalistic sympathy and took sides. Against Joe, the Yank major.

Joe's nearest ally was Adam, although a number of Americans with girls in tow had stopped to appraise the situation. Adam, bare footed and chested, was only yards away when two US MPs materialised from their watchful post outside Reflections. The sight of a GI wearing half a uniform, probably but not necessarily drunk, was too much for them. The first one, Private Felton, raised his white baton, hit first and didn't ask questions afterwards. It wasn't clear if he recognised Adam from their earlier meeting outside Reflections, although his humiliation at Joe's hand had probably helped make him feel somewhat insecure.

For the second time in five minutes Adam was knocked off his feet. This time he also cannoned into and bounced off a sandbagged shop window and fell flat on his front, seeing red before seeing black. Out cold.

Another nearby Aussie digger with drunken bloodshot eyes and a bullneck, hated all MPs, including his own, even more than he hated the Yankee imperialists who had taken over his women whilst purporting to save his country. He stepped in and swung at Felton's companion MP with a rock-like fist, connecting with the side of his head causing a stereophonic thunderclap in his middle ear, which left him stunned but still standing. Felton, flushed and vibrating from his first batonic success, went to his partner's aid, sensed a home run, and swung again, batting a hundred, transporting the drunken Aussie into nightmare land.

Meanwhile Joe was attempting to fight off the three beer-and-whisky-soured Aussie soldiers whose collective strength was more effective than their individual aims. Not appreciating the odds, two US sailors went to their army compatriot's aid with drawn knives, ignoring the fact he was an officer and didn't deserve their support. Joe was grateful for the rescue but was becoming confused about which side he was supposed to be on. Law and order perhaps, but that seemed inappropriate right now. Suddenly a relatively simple pursuit had metamorphosed into a fight to the death, and he wasn't sure why, not having the time at this moment to appreciate that the real causes were deep rooted and long simmering and had needed only to be triggered by booze plus incident.

When two of the sailors dug their knives into the ribs of two of the Aussie soldiers, Joe felt sick. He felt even sicker when Crowbar MacPherson returned to the fray, having dislodged his knife from his shoulder and, although weak from loss of blood, slashed at Joe's chest. Joe parried with his arms and felt a slash along his left forearm, which immediately turned the sleeve of his forest-green jacket woodland brown. Two more MPs arrived and clubbed at Crowbar, who seemed to have a head as hard as a bowling ball. Joe took the opportunity to look for Adam's fallen money, but it was being tattered and torn beneath the scuffling feet, except for some which had been inadvertently kicked into the gutter away from the cover of the shop awnings.

Two SPs appeared, swinging their navy clubs at the sailors. To each his own. One of the sailors was too quick and knifed one of the SPs. The other SP swung his baton like a drum major and split the ears of the sailors and one of the Aussies, who accidentally put his head in the way. He ran off down the dark and narrow Orwell Street looking for allies. All he found, however, were a number of US servicemen with open

• THE CIVILIAN WAR ZONE •

flies, taking advantage of the dark with ultra-willing girls with skirts high and panties low, standing up in shuttered doorways. If nothing else it was a testament to their youth, vigour, impatience and remarkably supple spines. To say nothing of their powers of concentration seeing that only yards away round the corner a street battle royal was in progress.

Back round the corner a number of Aussie soldiers ran across Macleay Street into a US canteen, scrambled over the bar and grabbed handfuls of beer bottles and much coveted cut-price American cigarettes. The few drinking US servicemen present didn't attempt to stop them at first. They waited until they had drained their glasses then they streamed out of the canteen, some with combat knives drawn, and chased the Aussies who had depleted their recreational rations.

Then the first platoon of US reinforcement MPs arrived, three jeeploads of them, including a population control squad armed with riot shotguns and tear gas grenades. They started to whale into all and sundry with their clubs, Aussies and Yanks alike, even some civilians.

After a brief snooze on the hard pavement, Adam came to amidst a scrum of scuffling olive drab and khaki legs. He decided to stay on the ground for a while, feigning oblivion until he saw a path to safety.

Joe, with throbbing left arm beneath his shirt sleeve, which he'd managed to wind tight, was still reluctant to draw his pistol, not wishing to escalate the level of violence. Instead he bent down and retrieved a fallen MP baton and hurled it at Crowbar, aiming for the now seeping wound in his shoulder. It connected, and another rich red fountain started to gush, partially in Crowbar's eyes, allowing Joe to finish him off with a blow to the back of his neck that journeyed down his spine and introduced him to temporary paralysis.

From somewhere deep within Cynthia's tortured soul there was a glimmer of undying determination, a resolve never to give in. She had to get free before the beast returned to finish her off or before the enforced immobility, her injuries and the elements did.

Between her wrist and the steel manacles there was a

quarter-inch of space. A quarter-inch of space. The colonel had not pressed the bands to their full enclose. It was, she felt, a quarter-inch of hope. Her only hope, however dim. She opened her eyes and was nearly blinded by the rain cascading down not only from the sky but in accumulated drops from the branches of her prison tree. If only she could turn over onto her stomach, or even her side, it would not be as bad, but there was no way.

She tugged her left arm to the limit until the steel cuff bit into her wrist and drew blood, pressing down against the articular cartilage in her wrist joint, which sent a bolt of pain right up her arm and into her neck and shoulder. She also managed to tear the epidermous and fibrous tissue of her wrist and blood poured down her arm, mixing with the rain and seeping into the earth. Now the tearing in her vulva was displaced by the pain in her wrist and she wondered, in her agonised mind, just how far she could pull her arm without fracturing the joint. And then she wondered whether it was better to fracture the joint or even lose her whole hand than lie around until she died from exposure or execution.

She marvelled at her pain threshold. The pain in her wrist and arm came and went, throbbing constantly but sending its messages to the brain in waves. She started to try and breathe in the same waves. Violent deep breaths, in and out, synchronising with the pain waves. In on the pain, out on the lull. At times the rain threatened to choke her, yet she had to keep her mouth open to expel as much oxygen as she could with each wave. She kept her eyes clamped shut, seeing all she needed to see in her imagination, which summoned up motivating images of warmth and comfort: the beach on a summer's day, her warm bed, a wonderful meal and soothing Benny Goodman music and the company of that sympathetic, loving soldier with the name like an English town.

She felt her chest heaving with the exertion and eventually her whole body arched with each inhalation. And she pulled, sickeningly, straining her biceps and deltoids, adding excruciating tension to the trapezius muscles in the back of her neck. The steel band ripped all the skin and fibrous tissue from her wrist joint, scraped the bone and lodged in the metacarpus of her hand, and it seemed that that was as far as it could possibly go.

Possibly? Impossibly? Thus far and no further. Give up. Die. Can't be done. Words, just words. She wasn't thinking words any longer. Nor even logic. There was no logic in this situation. There was only death or survival. States of being. Emotions. Guts. Logic said give in. That was no logic. That was death. Life was pain. Pain was life. The pain became a means of her survival, a means of life. Death was numbness. She wanted pain.

She arched herself again and tugged with every muscle, nerve and fibre screaming, her mind blacking out the nice visions, slotting in newsreels of dive bombers, eruptions, torn limbs, flames, destruction, death waves rolling back life but not extinguishing it, blackness and red, vivid shapes, livid faces, contortions of agony shutting out comfort, substituting searing heat for shivering cold, until the steel moved, crunching the tendon, flexor muscle and knucklebone of the thumb.

Now the waves of pain transformed into fire, constant unrelieved agony all the way up her arm, into her neck and brain, and she screamed non-stop, a siren of torment, feeling that the waves of giddiness were going to black her out and sabotage the whole escape operation. An operation without anaesthetic. But she held on by a very thin thread and the willpower of a goddess.

Just a little further and all her knuckles would crack. She could feel them splitting already, an indefatigable squeeze. Crunching like biscuit. The shock waves engulfed her as the bones fractured. But she utilised the strength of her entire body against the brittleness of all the bones in her hand. The body won.

Her hand, bloodied and pulped, snapped out of the steel ring. It thudded against the rocky ground, compounding the agony, sending a jarring message that overwhelmed everything before it.

Then she just lay there, gasping, praying for relief, engulfed in reality, no longer able to summon up imaginary images, the sky rolling around in waves of fluid grey and she felt a vice enclosing her head and numbing her brain. She tried to

· HOSTILITIES ·

keep her eyes open, despite the blurring rain, but now the vice was unstoppable and there were whirlpools washing over her, until the total night descended on her and she felt no more.

13

The point at which a brawl turns into insurgency or insurgency turns into a riot is seldom clear. But by 2 a.m. the streets of Potts Point, which was usually referred to as Kings Cross, appeared to be in stage three. And if it wasn't exactly a riot, it was at least a melee en masse, and the nearest thing to warfare that this part of the world was to directly experience.

Unfortunately for all concerned, the battlelines were somewhat blurred. Not only by the rain and the brownout, but by the boozed state of most of the participants and by their varying intentions. Certainly, most of the Aussie soldiers in the vicinity allowed their latent resentment and jealousy of all the Yanks to bubble over, and that meant obvious retaliation. Then there were the two sets of MPs, and they became targets from all sides. Throw in some civilians, most of whom had a love/hate regard for the American visitors, and the person nearest to each aggressive soul automatically became a target for his fists, feet, bottle, knife, club and eventually, firearm.

There was, for those disinclined to become involved hand-to-hand, plenty of cover down adjoining side streets and in some restaurants and nightspots, but it seemed, at first, that most males in the area, both in and out of uniform, were only too happy to join in. Perhaps too, it might have run a short sharp bloody course, dying away as the significance of personal injury and even death set in. But the official peacekeepers descended and, almost without trying, escalated the conflict and set it on target for a prolonged riot of attrition.

A jabberwocky of jeeps bounced up Macleay Street from the direction of the city via the tenemented depths of Woolloomooloo and disgorged a detachment of US MP reinforcements headed by the Provost Marshal himself, the

· HOSTILITIES ·

unrequited Colonel Tunks, armed with an M1 carbine and looking forward to finally being able to discharge his load. He was supported by platoon leader Captain Harris and the ubiquitous Master Sergeant Struther who was happily sporting a riot shotgun and a tear gas grenade launcher.

Tunks set up static checkpoints at the lower end of Macleay Street where the road curved down towards Woolloomooloo and the docks area, and at the intersection of Darlinghurst Road and William Street, which was the main entrance to the Kings Cross bohemian night-life area. They immediately increased street tension by carrying out non-selective cordon and search operations, personnel identification procedures and traffic control. Then Tunks instituted a command post halfway between the two checkpoints, at the right-angle of the two main Kings Cross arteries — Darlinghurst Road and Macleay Street — which threatened to become the meat in the sandwich of marauding Aussie and American battlers. Tunks sent juntas of MPs down the street in both directions, armed with spotlights, with orders to arrest everyone in sight, which was basically an unlawful command, as their jurisdiction was restricted to US personnel. Thus he immediately succeeded in making his men the common enemy. And when one panic-stricken MP private discharged his riot shotgun into a mixed mob of khaki and victory-suited Australian soldiers and civilians respectively, the white MP brassard became as despised as General Tojo. One Aussie soldier, nearest to the blast, lost both his eyes and had his face tattooed with pellets as numerous as freckles, though twice as deep. Others found themselves peppered with lead hickeys which stung like bees and threatened tetanus.

Some Aussie soldiers removed their belts and tried to lash MPs with them. But they were no match for the long white clubs. The GIs in the street varied their assaults and counterattacks between the increasingly angry Aussies and their own MPs, holding their own mainly through numbers not weaponry.

Tunks used his organic radio to request Divisional Headquarters to confine all US personnel to barracks until further notice, which didn't take stock of the fact that many GIs on

• THE CIVILIAN WAR ZONE •

leave in Sydney had rented flats or were billeted temporarily in hotel rooms or even private homes. So the flow into the riot area could not be fully stemmed. The Australian MPs issued no such request to Victoria Barracks, the showground or Lindfield Barracks, or for that matter to the crypt in St James Church, which was also billeting many in-transit troops in the city. They seemed to be ready to allow a build-up of Australian troops in the area, hoping for numerical superiority for the local boys. The first civilian police to arrive held back, unsure of who the culpable aggressors were and also feeling outnumbered and outarmed. They seemed prepared to let the US MPs bear the brunt.

Before long some Australian reinforcements arrived in response to news of an "all-in gutzer with the Yanks up at the Cross" on the grapevine. They had been able to leave Victoria Barracks, just half a mile south, armed with bayonets and a few grenades, whilst their officers turned a blind eye.

Tunks smelt bear. He sensed it had only just begun and before long all facilities would be stretched to the limit. He radioed Australian Army HQ Sydney Military District and requested a suitable area for a handy detainee detention point. They offered the showground.

Meanwhile Joe, trying to focus on his own patch of altercation, collected Adam's wallet, which had triggered the whole shebang, and tried to revive Adam, whose pavement bed was being thoroughly trampled on. Then, fully realising they were stranded in an unjust, ill-timed, unjustifiable war, in which they had no part to play, Joe looked for a way out. But all obvious side streets now seemed to contain MP checkpoints manned by over-conscientious "sadistic sheriffs" cordoning, searching, arresting and clubbing down, not necessarily in that order, everyone trying to enter or leave the vicinity. In fact clubbing seemed to be taking precedence over arrest, as the required transport to the temporary detainee detention point had not yet arrived. There were some ambulances, however, and the MPs obligingly made the ambulance drivers feel wanted.

Adam was not yet in good enough condition to make a run for it, so Joe carefully eased him over to the shelter of a sandbagged doorway to give him time to recover, whilst

258

• HOSTILITIES •

he further assessed their escape chances. He also removed his pistol from its holster, feeling no longer reluctant to use it, as the combatants became more desperate and consequently more dangerous.

The increasingly heavy rain was both a salve and a shield. It blurred aims, upset balance, thwarted grips and even helped soothe bumps and bruises, washed bloody noses, to some extent refreshed, and made the street shine and reflect. God's own lubrication for the battle weary.

Tunks, most of all, was refreshed. More than that. Reinvigorated. This was his moment of destiny. Wellington at Waterloo. Surveying the scene from his command post, megaphoning orders, radioing instructions, issuing command decrees, he decided that this was an ideal opportunity to institute his long-desired, unique brand of virtually ad hoc martial law.

He declared, in inspired tones, that henceforth his command post would be referred to as his TOC (Tactical Operations Centre) and he requested, no demanded, an armoured unit from Divisional Headquarters to protect his TOC. It wasn't clear how long it would take Divisional Headquarters to respond. He issued instructions to search and detain everybody in and around the entire Kings Cross area; ordered all weapons, ammunition, radios and cameras to be confiscated, including those of the press; ordered the breaking-up of any assembly of more than three persons; decreed that all detainees, whether military or civilian, be interred at the same detainee point and consequently fingerprinted, photographed and interrogated; requested military regulations to be broadcast by all the local commercial radio stations; authorised mobile and static checkpoints and roadblocks around the entire district; and announced that a 9 p.m. curfew of the Kings Cross area should be established forthwith. Then he topped it all by declaring that the normal brownout regulations in the inner city, including Kings Cross, should be immediately replaced by a total blackout.

He omitted to seek the approval of the Australian army or civilian authorities, which was established procedure, in the heat of the moment choosing to ignore anything remotely resembling established procedure. It didn't even concern him whether the full thrust of his decrees would be carried out

THE CIVILIAN WAR ZONE

or would result in a backlash. He was having a ball. This was *his* war, *his* command post, *his* jurisdiction. There was no time for negotiations. The battlelines were now clear. MPs versus the rest.

Right now there was not even time to consider the fate of the young lady he had left to rot in Cooper Park.

How long had it been? A matter of hours since she had been free, untrammelled, normal. Now just sitting up was a victory, although it made the world spin and the waves of nausea mitigated her triumph. She waited for them to pass before making the next advance. They didn't. She'd never felt so sick. It made gastroenteritis seem like a tonic. And her hand was a monstrosity. It was swelling up before her eyes and throbbing like a dredge.

Next step — standing up. She used a branch of the tree to pull herself up. The terrible tree. Her prison tree. Not easy. Her legs were not strong enough to support her. She toppled over. Tried not to use her monstrous hand as a cushion. Jarred her spine. Slowly this time. Used her good right hand, pulled herself up. Everything ached, something inside tore. God! A mess! Such a mess! Almost crippled. Everything ached so much, the slightest movement was an ordeal. But she was standing. Oh glory! Standing. Not without support. The blessed tree. But walking? That was something else. Her head felt light, she kept seeing odd shapes and lights pass before her eyes, and there was a roaring in her ears. Sweet delirium. And the shivers. Not just cold from the wet, but shivers deep from inside. Shaking with some sort of palsy. Perhaps, in shock.

She had to leave this place. Now. Not just the prison tree, the park. She moved forward, slowly, painstakingly, one step at a time, unsupported. The ground sloped down. She was high up, well above street level, above a creek whose waters were swollen and spilling down.

Downhill was better than uphill, but the route was rocky, wet, precarious. There must be some steps somewhere. Somewhere. Better to move sideways till she came to them. But sideways was slippery. She tripped on a rock and fell. Sideways, twisting her body away from her left to protect that hand. The main impact was thus on her right elbow. She could

• HOSTILITIES •

have broken it, but didn't. Now it too joined the ache parade. She had very few sound parts left. What next? Where were those steps? Without them there was just a rough, treacherous slide downhill. And she wouldn't survive that.

She was sitting down again. Maybe that was the way to travel. Standing up was for athletes. Not cripples. Going down now. Slow and unsteady. A foot at a time. She didn't care about scrapes and lacerations. They were nothing. Then she slid down a grassy verge on her bottom and the momentum raised the pain to new unbearable heights. No, not unbearable. She could bear anything now. She'd been through hell and anything less was heaven.

It was progress. Limited. Then, through the dark forbidding maze of trees and hillside, she saw the twinkle of some not quite browned-out houselights. So she kept descending, praying for speed to get it all over with, but proceeding at barely snail's pace, still finding each movement a bigger ordeal than the previous one.

Street level, when she reached it, was not as rewarding as she'd hoped. There was a long stretch of rough flat ground between her and the street, where the houses were. A hundred yard marathon. It meant either walking or crawling. A choice between bad and terrible. Some choice.

So she varied it, gritting her teeth, swallowing her agony, panting, using her breathing as an antidote, drawing in great gulps of air and water, choking up, hyperventilating, proceeding, getting there.

Her progression to the porch of the first house across the road at the foot of the park was even worse. For the road was hard and slippery and she kept falling over with weakness and fatigue, several times unintentionally cushioning her fall with her mangled hand and eradicating its numbness with fresh torrents of pain. And when the people in the house opened the front door in response to the dull thudding, Cynthia didn't even see their faces, for she was sitting with her back against the door frame, head slumped forward, blacked out again. Unaware of her unique triumph.

When Winnie arrived at Sydney Hospital she didn't know

whether to be relieved or terrified. She was relieved that her daughter had finally turned up, but was terrified when she found she was in surgery.

"They are reducing the fractures in Cynthia's carpal, metacarpals and phalanges," the sister said, and Winnie nearly fainted from incomprehension. "Wrist, hand and fingers, dear," the sister clarified.

That didn't sound so bad, at first. Of all the parts of the body, the hands seemed the most expendable, and yet, when Winnie thought about it, they were the parts one used the most.

"She's also being treated for shock and exposure plus a number of contusions, abrasions and lacerations," the sister explained, not quite matter of factly.

Winnie was overloaded with questions but the sister was frantically busy. So she passed her over to a police constable, who explained what he knew of Cynthia's ordeal which was not much except for the extent of her injuries. As yet they hadn't been able to question her.

Winnie told the constable who she was and asked him to try and find out where her husband was. The constable replied that probably, like most of the police force at the moment, he was up at the Cross, where a riot was going on. Winnie then called headquarters and spoke to Inspector Roberts of Joe's squad. Winnie explained the predicament and asked him to try and find Joe. Roberts said he would. Winnie then settled down nervously to wait, unable to do anything, not even sip tea or knit. She wondered whether to believe what the black American corporal had told her. It sounded so far-fetched. Winnie had been incredulous. She couldn't help thinking that Wells had invented that story to cover up his own designs on Cynthia. She had almost told him so and he had been quite offended. And how could she forget his words, the words he shouted when his mask of politeness had finally dropped and he had stormed out of the house:

"Lady! I know your trouble! Your own bigotry means more to you than the welfare of your daughter!"

What did he mean? She was only thinking about the welfare of her daughter. She didn't like her going out with

· HOSTILITIES ·

Americans at all, anyway. It was inviting trouble. All the Americans wanted was sex. And as for this black man, despite appearances, he was no different, surely. And now look what had happened. Some American had beaten her up, tortured her, even . . . dare she think it . . .? No. She couldn't imagine an MP colonel doing such a thing. It was fiction. And could you trust the word of a black man?

She always knew something like this was going to happen. She always feared the worst. This perhaps saved her some grief. Optimists felt grief the most, because tragedy was so unexpected. Basically though, she blamed Joe, because he had made no attempt to discipline his daughter or advise her. He always said she was so well put together and so perceptive and intelligent, it was unnecessary to treat her like a child or to interfere in her private life. What sort of a father was he?

He'd never been a good father. He was so rarely home. He seemed to think that children grew up all by themselves and the less guidance they received the better. Well, she'd see how he reacted now when he saw what had become of his lovely, perceptive, intelligent daughter. Mangled and beaten and . . . and . . . what else? The constable and the sister seem to have inferred that something else had happened to her, but it couldn't yet be confirmed.

14

A period of uneasy truce had set in. There were plenty of people still in the riot area, but mostly they hovered in dark corners or had escaped into buildings, deciding for the moment that survival was preferable to attack. It seemed as though the MPs had established control of the streets.

In the blackness of the night, amidst the swirl of the continuing rain, however, everybody remained on edge. The MPs continued to patrol, sometimes firing at shadows, suspecting every moving thing, their paranoia fuelled by the constant stream of new orders and instructions handed down the line from their commanding officer, who didn't want the emergency to end until he had increased his status and authority to the limit.

Despite an official radio blackout, news of the riot had travelled fast in army circles. From their inner-city bivouacs, Australian soldiers had rushed to take part with almost the same enthusiasm as had spurred them to enlist when the war began. But all around the area they were confronted by MP checkpoints. They argued rightly that the US MPs had no authority to deny them access to anywhere in their own city. But the MPs had the weaponry and the authority handed down to them from above to enforce their position.

There were a few side streets still unguarded however, so infiltrators did slip in.

At one of the main checkpoints in Darlinghurst Road, corner of William Street and Bayswater Road, the main artery to and from the city, two drunken Aussies started yelling at the MPs when they barred their entry. The MPs simply clubbed them about their heads until they were unconscious and then had them ambulanced away. Their actions did not go unnoticed.

The truce was over.

• HOSTILITIES •

A few moments later, a carload of Australian troops, not long back from their sandy, shell-shocked sojourn in North Africa, pulled up at the checkpoint, with the MP riot shotguns trained on their car. One khaki Aussie arm shot out of the car window and tossed a hand grenade at the feet of the MPs.

The MPs panicked, fired up in the air and dived for cover. The explosion amputated the foot of one of them and tore a hunk out of the stomach of another.

The Aussie soldiers smashed through the checkpoint barrier with wild bloodthirsty cheers and came under rifle fire from several other MPs further down the road. The car eventually cannoned to a stop against a sandbagged shopfront. The Aussies appeared to be unhurt as they spilled out of the car and found themselves surrounded by US MPs with guns trained.

Tunks left his command post for a tour of the combat zone, believing that the best generals were those who showed themselves to their men. Not that he could be readily noticed in his jeep with the hood up against the rain, riding through the dark streets with a coterie of armed MPs, one of whom was flashing a spotlight up and down the pavement.

"Stop!" Tunks suddenly yelled, and the jeep skidded on a wet patch before bouncing off the kerb. "Church! Detective Sergeant Church I want you!" Tunks screamed. But his voice needed amplification. He raised his megaphone and repeated his demand.

Just down the road, heading for the lower Macleay Street checkpoint, Joe was supporting Pfc Adam Goldhart, who seemed to be partially incapacitated or drunk.

Tunks clambered out of the jeep surrounded by his armed minions.

Joe stopped, turned. He recognised the voice, and picked out the white MP armbands and helmets, but the faces were anonymous. He had a wild thought. Maybe that abrasive colonel could help them get past the checkpoint. They seemed to be arresting everyone trying to leave, and he wasn't sure any more if his officer's uniform meant anything. But an Australian police wagon, heading towards the checkpoint, came between them. Inspector Roberts jumped out, all bulk and

• THE CIVILIAN WAR ZONE •

bluster, and ran up to Joe.

"Joe! Crikey! You're harder to find than a silkworm in a woolshed! You'd better come with me. It's your daughter! She's in the hospital!"

Joe thought he'd suffered enough shocks for one night, but suddenly everything else moved down a peg. Roberts started pulling him towards the paddy wagon. Tunks was breathing down his neck. Adam was a millstone. "Come on!" He urged Adam to join him in the wagon, but for some reason he seemed to be holding back and his attention was riveted elsewhere. Joe didn't have time to argue. Next moment he was in the driver's cabin and yelling out the window to Adam.

"Get yourself out of here! Get an ambulance! I'll see you at Sydney Hospital!"

He wasn't sure if Adam had heard him. He seemed to be in some sort of trance. He was swaying on his feet, his bare torso shiny and wet and his curly hair all plastered down. Something or someone had his attention. Transfixed. The thought crossed Joe's mind that Adam had recognised the man they were after. But he couldn't wait. Roberts had the van in motion. He leaned out the window.

"If you see anything, tell the colonel!"

Again Adam didn't react. The paddy wagon shot past the checkpoint and out of range.

Tunks was livid. "Where the hell's he going? Bring him back!" he commanded the MPs at the checkpoint, who stared at him blankly. They knew they weren't supposed to leave their posts. Besides the wagon was already out of sight, down the hill and round the bend. Tunks considered pursuing it in his own jeep but he didn't want to leave the area.

Adam didn't know if it was the beer, the beatings, the rain or the riot, but he seemed to be surrounded on all sides by MPs. All of them threatening. His pal Joe had gone off and left him, shouting incomprehensible words. And now MPs. Dozens of them. Nightsticks and guns, all the trappings of repression. And he felt as vulnerable as a child. It had to be the blows. His head was aching and he was seeing things. MPs. Tell the colonel! He'd heard that. If you see anything, tell the colonel! The colonel? Yes, he was seeing things. All

• HOSTILITIES •

of them MPs. Including that face. That almost familiar bloated face with the strange eyes, coming towards him in the gloom, underneath a white MP helmet. That didn't make sense. There seemed to be half a platoon of them, heavily armed, passing by the checkpoint, headed by that long-lost major. Tell the colonel. No. He was seeing things. The spotlight that had been picking them out was now shining directly at him, dazzling him so he couldn't see a thing.

"Hey you, soldier! Where's your uniform? You're a disgrace to your country!"

It was the colonel addressing him, but Adam didn't know it. He shielded his eyes, trying to locate that moon-faced creep. Then somebody prodded him with a rifle barrel.

"You're under arrest, soldier!"

They spun Adam around, preparing to handcuff him. But he twisted his body away, more intent on picking out that face again than resisting arrest. But the MPs didn't know that, and the colonel who should have been available to receive information concerning a much-wanted suspect was far more interested in taming rioters and minor offenders, like this half-dressed inattentive soldier. So one MP piledrove him in the stomach with a rifle butt whilst another clubbed him across the back of his skull. For Adam it was third time unlucky and a severe dent in his potential as a witness.

He slumped forward, semi-conscious. Handcuffs were snapped on him and he was dragged to the six ton Corbitt truck that was being used to transport arrestees to the insurgent detainee detention point.

15

Sherbrook Wells had over-subsidised another Sydney taxi driver, when he trailed Tunks' jeep up to the Cross from the city. The driver charged him double because Wells asked him to "follow that jeep" which, according to the cabbie, entitled him to danger money.

The driver disgorged Wells not too far away from Tunks' TOC, before orders were issued to cordon off the area. Wells realised he'd just sailed into a battle zone but, getting his priorities right, he skulked around shop doorways and in one of the few coffee lounges that remained open, trying to keep Tunks in sight. It didn't take him long to realise that, with this new emergency, Tunks was unlikely to lead him to Cynthia, assuming he had done something with her. Or *to* her. So Wells turned his attention from surveillance to survival.

There were very few black soldiers about. This riot was not their concern. Remaining uninvolved was Wells' main concern. One day, he surmised, he might write about it. Perhaps even now. He saw journalism as his forte, his future. He wondered if one of the papers back home would be interested. If it got past the censors. He had no doubt it would be squelched in the local papers. Bad for morale. That was a laugh. Right now it was bad for his health.

Survival and surveillance. It meant keep moving. The rioting was fluid. It wasn't contained in a small area, but had spread along the main thoroughfare for nearly a mile, overlapping into side streets and back alleys.

Urban warfare. Scattered. Building to building. Short deadly bursts. Firing at shapes and shadows.

Urbane warfare. "Got a light, mate?"

"Sure."

Flare in the dark. Grunt. Knife in the ribs. Fatal cough.

• HOSTILITIES •

Flood of blood.

Open warfare. Bottles, sticks, bayonets, fists, guns, grenades. Hit and run. Shoot and fall. Charge and retreat. Sometimes hit and miss. Warning shots, often badly aimed. Tear gas. Dash for cover. Back out of sight.

If he was cautious, with keen eyesight, there was space enough to survey and survive.

Tunks wasn't a hard target. He was so involved with issuing decrees, receiving reports and behaving like Robespierre in heat, he wouldn't have noticed the Hound of the Baskervilles sniffing around.

Tunks was his only lead, so Brook hung on, narrowly avoiding the enemy, which appeared to consist of all human beings in the vicinity. Eventually he was almost rewarded.

When Tunks started touring the riot area in his jeep, asserting his authority behind his protective barrier of armed vassals, Wells almost lost him. A few times he had to sprint down the middle of the dark wet shiny street, which he found was safer than the pavement where most of the MPs and battlers were. And when the jeep stopped and Tunks hailed a US major, Wells couldn't believe his eyes. The major looked just like Cynthia's old man.

He couldn't quite fathom that. He crossed the road quickly and kept running down under the awnings, cannoning into some Australian soldiers, who would've retaliated except that Wells was sprinting and they were sluggish. But the hefty MP he next cannoned into was far from sluggish. Brook almost bounced off this steadfast symbol of astringency, who looked at him with a baleful eye and said:

"You're under arrest for not lookin' where you're goin', nigger!"

Brook refused to be cowed. He stuck a defiant chin out. "You're wrong, corporal! I was lookin' where I was goin'. I was goin' straight at you!" After a perfectly timed Golden Gloves feint with his left, Brook uppercut the surprised MP right on the chin, which didn't so much lay him low as stop him short. Then he continued on his speedy way down the dark street.

Right before the checkpoint, beneath a stately vigilant block of red brick flats, Brook overheard Tunks megaphoning

THE CIVILIAN WAR ZONE

Cynthia's father's name. But he was too late. He watched with dismay as Church climbed hastily into the police wagon, but he continued his futile dash, in the wake of the wagon, towards the checkpoint, throwing caution to the rain.

The eagle-eyed colonel Tunks, smelling blood at every step, caught sight of Wells. Another of his chickens. This one he wouldn't miss.

"Get that nigger! Shoot the sonofabitch!"

Master Sergeant Struther obeyed his colonel's order without hesitation, trying not to grin as he sighted his M1 carbine, which, at this range, was as accurate as a rifle.

He couldn't miss. And he didn't want to.

Brook felt a pattern of searing pains in his back and legs and the momentum of his flight increased by 300 per cent. For about three seconds. Then he crashed, face down on the bitumen with a bone-shattering impact. He twitched a few times, and then lay still as a corpse.

Tunks was elated. That left only Church. And he'd get him before the night was through. He used his organic radio to communicate with his RWI station. He then asked the station to connect him with Darlinghurst Police Station. He was so high on battle energy his voice crackled through the ether with unassailable authority.

"This is Colonel Bastien Tunks, Provost Marshal, US Military Police Company attached to Divisional Headquarters. I'm after your Detective Sergeant Church, who's been assigned to me. He just left me in a police wagon and I want to know where he's going. It's top priority!"

Despite the priority they kept him waiting five minutes, during which Tunks burned with impatience. Then they succeeded in knocking the battle high out of him. They told him that Church was on his way to Sydney Hospital to see his daughter, who had had some sort of accident.

Tunks turned as white as his MP brassard.

Sydney Hospital was like a casualty way station. As Joe strode past the mobile injured with their blood-soaked bandages, towards the women's ward, his imagination fed his anxiety. Had she somehow been caught in the riot? Had she been shot,

• HOSTILITIES •

knifed, assaulted, raped? Nothing else mattered now except her. Not that mass murderer, or the rioting troops, nor even the war itself. He suddenly realised for the first time, what the war was all about. It wasn't defeat or victory, or even national survival. It wasn't statistics or territory. It wasn't churning out the implements of death or rationing; it wasn't calls for patriotic duty or glory or hate for the enemy. It was personal tragedy.

With millions dying all over the world, each death meant bereavement for someone, who perhaps didn't really care who won or lost at all. All they cared about was that they had lost someone they loved. And when the fighting was eventually over, that simple personal fact would remain. Perhaps for ever.

Then Joe chided himself for his morbidity. Cynthia wasn't dead. Roberts hadn't said that. She'd had an accident. But that in itself was terrifying. An accident. That could mean anything.

He imagined her lying there with her legs amputated, scarred and disfigured all over. His mind sifted through images of all the accidents and violence he had ever seen. A monumental list. He had been the victim of violence himself: razor slashings, broken legs, contusions, lacerations, a bullet wound, to say nothing of his worst experience of all. Syphilis. Way back. In his twenties. The cure for which was almost worse than the disease. But he had come through. By God, he had come through! But he was a tough man, resilient as hell. A fighter. She was only a girl, his fragile lovely daughter, who should be loved and cherished by everyone.

He saw Winnie by the bed and a nurse hovering around looking busy, and he sprinted the last few yards.

Cynthia was not long out of recovery. Her left hand and arm was in plaster and outside the covers. An IV drip was attached to her other hand. There were dressings on her face, but she looked relatively comfortable and semi-awake.

When Joe sat down on a bedside chair, Winnie on the other side said nothing, but gave him a look of such hostility he felt for a moment as if he was the person who had hurt her.

It wasn't an accident. He could see that. He could read

• THE CIVILIAN WAR ZONE •

the wounds, the placement. Who was to blame?

When Cynthia told him, quietly, in a weak almost incoherent voice, he had to ask her to repeat it. His head spun. It didn't figure. The element of coincidence was too overwhelming, too disturbing.

"Are you sure?" he asked, after she'd already repeated the accusation.

Of course she was sure. Why would she dream up a name like that?

"How did you meet this man?" It didn't make sense.

She told him, but he still found it hard to accept. Then she seemed to run out of strength and the nurse suggested they should let her rest. But Joe needed to know more. Cynthia was just able to utter single words. Nouns, without verbs or adverbs. Just an occasional adjective, a loaded word. And Joe was good at such word games. He pieced it all together and added one of his own, silently. Vengeance.

Winnie just sat and listened, not really surprised, except at the fact that the man that she had so wanted to hate had actually told her the truth. And now she couldn't hate him any more. She could only hate some colonel she had never met. Or else she could hate all Americans. That was easier. Blame them all for the sins of one. A common enough reaction, particularly in wartime.

16

Joe felt surprisingly calm. It was not his first reaction. The hate was certainly there. It was making his stomach churn. But he was calm because he knew what he was going to do. He was going to get that bastard.

Absolutely crystal clear. There was a riot. People were attacking each other in the streets for no good reason. And getting away with it. Some of them anyhow. He would just shoot Tunks and disappear into the crowd.

He'd be surrounded by allies. The MPs were everybody's target. He was going to get the top dog.

Justifiable homicide. Calm. Ultra calm. His hands weren't shaking, even his back felt good for a change. But the hate was down there in the pit of his stomach. It was as much a part of him as his love for his daughter.

Yes, he would shoot the bastard.

But there was something else. He was a policeman as well as a father. And he had taken Inspector Roberts with him. Why?

To make the arrest.

Oh, he would still shoot him. He knew the man. He would not just stand there and allow himself to be taken into custody by a civilian cop. Joe would have to shoot him. It would be self-defence. The colonel would no doubt order his men to shoot Joe.

The law was on Joe's side. Civil law. The man had broken the law of the land. Military personnel were not immune.

Not a normal calm. Pathological.

The police van passed through the checkpoint without too much trouble. Then they drove slowly up the street ignoring the roving bands of hunters and hunted. It looked more like the aftermath of a battle than all-out warfare: a shuttle

• THE CIVILIAN WAR ZONE •

ambulance service, handcuffed arrestees, vigilant patrols, civilian police still in more of an observer role, isolated palls of smoke, constant light rain, intermittent illumination, perhaps more of everything waiting in the dark shadows, mopping up.

They stopped near three MPs scouring the street for stragglers. Joe leaned out the window.

"Where's Colonel Tunks, soldier?" Joe utilised his best US accent.

The MP saluted. "I guess you could say he's everywhere, sir," the MP replied with a grin. "There's a command post at the top of the road. You could try there."

Joe's stomach turned over. He was getting warm now. The calm was just a veneer. Agitation was setting in. And impatience. His heart was thumping so much he felt it was going to burst through his chest. When the moment came, he might not be able to control himself.

Roberts was driving and Joe stared out the window, his eyes X-raying the shadows. The brownout had become a virtual blackout now, except for the odd splashes of light from MP spotlights, some mounted on patrolling jeeps. Joe thought he saw some faces staring down from the residential building windows, safely anonymous. For the first time since the American invasion, not a single street lamp, shop light, neon or sign was showing at Kings Cross. Up on high, the moon was weeping and the stars were nowhere in sight. Down below, you could hear voices, muffled commands, shouted incoherencies, even some snatches of drunken ditties and patriotic songs.

At the Kings Cross end of Darlinghurst Road, behind the checkpoint, a crowd of curious civilians had gathered, hoping to see some warfare at first hand with comparative safety. Most of them were soldiers' women anxious to see the result of what they had obliquely motivated.

Then, at the corner of the right-angle, Joe spotted Tunks, standing by his jeep under a portable bullseye lantern, barking orders into his organic radio. He was surrounded by his security platoon who were holding their shotguns and M1 rifles at the ready, as if anticipating an enemy assault.

"Stop here. We'll walk the rest," Joe said. They left the

wagon about thirty yards away from the command post and walked slowly towards Tunks — Joe, the would-be major, Roberts the civvie-clad cop with nothing to mark him out as such except his bulk, his knotty features, broken nose, bull-like neck and aggressive stance, to say nothing of his feet.

Joe didn't stop to consider the fact that they were outnumbered, outgunned, outorganised. They didn't have a show. They were walking into the lion's den without a prayer. That was the reality. But the motivating factors were all-consuming. Hate, revenge, justice. They didn't need to have their own platoon. That would just produce another battle scene and no sense of justice achieved. This way, they had the advantage of being the underdogs. A certain diffuse, contrary psychological advantage.

Tunks saw Joe when he was fifteen yards away, and the guards' M1s picked them out as potential enemies. Joe and Roberts kept approaching, trying to look casual, not wanting to activate those itchy trigger fingers.

"I've been waiting for you, Church!" Tunks called out, ominously. He had his own .45 automatic in his hand, pointing at the ground. His steel pot helmet with the white "MP" on it gave his mean head a look of invulnerability. Or maybe it was his authoritarian relish that did it. He was wearing an Ike jacket over camouflage fatigues, which illustrated his belief that he was in a war zone.

Joe didn't say a word until they were within spitting distance. When he did speak, his voice was deep and controlled, for he knew that any overt sign of emotion at this juncture would be counterproductive.

"Colonel Tunks, I'm arresting you for causing grievous bodily harm, unlawful sexual intercourse, attempted murder and abduction, all upon the person of an Australian national, Cynthia Church. Inspector Roberts has a warrant for this arrest and I advise you to come with us peacefully." Joe could feel his temples throbbing and his voice seemed to echo as he strove to keep his emotions under control. But it wasn't going to take much to tip them over the edge.

Tunks did the worst possible thing. He laughed. Not with amusement, but with scorn. A scathing rebuttal aided and

• THE CIVILIAN WAR ZONE •

abetted by the armoury that was pointing straight at Joe and his companion.

Joe didn't see the weapons or the security platoon. He saw only Tunks' leering face. He took two paces forward and hit him with the weight of his whole body behind his fist and the agony of his beloved daughter fuelling the weight.

The laugh caught in Tunks' throat as his head snapped back almost sharply enough for whiplash, the impact on his jawbone forcing him back against a stone pillar. His face turned grey and the sneer turned to equal parts of fury and fear. He swung his gun up in an arc and held it, quiveringly, at Joe's head. His escort clicked their safety catches and formed a firing squad, targeted at Joe.

"You saw that!" Tunks screamed. "You saw that! Arrest him! Arrest them both! It's treason! And if they resist, shoot them!"

Two MPs stepped forward and tried to handcuff Joe and Roberts. Roberts, out of his depth, gave in easily. But Joe angrily knocked them aside and went after Tunks. He landed another hefty punch and knocked Tunks' pistol aside, then kicked the colonel in the groin, doubling him up.

Four MPs then subdued Joe with a gun butt to the back of his neck, an arm round his throat. His arms were pinioned behind his back whilst they handcuffed him. Joe, much to his own surprise, and perhaps because of the satisfaction involved in unleashing an assault upon Tunks, remained self-possessed. The entire American army couldn't have got under his skin now. He knew Tunks' days were numbered.

Tunks, with a red splotch on his jaw and pulsating malevolence in his heart, tempered somewhat by the realisation that the ground was shifting beneath him, stepped in and whacked Joe across the mouth, drawing blood. Joe kept his head up and his gaze defiantly direct. He knew Tunks wanted to obliterate him, but he also knew he didn't have the guts to do it in front of all these witnesses. After all, Joe was no drunken dogface to be cut down in cold blood. Furthermore, although his men were primed to obey orders, this appeared to be an extraordinary situation and their colonel, unloved at the best of times, seemed to be getting out of his depth.

HOSTILITIES

Or was he?

"Why are you wearing that uniform?" Tunks asked, slyness replacing his fury.

"You know why!" Joe spat out.

Tunks looked pleased. "You're right. I do know why. Release him!"

Sergeant Struther unlocked Joe's handcuffs.

Tunks levelled his automatic pistol at Joe's head. It was obvious now. Joe had miscalculated. Tunks was going to shoot him after all. He should've realised that. He had no choice. He was gambling that it was better to have shot a man during the course of a riot than to be accused of abducting and raping an innocent girl.

The MP platoon had moved to one side now. It was just Tunks facing Joe and Roberts.

"And the other one!"

Struther unlocked Roberts' cuffs. Roberts was quite confused. He looked at Joe for a lead, but Joe had his gaze fixed on Tunks.

"I'm using my authority as Military Governor of this area to arrest these men as enemy agents. One of them, for the purpose of aiding and abetting the enemy, has impersonated a US military officer and has also resisted arrest and assaulted the Military Governor."

"Joe?" Roberts asked, not sure why Tunks had had their cuffs removed, if they were under arrest.

But Joe knew.

Tunks' eyes blazed obsessively. He waited a moment longer before squeezing the trigger. He knew that Joe knew that he was going to shoot them. He also knew that, given half a chance, Joe would try to jump him, which would supply some justification. So he gave him half a chance. He lowered the gun.

Joe hesitated, then went for him. Six yards. It was his gamble. Half a second to live. Stretched. Frozen in time. He wasn't going to make it. Tunks had the gun levelled again. Point-blank range. Between the eyes. Squeezing the trigger. Joe twisted his body, trying to escape the bullet path. Futility. Moving target, still target. Either way. Dead.

• THE CIVILIAN WAR ZONE •

But as Tunks squeezed the trigger, hoping to dispose of all his demons, five anonymous MPs, who had been standing twenty yards away in the shadows of a shop awning, fired directly at Tunks and his security platoon at the command post.

The first ten rounds from Carl Goyt's M1 carbine thudded into Tunks' face and neck, disintegrating most of his features, splintering part of his skull and spraying blood, grey matter and pieces of shattered bone in the air. Five rounds lodged, five rounds exited from the rear. Brain death in seconds.

"We regret to have to inform you that your son was killed while attempting to execute his duty in the service of his country."

Joe and Roberts hit the road, unmarked, and crawled out of the way on their stomachs. Three other MPs, excluding Sergeant Struther, went down with bullet wounds. Two dead. The rest scattered, totally confused, not sure whether to return fire, but sure that the hip-shooting MPs were part of some savage mistake.

BOOK IV

CASUALTIES

"One day President Roosevelt told me that he was asking publicly for suggestions about what the war should be called. I said at once 'the Unnecessary War'."

WINSTON CHURCHILL

1

The next morning all the detainees in the cattle pavilion at the showground were addressed by an MP lieutenant who seemed to love the sound of his own voice, because he stretched out the orders like a retiring headmaster to his captive school audience. At least, that was Adam's assessment, as he wondered what was in store for him.

"I am your confinement officer. My name is Lieutenant Moyes. Shortly you will all be transferred to a proper military confinement facility. . ."

"What hotel will that be, lieutenant sir?" a deadpan private asked.

"I would remind you that although you have been classified as casual prisoners in temporary custody pending court martial proceedings, you are still fully subject to normal US army regulation and discipline. And that includes due respect for rank." Moyes paused to allow a suitable impression to be made.

"At that facility, you will be given administrative and operational processing, which will include a personal search, classification of your possessions, examination of your army service record, medical and mental hygiene examination, an appropriate custody grade, assignment of particular military duties to be carried out during your period of confinement and legal briefing in preparation for the court martial. Now, I understand there are some civilians here and some members of the Australian armed forces. You will shortly be transferred to the State Police authorities and your own Military Police respectively, who will conduct their particular trial and punishment procedures."

"Excuse me, sir," Adam called out. "Some of the men here need medical attention. In fact, that includes me."

• THE CIVILIAN WAR ZONE •

"Nothing can be done about this until you reach the proper confinement facility. All of those with more than superficial wounds were taken away by ambulance, so you'll just have to exercise some of the fortitude expected of fighting men until you see a medical officer."

Adam's problem was mainly a splitting headache and, he suspected, oncoming concussion. The swelling in his jaw he could live with for the moment. Likewise his inflamed shoulder wound.

There were about thirty prisoners in the pavilion, guarded by five armed MPs. Straw was the only furniture and during the night those wishing to go to the toilet were escorted out of the pavilion to a nearby "excretion facility" by one of the guards.

"During the transfer you will march and ride in strict formation in orderly units. Anyone attempting to escape will be shot. At all times, strict military discipline must be adhered to. You are still in the army no matter what your confinement. Any deviation from military discipline will result in further punishment and reconfinement in a high security solitary cell."

Adam sighed. It all seemed so useless and bureaucratic to him. Rules and regulations. He hated the sound of them. He wanted to be free, but the entire world was in the shackles of war. There was no freedom any more. Not even freedom of thought, let alone of action. Not even freedom to go to the toilet alone. Here he was in a cattle pavilion soon to be escorted under armed guard to some prison compound prior to no doubt being transferred to a stockade where he'd probably be beaten to death by either a brutal guard or a frustrated fellow prisoner. Not much to look forward to. He hated the army. He wanted to fight the Japanese, but he'd rather belong to some undisciplined highly motivated guerilla force.

Adam's musings were almost prophetic. First some civilian police came and escorted the civilian prisoners away. Then some Australian MPs took care of their army compatriots. That left about fifteen US army prisoners, including Adam. And it appeared they were to be moved in two batches. Why, it wasn't made clear, but the MP guards and the prisoners themselves didn't ask questions, as this would have been in contravention of military regulations.

Adam was in the first batch of eight, seemingly selected at random and marched out of the cattle pavilion. At first he was as compliant as the rest. A simple transfer to a military confinement facility. No doubt they'd be given some breakfast there. That thought made the transfer seem quite desirable. Yet, as they were being marched for almost a mile around the showground, past other animal pavilions, bare display stands, by the woodchopping ring now transformed into an Australian army drill compound, over worn grass, dirt and tarred road, Adam sensed there was something curious about this so-called transfer. Their armed MP escort bothered him, as well as the long march. He had expected that there would be an army wagon waiting for them outside the pavilion. The lieutenant hadn't said where the facility was going to be, but surely it was not here in the showground. Yet, it was.

The armed escort, despite their uniforms and MP brassards, looked to Adam like a real sad sack army. There were three of them, all unhealthy-looking, shifty-eyed, slouched rather than rigid, cruel rather than authoritarian, ruthless, perhaps even untrained. In other words, not what they seemed to be.

"Where exactly are you taking us?" Adam asked.

"Shut your face or you'll be wearin' my bayonet on your arse!" one of the guards said, in a most unmilitary tone. Furthermore, the accent was definitely unAmerican.

Curious. Definitely curious, thought Adam. His mind jerked back to his dead friend Salome, and his discussions with Joe Church, and it all started to come clear. In a confused kind of way. This was not a kosher MP escort. Yet the showground was definitely a military facility, albeit an Australian one. There were army vehicles and a variety of Australian army personnel in view. Adam thought he might make a dash for freedom, throw himself upon the mercy of one of these Australian units. But then it was obvious he was a prisoner, and the armed escort, whoever they were, would not hesitate to shoot. Or, like the man said, decorate his ass with a bayonet.

Then they were outside another animal pavilion. The guards ruthlessly ushered them inside, prodding them with the

• THE CIVILIAN WAR ZONE •

aforementioned bayonets, which were attached to their M1s.

No doubt this was their new confinement facility, but not the one officially designated. For, inside the smelly, dank, dark pavilion, Adam found himself face-to-face with his new confinement officer, and the ache in his semi-concussed head reached stunning proportions. This confinement officer was definitely an imposter. Adam immediately recognised the moon-faced major with the liquid moonscape eyes. He looked around for an escape route, but it was too late. In a matter of seconds he and the other seven prisoners were in handcuffs and chains and their esoteric confinement officer was about to prescribe the elements of his regime, which would rival in application the worst kind of Nazi facility.

By dawn the riot had run out of steam, as had most of the MPs. They were now rudderless owing to the demise of their commanding officer, shot down in the line of duty by unknown MP assassins.

Government censorship ensured that the full extent of the riot went unreported. The morning papers carried stories on page five about a "drunken rampage by soldiers on leave at Kings Cross". And added that the shenanigans were soon put down by US and Australian MPs in their characteristically efficient manner.

In the normal course of events, a fully fledged Royal Commission or legal inquiry would have been held into the causes and effects of the riot, the shooting of the MP Provost Marshal and the allegations against him concerning an Australian girl. But there was a war on. And, as everybody knows, when there is a war on, matters on the home front, however severe, are pushed aside. Governments of all kinds, during wartime, find it impossible to be constructive on both the home front and the battle front at the same time. They also know that most civilians are more concerned with the fate of their fighting men overseas and the possibility of invasion than they are with domestic affairs. Which is why so many ailing governments find it propitious to go to war.

So the riot produced no such legal indulgence as a civilian inquiry. Instead there was an official inter-services inquiry,

• CASUALTIES •

behind closed doors, between the New South Wales Police Commissioner, an Assistant Police Commissioner, who was also head of the Criminal Investigation Branch, the new acting Provost Marshal of the US Military Police (the newly promoted Major Harris), General Richard Marshall representing General MacArthur, and General Sir Thomas Blamey, CIC of the Australian army and allied land forces in the South-West Pacific, who was also a former Chief Commissioner of the Victorian Police Force.

The inquiry produced much discussion and no results. Various witnesses were called, including Detective Sergeant Church, whose accusations against the deceased Colonel Tunks were noted but disregarded. The late colonel's record was not about to be officially besmirched.

It was acknowledged that MPs were generally quite unpopular with members of the armed forces, which was taken to mean that the MPs were obviously doing their job well. General Blamey commented:

"MPs are like generals. If you're not hated by the common soldier, it's an indication that you're not doing your duty. I should know."

Excessive alcohol was attributed as the cause of the riot and it was suggested that the Commissioner for Police should move against those black market grog sellers who were defying the licensing laws. The Commissioner pointed out that when they had previously done this, they had been requested to be more tolerant by the US military command as their troops on furlough needed an adequate supply of alcoholic beverages at all hours.

It was decided that an army inquest into Colonel Tunks' killing would be held but, as far as the inquiry was concerned, it was accepted that he was shot by unknown assassins in MP uniforms during riot conditions, which made it impractical to locate the perpetrators. The same applied in relation to the five other deaths that occurred during the fray. It was generally agreed that there was no more purpose in instituting a formal investigation into these deaths than there was in investigating deaths in Buna or Kokoda. It was all part of the war effort.

• THE CIVILIAN WAR ZONE •

Finally it was noted that a number of prisoners had apparently escaped from custody at the temporary detention point. Such men were now officially listed as deserters.

2

It was indeed unfortunate for Adam Goldhart that Crowbar MacPherson had been released from custody in his animal stall at the showground by his confrères in the British Empire Territorial Army. Being a well-conditioned punching bag with more scars than Caligula's sister, Crowbar had absorbed his punishment from the night before and was now as good as old. Except that when he saw Adam amongst Goyt's new American prisoners of war, he demanded his pound of flesh. Goyt, happy to gratify his abrasive abetter, granted him carte blanche.

Adam, helpless, chained, hungry, headachey, confused and smarting at his minefield of a fate, broke into a cold sweat when he saw the baboon-like Crowbar looking down at him mercilessly in his goat pen. Mutual recognition. Triumph and trepidation respectively.

"If you want my wallet back, I'd gladly give it to you," Adam said, "but I'm afraid it got lost during the riot. However, you can have my marker." A feeble grin. Wasted.

Crowbar not only had no sense of humour, he was both illiterate and inarticulate. He had always found that action spoke louder than words. Action meaning violence. He had spent half his life shutting up people who talked too much, because he didn't understand what they were talking about.

Adam, despite his innate optimism, now expected to die. He had no way of resisting the beating that Crowbar was about to inflict on him and even if his chains were removed, the mad major, having come down from colonel to MP captain despite remaining, internally at least, field marshal of his tiny but expanding British Empire Territorial Army, was poised to penetrate Adam's anatomy with his own sharp-pointed weapon, as soon as Crowbar had done his worst.

• THE CIVILIAN WAR ZONE •

Adam's deliberately unfocused mind wondered how his family would react to the official black-bordered telegram that would be hand-delivered to their front door. His mother would burst into tears, as he had seen her do on much less significant occasions. His father would probably plunge himself into his work as president and founder of Goldhart Industries Inc. — a pretentious name for a firm that churned out watchbands, belts and men's suspenders. Before Adam had been drafted, his father had been offered, or rather allocated, a government contract to switch over to manufacturing gun holsters and webbing belts for the army. The fortunes of war, Adam thought grimly. At least now he won't expect me to take over the business, which suggestion Adam had always resisted.

Before commencing his task, Crowbar unlocked Adam's chains. He wanted no restrictions on his freedom to bounce his victim all over the POW goat compound. For a moment Adam thought he might now have the chance to make a run for it, but there were M1 carbines trained on him from those guarding the only exit, which seemed to be firmly shuttered anyway. Then he wondered if it was better to be shot down trying to run than to just lie there and take the punishment that was about to descend on him.

He hadn't arrived at a decision when Crowbar's first blow struck. It caught him flush in the face, whilst being hoisted roofwise by Crowbar's other hand. It jarred him all over and was hard enough to make it a one punch victory for MacPherson. But it was only the beginning. Adam heard his own voice yelling in agony, disembodied, and the Milky Way flashed before his eyes as his body catapulted backwards into the wooden boards that made up the stall.

But the curious MP captain, who had been observing from a safe distance, suddenly blocked Crowbar's next assault, using his carbine bayonet and disputable authority as a wedge. His eyes seemed to have a feverish quality as he stared down at the hapless Adam sprawled in the goat pen with a freshly bloodied face and dazed expression.

"Haven't we met before, soldier?" Goyt asked.

Adam, fighting off waves of nausea and a pain in his jaw that he knew was going to escalate at the slightest movement, barely moved his lips when he spoke.

"I don't think you're in my unit."

"What was that? Speak up!" Goyt barked.

"I said I don't think you're in my unit." Adam shut his eyes for a moment as the pain enveloped his face and even halfway to the back of his skull. Probably a fractured jaw.

"Yes. We've met alright. I never forget a face."

Adam remained mute. Let the sonofabitch do all the talking. Why should he increase his own suffering?

"Where was it?" Goyt's memory wasn't really as good as Adam's.

Adam wasn't going to help him out.

"It seems we have to interrogate this soldier. Shackle him!" Goyt's command was immediately acted upon by the precious weed, Corporal Seldom. "Now, sit this apology for a soldier up! I don't want to have to stoop to his level."

The sly slinky private called Blunt, who was anything but, and Seldom, so deceptively delicate and benignly remorseless, hoisted Adam to a sitting position on the straw.

"Get him something to sit on!"

A wooden packing case. But Adam swayed and crashed back on the straw. He seemed to have lost his sense of balance. Seldom and Blunt hoisted him back on the wooden case, with his back against the beaverboard and chained his wrists above his head, shortening the chains by winding the slack around an iron bracket on two tethering posts. Adam was now as secure and vulnerable as if crucified.

Goyt wasn't satisfied.

"He's far too comfortable. Interrogation relies on discomfort. Let's have his arms higher and get rid of that packing case."

Now Adam was virtually suspended with his feet just touching the straw but not enough to support his weight. The strain was mostly upon his wrists and shoulders and he felt that with any great movement he'd dislocate his shoulder joints.

Goyt seemed pleased. "Private MacPherson, the cat! If you please."

"The cat? I don't have no cat!"

"I know where it is," Seldom volunteered.

He dived into an ordinance crate and produced the cat-o'-nine-tails, which Goyt fondled lovingly before handing it to MacPherson.

"Strength is of the utmost importance in this form of interrogation, coupled with a total lack of sympathy for the victim. Private MacPherson. Do the honours."

Crowbar grunted, quite happy to oblige.

"The British army has long cherished the cat as the leading instrument of efficient interrogation. Rather more effective than fists and clubs, don't you think?" Goyt had now reverted to clipped English tones, rendering his US MP regalia ludicrous. Adam wondered if it was all a nightmare, and yet he could smell the straw, the animal miasma, and the foul breath of the barbarous goon-like MacPherson, who was breathing a lifetime of bad diet, nicotine and booze through his stained teeth. And his vision was clear and undistorted — shaded daylight with sunshine shafts stabbing down from the skylight windows.

And he was awake because the throbbing pain and stretched discomfort wouldn't let his concussed brain black him out. Yet it seemed so pointless. He had nothing to offer this nutcase of an officer except some identification which was really only a painful trauma of no real substance. Was this all a sidelight of the real war with its booming guns, shattered bodies and lives, disintegrated landscapes and buildings, engendered by frustrated politicians, played out by mindless lackeys? It was no better except in degree and he was always going to be a part of it from the moment of his drafting. Fight for democracy! Revenge Pearl Harbor! Protect our beloved country from invasion! All thoroughly worthwhile sentiments. And yet the means and the sidelights, the illogical logistics and the prejudiced reactions were all part of the whole, were all equally reprehensible. Interrogation, torture, needless agony, futile death. What did it matter? Civilian or soldier? Innocent or guilty? Paid or unpaid? All crumbs to be fed to the masters of destiny, the distorters of history. And outside, the golden sun wreathed the cityscape in nature's smiles, with a flawless blue alabaster sky and a mild warmth, not too hot nor too cold. A truly beautiful autumn day, redolent with calm and comfort. How could anyone be sick or sad or savage on such a glorious God-given day? Yet inside:

"Where've I seen you before, soldier?" Goyt's staccato question, ludicrous in the extreme, forcing a man to jog his own inadequate memory, was a prelude to incontinent savagery. Adam certainly would have told him, without hesitation, except his own brain was on the verge of malfunction and his cracked jaw was issuing a painful warning against the slightest lip movement. So Crowbar MacPherson commenced utilising his new/old weapon in the very best nineteenth century British army tradition, connecting with Adam's chest, making his earlier sunburn seem like an angel's kiss.

Goyt's smile of satisfaction at the agony of his young enemy was quickly tempered by a rapid rise in his respiratory rate, a foretaste of further breathing difficulty which only his carbine bayonet could assuage.

If nothing else, the riot had resulted in efforts to ensure a greater degree of cooperation between the allies. The acting Provost Marshal assigned Sergeant Struther to work closely with Detective Sergeant Church on the investigation into the killings of US personnel.

Joe found Struther to be ambivalently professional in his attitude, stemming from his abrupt termination as Tunks' hatchet man. Having seen Joe fearlessly confront and even assault his leader that disturbing night enabled him to endow Joe with a certain amount of sycophantic loyalty, almost as if Joe had toppled the king and was now king himself. At the same time Struther found it hard to work with a civilian cop like Joe who seemed to have such a relaxed, almost casual, attitude to discipline.

Joe himself was ambivalent about everything. He was glad that the man who had defiled his daughter had received the ultimate come-uppance, yet it was not a satisfying retribution. Almost an accident. Perhaps a fortuitous one though, for he had not placed his own position in jeopardy by carrying out the execution himself.

Joe still wanted to use Private Goldhart in the investigation, as he was the only recorded person to have identified a suspect in the case. But Adam was not at his barracks and had been listed as AWOL. Struther suggested that he may have been arrested during the riot and, sure enough, his name was on the detainee list. However, it seems he was one of the eight who had apparently fled from custody at the detainee detention point, which gave Joe cause for thought. Why would he even attempt to escape? And then he noted that the detainee detention point was at the showground. The showground? From somewhere back in his recollections, made hazy by recent events, he revived his theory concerning the animal traces on some of the GI victims' bodies. The showground.

Certainly it was only a hunch, but they had little else to go on.

They went to the headquarters of the Commonwealth Military Forces in the so-called Hall of Industries at the showground and received a briefing as to what use every pavilion, stand and building was being put by the Australian army. Six animal pavilions were not listed for any specific use. Upon further questioning from Joe, the army clerk informed them that three of those pavilions — one horse, one pig and one cattle — had been temporarily turned over to the US Military Police for use as detainee points. That still left three animal pavilions not being used by the army for either personnel bunking or storage.

Joe asked if any of these pavilions had been recently used to house animals, and it seemed that all three had, at various times. As the showground had become a self-contained army town, they had found it convenient to house some animals for the mess unit. Mainly cows, pigs and goats.

Joe decided it was reasonable to assume that one of these three pavilions had been the last resting place for those GI victims whose bodies showed animal stains. He wasn't at all sure what they would find in these pavilions, if anything. Perhaps some traces of animal blood and excrement, which he could then have analysed. Perhaps even some further evidence that killings and/or torture had occurred there. But he really wasn't expecting to find anything other than three empty sheds. So he and Struther set off alone, on foot, around the showground's endless winding roads to examine these

· CASUALTIES ·

pavilions. Joe had his regulation pistol in his shoulder holster, whilst Struther had his on his belt, together with his white club and combat knife.

It was a lovely sunny day. The showground was like a summer holiday camp, and most of the troops were barechested, some just in khaki shorts and slouch hats. All of them looked relaxed, even those at drill. Sure there was a war on, but it was a million miles up north. This was just army games. New recruits being honed at a leisurely pace. Rifle fire at the practice range, carried out as sport rather than as warfare. Brown vehicles trundling along going nowhere in particular. And one civilian, Joe, about to barge in on the enemy. Unwittingly.

3

Compared to an ordinary, single-strand whip, a cat-o'-nine-tails is like an axe compared to a knife. It has short thick strands which don't cut in like an ordinary whip but which thud in jarringly according to the strength of the flogger. After the first half-dozen thumps Adam felt his ribs crack and he deposited a stomachful of bile on the straw, which he regretted hadn't landed on the mad captain's face.

Then they turned him round from front to back, so as to vary the punishment and spread the pain. He'd never felt so sick in all his born days and each thud seemed to jar his already deeply shaken brain. He prayed for unconsciousness but was thudded awake again and again to further suffering. His only outward expression was one long continuous groan which reverberated uncontrollably from his chest. Goyt was using the flogging as an object lesson to the other seven prisoners, chained to their stalls. Their turn was next.

Adam had always felt, deep within his psyche, that he was born to suffer. It was a certain, definable Jewish reaction. Suffering had always been almost an obligation — a way of paying one's dues to the human race. But that was in contemplation. Now, in reality, it was just an unendurable ordeal with no nobility, no salvation, no meaning. He wasn't even suffering because he was a Jew, but because he was an American.

The original reason for the interrogation seemed to have vanished. Goyt no longer seemed interested as to where he had seen Adam previously. Now it was all part of his holy crusade to prevent the American dilution of his country's ties with the British Empire. Goyt's very own Victorian fantasy.

"You are here under false premises, soldier!" Goyt intoned, as Crowbar kept flogging at five second intervals. "We are in this war not to help America revenge Pearl Harbor, but to support the retention of the glorious British Empire which has helped to civilise the savage world."

Adam didn't actually hear a word Goyt was saying. He heard only his own incessant agonised groans and the thwack of hide upon his own tortured, reddened flesh, coupled with the howls of tortured humanity that were blanking out logical speech and thought everywhere.

He had long ago lost count of the blows. All he knew was that when, sooner or later, it stopped, he would die. Strangely the blows were now actually seeming to keep him alive. Pain and suffering had become life itself. Anything else was blackness and probable death.

But now there were shouts from the other prisoners urging Goyt to stop, so he instructed his uninvolved troops — Seldom, Blunt, Kroeger and his latest confused deserter, a callow fool named Smithson — to shut them up with blows to the head, and then to gag them.

Then MacPherson, sweating and strained and fresh out of satisfaction, decided it was time to rest and ascertain the purpose of his labours. As the flogging ceased Adam slumped into merciful blackness deep at the bottom of a mental whirlpool.

Joe and Struther barely conversed as they unhurriedly traversed the showground. There was little that was comradely between them. Joe's thoughts segued between sadness at the ordeal inflicted on his daughter, who still had a long recuperative period ahead of her, his wife Winnie who had retreated into a morose silence since Cynthia's escape, and a doubtful hope that they would find some new evidence to enable him to make progress on this so far baffling case.

Struther's thoughts were equally diverse. He pondered his promotion possibilities now that his mentor was dead, and thought about the young Air Corps warrant officer who had tempted him in a back street at Kings Cross a week ago, had sucked him off in a hotel room and then attempted to roll him. Struther had not been wearing his MP brassard that night and the young faggot had hightailed it off before Struther could smash his skull in, as he'd wanted to.

They passed the Standard Cars permanent display Building, which was being used to store non-perishable equipment like barbed wire and steel pipes, then the horse exercise ring area, being used for unarmed combat training, past the Red Indian village site, being used for idle sunbaking, and up to three horse pavilions. These were hangar-like brick sheds with skylight windows covered by wire netting set high above blank walls, just below wrought-iron roofing.

Horse Pavilions A and B had armed sentries stationed outside. According to Joe's list, they were being used by the Munitions Department. Horse Pavilion D however was unguarded. They pushed open the heavy wooden doors, which were unbolted, and went inside.

It was as advertised. Horses.

"Why have you stopped? I didn't give the order to stop!" Goyt rounded on Crowbar, who'd tossed away the cat and had sunk down on his haunches, not exactly exhausted, but weary and resentful.

"What's the point?" MacPherson mumbled, running one tattooed hand through his thinning sandy hair, the sweat on his face making him look more pugilistic than ever.

"Stand up when you speak to me!" Goyt bawled, twitching with impatience, his chest heaving.

MacPherson just looked up at him, no longer particularly interested in his CO's campaign. "Whatta you want me to keep hittin' him for? He's near dead. Why don't we just finish him off and get outa here. None of these bastards has got any moolah on 'em. They ain't worth fuckin' about with."

Goyt fumed. "Have you forgotten who we are? Have you? We are not common criminals! This is insubordination and it won't be tolerated!"

MacPherson sneered. His expression suggested he thought Goyt talked too much. In a moment he'd have to shut him up.

"I'll give you one more chance! Get back to your duty or suffer the ultimate discipline!" Goyt's voice was singsong, and slightly cracked. He felt his authority waning, and this confused him. It smelt like mutiny. Or at least, treason.

• CASUALTIES •

Crowbar picked up the cat and hurled it at Goyt. It struck him on the face, leaving a red blotch. "Flog him yourself! I'm leavin'!" Crowbar stood up, brushed some straw off his crumpled Australian army fatigues, picked up an M1 rifle (which would be a giveaway as the Australian army used 303s), and lumbered towards the exit.

"You'll leave when I tell you to!" Goyt screamed.

Crowbar kept going.

Goyt withdrew his .45 service revolver and pointed it at Crowbar's back, his breathing difficulty escalating.

Goat Pavilion B was situated almost against the high prison wall of the showground, well away from all the other animal huts. As they approached it, Joe felt a strange sensation in the pit of his stomach. This pavilion was unguarded on the outside, but its doors were firmly shut. Nothing particularly strange. The other two on their list, which had housed animals, were similar. But this was the last. Joe decided that the strange sensation in his stomach was probably disappointment. This was one big wild goose chase. Back to square one.

He didn't transmit any of his feelings to Struther. The American seemed quite preoccupied now. Contemplating his own obsessions. Joe thought him rather world-weary and disturbingly sceptical for a thirty-year-old. Maybe that went with being a member of the Military Police in a foreign land. Maybe he was just homesick. In a way he sympathised with him. Joe had spent much of his own police life apprehending vice offenders. The US Military Police spent most of their time rounding up drunken, whoring, fighting soldiers. And perhaps, he thought, getting somewhere near the truth, Struther had to fight the same inclinations in himself that he had to thwart in others. Joe knew his type well.

Joe's mind then was not really on the task, when he started to push open the arched wooden door of Goat Pavilion B. He had pushed it barely an inch when three muffled shots rang out, startling the life out of him. He immediately ducked back, away from the door, assuming that Struther would do the same. Then he noticed that one of the bullets had penetrated the wood.

• THE CIVILIAN WAR ZONE •

"Get back!" he hissed at Struther, who seemed to just stand there, as if rooted to the spot, right near the bullet hole.

Struther slowly turned to face Joe, moving like a ballet dancer in a slow-motion pirouette. He had a shocked look on his face. His eyes were wide open, as was his mouth, except that his tongue was sticking straight out. For a moment Joe thought he looked like a clown, caught in the act. Then he noticed that really only one of Struther's eyes was open. The right one. The left was a sunken hole, charred round the edges, with blood seeping out, apparently blasted inside by the stray bullet, which was either now embedded in his brain or had blown a jagged exit hole out the back of his skull.

Then Struther completed his slow-motion pirouette and crumpled like a dying swan.

4

Joe flung himself to the ground and crawled over to the fallen Struther, who was now flat on his back, body slightly twisted, staring blindly up at the unsympathetic sun. Joe felt his wrists and his neck. No discernible pulse. Blood seeping out of his eye socket and from the back of his skull, next to some expunged brain matter.

Joe then crawled back around the side of the pavilion, trying to still his shakes. He looked around. There was no one in sight. This part of the showground was out to lunch. Not far away was a brick toilet block, some grey scaffolding, some roller coaster framework and the massive art deco Commemorative Pavilion with its sandstone and glass panels.

He drew his pistol and waited for someone to come through the door. And waited. No one. Then he realised that the shooting was not at them. There were no windows. Those inside wouldn't have seen them at the door. Struther was just unlucky enough to catch a stray bullet intended for someone inside.

He had two options. Go for help, or go inside. If he went for help, those inside might leave. The nearest phone would be in one of the large halls or stands being utilised as army offices. The nearest available army personnel were well out of sight and sound. He was also curious. Who had done the shooting? Perhaps it was only an accidental army discharge. But not a rifle. It was a handgun. He could tell that much. He had to find out. Now.

There was a door down the side. He tested it. It was bolted on the inside. He leaned his head against the wall. He could hear some muffled indistinct voices. Shouting perhaps.

Well, no point in venturing into the lion's den. Maybe he could get the lions to come out?

• THE CIVILIAN WAR ZONE •

Joe had always been a bit of a loner. He couldn't help himself. Perhaps because when he had first joined the police force he had found that most of his fellow officers were self-seeking, corrupt and therefore unreliable. He had forged an enviable reputation as the most effective cop in the country largely through his own resourcefulness, only bringing his men in at the last moment. Right now, not very far away, he had half the Australian army and buildings loaded with munitions. Yet here he was, one crazy cop all alone against an unknown enemy.

To hell with it. He'd been in the field too long to feel insecure. He liked to feel outnumbered; relished unknown odds; thrived on the unpredictable. It made the Joe Church juices flow.

He thumped on the door with the bullet hole.

Then stepped back so that the door would hide him when it opened. Delay. Tension.

He was about to slide forward and thump again, when the door swung slowly open. A gun barrel stuck out. Short, snubbed. A US carbine. The door opened more, shielding the person from Joe's view. The person eased forward, looking around, beyond the door. Joe moved.

He slammed the door shut. Rammed his pistol into the man's neck, below his steel helmet, which had a white "MP" on it.

It was a youngish chubby man, slow, watery-eyed, out of condition. For an MP, Joe thought, he's badly out of shape.

"Drop it!" he said. "Or I'll blow your head off!"

Kroeger dropped his carbine. Joe picked it up. He'd never handled a carbine before; he'd heard they were reactive but inaccurate. He dragged Kroeger round to the side of the building, which was a narrow pathway alongside a high bank of rock. Jamming Kroeger against the wall he stuck the barrel of the carbine in his neck. He had holstered his own pistol.

"For your information I'm a police officer. I want to know what's going on in there."

"Nothin'."

"But you just shot one of your own men."

"Some guy was tryin' to escape."

• CASUALTIES •

"No, I mean outside. Look!" Joe pointed to Struther's body.

"Sheeit! Where'd he come from?"

"Who's in charge in there?"

"The captain I guess." Kroeger looked relatively unconcerned at Joe's prodding. He kept chewing gum and his watery eyes were focused somewhere away from Joe's face, in communication with some other non-existent presence.

"We're going in there." Joe prodded him with the carbine. "You first."

Kroeger nodded. "Sure. But I don't think the captain's gonna like it."

The first thing that Joe noticed was Crowbar MacPherson's lifeless bloodstained body stretched out on the straw, just inside the door. "He's an Australian. Why did you shoot an Australian?"

"I told ya. He was tryin' to escape," Kroeger chewed.

Joe bent over Crowbar, keeping his carbine pointed approximately up at Kroeger. Crowbar's face registered.

Joe frowned, looked up. An MP captain had moved closer to him and was staring at him. Adam's description of the elusive major swam before his eyes. He wasn't absolutely certain yet, but it seemed he'd stumbled on the right place.

"Civilians are forbidden to enter these premises!" Goyt snapped, his eyes reducing the space and reflecting through the gloom.

Joe straightened up. "I'm a police officer."

"You're still a civilian! And return that gun to my man!"

Joe ignored the request, moving the carbine in a slow arc. His gaze fell on a nearby stall containing a chained GI. "Mind if I look around?"

He didn't wait for a reply but started to move down the row of stalls.

"I don't think you heard me!" Goyt intoned. "I said civilians are not allowed in here!"

Joe didn't respond. When the odds are against you, he'd learnt long ago, the best policy was to throw the enemy off balance by enigmatically redirecting the conversation. "You're under arrest. Murder, torture, maiming and, it seems, forcible abduction." Joe stopped at Adam's stall.

Goyt seethed with indignation. "No soldier, in his military capacity, can be guilty of any crime. This is war. I am a soldier. You are only a civilian. It is my duty to kill and maim!" Adam was unconscious, bleeding, suspended, perhaps near his final gasp. "Gimme the keys!" Now Joe gave Goyt a hard look.

"What are you talking about?"

"The keys! This man shouldn't be chained! I want the padlock keys! Now!" Joe's shout almost unnerved Goyt. Such authority from this stranger was more than he could handle.

"We can't do that. You're a civilian. This is nothing to do with you!" Goyt's tone was strangely subdued, almost a whine. Joe reasoned that the man was cowed by authority, but authoritative with those who cowered. The classic bully syndrome.

"It takes one to know one," Joe said, half joking, but keeping his carbine trained on the captain.

"What was that?" Goyt was feeling more insecure by the minute and his breathing was becoming difficult. He wanted to shoot this man down, but he seemed to know more than he should and Goyt had to know why.

"I am implying that you are a civilian too, *captain*. To start with, that American uniform doesn't seem to fit you very well. If there's one thing I've noticed about American servicemen, their uniforms are tailored to fit. Secondly, as a lifelong undercover detective, I know a good accent when I hear it, and your American one, wide ranging from Boston New England to the plains of Oklahoma, seems strangely inconsistent. And I suggest that you immediately have all these men unchained or I'll be forced to drill holes in that ill-fitting uniform of yours." Joe's tone was consistently matter-of-fact. A miscalculation. Goyt could handle that. He could cope with affability, understatement, ambivalence, even sinister undertones. He knew them all well and utilised them himself. What he couldn't cope with as well was bluster, overt abuse or rage aimed directly at him. This was too like his father — his eternal Achilles heel.

Goyt gave Joe a crafty smile. He even holstered his own revolver and he narrowed the gap between them. "I'm glad you've seen through our little deception, officer. Truly glad.

• CASUALTIES •

It's true we are not what we seem. But then, there is, as you know, a war on. And one must do everything necessary to defeat the enemy. Espionage and deception are simply legitimate tools of warfare. We, as you know, live in an occupied country, a country occupied by a mongrel nation hell-bent on destroying our traditional ties with the British Empire. And so it is up to us, and you, as a civilian upholder of the law, to fight this invasion with all the means at our disposal. Allow me to introduce myself." Goyt offered his hand to Joe. "I am Field Marshal Carl Goyt, CIC of the British Empire Territorial Army, elements of which you see before you." Goyt paused, took several deep breaths, tried to still the constriction in his lungs. Then went on: "You, my friend, are one of the few who have seen, at close quarters, some of our patriotic endeavour. Before you, in this place, you can see that the invading enemy has been thoroughly subdued. They are not conquerors but bits of sub-human flotsam and jetsam, who crumble when the slightest pressure is put upon them. Only last evening we succeeded in destroying one of the occupation's leading commanding officers. A feat that ranks with the recent assassination of the German Heydrich, which you may have read about."

What was he talking about? Then Joe suddenly remembered seeing the newspaper headlines concerning the death of one of the better known SS officers. But Goyt's speech was now beginning to unnerve Joe more than the chained prisoners, his armed acolytes and perhaps more than the riot. There was an eeriness about the whole situation. The man was obviously a case, but a dangerous one. Here in the half light of the evil-smelling animal pavilion, the man's high-pitched tones indicated a pathological logic, the likes of which Joe had not encountered before. He didn't want to shoot the man dead, because nobody would believe the type of man he was or that he was responsible for all those killings. Joe realised he had to take him alive, so that he could tell his own story.

So Joe accepted Goyt's handshake, which he found clammy and weak. And he worked towards gently undermining the man.

"I am amazed, sir," Joe said, lowering his carbine until

• THE CIVILIAN WAR ZONE •

it was aimed at the ground, "that there is little public awareness of your army. Perhaps we can do something to change this?"

Jackpot. Goyt's expression lit up and then faded. "I would be grateful if you could, officer. But the press has seen fit to ignore us up to now and I'm not sure yet whether the time is ripe to reveal all our achievements. After all, our work is not yet finished. And we don't wish to compromise this in the glare of public acceptance."

"True. But, until the public gets to know about what you are doing, your ranks will remain thin. And I'm sure you're interested in recruitment."

"What do you suggest?" Goyt's suspicions were not fully stilled. He still distrusted Joe, his depth of understanding in itself being cause for suspicion.

"I suggest you allow me to bring some influential people here from the press, the government and the Australian army and you can tell them your story and show them just what you've . . . achieved here in this place, which is, as you know, one of the AIF's most important installations. But I'd also like to take this fellow here with me . . ." referring to Adam, "to excite their interest. Otherwise I doubt if they'll believe me."

Goyt seemed to be seriously considering Joe's proposition, but his breathing difficulty had been growing all the while. Then there were the voices inside his head. His father's mostly. These factors eschewed all logical progression. Like most paranoid schizophrenics, persuasion had to be multifaceted and as illogical as the factors that governed their own behaviour. Joe's desire to take the man alive was going to prove quite impractical. For Goyt's mood had started to shift, for no apparent reason.

"The civilian mind is not to be trusted," his father said. "Only the military mind is worthy of loyalty. In peacetime the civilians put the military on trial, and in wartime they expect you to die for them. Trust them the way you'd trust a mad dog."

Goyt's eyes flickered. "Return that weapon to its rightful owner, officer. We cannot allow you to leave with it."

Joe hesitated. He could feel sweat break out on his

forehead, but this man was a sensor. He used all his resources to retain calm authority.

"I'll be glad to, as soon as you've given me the key to release this man."

"Give him the keys," Goyt said to Seldom, who hesitated. "That's an order!"

Seldom blanched, then handed Joe a bunch of keys, which Joe handed back. "You release him."

Seldom looked to Goyt for advice. Joe knew better than to drop his guard whilst fumbling with keys.

"Don't . . ." Goyt started to say, but he had a sudden shortness of breath. Furthermore, although the gloom and contrasting shafts of sunlight made visibility deceptive, his skin was taking on a bluish tint caused by cyanosis. He began to cough, drawing in great gulps of air.

Joe recognised the symptoms. "It's probably the straw or the animal odours, but tell me, Field Marshal, how long have you had asthma?"

A perfectly reasonable question.

Goyt started to choke, but managed to spit out: "What did . . . you say?" It would have been better for him if he hadn't asked for a reiteration.

"I said how long have you had asthma?"

Something in Goyt's agonised expression alerted Joe, so that he gripped his carbine more firmly and raised it up.

Goyt, galvanised by the dreaded word which was heightening his all-engulfing respiratory symptoms, advanced the five yards towards Joe with his carbine bayonet extended.

Joe managed a half twist and the blade ripped his left side, just above his waist, puncturing skin and ribcage, sending an electric current of pain right up his chest and side. In an involuntary reaction, his thumb released the cross lock safety catch and his index finger lightly squeezed the trigger. He hadn't intended to shoot and was not consciously aiming. But the weapon was so sensitive to the touch, he'd loosed off ten rounds before he knew it. And three of them had found a target. One in Goyt's stomach and one in his heart. The other found the kneecap of the hapless deserter, Kroeger, who reacted to this physical stimuli with a howl of pain that quickly degenerated into a prolonged whine.

Carl Goyt didn't seem to die immediately. His punctured heart had a few beats left and the burning, tearing sensation in his guts made him dance like a spastic zombie for some seconds, before he crashed into a wooden cross-bar on a stall. He tipped over head first into a mound of animal excreta, where he expired, his face buried in what his mind had previously been full of.

The other members of Goyt's rabble, seeing their unpredictable redeemer and meal ticket shot down, yelled like banshees and took to their heels, fleeing the pavilion before Joe had recovered his presence of mind. He had just shot two men, accidentally. Or was it? Justifiably? Yes. Regrettably? Yes. He hurled his carbine across the hut, disgusted with his own lack of control and yet, deep down, aware that he had just won a crucial battle. The enemy, the insane enemy was dead. Demons and all. Asthma and all.

Joe wondered if anyone would believe him, for the moment ignoring the fact that the stinking animal penitentiary was full of dazed and gagged witnesses. And when they picked up those remnant deserters, as they surely would, they would spill their guts out for a song.

Then he remembered Adam, still suspended, still breathing, mercifully unconscious, but young enough and strong enough to survive. He found the keys that Seldom had dropped before his flight and released the chains. He laid him gently down on the straw, covered him with his own jacket, pillowed his head and started to go for help, realising he himself was growing weaker from the blood that was spilling out of his torn side.

He was just halfway to the door in the centre aisle, when it swung open from the outside.

A thick, bull-necked figure was silhouetted there, skull partially caved in, one eye obliterated in an empty socket, face twisted with perplexed palsy, body swaying out of control, operating on half a central nervous system, half a brain and a modicum of surviving instinct. A terrifying spectre, shooting from the hip, spraying a chamber full of .45 cartridges all around the dark interior, determined to destroy the anonymous

· CASUALTIES ·

citizen responsible for the bullet that had killed his eye and part of his brain, the results of which were going to reduce him to vegetable status in a matter of a few more seconds.

5

The day that Brook Wells rejoined the human race was crisp, clear and sunny, and it reflected his relief at successfully passing through the alternating pain and morphine fog components of his recent precarious existence. At times he thought he was dead, but wasn't because he thought so. At other times he wanted to be, but couldn't because they wouldn't let him.

Three carbine bullets in the back had given him pneumothorax which amounted to unwanted and unneeded air in the chest, a collapsed lung, five holes in his body (three back, two front for exit purposes), a damaged intercostal muscle between the ribs, and great difficulty in breathing, which added a degree of constant panic to his pain. They gave him a thoractomy to open his chest and remove the bullet which was still in one lung near the bronchia artery; a chest drain, which he felt was like some kind of medieval torture implement; lots of oxygen, which he grew to need and love; padded dressings, which were neither here nor there but almost everywhere; and vast quantities of drugs, to combat the pain and infection, which were a mixed blessing.

Time passed with painful slowness and it felt like six months from shooting to surfacing. But it was only a few weeks.

The surgery, of course, didn't register, but the recuperation was hell. And all the time his mind struggled with recurring doubts and anxieties, not so much about himself but about someone else to whom he was deeply attached. Yet, for some time, he didn't know who it was that kept prodding his subconscious and perhaps even keeping him alive. It was something he had to know about someone. But who? What? Why?

The remembrance of Cynthia finally came clear the first

day they allowed him to sit up. He wondered what had happened to her. Was she dead or alive? Where was she? But they wouldn't let him use a phone and he wasn't capable as yet of letter writing. Soon.

More long days passed. They spoke to him about going home. To Philadelphia. He wasn't going to be much use in fighting the Japanese now. He wasn't sure whether to be glad or sad. He actually wanted to be part of this war. He'd already been part of it. Unintentionally. Or was that another war?

Yes and no. All wars are related in a way. They all stem from people's inability to communicate. No, that was glib. It wasn't that simple. He wanted to write something about it. Crystallise his feelings. Find reasons. Define attitudes. Wars are started by clever people and fought by stupid people. Mainly men. That wasn't true either. Most people weren't given a choice. Whether they were clever or stupid. And if people were clever why would they be stupid enough to start a war? When he was stronger, he would write it all down and see what conclusions would result. Maybe none. Maybe just further questions.

First he had to solve that other problem. What had happened to Cynthia?

Did she know she'd been haunting him all the way through? Her face, her lips, her eyes, her gentle voice. Portions of her kept cropping up in his imagination. And for weeks he didn't know who she was. Now he knew who but he didn't know where.

They then let him get out of bed for half an hour. Telephone.

He wheeled himself to a telephone. His fingers kept trembling as he dialled. In fact he dialled the wrong number three times. Christ! He felt so weak.

Her mother answered. Difficult woman.

"Mrs Church? This is Sherbrook Wells."

He could've cut that pause with a knife.

She's going to hang up. But no.

"Oh yes. How are you, corporal?"

Did she really want to know? Well, whether she did or not, he was going to tell her.

• THE CIVILIAN WAR ZONE •

"Well, for a man who's just had three uninvited bullets passing through his body, I'm okay. Thanks to Dr Morphine."

"Three bullets? I don't understand. Were you shot?"

Brook had to bite his tongue. But he knew her inanity was a cover-up while she sorted out.

"You could say that."

"Who did it?"

"The MPs."

"Why?"

"For no good reason, Mrs Church. Like always."

Winnie tut-tutted, hiding her true response, which was akin to horror.

"What did you say, Mrs Church?" Brook wanted to draw her out. This was an extremely frightened repressed woman. Probably having become so with the onset of age and war. He sensed that she had not always been like this. After all, with a vice cop for a husband and a highly intelligent and well-balanced daughter, she must've been hit with a barrage of worldliness. Some people grow with age, others wither.

"Oh my God, I don't really understand what's happening." She was opening up now. "I thought we were all supposed to be fighting the Japanese, but we seem to be fighting each other. I really don't understand."

"You're not the only one, Mrs Church. But I think you could say that war brings out the hate in people and it's not always well directed."

Another long pause, but this one was more thoughtful.

"You might be right, corporal. I've never thought of it quite like that."

He couldn't wait any longer. "Look Mrs Church. I've been burning up here. This is my first day out of bed. I've gotta know. Cynthia . . . ?"

"What do you mean? Didn't you know what happened to her? Oh I'm sorry. With all the terrible goings on . . . someone should've told you I suppose . . ."

Brook felt like dying. Winnie had just started to paint a terrible picture which he filled in. He didn't want to hear the rest. Not even the morphine could stop this new pain.

"She is recovering, thank God . . ."

• CASUALTIES •

"What?"

"She is recovering."

"From what? Please tell me!"

She gave him a brief summary of Cynthia's ordeal and the outcome. Brook almost felt sorry. He would've liked to have killed that sonofabitch himself. "Where is she, Mrs Church? I must see her."

"I'll ask her to phone you, corporal. Where are you?"

"Royal Prince Alfred Hospital. In the US section. Please get her to call me right away. I'm burnin' up here!"

"I will, corporal. I will." She hung up and wondered what had happened to her. She was relating to this person just like she related to other people. White people. What was happening to her? This man felt for her daughter which meant that Cynthia and he might . . .? How would that look? A Negro and her daughter? Despite everything, she still felt frightened. It was all so much beyond her previous experience. But then, she consoled herself, so was wartime; and she was learning to cope, like everyone else. The war would end one day, and maybe so would this.

EPILOGUE

It was a fine party. All the guests had been required to contribute ten ration coupons each, so that Winnie could provide a variety of savouries, sandwiches, frankfurters, rolls, soft drinks, tea, coffee and some cakes. Joe, bending a little as a matter of wartime necessity, managed to get his hands on a considerable quantity of sly grog, including several dozen bottles of beer, champagne and several bottles of Scotch. He, of course, despite being the reason for the party, stuck to the soft drinks and tea.

They all toasted Joe to the very last drop, for being one of the very few wartime recipients of the civilian George Medal for heroism. And there was also his ascension to the rank of Detective Inspector, after twenty-eight years on the force.

Being wartime, the guests included a number of walking wounded, including Cynthia Church, left hand still in plaster and some remaining discolouration on her face, skilfully covered by black market cosmetics. She seemed to spend most of her time in the company of Corporal Wells, who had grown considerably thinner despite the augmentation of some bulky bandages under his shirt. He remained mostly at her right side, so that he could hold her only available hand. A number of the Church family and friends seemed embarrassed that Cynthia was consorting with a black American, until they noticed that Cynthia's parents seemed to take it for granted.

Then there was the other American, Private Adam Goldhart, whom everybody knew had figured in Joe's daring escapade at the showground. He looked very pale and drawn, was wearing some very constricting bandages around his middle and his jaw was wired. Now unfit for active service, his application for transfer to the Judge Advocate General's Department had come through, and he was looking forward to trying to inculcate an element of justice into the system, utilising his own experiences on the receiving end as motivation. What effect such reforming zeal would have on the system remained to be seen, but at least he was going to try.

The guest of honour looked buoyant despite his well-dressed injuries — the deep knife wound in his side and the two surface bullet grazes on arm and leg. But they were nothing compared with some of his previous wounds incurred during peacetime vice raids. He was able to further enhance the occasion by pinning his George Medal onto his daughter's wide butterfly collar. Sealed with a kiss. No one disagreed when he announced that she was actually the true recipient.

Yet inside he was deeply disturbed, as were most of the others. They had all come face-to-face with evil and it had been wearing a very human face. The recurring problem seemed to be a matter of distinguishing friend from enemy, without becoming paranoid.

I was angry with my friend:
I told my wrath, my wrath did end.
I was angry with my foe:
I told it not, my wrath did grow.

And I water'd it in fears,
Night and morning with my tears;
And I sunned it with smiles,
And with soft deceitful wiles.

And it grew both day and night,
Till it bore an apple bright;
And my foe beheld it shine,
And he knew that it was mine,

And into my garden stole
When the night had veil'd the pole:
In the morning glad I see
My foe outstretched beneath the tree.

WILLIAM BLAKE
"The Poison Tree"